Chapter 1   the homecoming

Aulay Mackay stepped into the blend of stale beer, old men and fried eggs. The Stushie, a pub on Glasgow's south side, served all day breakfast. In the gloom were two booths; one for Eddie Curren's inner circle, the other for hangers on.

"Hi, Uncle Eddie... and you other wasters," said Aulay.

Eddie's disciples gave him a nod or a smile.

"Here." Eddie patted the seat next to him. "You sit here Aulay."

"No' today, I'm off to the bookies. You fancy a bet put on?"

"I'm all right the-now. Put a tenner on Bloody Nose in the 3:15 at Ayr. She's worth a sniff, son"

Eddie downed his whisky then eased his seventy three year old frame round the booth. He patted his pocket for the makings. "Let's light a fire, Aulay."

Before he burst into the daylight, Eddie signalled for another round of drinks. It was nine o'clock in the morning. Outside, both men rolled their own.

The Stushie stood alone, her neighbours bulldozed to make way for the M74 as it sliced through Polmadie on its way to merge with the M8 in the city centre. The pub's survival came down to an architectural quirk above the false ceiling. It gave the Stushie a Grade A listing. The new motorway had to move sideways. The surrounding tenement streets, Aulay's streets, were gone, replaced by concrete and tarmac, which let the wind blow.

"How you finding being back?" asked Eddie as they huddled together to light up.

"No' bad. Everything's the same but different, you know?"

3

"No, son. Last time I went abroad... was for your Uncle Harry's wedding... in Edinburgh."

Aulay joined the army on his eighteenth birthday. Seven years on, and a civilian again, he was still taking orders. He didn't like it but the spooks had him by the short and curlies.

His last instruction. "Go back home. Catch up with your Uncle Eddie. He's your way in."

"Way in to what?"

"The Polmadie."

The pair watched the commuters on the new motorway. Sometimes the cars moved.

Eddie took a long draw. "You getting anywhere with what I asked?"

"If Kenny Finlayson's making any moves, I've no' seen them."

"I don't trust the bastard, Aulay. He's been sniffing around too long and she's still young yet, doesn't understand these things. I can't let her-"

One of Eddie's cronies sauntered along pulling his fags out. Eddie raised an eyebrow. The man turned into The Stushie with a, "See youz inside, eh?"

"I can't let her do this," Eddie went on. "She'd never live it down."

This wasn't about his daughter's feelings. Eddie was pasting woodchip over his own cracks.

"When I hear something Eddie, I'll let you know."

"I know son, but ... I'm no' a good worrier."

A trace of menace? The stakes were high, even for Aulay, who was a True One. Long past the deference of Eddie's followers, Aulay looked him square in the face.

"Anything at all an' I'll give you a bell. Stay sane, Eddie."

Aulay headed for the bookmakers. Uncle Eddie was wrong. Bloody Nose was a nag. His money was going on Rotund Relative, a dead cert.

***

Aulay followed the small Citroen into one of those oddly shaped developments which had sprung up while he'd been away. Pale coloured bricks, a mix of expensive houses and flats, with ordered parking behind shiny metal railings. He watched Kenny Finlayson park up, walk to a mid terrace house and ring the bell. Slipping his car into a space down the street, Aulay dialled Eddie's number.

It was getting dark when a big Chrysler 220 launched into the back of the Citroen with a good thump. The little car leapt forward, its rear end crumpling. The lull ended when, as if in sympathy for one of their own, other cars joined the Citroen's wailing. Eddie climbed out of the Chrysler, leaned on his unmarked bonnet and lit up. A concerned member of the public made his way over. Twenty feet from the Chrysler, the man coughed, checked his watch and walked away.

Time ticked on. Aulay wondered if the not so secret lovers had sneaked out the back door.

A kafuffle at the corner. Two heavies dragged along a dishevelled Kenny Finlayson. They levered him into the back of the Chrysler. A terrace door opened. Shaz Curren, hair a shambles, stockings torn, blouse buttons in the wrong sequence, tottered down the steps.

"Leave Kenny alone, you auld bastard." She waved a pretty .22 special at her dad. "What gives you the right?"

Eyes closed, she fired off a couple and the evening echoed to the high pitched cracks from the small gun. She fired a few more. After a second hollow click, Aulay watched the only woman he'd ever loved, drop the gun, sit on the pavement and howl.

Sliding down in his seat, Aulay reversed out and drove away. He didn't see Eddie fall.

***

When Shaz Curren made her entrance into the world, Aulay was two days old. They shared a cot in the maternity ward of the Southern General. Growing up in the same tenement, they stayed glued together until Shaz went to university and Aulay took the Queen's shilling.

The day before shipping out for his second stint in Iraq, Aulay phoned his mum and she dropped the big one.

"Oh, and dear, Shaz is seeing a nice boy from Yooni. Francis something or other, from Coatbridge."

Aulay sank into a dark hole where Francis Shite Bastard threw a spotlight onto his last home leave. Shaz had been distant, impatient. Had their relationship withered in the barren waste of the text message? Going on line had worked for a while but there's no spark when you know the person on the other side of ether-ville. The phone sex had been great until the novelty wore off after a fortnight.

In the depths, Aulay remembered what the old hands had said. A long distance love affair takes work. What made him think Shaz Curren would knit by the fire while he played the hero? Aulay launched a barrage of texts and emails. No replies. In a last-ditch effort he wrote a letter, his first. It went through numerous drafts and took a week. Still nothing.

For the next few years Aulay spent his leaves drinking vodka as he chased Shaz look-a-likes round the Costa del Sol, or was it the Costa Brava? After a dodgy tour in Afghanistan he took the three months they gave him and crossed America by iPod. The New York shop assistant recognised his type and preloaded the pocket juke box with

6

American sad classics. The songs reeked of longing, loss and betrayal. He wasn't alone. Still, it was ages before he stopped putting the light out with, 'night night, Shaz babe'.

He returned to Glasgow to find Shaz and her current Shite Bastard in trouble with her dad. Not a place Aulay would recommend anyone spend too much time.

***

Wearing his black tie, Aulay walked through Craigton Cemetery. Two square miles of Victorian decay where the older gravestones lie buried in the weeds. He knew every road, track and path. Their playground until he and Shaz were old enough to appreciate its isolation. Happy days.

"Hi Shaz, how you doin'?"

"No' bad, Aulay. Howz you?"

"Fine. Good day for it, eh?"

The greeting manoeuvres were a struggle. The stinging sleet didn't help. Shaz offered to share her umbrella. It was the grizzled scene from countless films, or filums as they say in Glasgow. A gray slab for a sky with two gravediggers huddled under a tree, eager to fill in the hole and get to the pub. The smell of fresh soil drifted from under green plastic sheets.

As the coffin scraped its way to the bottom, Shaz's body moved in time with her sobs. Aulay put his arms round her. She felt thin.

"Let it go," he said. "You've been through a lot in the past week."

Three days after Shaz shot her dad in the leg, Kenny Finlayson died in a hit and run. Hospital bed or not, Eddie Curren could still organise things.

The sleet changed direction to horizontal, reducing the mourners to Aulay, Shaz and Irene Finlayson, Kenny's stricken mum. The story goes that the teenage Irene went camping where she hooked up with an American sailor out of the Holy Loch. Introduced to Jack Daniels, Irene woke up in her tent naked, sore with no Leroy. Nine months later young Kenny arrived.

"Kenny wasn't a bad guy," said Shaz through her hankie.

Aulay knew Kenny Finlayson through conversations. He drank in the Pandora. Did a bit of trading at the Barras Market and could plaster a fine wall, for cash.

"When Da' first found out, he hauled Kenny in..." Shaz paused for more sniffling. "But Kenny wouldn't listen, figured Da' was ancient. I tried to end it, believe me, but Kenny kept coming."

Aulay ignored the pun.

Shaz looked at him but saw something else. "He wasn't blazin' saddles, in or out the scratcher. He was cute and good fun and... Know what I mean?"

He nodded. Shaz had been enjoying Kenny until someone better turned up. Aulay had done the same, but Shazs are hard to find.

"I should have tried harder;" she said, "but... part of me used Kenny. Me with my educated liberal bollocks. I used him to stick two fingers up at Da' and... Fuck me, Aulay; I got the poor bugger killed."

More sobs came.

Kenny didn't deserve to die but, looking at Shaz, Aulay could see why he'd risk it. Think Uma Thurman with or without the sword.

Aulay felt a bit guilty too but hey, he'd get over it.
***

Aulay and Shaz did all their early fumbling together. Not just sex, but all the adolescent stuff, booze, drugs, theft and extortion. They kicked vandalism after one night, neither of

8

them got it. Their thieving was small time, shoplifting mostly and that stopped when they started working in Woollies at the weekends where stealing was a perk.

The extortion was more of a scam. Shaz developed early. They charged a pound for a look, two quid if you wanted her to jiggle them about. A fanny flash? No chance; or so Aulay thought.

Johnnie Smote saved for weeks and put up £25.

"Smote," said Shaz buttoning her blouse. "Double it and you're on."

Any youthful qualms Aulay had about being a pimp, evaporated. He wasn't in charge. Had he ever been?

Last button done, Shaz looked at the Smote. "It'll be our little secret. Anyone hears about this, anyone finds out... If I hear a fuckin' rumour about a rumour..."

The wide-eyed Smote shook his head. "Right, honest Shaz, sure."

"Ok, Smote. Let us know when you've got the money." Shaz winked. "Off you go."

Two weeks later a trembling Smote turned up at the usual place. The tenement's bin store didn't have a roof but the walls were high enough to prevent any gawkers from the third floor looking in for free. It didn't smell too bad.

"Here's the rules." Aulay put authority into his recently broken voice. "You need to stand there and no' move... nothing."

"For fifty quid I want ten seconds worth," squeaked The Smote.

"Fu-"

Shaz broke in. "Smote, you'll get three seconds."

With The Smote struggling and tears nearby, Shaz switched to a softer tone.

"Kneel down. You'll get a better angle."

If Shaz'd told The Smote to eat his thumb he'd have asked, 'Which one?'

With The Smote in position, Shaz surprised them both when she turned, lifted her short skirt and bent over. Aulay watched The Smote explode before the gateway to heaven swung into view.

***

Giggling at the memory wasn't the most diplomatic thing to do, at a graveside. Shaz elbowed Aulay away.

"You findin' anythin' funny here?"

"Sorry, got stuck in a memory there. Look, let's get out of here before we drown."

The sleet had matured into a biblical deluge. Shaz waved to the unseeing Irene Finlayson. They left Kenny's mum alone with her grief.

"You fancy a wee drink then?"

They'd reached the war memorial where Aulay used to chase the screeching Shaz to the top. His mouth was dry. Would she?

Her green eyes looked up. "I was sloshed when I shot Da'. You must have heard?"

He nodded.

"I wanted Kenny to go out on a high, you know. Our last time together. I bought champagne... prawns with all the dips... I borrowed a house from this girl at work..."

He waited.

"How the fuck did Da' find us?"

Aulay tucked his guilt behind shrugging shoulders.

"My brain's gone, Aulay. Let's get a bottle and go to your place. We'll shag for Scotland."

How could he refuse and anyway, he was safe. Aulay was white.

"Mr Mackay?" A British army Major put his hand through the bars of Aulay's cell. "My name is Storm."

They shook hands. The cell door slid open.

"Hurricane," said Aulay, "have a seat."

Major Storm sat on the bunk. The look on his face said he'd heard them all before.

Aulay sat on the toilet. The cell door shut with a clunk. The key turned. The sound was getting familiar. Aulay was staring at a long stretch in an Iraqi jail for something he didn't do. What he did do was capable of sending him away for a long time too.

After checking his general health and wellbeing, Hurricane got down to it.

"So, Aulay, tell me your story."

First name terms already? Young for a Major, Hurricane was either bright or had blue blood.

"Before we get to that." Aulay hoped the Major was bright. "I'm a civilian. What are you doing here?"

After five years service, Aulay left the army to work in the private sector. A bodyguard in Iraq earned more in a month than a British army sergeant did in a year. He had other reasons for leaving but money was the simplest answer.

"Aulay, you are a British citizen charged with the murder of a US citizen, in Iraq. We want to ensure nothing is overlooked."

"Who's we?"

Hurricane ignored the question. "Before his death, did your employer mention his illegitimate son?"

"Maybe."

Aulay's last boss, Coulfield Waincross III, an industrialist bidding for the multi-billion dollar contracts to rebuild Iraq, had been shot in the head by a sniper. Married with two daughters, Coulfield Waincross III hailed from the US Bible belt. News of an illegitimate son, from his student days, would create more than a few ripples. Coulfield had political ambitions.

"Do you know the boy's name?" asked Hurricane.

Aulay shrugged. His American interrogators had questioned him for days. Coulfield's son hadn't got a mention.

"I'm trying to ascertain the extent of your relationship with Mr Waincross. It may help with... your situation."

Aulay's situation was dire and Coulfield was dead. What the hell.

"The bastard is eighteen. He doesn't know who his father is. His mother gets a monthly cheque and will do 'til Todd's twenty-five. Mr Waincross set up a trust fund. Todd believes his father died doing government work, to explain the cheques."

Clasping his hands together Hurricane settled back. He was staying. Aulay's tension level went up a notch. He'd passed a test.

"Please start at the beginning, Aulay."

***

For the post of Coulfield Waincross III's bodyguard, Aulay flew to Los Angeles where the Waincross family had one of their homes. For a week he needed to prove he could mix in swell company... that he didn't dribble at table.

The first attempt on Coulfield's life took place at Gio's, a restaurant perched high above the Pacific. Two armed security guards manned the electric gates. An elevator rose from reception to the eating terrace. Brutally expensive,

Gio's boasted a clientele in the upper strata of L.A. society. Charlotte, Mrs Waincross III, liked to mix with people from the media and Hollywood. There was a uniform for these occasions. Jeans and sneakers for the Celebs. Silk suits and slicked back hair for the hoodlums. Add shades for their bodyguards.

Mrs Waincross chose to eat in the sunshine. At an adjoining table, Aulay sat with Sal, an ex US marine protecting a mob family having a birthday bash. They exchanged Middle East stories.

"You know I hate this place," said Coulfield.

The tables were close. Aulay could follow the family chit chat.

"Now darling it's a family day," said Charlotte without a pause in her sweep of the room.

A more detailed scan would take place under the illusion of eating. Aulay quickly worked out that eating is what most people in Gio's spent a fortune not doing.

"Ciao, Giuseppe," called Coulfield.

"Buongiorno, Signore Waincross"

"Usuale per me, Giuseppe"

"Pizza vesuvius con supplementare jalapeno, e chilli olio?"

"Si, grazie."

"Coulfield?" said Charlotte. "When you have pizza the girls insist on it. You know their dietician has imposed a regime."

"Do you think I give a shit what... whatever his name is, says?"

"We need to ensure they have a proper diet, Maurice…"

"Fuck Maurice. Sorry, you can't, he's gay aint he?"

"Do you know the scale of obesity in this country?"

"Charlotte, we have a dietician because you can't show your face in this town without one."

Coulfield pointed. Their two girls were running round the soft play area.

"They're fitter than Olympic gymnasts."

It was the first time Aulay had seen the combination in action. Stinking rich and miserable.

Following Coulfield's lead, Aulay discovered another first; Pizza can set your mouth on fire. Reaching for a jug of iced water he heard a familiar sound. The zing a bullet leaves in its wake. He crashed into Coulfield dragging him to the floor.

The round struck the wrist of the host at the next table. He was toasting his nephew's twelfth birthday. The birthday boy followed his uncle's hand as it spun through the air, until the next bullet arrived.

Among the blood spatter, the clattering furniture and customers' screams, Coulfield Waincross III fought like a cornered cat to free himself from Aulay's grip. Aulay forced his prospective boss's head round. The gaping hole, that was once the birthday boy's left eye, stared back.

"Mr Waincross." Aulay kept his voice conversational. "Stay here and keep down."

More bullets punctured the air. Aulay counted seven, all silent. Long range shooting or high velocity silencers?

"My girls?" said Coulfield.

Not, 'my wife' or 'my family'.

Aulay turned. Mrs Waincross lay in the foetal position, a marble pillar between her and the shooters.

"Shite."

Aulay got up and ran, scooping both girls into his arms. All three crashed into the soft play, landing with a pleasant plop, on the blue and pink cushions.

With the Waincross family secure in their limousine, a Cadillac with more armour plating than a Challenger tank, Aulay clambered up the cliff to the only spot the shots could have come from. In the scrub he found empty shells and Sal.

"I don't get it," said Sal. "This is either a warning or a right screw up."

"Who's the guy who lost his hand?" asked Aulay.

"Angelino Carbretti. The second assistant accountant to the third accountant. He's way down the food chain."

"Why are you here?"

"Guests from out of town. I'm here for show. Angelino wanted to impress his wife's folks."

Aulay followed the line of fire. If the shooters wanted Coulfield dead, he'd be dead. Shooters? No single rifleman could fire the first four shots in three seconds.

"Who's your guy?" asked Sal.

"Business man. Works overseas."

"Where?"

"Iraq."

Sal raised an eyebrow. "Why are you here?

"I'm doing my interview. They're checking I don't lust after pre-pubescent females."

Sal laughed.

One thing troubled Aulay. "I thought you mafia types didn't go in for the military?"

"You been watchin' too many movies. Where's your skirt thing?"

"Touché"

During the endless tangle with the L.A.P.D, Aulay and Sal talked. They agreed to stay in touch. Aulay kept Sal up-to-date with Coulfield. Sal kept him up-to-date with Angelino...

Angelino Carbretti's books got the twice over. Every illegal cent was accounted for. He was clean. This didn't stop the bosses putting Angelino under 24-hour surveillance. They bugged his office, his house and the bachelor apartment he kept hidden from everyone.

When Angelino returned to work, he revelled in his first street name, Capitano Hook. Good with the prosthetic, Angelino could lift a glass and use a knife. Mrs Carbretti hated it.

"Don't you think about entering the bedroom with... that thing."

"But honey, I-"

"No buts. Leave it in the kitchen drawer and cover yourself up. It's disgusting."

Claudia, on the other hand... "Il mio Capitano, please be gentle."

Using a variety of attachments, Angelino unhooked her straps, snipped the ties then cut until Claudia lay naked and cowering. It cost him a fortune in lingerie, which was of no concern at all to Il Capitano.

***

Coulfield Waincross III took the philosophical view. The wrong place at the wrong time. Mrs Waincross wiped Gio's from the list of places to be seen and life returned to normal.

Aulay got the job.

For the next 18 months, especially during the long negotiations in Iraq, Aulay and Coulfield were rarely more than two metres apart. On many a boozy night they'd sort out the world's problems before blurting out their worst

17

nightmares. It's what drunken sad bastards do. On the last night, in their Baghdad hotel suite, it was late, they'd finished off two bottles of Jura, a malt whisky from the isle of the same name and Cooly's favourite. Aulay only said 'Cooly' in private.

They were on the final lap. A place where confessions live. Where trust, self sacrifice and lifelong kinship are sealed tighter than a jar of beetroot. They'd dispensed with Mrs Waincross, US foreign policy and why some Iraqi women, wearing the full burqa, are sexier than a lap dancer on speed.

The shooting at Gio's came up again.

"Aulay, you got me to the floor, you checked Mrs Waincross and... I owe you my daughters. You strolled through it all like... like a walk in the park. How did you do it?"

During previous conversations Aulay'd said, "Hey, it's my job."

This time, the Jura spoke. "It's 'cos I don't give a shite."

"You..." Cooly leaned forward. "You don't care if you live or die?"

Aulay shrugged. He'd let his stoical disguise slip.

Cooly probed further but Aulay refused to expand on his revelation, his loneliness, the empty hole he filled most nights with the shadow of Shaz Curren.

"I've received another death threat," said Cooly. "A final warning."

"KBC aint goin' to do nothin'." Aulay slipped into talking American when he drank with Cooly.

The Kendler Brand Corporation, Coulfield's competition in the multi-billion dollar game, and their preferred bogey man, were struggling. Word was they needed to win the next round of tenders or face going belly up.

"Anyway, Cooly. Nothing's goin' to happen to you. You got me, remember?"

Rounding the last bend they entered the home straight where a tearful Cooly told Aulay about his son, again. It lasted the first half of the third bottle.

"He's a good boy, Aulay, eighteen now. Likes engines and made the grade, he's going to M.I.T."

Cooly puffed out his chest. "Todd reckons he got a scholarship, but I'm picking up the tab, like a good father should, don't ya think?"

"That's cool, Cooly."

"I've seen him but he don't know me." More tears came. "Aulay, my friend, my one true friend, promise me..."

Cooly's reality balance sank under the weight of the Jura.

"...if anything happens to me, I want you to go see Todd ... when he's twenty five. Tell him about me; tell him what his father was like."

"Sure, Cooly. You got it."

The two stalwarts stood and embraced. Was there enough malarkey left for the grand gesture? Cooly weaved his way to his bedroom and returned with the family bible. Aulay placed his right hand on the leather bound volume and solemnly swore.

"Fuckin-A, Cooly. I will go see Todd and tell him you were the best buddy a man ever had."

Tumblers met across the now whisky-splashed tome as the two warriors entered the *Order of the Blootered Knights of Jura*, whose motto, *best-est friends ever*, they'd have had emblazoned across their chests if only a tattoo artist had been handy.

Cooly slumped onto the couch, crossed the Rubicon and passed out. Taking a last quaff of Jura, Aulay too crossed the water.

Next morning, Aulay was puking up in the toilet when he heard the shot. He'd been too drunk to check all the curtains.

Chapter 3   the departure lounge

It was Aulay's first time seeing an old Uncle Eddie. The striped pyjamas hung loose, his skin didn't fit and looked pasty. Eddie was dying from cancer, walking dead before Shaz put a bullet in his thigh. He was in command of the hospital ward though. When Aulay arrived, two old blokes scurried back to their beds.

What do the young and alive say to the old and dying?

"Hi, Eddie. Howz you?"

"I'm fucked, son... bet the 2nd favourite in a one horse race."

The eyes still had it.

"Fancy a bet put on, Eddie? I've got a tip for the 4.15 at Doncaster..." the blood left Aulay's face.

"Christ, son, you're sharp the-day."

Eddie tried a guffaw but it fell short. The tubes up his nose didn't help. After the spasm he nudged a finger at the newspaper on the bedside cabinet. "Reach me that Daily Snot."

Eddie turned to the red top's horse racing section where Aulay's fuck up was underlined in red.

- Number 6, running in the 4.15 at Doncaster. The even money favourite - Daughter's Revenge.

"She's a shoo in," said Eddie. "Put your house on it. Get my wallet."

Eddie grinned as Aulay took the twenty. "On the nose, mind."

"Sure, Eddie."

Awkward places, hospitals. The act of trying to be normal prevents it. In the silence Aulay wondered if pregnant pauses were longer in the maternity ward.

"Pull the screen round, son."

As he pulled at the thin curtain, a nurse caught Aulay's eye. She gave him a knowing smile. When he turned back, Eddie was rolling a fat cigarette.

"You can't smoke-"

"Wheesht." Eddie slipped his tongue along the dark liquorice paper. "It's all fine."

After lighting up, and savouring the opening draw, Eddie motioned at the bedside cabinet.

"The nurses get one a day."

In the drawer was a healthy stack of £10 M&S vouchers.

"It's no' bribery, Aulay, it's a present. Nurses are allowed wee presents."

Three nurses on three shifts added up. "Expensive habit."

"Och, money's the least of my worries." Eddie held out his tobacco tin. "You fancy one?"

"I'm ok, thanks. Stoked up before I came in. How many fags you allowed?"

"One in between doctor's rounds and..." Eddie twirled the lit end. "...I think night shift Betty fancies me 'cos..." He paused to purse his lips in a kiss before exhaling. "... She wakes me up before breakfast, for a quickie."

Eddie sniggered and Aulay joined in. A good smoker, Eddie puffed with style.

Using a thermos for an ashtray, Eddie dropped the smouldering fag-end in before screwing both lids on. After spraying around the stuff you see in posh toilets, he winked and lowered his head onto the pillow.

"I'm going to savour this one, Aulay. I'll be bursting into different flames soon enough."

Did he mean hell or the oncoming cremation?

A few minutes later he stirred. "Bottom shelf, Aulay. The black bag, take it."

"What?"

"Christ, son. I'm cackin' it here and you're messin' about."

Eddie fiddled with his insides, coughing up a couple of weak ones. Aulay wiped away the spume with a paper hankie. There's a box of hankies by every hospital bed, like a mini tombstone.

"You remember when Mrs Eddie went, Aulay?"

"Aye."

"Good do. Fair old turn out, eh?"

Did Eddie think he'd match it? No chance. Half the south side turned out for Mrs Eddie. A minister and a priest did the honours. The police turned up, to divert the traffic.

"I'd do well to match that," said Eddie, "more there than at Gory's send off."

This'll do, thought Aulay, the days of yore. Familiar ground.

"The Polmadie's first Top Banana was a proper hard man. No messing with Gory, or his team. Not like these days, son."

Eddie joined The Polmadie in the fifties when being a hoodlum carried some community spirit and the Top Banana lived in your street. As Eddie warbled through a few favourites Aulay nodded at all the right bits. From sitting on the man's knee to cigarette rolling lessons, Aulay had been brought up on Eddie's in-his-prime stories. He'd learned a lot, which was the plan.

After a bit, the cheery reminiscing dipped. "I've always regretted not being there. I could maybe have done something."

Eddie lay unconscious in a dentist's chair when Davy 'Gory' McGlorry was gunned down in '89. After a suitable pause, to respect the memory of the divine Gory, Eddie carried on.

"When Mad Rab took over, he ran The Polmadie with his fists. We were a tight ship though, son."

"How come he got launched into the Clyde then?"

"You no' hear about it, Aulay?"

"Chinese whispers."

Aulay lied to keep Eddie talking. The man was slipping away but some supernatural nonsense clung on, pumping up the thing called hope.

"Well, son, Mad Rab went mental and two broken bodies wasn't enough. He picked on the wrong bloke to be next."

Eddie slumped a bit so Aulay gave him a prod. "He went for Chancer MacKinnon?"

"Aye... and after pulling the knife out of Mad Rab's chest, this Chancer declared himself Top Banana. You know him?"

"No' really."

Regime change in Glasgow gangs didn't happen often. The Polmadie were now run by a younger generation, Aulay's generation.

"You heard if the new Banana's made many changes, son?"

Retired and three generations removed, Eddie was Polmadie down to his leather brogues which lay, optimistically, under the bed.

"I've heard the new Banana's thing is computers and stuff."

Eddie raised an eyebrow. "And?"

"He's I.T.'d the tanning shops, the Fat Controller ice cream vans and The Bull's Security. The pubs and bookies are said to be next."

"What about the Depot, anything happening there? Have things changed?"

There was a trace of desperation in Eddie's voice, which was fresh.

"Christ, Eddie. No one's going to talk to me about that. More than a life's worth."

The Depot, the drug gang's distribution centre, where the smack went out and the cash came in.

"Aye, s'pose you're right. Anyway, not enough time to make big changes there."

Eddie looked exhausted. Lying back, he squirmed a bit before launching into more stories from the good old days. He stopped halfway through one of Aulay's favourites.

"Howz Sharon doin'?"

"No' too bad, Eddie. Bit stressed out."

"Was she hooked on that nig...?"

Even Eddie understood the potential fallout in a place like this.

"Kenny Finlayson had his hooks in," said Aulay, "Shaz didn't and tried to end it. If you'd left it a wee while-"

"Shite. I left it twice already. Christ, if..." a cough developed into a bout of wheezing.

Hospitals put your inadequacy in the spotlight. If Eddie had a shrapnel wound, Aulay could do something...

Eddie resurfaced. "I did it for you, Aulay." It was nearly a whisper.

Aulay leaned in. "Did what, Eddie?"

"That black bastard Finlayson's out the way now, son. You're the only one for Sharon. She was a shambles after you left... first thing she did? Go out with a fenian for Christ's sake."

Eddie went crimson. A hefty coughing and spluttering developed into a beep beep beep from one of the machines. Before the cavalry arrived Aulay slipped a half bottle of whisky into the voucher drawer. The nurses would understand. Incoming medics shoved him to the side. The curtain swished round a purple Eddie, a black doctor and two brown nurses.

Aulay paced the corridor. Eddie had Kenny killed so he and Shaz could get back together? The cold sweat on his back said yes.

After an age a nurse appeared. Another hospital rule, time slows down.

"Mr Curren is heavily sedated... he'll be out... until morning."

She kept her look of concern from sliding into pity, a pro.

His spell in the Grim Reaper's departure lounge left Aulay feeling uneasy as he walked through the labyrinth that is the Victoria Infirmary. It took ten minutes before he reached a place he could light up, a retired bus shelter. Behind adolescent smoke rings, he wondered how he was supposed to join The Polmadie now. The old plan, using Uncle Eddie as a reference, was at death's door.

A doctor appeared asking for a light. He introduced himself as Iain MacCrimmon from the Isle of Skye.

Aulay had to ask. "You play the bagpipes?"

"Och, aye."

"Fantastic."

They smoked in silence until the doctor answered his phone and prattled away in gibberish that Aulay assumed was Gaelic. Whatever the lingo, Dr MacCrimmon was in love with the caller.

The wee black bag didn't weigh much.

Major Storm sat forward. "You need to convince me about the rifle."

Bloody forensics. The bullet that killed Coulfield Waincross III came through the barrel of Aulay's L11 sniper rifle.

"My L11 was stolen. I must have filled in a dozen bloody forms."

"The TC scope..."

Aulay interrupted. "TC scopes are shite. I had a B4 fitted, and it was broken."

"Can you prove that?"

"Lieutenant Forbes Ogg, 4th Battalion, the Highlanders, he broke it, check with him."

Hurricane didn't take notes. Aulay hoped the major had a good memory.

"In your statement you claim to have won a lot of money from Mr Waincross."

Having three hundred thousand dollars stashed under his hotel bed added to the body of evidence.

"Aye, Coulfield was a crap poker player. Ask around. There's a few big shots took a pile off him every week. He didn't care, had more money than God and loved playing, like a kid."

"If Mr Waincross left you something in his will, with a condition attached, would you know what that condition might be?"

This was news. Cooly never mentioned anything about... Ah, the Order of the Blootered Knights of Jura.

"Seven years from now, I'll need to visit somewhere in Alabama."

"To do what?"

"Track down a twenty five year old called Todd and take him out for a beer."

Hurricane stood up. "Thank you, Aulay." He straightened his uniform. "I'll be in touch."

What the fuck did that mean? Aulay wanted to throttle the guy. Confinement didn't suit him. It nibbled away and when his hopes rose, even a smidgen, the fires burned.

***

British Military Compound, Basra, Iraq – 2 months later.

Aulay found himself sitting opposite Major Storm once more. Not in a cell this time but the NCOs' mess. Unlike the Americans in Baghdad, there was no air-conditioning. The place stank of bacon, eggs and black pudding. It felt like home.

"You are fortunate," said Hurricane. "The Americans took a little persuading and there are certain...em, caveats to your being released to us."

Fuck the caveats, whatever they were, Aulay was in the clouds.

"The TC scope fitted to your rifle at the time Mr Waincross was shot arrived in a batch two months after you reported your rifle stolen. Not absolute proof but enough to sow a seed of doubt in our American cousins."

"And..."

"An inventory accounted for all but one scope, the one in question. A Quartermaster Sergeant is now under arrest."

Aulay stayed quiet. His heart pumped though.

"In order to ingratiate himself, the QMS gave us a name. Luther Black."

Oops, thought Aulay, this could be tricky.

"Unfortunately, that individual's corpse was discovered on the same day Mr Waincross was shot."

Aulay stared into the eye of the Storm. He had no guilt. There was nothing to give away.

***

Coulfield's body was still warm when Aulay crashed into another hotel suite. A stupid thing to do and probably why he got away with it.

Inside, two men played pool, jackets off. They were drinking scotch rocks. It took Aulay three months to persuade Cooly to stop polluting the Jura with ice. He was still working on these two.

A gun in each hand, Aulay asked, "Why?"

One man twitched.

"Stay still, Luther."

Luther Black would have fired the shot that killed Coulfield but his boss gave the order. Aulay was prepared to let Luther live.

"Tell me why?"

Luther's boss didn't look too good. "Aulay..."

So, they were still pals. Aulay liked both these men. He'd drunk long into the night with them.

"I just heard about Coulfield. I'm so sorry, a terrible thing. He was-"

Luther moved. Everything slowed. Aulay put the first bullet into Luther's head, as per the manual. The second and third pierced his chest. Not too shoddy, thought Aulay, for someone sweating malt whisky. Luther managed to fire one into the floor.

Luther's boss shrieked. ""Aulay, please... I'll give you anything, five mill... ten."

"This is not about money."

The C.E.O. of Kendler Brand stayed alive for another half second.

***

"We suspect you killed both men," said Hurricane.

"Why am I here then?"

"No evidence and... your conduct at the Anfursati mosque is still highly regarded."

Aulay was a hero then.

"... It's the primary reason the Americans have allowed us some leeway."

Aulay knew it was pure cheek but... "What about my three hundred grand?"

"You'll get it in stages."

"One of the caveats?"

"Yes, and there's something we want you to do... for us."

"What if I say no?"

"It's back to Baghdad. Take your chances with the Iraqi legal system. You might be found innocent... though I doubt it. Could take years."

Four months in a cell was enough. "What do you want me to do?"

"All in good time."

Still buzzed up, Aulay couldn't resist it. "Will I be a double '0'?"

A trace of a smile crossed Major Storm's face. "Not initially."

Chapter 5   Glasgow

Aulay's bedsit was a six by fourteen foot cupboard on the first floor landing of a big sandstone villa he shared with ten other loners. The rent was minimal and he didn't have much stuff. A one ring Baby Belling reheated any leftover take-away. A lonely TV aerial cable lay curled on the carpet. His years away had stifled any longing for crap telly.

He picked up his book, a Tom Clancy, and flipped the latch to release his bed from daytime vertical to night time horizontal. There was a lot of hanging about in the army and Aulay had caught the reading bug. It was serious. He'd read anything, a list, a thesis, an instruction manual.

Uncle Eddie's revelation, and the look on the face of the ICU nurse, 'you've seen the last of Mr Curren', joined forces. Unable to concentrate on Mr Clancy's hero, Aulay left the cupboard. He headed along Shields Road in search of a drink.

The district of Pollokshields is split in two. On the east side of Shields Road are square blocks of three storey tenements with a large Asian population. The shops are colourful, smell great and are full of stuff Aulay didn't know anything about. To the west are long wide avenues lined with grand mansions, built when Glasgow was the empire's second city. The further west you travel, the more likely the monoliths are still single family homes, where the seriously wealthy live.

Marooned at one end of the bar, Aulay was on his sixth Heineken when Eileen McCloy appeared at his shoulder.

"Aulay Mackay, well, well. Here's a delightful surprise."

If a cheroot rolled on the humid thigh of a fat bird is your bag, Eileen McCloy will fire your torpedoes. Aulay blamed the lager for mixing his phora-mets.

31

"Eileen, howz you, doll?"

"I'm fair to fabulous, and all the better for seeing you, handsome. A wee drink, Aulay?"

"Sure. A Shite & Mackay."

On the wrong side of fifty, Eileen didn't hide her assets. Her chest announced her presence before she entered the building and straining thigh high leather boots drew the eye up to where fantasies lived. Eileen McCloy could round up her followers with a whisper. One of the faithful, the tittle-tattle had, was Eddie Curren.

They were in Sammy Dows, a pub taking up the ground floor of a tenement in Strathbungo. Even after a fresh coat of paint Sammy's looked tired. A pub with a hangover. There were a few regulars in, some Aulay knew, others he was on nodding terms with. He arrived wearing his solo-flight badge so everyone gave him a wide berth. Eileen ignored badges.

They moved to one of the window seats. A gamble as it wasn't unknown for a brick to come flying through from an ejected punter. After the weather, the football, the state of the union and a couple of house whiskies, Eileen got round to it.

"Eddie's a goner then, I hear?"

"Yep, auld bastard's riddled with it, Eileen."

"You'll have something comin' to you then?"

Aulay supposed he would.

"What you planning to do with it?"

"With what? The family estate?"

Aulay laughed until he noticed Eileen wasn't.

"You've no' looked in the black bag yet?"

This was the genius of Heineken mixed with cheap blended whisky. They swam together but not too synchronised. Aulay threw back his latest dram as Eileen scribbled something on the back of a business card. She handed it over and stood up.

"Come and see us on Tuesday night, Aulay."

"Us?"

"The Strathbungo Cellists. Home safe, now."

"Shhhure thing, doll."

Too far gone to read, Aulay stuffed the card into his jeans and slipped back into the warm slime of self pity. His return to Glasgow was going swimmingly. Uncle Eddie would soon be joining Kenny Finlayson in the hereafter, and Shaz Curren still pushed all his buttons.

'It's only a comfort shag,' she'd said after their post-funeral session. He'd since sent the odd text, keeping it light. No replies. The hole Aulay had fallen into when Shaz dumped him was deep. In the years that followed, he'd only managed to peek over the top a couple of times.

Aulay woke with a pounding head and a mouth like the floor of an Airdrie butcher's. After scratching various bits of himself, he coughed up a little phlegm, took a swig from a half-empty Irn Bru tin, rummaged for the makings and rolled a thin one. He flicked the Zippo, drew in a good belt of Golden Virginia and coughed for five minutes. In the mirror he looked at the result of the previous evening's intake. He needed stronger tobacco.

After a shower in the communal bathroom, Aulay spent the next eight hours delving through the black bag's contents. Mobile on silent, he ate corned beef from a tin, with Jaffa cakes. Uncle Eddie and The Strathbungo Cellists had the mother of all scams mapped out. A raid on The Polmadie's Depot. It was beautiful, poetic and fuckin' crazy.

Searching for cigarette papers he found Eileen's card.

The Fotheringay, Tue @ 8pm. Come to the back door.

33

He had five days. Checking his phone, there was a missed call from Shaz. His insides turned over when she answered.

"Hi Shaz," he said.

"Da' died. Thought you should know."

Chapter 6   a sad day

In Eddie Curren's funeral cortege, Aulay sat in the second car. Shaz wasn't going to attend.

"The auld bastard can dance all the way to hell," she'd said. "I don't give a shite."

"Can you no' remember him as he used to be?

"When we were young?" Shaz stopped with one long leg in her smart suit skirt. "He was no different then. We changed, Aulay. No' my Da'."

Her hips filled the material. She reached for her bra.

"He was a bigoted, racist bully and stayed that way 'till his last breath."

That was true, Aulay was there.

"People are no' the stereotypes Da' made us believe. When I went to Yooni the world opened up for me."

"It opened up for me too."

"No' soon enough, Aulay. You came swaggering home after your first tour bragging about wiping out the Ragheads. You made me sick."

"I was only eighteen."

Shaz stepped into her four-inch heels, did a quick check in the mirror and walked over. It wasn't a long walk. They were in Aulay's cupboard.

"Aye, but you're no' a teenager anymore. You've changed too. It's taken you a bit longer than me, but you've moved on."

"How do you know?"

Hands on hips, Shaz squared up. "You think Kenny Finlayson should be in the ground?"

Uncle Eddie's deathbed confession came back. It gave Aulay a jolt. Shaz took it as his endorsement. She put her arms round him. On four-inch heels, she looked him straight in the eye.

"If you hadn't left Glasgow you'd have stuck with Da'. Christ, Aulay, you'd have been there when Kenny got picked up."

Aulay screamed at his eyelids not to blink. He waited for something else to give him away. His throat finally loosened. "You sure?"

"Oh, come on, Aulay, you were Da's Mini-Me." Shaz laughed then. "You even smoked like him."

Time moves on. Aulay had since studied Mickey Rourke playing Marv in Sin City. The slow draw and release, with the cigarette effortlessly poised.

Shaz picked up her briefcase.

He asked the question. "What are we doing, Shaz?" Aulay's hooks were so tender they were bleeding.

"I'm no' sure. Let's play it by ear, eh?"

Play it by ear. Was that good?

Shaz looked at her watch. "Got to go. I've an appointment at ten."

"Who with?"

"John Maclean, he's a reporter with the Daily Snot."

An image of Bruce Willis appeared in Aulay's head. "He wear a vest?"

"Eh?" Shaz raised an eyebrow.

Aulay's brain scanned the possibilities. Was he just another Kenny Finlayson? Was Shaz biding her time until someone more worthy came along? The odd shag until the white knight rode over the horizon?

"Never mind," said Aulay. "What's this Maclean guy want?"

"He's looking for a bit of background."

"And?"

"Yes, he wants into my knickers but this is one lawyer who keeps contact with the press to a minimum. No tongues."

Shaz was coming back up. Looked a million dollars at her lowest, now, wow, power gear on, hair crazy, a true ARSF; Absolutely Ravishing Stunningly Fabulous.

"He wants to talk about Eddie?"

"Aye, they all do. Da' was the last of the breed and all that shite."

"You doin' the right thing?"

"What? Seein' a journo, shaggin' you, or not goin' to the pyre?"

There was an edge there, the old edge. Aulay loved it, always had.

***

The black limousines crawled along the familiar streets. Aulay remembered his last cremation, when Mrs Eddie went up in smoke. Two weeks after the wake, he was in the army with all his prejudices intact. During basic training, his first set of blinkers fell off when Tim Curtis pulled him through the pipe. Aulay had been drowning at the time and Tim didn't have to, it slowed him down. Tim was English, Aulay's first. Coming home this time he'd no blinkers left. Eddie suspected as much. It's why he put him on the Kenny Finlayson thing.

Eddie'd opened with a bulls-eye. "There's a problem with Sharon."

Aulay no longer whispered her name in the dark, but he still lived with her ghost. Today's Shaz was not the Shaz of his nights. She's different. Older. His Shaz unzipped him in the Odeon during Titanic. He got a two hour thank you for coming... which he did, just as Leonardo slipped below the surface and the tears ran down Shaz's face. Even now, Aulay flinched whenever that Canadian bird launched into the song.

Shaz had sailed through school. Glasgow University accepted her application almost before she'd applied. Her teachers, Aulay's teachers, extolled her virtues and the invitation to study whatever she wanted was taken up. She came top of the class in both law and economics. Glasgow's top law firms laid out the red carpet.

He'd bumped into Shaz once during this time, when he came home for a mutual friend's twenty-first birthday party.

***

Aulay was waxing lyrical about heroic deeds to an enthralled audience of old pals when Shaz pierced his armour.

"Hi, Aulay."

His Shaz Curren resentment file, with its images of plump thighs and love handles, sank like Leonardo.

"This is Francis. Francis this is my cousin Aulay. He's not my real cousin. My granny adopted his dad."

Mr Francis O'Rourke shook hands like a front row forward. Aulay knew a front row forward, Corporal Hendry. The corporal had a very small willy. Aulay relaxed, a bit.

"How do?" said Shite Bastard. "Shaz tells me you're in the army,"

He'd got a mention in dispatches.

"Aye, for Queen and country."

A little catholic baiting can do wonders. Not all his blinkers were off then, and the beer was working. Francis ignored the comment. Shaz threw a warning look.

"Shame the IRA have packed it in," he said. "I'd have enjoyed a stint in Ulster."

Nothing. Getting this Francis geezer to bite was proving difficult. Aulay launched into the cardinal having a heart transplant gag. Before the punch line Francis saw the direction it was going.

Shaz nipped in. "You're being a real tosser, Aulay. Francis, let's go."

Shite Bastard left with, "Good to meet you."

Aulay spent the rest of the evening watching Shaz and Francis schmooze round the function suite laughing, laughing with other people. Dancing, all the old gang wanted to dance with Shaz. Aulay massaged his frustration with vodka.

Yvonne was drunk enough. "Hey, Yvonne doll, come here."

With everything in position, Aulay arranged for the table cloth to slip as Shaz and Francis returned to their seats after a strenuous rendition of Delilah from someone's Uncle Charlie. Aulay's hands held the back of Yvonne's head as it bobbed up and down.

It took a second, a look, the swipe of shock. The jealousy Aulay had aimed for turned out to be disgust. Shaz grabbed Francis and marched off. A scream went up from Granny MacLauchlan who'd sat in Aulay's booth for a well earned breather. Silence descended. Everyone turned. Sensing a change, Yvonne opened her eyes, screeched, threw her head back and crashed into the table. Drinks fell about and pandemonium reigned. For Aulay, the rest of the evening passed in a bit of a haze.

When he woke up, 'Woke up' is a bit gentle. An old dosser was kicking lumps out of him.

"Son, you better get up. There's two polis comin'."

"Wha'... eh?"

"Get up. Ye can't have booze on the street."

Aulay was cuddling a can of Special Brew in a bus shelter on the Cathcart Road. Sitting up, he wished he hadn't. The world was spinning. The dosser grabbed Aulay's can of father's ruin and stuffed it into one of his coats.

"Jimmy, you ok?" said the taller PC.

"I'm awright, PC Cameron, youz?"

"This one givin' you any bother, Jimmy?"

"Naw, this is my pal, Aulay."

Jimmy put a wide grin onto his wrecked, bearded face. He patted his new pal on the head. Aulay nearly passed out.

With no obvious crime being committed, the policemen left with, "Ok, Jimmy. You go easy now."

When the PC's turned the corner Jimmy retrieved the can of Special Brew. He gave it a long look before handing it over.

"No, you have it, Jimmy... hic ...I've had enough"

Aulay didn't know that hiccups could light a banger inside your skull.

"Cheers, pal." Jimmy tugged the ring-pull.

In Aulay's vodka-sodden brain something monumental tried to break through.

"What am I doing here?"

Jimmy paused mid-guzzle.

"You fell out wi' yer bird and she waltzed off with some fenian wanker called Francis. You no' remember tellin' me about it?"

Everything came crashing back. Star billing went to the look of disgust on Shaz's face. A look that haunted Aulay's nights for months. His bridge to Shaz Curren had been tottering on a skelf and he'd set it on fire.

He forced a twenty onto his new friend and crawled out of Glasgow.

***

Eddie's hearse was stuck. To let the previous lot leave the crematorium the driver edged off the tarmac and paid the price. He approached the second car.

"I'm sorry, gents. Can I ask the bearers?"

Aulay and five others put their shoulders to the big Daimler and pushed. Nothing happened. Sweating, his polished black sleeks smeared in mud, Uncle Harry looked in at the coffin and let slip the communal thought.

"Eddie might be dead but he's still givin' us grief."

They couldn't do it. The bearers stood and roared the laugh of the stressed and uneasy.

Eddie's coffin slipped through the curtain while Sinatra sang 'My Way'. The cheap sound system was no match for the vaulted crematorium acoustics and Frank sounded distant. No matter. It worked. There were tears.

After the service came the car park loitering. Aulay rolled one and loitered solo. The man who'd shown him the ropes, and how to untie most of the knots, was gone. To think about something else, he scanned the faces. A mixed bag. Eileen McCloy worked a group of past their prime hoodlums in ill fitting suits. Aulay wondered how many played a stringed instrument. Eddie's cronies from The Stushie wandered aimlessly, lost without their leader. The family stood apart, tight-lipped. True Ones didn't get involved in scams or belong to a crew. Not strictly blood, Aulay's dad ran the odd errand. He'd been on an errand when the accident happened. Aulay was four and grew up with a twelve year old father. Everything was fine until Aulay turned fifteen, when a sleeveless v-neck wearing kling-on, with a five o'clock shadow, became an embarrassment.

Aulay's mum kept his dad on a loose leash. Dad walked the city every day, tidied his own room and filled the space with model ships and aircraft. With good hands and the diligence of an archaeologist, Dad's world was full of discovery, success and satisfaction. Sometimes Aulay wondered.

The night before he left for basic training, his mum sat him down for the 'boyfriend' conversation.

***

"Aulay, you know I'd never get rid of Dad. Put him in a home or anything."

"Aye, of course." He'd never thought about it.

"Well... There's something I need to discuss with you. You're off to the army now, grown up and..."

Tears were rare. Outside of her latest bodice ripper, when the heroine plucked an eyebrow, Aulay'd never seen any. This was serious.

"What I'm trying to say..."

Mum had been seeing her boyfriend for ages, in what she thought was secret. Aulay jumped in.

"Stan's a good bloke. Dad likes him and it's time you enjoyed yourself, in public."

It was a life-changing moment; letting sex out of the bottle. Anyway, Stan the Man had long since stopped paying Aulay silence money.

***

As the funeral cortege filled up for the return journey, Stan the Man approached.

"Sad day, young Mackay. You and Eddie were close."

"Aye, Stan. You got a light? How's Dad doin'?"

"Dad's a little confused and smoking's bad for you."

Everyone called Aulay's dad, Dad.

"Dad keeps asking for Eddie, it's all a bit much for him."

Stan paused as they both lit up.

"I've got a 420 piece Airbus 380 waiting. It'll take Dad out of himself."

"Good plan, Stan."

Aulay left the wake when two of Eddie's cronies started crying on each other's shoulders. Whisky-sodden, they'd been swinging punches at each other moments earlier.

"So... How was the bonfire?" asked Shaz.

They were in Aulay's cupboard. He'd spent the previous fifteen minutes in the communal shower trying to wash off the lingering crematorium smell.

"Busy," said Aulay towelling himself down.

"Did anyone leap into the flames after him?"

Aulay remained quiet. He wasn't in the mood for Shaz making light of it.

"I'm sorry."

Her tone rang true. He looked up. "When I was younger," he said. "I worshipped the guy. Still do in a way. Eddie gave me stuff you can't buy."

He got a cuddle then. The tears nearly came but Aulay had standards. He'd zipped up too many body bags to let himself go. The minutes passed.

"Here, use this." Shaz held out a tissue.

After his blub-fest, Aulay felt better.

"How'd you get on with the journalist?"
***

Shaz's office at Birltoni, Donald & Pratt is on the second floor of the Georgian building opposite Glasgow's High Court. BD&P's public space oozes success with polished hardwood floors and dark brown chesterfields. Austere looking plants, in floor-standing vases, parade across the reception hall.

Within months of joining the firm, Shaz was part of the place and the senior partners fought over her diary.

Bucking the firm's conservative tastes, Shaz decorated her office in pastel shades, beige leather and shiny chrome. The blinds were pink and Vincent van Gogh prints, from his

Arles period, hung on the walls. It was bling with style, she insisted.

Having head-hunted, and secured, the top achiever from Glasgow University, some unexpected side effects began to percolate through BD&P. Dressing like someone in advertising, Shaz introduced glamour into their dour world. After two days, Mr Birltoni reconnected with his Italian ancestry and silk ties appeared. The following Monday, before Mr Findlay Donald reached his first floor office, everyone knew that his tan loafers had been ditched in favour of leather oxfords. The firm's doyen held out for nearly a year. Returning from a Tuscan holiday, Miss Linda Pratt breezed in sporting a bob haircut and designer glasses. The receptionist asked, "Do you have an appointment?"

Shaz only agreed to the interview with John Maclean after a senior partner pushed. He'd laid it on thick... "We're a high profile criminal practice, Miss Curren... Have to keep in with the press... Having an old-school hoodlum's daughter here, as a junior partner, makes you newsworthy Sharon... Especially at this time."

There had been enquiring looks when Shaz announced that she wouldn't be attending her father's funeral.

"But John Maclean's a low-life letch," Shaz pleaded. "Why him?"

When Mr Birltoni bristled and responded with, "Miss Curren..." The outcome went beyond appeal.

Shaz first met Maclean during a dancing lesson. Maclean wasn't there to learn the tango. He had a sideline, collecting rent for The Polmadie.

The dancing instructor hired the Pennant Bar's basement for three afternoons a week to give modern, tap and Latin classes to bored housewives. A surge in all things Latin had produced a swelling in numbers and some weren't bored, or housewives. Two straight blokes turned up one day.

Maclean strode in shouting over the music, "Oi, Nine-Bob!"

George winced, hit pause on the remote and turned to his class. "Won't be a mo', ladies."

Sashaying over to his man bag, George foutered inside, pulled out an envelope and minced over to Maclean.

"It's all there, choochie-bum." George turned back to his class.

"Hold on." Maclean grabbed George's braces.

George's latest squeeze, Hugo, who stood next to Shaz, took a step forward. Shaz held his arm. It's ok," she said. "Georgie boy can take care of himself."

George faced Maclean. "Yes, my stallion?"

"Who's the bird in the black leather mini?"

"Och, are we smitten, love god?" George fluttered his eyelids.

"Cut the shite, Nine-Bob."

"Hang about. We're nearly done." George flicked something invisible from his sleeve. "May I go now, oh Lord of lust?"

Maclean hung about.

Overweight but not ugly in the conventional sense, Maclean carted his sleaze around on his face. His too full lips always seemed on the point of drooling. Throughout what remained of the tango lesson, his eyes flitted from Shaz's crotch, to her chest, and back again. As subtle as a wheel clamp.

At the end of the lesson Shaz gathered up her gear. Maclean walked over.

"Hey, doll," he said, "You fancy workin' out some more?"

"You're out of luck." Shaz sighed. "I wear knickers on a Tuesday."

The put-down produced a flicker of pleasure. Shaz cottoned on. Maclean bent to the masochistic wind.

An hour later, Shaz's mobile received a photograph of a stubby erection. There was no return number. Lawyers and crime reporters share the same spaces and, whenever their future paths crossed, another photograph would wing its way through the ether.

***

Shaz took a deep breath before ushering John Maclean into her office. She wasn't a student anymore. She'd climbed out of Polmadie. She was an up and coming lawyer. Dealing with the likes of Maclean would be a doddle.

Already sweating, Maclean's clammy palm slipped into Shaz's hand.

"Sorry I'm late," he said.

Shaz fell at the first fence.

"I heard that you only apologised for coming early."

Maclean's eyes widened. "Sorry, what did you...?"

She waved him away. "Mr Maclean, no need to apologise. Now, what can I do for you?"

Shaz can speak best-telephone. Her stint at university honed the rough edges off her street Glasgow. Maclean squeezed his frame into a chair making his ill-fitting suit struggle. He adjusted his black tie.

"You no' going to the crematorium then?"

The guy emitted cheap cologne in waves.

"No," said Shaz leaning back.

"How no'?"

"Been there, done that... when Mum died."

"Aye, there was a big do for Mrs Eddie."

Maclean leaned forward. "Shaz doll, any light to shed on the rumour your da' was shot?"

"My father died of cancer... without complications."

"But the shooting took place outside one of your colleagues' flat. The rumour is an eyewitness withdrew his statement."

Shaz had wondered what her dad offered the eyewitness. Life in a wheelchair? The negotiations wouldn't have lasted long.

"Sorry, Mr Maclean. Can't help you. Anything else?"

Maclean checked his notes.

"Eddie was old Polmadie and a little birdie tells me your da' was putting a new crew together."

Shaz wouldn't have put it past the auld bastard. "My father was too old to go sailing."

Maclean grinned. "Let me try another tack."

The limp nautical pun met a blank look.

"Did Eddie ever mention a group of classical musicians?"

"No."

When Maclean leaned forward a shirt button popped open revealing a white cotton vest. Shaz got it then. Aulay'd said, 'Does he wear a vest?' ...of course, Bruce Willis played... John McLane... in the Die Hard filums. Shaz smiled then watched Maclean take the smile and caress it.

"I've a source says the Top Banana of The Polmadie was seen leaving this office. More than once."

"Everything said within these walls is confidential, Mr Maclean. You know this."

"Ah, so you know Chancer MacKinnon is the new Banana?"

"I believe it's in your newspaper."

Shaz lifted a copy of the Daily Snot from her bin.

New Order at The Polmadie

An exclusive from our Organised Crime Reporter, John Maclean.

Today, Eddie Curren, the last link to the grim days of Davy 'Gory' McGlorry, is laid to rest in what will be the biggest collection of Glasgow hoodlums since Gory himself was slain back in 1989. The new Top Bannana of The Polmadie, Alec 'Chancer' MacKinnon is one of a new breed of gangster...

"There is one thing, Mr Maclean."

"Aye?"

"There are only two n's in banana."

'Some say Chancer MacKinnon is linked to the death of Mad Rab Smillie whose body was recently fished from the Clyde. The Strathclyde police are refusing to confirm that they are investigating a murder pending further forensic investigations.'

There was more tittle-tattle gleaned from the pubs on the south-side where Maclean did most of his 'investigating'.

"Shaz, please." Maclean leaned back, legs spread. "I'm under pressure here."

Keeping her eyes fixed on Maclean's reddening face, Shaz struggled to keep her fury in check.

She lowered her voice. "Relieving your pressure is not my game, Maclean."

A beetroot Maclean put his briefcase on his lap. He looked out the window, which was difficult as the blinds were down.

Shaz stood. "Your time's up."

Maclean's briefcase didn't move, relatively speaking, all the way to the door. Shaz waited. Masochists, even those with an erection, can rally for one last effort.

Maclean was a trooper. "Shaz doll, you'd get my last Rolo."

Shaz's composure lost the inner battle. "I'd shove it up your arse with a fork."

Maclean's expression suggested that a fork up his arse would be do-able.

***

"So," said Aulay, "Maclean left with what he came for?

"Aye, a fucking hard-on."

Aulay put a dod of gel in his hair. "And you've met Chancer MacKinnon?"

"Aye."

"What's he like?"

"Different. No' what I expected."

"How so?"

***

Not long after Mad Rab Smillie 'disappeared', a guy walked into Shaz's office. Average height, late twenties, unassuming. She'd pass him on the street without a glance.

"Miss Curren. Very pleased to meet you, and please, call me Chancer."

And there it was; the smile, it radiated.

It was too early for first names. "I know who you are, Mr MacKinnon."

"I'm not surprised, Miss Curren."

Chancer MacKinnon had another trait not associated with Top Bananas; he too could speak best-telephone.

"Can you come straight to the point?" said Shaz.

"Let's talk over lunch. I don't like offices."

Shaz didn't do business lunches. They too often turned into the client looking for more than legal advice. However, when the Senior Partners discovered who was in her diary they stressed the importance of securing such a high-profile client.

"Do whatever is necessary, Miss Curren." It wasn't a request.

Sitting in the vaulted bar of the Corinthian, Shaz tried to gauge the Banana, a murderer... allegedly. Raised eyebrows from legal eagles she knew, and the deference shown to Chancer MacKinnon by the staff, fed her unease, and her excitement.

"Why this place?" she asked after a light lunch of pasta, salad and chit chat about nothing.

In the dim and distant the Corinthian used to be the Sheriff Court. It was now a magnificent space laid out in booths where the city's wheelers and dealers did their business. The ceiling, half a mile up, was a concoction of Victorian sculpture and the plasterer's art. The outrageous pricing policy kept the hoi polloi at bay.

"Public place the Corinthian," said Chancer looking around. "You'll find more dodgy people here than in Queens Park at midnight."

"Why are we here and not in my office?"

Chancer produced an MP3 player and fiddled a bit. "Have a listen."

Shaz took the offered earpiece.

"Listen, hen. If I do time for this it's your stunnin' arse that's goin' to be on fire... and I don't give a shite who your father is."

She was listening to Mack the Knife, a new client who'd been in her office two weeks before.

Shaz heard her own voice...

"Mr MacNieve, the victim died from multiple stab wounds and your semen was discovered inside the dead

51

woman's body. In her left ear I grant you but, it puts you within range of her murder. You need to tell me everything or I can't help you."

Shaz removed the earpiece. "How did you get..."

Chancer pointed at her empty glass. "You want another?"

"No, thank you." What else did the Banana know? "So, Mr MacKinnon, what can I do for you?"

"I've got a handle on how The Polmadie works. It's taken me a while but things are coming together."

"What things?"

"Miss Curren, it's my intention is to make The Polmadie legit."

Shaz blinked. She'd assumed the Banana wanted to discuss legal strategy about his involvement in the 'disappearance' of Mad Rab Smillie. Now? The guy had gone all *Michael Corleone* on her.

Chancer held out a memory stick.

"My proposal. I'd like you to go over it. Look for stuff I've missed. To exit securely I need to keep the Revenue & Customs people happy."

"Should you not be more worried about Serious Crime?"

"A couple of things about the polis, Miss Curren. They need evidence to convince the Procurator Fiscal to go to trial. There is no evidence."

Chancer took a sip of his Irn-bru.

"As for my plan for the Polmadie, the polis investigate crimes already committed, not what the future holds. Crime prevention is an advertising slogan."

"And Revenue & Customs?"

"Those bastards, well, they can do what they like without a reason. They're answerable to no one. They can go back years and squeeze your ba... em, that's where you come in. I need to create legitimate businesses with clean money."

Top marks.

"Why me? There are more experienced people at BD&P."

"You come recommended and... let's say you understand my situation more than most."

The pair talked for three hours. When they'd finished, an impressed Shaz wondered what was next. Dinner maybe?

Chancer stood up wearing his big smile. Shaz followed his gaze to a heavily made-up redhead.

"Jem, hiya."

The Banana gave the girl a hug, a full on embrace. Not his sister then.

As Chancer did the introductions, the floozy tottered on six inch heels, her impressive chest to the fore.

Shaz's Chancer rating slipped.

"Hi, Sharon, nice to meet you," said the big busted tart.

Chancer headed for the bar.

Jemima MacAskill sat down smoothing her short skirt. Shaz waited for the thick red hair to be flicked, or a scan of the place to see who was looking her way. Neither happened.

"You're the lawyer then," Jemima said with an open smile. "Chancer needs a good one. You any good?"

Not the sort of question Shaz expected from a gangster's moll.

"Depends on the evidence."

"Good answer. You're everything Chancer said you'd be."

"Eh... sorry?"

"Chancer said he was meeting the most beaut... no, what he actually said was, 'I'm meeting an ARSF.'

Shaz snorted. Jemima MacAskill wasn't one of them. Them? Shaz had stopped counting insecure females after a thousand or so. Drooling husbands and boyfriends needed ditching. Lots of women didn't get it.

Shaz rewound. The office meeting, the invitation to lunch, the chat. Proper business chat, she reminded herself. With Chancer MacKinnon she'd got it wrong. How'd that happen? The smile. Shaz was angry with herself, and the Banana's fucking smile.

"What do you do?" Shaz asked.

"In my last year, I'm doing medicine at Glasgow."

The tart was nearly a doctor. Shaz started to laugh. How could she be so wrong? The bimbo floozy turned out to be a seriously bright medical person.

"I'm sorry, Jemima," Shaz snorted, "'cos you're with... I assumed..." she couldn't go on.

Jemima giggled too. "First impressions, eh?"

"Aye," cackled Shaz, "it's those tits, they give you away."

Both girls lost it then.

"You guys OK?" asked Chancer returning with a tray.

His arrival didn't help. The doubled-up females quadrupled. Chancer gave up, put the tray on the table and said, "I'm goin' for a pish."

It was the funniest thing Shaz and Jemima had ever heard.

***

Back in Aulay's cupboard, he was intrigued. "So, you fancy the new Banana?"

"This was months ago and, well... if he'd been free, who knows. He's got a nice smile."

Aulay slued off the conversational tone. "Aye, for a murderer."

"You jealous, immature or being a fanny?"

"All three."

54

Aulay didn't mention that Kenny Finlayson would still be alive if the Banana had been unattached.

"Anyway," he said, "how big are Jemima MacAskill's tits then?"

A smile spread across Shaz's face. She couldn't hold it back. Shaz Curren laughing was the sweetest sound Aulay knew... well, maybe a close second to the little squeals she made a short time later.

After Shaz left, Aulay spent the time, in his second shower of the day, collating what he knew or thought he knew.

John Maclean's information meant the Strathbungo Cellists had a broken string. Chancer MacKinnon taking the Polmadie down the righteous path was bollocks, a means to another end. Would infiltrating the gang be more complicated with Shaz as the Top Banana's lawyer? Dead right. And by Shaz's reckoning, Jemima MacAskill sported a fine pair of 34 DDs.

Aulay's phone vibrated. His spook. Hector had introduced himself in the Yadgar. A Pakistani cafe on Calder Street.

"Mr Mackay?"

Aulay looked up. The bloke by his table was over sixty and tall.

"My name is Hector. Force 12 says hello."

"How is Light Breeze?"

"He's very well."

The man's accent was off kilter, not Glasgow or Edinburgh, north and west maybe. Hector sported a slim moustache with combed back grey hair. He dressed well, nothing flashy but well made. Expensive shoes. Two years working for an American zillionaire had given Aulay insights. Dapper, an Uncle Eddie word, sprang to mind.

Hector carried a cane and from the awkward way he slipped into the seat opposite, the stick wasn't an ornament.

"That smells good," said Hector.

The waiter, Yousef, approached their table. Dismissing the menu with a wave Hector launched into Urdu. Yousef scribbled on his pad. After checking the details, the smiling waiter retreated.

"How did you find this place?" asked Hector.

"I walked past one day and the place was full of Asians. Thought I'd give it a try. Been coming ever since."

Aulay didn't mention his first visit to the Yadgar.

***

Scanning the menu, he saw a raft of things he didn't recognise. A dark skinned bloke sat in one corner drooling over a plate of bright red chops. When another flick through the menu didn't produce a result, he wandered over to the bloke in the corner.

"Excuse me, pal..." Aulay waved the menu. "If I wanted to order what you've got, what should I ask for?"

The man gave him a sad look and said, "Lamb chops."

***

If Aulay was to work for Hector, it wouldn't do any harm to probe a little.

"Where'd you get the lingo?"

His probe blew up on the launch pad.

"Mr Mackay, can you remember a number?"

Hector read out eleven digits. A mobile phone? Aulay repeated the number, backwards. Hector looked impressed.

"Do you know Alec 'Chancer' MacKinnon of the Polmadie?"

"The new Banana? Only to see. We're no' on speaking terms."

Yousef arrived with two chapattis, fish pakora and what looked like lamb in a thick dark gravy, and another wee chat in Urdu. Hector checked and sampled each of the plates in front of him.

"Serious Crime," said Aulay, "are halfway up Chancer MacKinnon's arse."

Hector dragged his gaze from his plate. "Are you talking about Mr MacKinnon's part in the previous Banana's sad demise?"

"Aye."

"Serious Crime are floundering. They have a rotting corpse but, without a witness, they've got nothing."

Hector selected a piece of haddock and dipped it into both the white and red pakora sauces.

"I'm after bigger fish," he said.

The guy could eat. He didn't wolf it down, more sensual. No two mouthfuls were the same as he dipped and scooped with bits of chapatti. After savouring each creation he'd sip from the newly arrived glass of sweet lasse.

Aulay's remaining lamb chop looked staid, his side of the table a little threadbare. He made a note to have Yousef bring him what Hector was having, next time.

"What bigger fish?"

"That can wait." Hector manoeuvred an elusive mix of lamb and chopped onion. With the delicacy finely balanced he looked around the cafe.

"You can be reckless, Mr Mackay and... I'm surprised I've not heard of this place."

So, Hector knew Glasgow well but wasn't up to date with this part of the south side. He'd also read Aulay's service record.

"The Yadgar used to be a kebab shop. They bought out the hair dresser next door."

Aulay pointed to one wall where the plumbing for 6 sinks was still visible below an array of electrical sockets for blow driers, tongs and the like.

"Tell me about the Anfursati Mosque," said Hector behind a mouthful.

Ah, the pinnacle. Not the finest action of Aulay's military career but the one with the furthest-reaching consequences. The incident gave him some notoriety.

***

Anfursati, Iraq

It was a local dignitary's funeral and Aulay's company patrolled the mosque's perimeter. An Arab boy shuffled along. Aulay ignored him until something made him look twice.

"He wore one brown sandal and one black sandal. My eyes lied to me. I'd been expecting a pair so that's what I saw."

Something clicked. Aulay barked an order as he ran up the steps of the mosque. Barging his way through, he ignored the desecrating howls from family and mourners. She was twenty metres away, full burqa with gold thread. She turned at the commotion. Aulay shot her in the head, twice.

Mourners screamed and scattered in panic.

Aulay stood over the body as the rest of his unit caught up. They looked scared and mystified, but followed Aulay's barked instructions to form a ring round him and the body.

The crowd's hostility grew. The noise increased inside and outside the mosque. Furious young Arab men steeled themselves, flexing their fundamentalist muscles against this unholy outrage.

Aulay shouted into the ear of his Iraqi interpreter. "Tell everyone to stay back."

Abdul stared through startled eyes. Before the war he'd been a civil servant in the Ministry of Education. Books were his thing, not bellowing fellow countrymen bent on eating his liver. The first row closed in, pushed from behind by a growing mass of indignant mourners. Aulay's men fidgeted. It would be a bloodbath. Aulay rammed his gun into his interpreter's shin. Out of his stupor, Abdul screamed at the crowd to stand back.

The Imam stood in the pulpit, is it a pulpit? Aulay signalled for him to come over. When the Imam didn't move Aulay pointed his pistol. The Imam hesitated again. Aulay fired a round past his left ear. The man hurried over. What looked like an attempt to shoot the Imam didn't boost Aulay's fan base.

Handle first, Aulay held out his knife and pointed at the corpse. The Imam was having none of it. Aulay grabbed the man's wrist forcing his hand onto the dead body. The Imam felt the irregular lumps. He took the knife. Aulay cleared two of his guys away so the frenzied mob could watch. The

Imam's slicing revealed a copy of the Quran strapped onto explosives, and a week's stubble.

When he'd scanned the mourners Aulay had dismissed her. The Arab boy's odd shoes made him rewind. The shoulders. They were neither female nor mournful. They were of a man about to enter a state of grace and claim his 72 virgins.

The incident passed into legend as, *The Mourn Identity*. Aulay got a medal from the Brits, the Americans, the Iraqis and an invitation to the post-funeral activities. He stayed for three days. Two of the dead dignitary's wives were particularly grateful. Eighty-three members of their family were in the mosque along with a good number of the Iraqi ruling elite.

Aulay's telling of the story left out the widows' generosity.

***

"It's a minbar," said Hector.

"Eh?"

"The pulpit in a mosque is called a minbar."

"I'll remember that."

Hector finished his meal, sat back, mopped the thin sheen of sweat from his brow, blew his nose and basked in the glow.

"Ah, the spices," he said, "almost to the point of pain. A gastronomic delight".

Yousef arrived to clear the debris.

Alone again, Hector smiled. "A big risk, charging into a mosque on such flimsy evidence?"

"I got lucky."

During his rampage through the holy place, Aulay's brain had screamed, 'what the fuck are you doing?' Gambling with his own life didn't give him any grief, but his men?

60

"I was on autopilot." Aulay shrugged. "It worked out."

"What made you leave the army and join the private sector?"

What to say? What to say? Five years is a lot. Was his luck running out? Special Ops is full-time, even asleep. He'd lost good friends, people closer than family, as well as a grip on the reasons why they were over there.

"The money's better."

"Aye, right," said Hector. He left it there.

Looking into the man opposite, Aulay sensed a kindred spirit. Hector had been round the block. He was tempted to ask about the cane but held back. A story for another time.

"This will be our link." Hector passed over a business card. "The web address will need a password. Use the number I gave you." He took the card back. "I will give you a time. You will then call the same number from a public phone box or a *pay-as-you-go*."

"Bit laborious, isn't it?"

"Get a Blackberry," said Hector, "get two."

He showed Aulay his trick mobile phone.

"Set up a few email accounts. Keep one phone on top up, pay cash and only use it if you're entering The Dire Straits. Register both phones via the web link."

Hector stood up. "Goodbye, Mr Mackay." They shook hands.

Aulay watched his spook cross Calder Street. The cane was an accompaniment to the rhythm of the man. Hector limped like he meant it.

He wondered about 'The Dire Straits'?

Since that first meeting, Aulay'd sent the odd cryptic 'progress' report and a few bits of gossip. If he was one of Hector's agents, it was very low key.

Chapter 9   band practice

Tuesday, 7.55pm.

Aulay approached the Fotheringay down the back lanes of Strathbungo with two heavy hearts. Uncle Eddie was gone and, no matter how slick his plan looked, meeting his crew was going to be a disaster.

"Oh, be still my beating heart," whispered the lurking Eileen McCloy. "Howz about a quickie?"

"Sorry, Eileen. They're empty."

"What? You and Shaz back shaggin' again?"

Aulay and Shaz were still circling each other. He'd sensed her wariness along with a lingering hostility. He kept his distance. He didn't want to blow it, again.

"Why The Strathbungo Cellists?" he asked.

"Before the Fotheringay shut-up shop, they rehearsed in the back bar."

Eileen led the way. The Fotheringay took up the ground floor of a tenement on Nithsdale Road. The pub used to be the place to go. It went downhill when the last owner started drinking the stock and throwing darts at customers. They went through a gate and walked across the back-green to a metal door. After Eileen gave the secret knock, the door opened and they entered the boarded up boozer. In the dimly lit lounge sat six cellists. There were no instruments. All eyes followed Aulay's wee black bag.

The Fotheringay had the lonely look of the abandoned with dusty shelves and bare patches on the walls where landscapes of old Glasgow and the dart board once ruled. A dirty pint glass lay on the floor, its future bleak.

"Let me introduce you to our players," said Eileen. "Arnold 'Fang' Leadbetter. A Fat Controller ice-cream-van driver. Fang delivers the scag and knows the timetable."

"Aulay, you in?" whistled Fang.

One of Fang's vampire teeth stuck straight out. With his top lip forever snagging, he spoke and whistled at the same time. Aulay always wondered why he never got it fixed.

"I'm here to learn, Fang. Howz Ivy?"

"Och, no' bad now the ramp's in. She can get out to the garden."

"She know about this?"

"Jesus, Aulay, you know Ivy. She thinks I'm at the bowlin'."

"Why you here?"

"Need the money."

"Must need it pretty bad. The new Top Banana's no wimp. He'll come after you." Aulay looked round. "All of you."

"He won't know it's us," whistled Fang. "It's all in the Plan."

"What you need the money for?"

An armed robber needed lots of motivation.

"I've got bugger all and nothing in the pipeline. Ivy dreams of retiring to the sun. If we don't do this, I'm goin' to be sauntering down the social for a few quid a week, 'til the end."

Aulay nodded. Eileen moved on.

"Liam 'Meow' McGuire. Best burglar on the south side. Meow's been in more bedrooms than Tiger Woods."

Aulay stayed with the golfing theme. Meow had the air and build of Gary Player about him. Mr Player must be seventy-odds by now.

"Hi, Meow, when'd you get out?"

"Three months ago."

Meow's script never changed. His security consultant business cards were all over the place. He'd carry out a

63

survey, complete an inventory of items worth stealing and produce a security report, for a fee.

The fee was Meow's wanker filter. "If the bastard's no' willing to pay a consultant then he's too tight to have anything worth nicking."

Meow relayed successful tenders to legitimate security companies, for a percentage. A lucrative inventory would result in a return visit, in the dark, eighteen months later.

"Still dishing out the business cards?"

"No' anymore, Aulay. Got a web site."

"Of course."

"You still gettin' blowjobs in public?"

Aulay was famous.

"Only when the money's right."

There were a few smirks and the tension in the room eased.

Meow's motivation was crime, a livelong devotee.

"There'll be guns involved."

Shooters weren't Meow's thing.

"In the plan, I'm on the roof. No need for a gun up there, Aulay."

There it was again. The plan of the prophet, St Eddie, patron-saint of old crooks. This crew were true-believers. Eileen moved on.

"Ivor 'Paki' Solomon. A Polmadie Recipient until Mad Rab Smillie threw him out. Paki knows all the routes."

A Recipient delivered the hard drugs to the street dealers which kept the crack-heads away from the Depot. Paki was a dead-ringer for Liza Minnelli's fourth husband. Aulay could never remember that guy's name.

"Shalom, Paki. Why'd you get the chop?"

"Two light loads in a row. I was on the ran-dan and let my boy pick up the shipments. He... em, lifted a few samples."

"How is Morris?"

"No' bad. He's off the scag and got a bird."

Mad Rab Smillie had beaten so much crap out of Paki's son, the teenager needed six operations. Aulay had bumped into Morris the other day. His face was still squinty and he poured lager in one side of his mouth. His bird wasn't a stunner either but they were happy, Aulay could tell.

"Why you still out, Paki?"

"The new Banana's got a thing about drinking on the job. I fell foul."

When Aulay found out that the Polmadie Capo's carried breathalyzers, he was stunned.

"How long you been on the wagon?"

"Three months, Aulay. I'm clean."

Paki had the only corner shop in Kinning Park not run by Pakistanis. Cut Kinning Park; the entire city.

"What's your story, Paki?"

"The Polmadie owe me. I've been running their drugs for years. Taking all the risks while they raked in all the cash. I'm due some."

It made sense.

"Mohamed 'Osama' Bin Al Alludie," continued Eileen. "Did the Albert Drive bank job with the Farzzi brothers."

"What you doin' here, Osama? You're loaded."

"Was, my friend. Turns out I was working for foreign masters. It all went overseas."

"Serious Crime or any others been sniffing after you?"

The mention of Serious Crime shook more than one cellist. The police were bad enough but Serious Crime were a law unto themselves, especially these days when every brown skinned bloke was suspected of keeping quiet, at least.

"I'm safe, Aulay. I can prove it."

"Any of your old Taliban pals keeping tabs on you?"

Another tremor rippled through the cellists.

"No, Aulay. I was three times removed."

"You got a plan?"

"Och aye. My kids are all married now. I'm going home to Beirut to open a computer shop."

Aulay nodded.

"Last but not least," said Eileen, "Stan the Man. Procurement and Storage. Stan's been buying what we need already. He still has the three containers he used to use for stock."

"Mum know about this then, Stan?"

"No, Aulay, of course not."

"What's your story?"

"B&Q took my life away. I spent everything to keep the shop going. I need a result. Your mum and I, we hope to get married soon. We'll keep Dad, of course."

Aulay's mum's boyfriend wants to marry his mum and have his dad along for the trip. Weird or what?

Aulay's mum divorced Dad when his mental age was diagnosed. You need to be sixteen to stay married in Scotland.

That left McCloy.

"What's your contribution to the Strathbungo Cellists then, Eileen?"

"I apply balm wherever and whenever necessary. You know me?"

So, the players...

A hard drugs delivery driver on every police radar.

A burglar who spent more time in jail than out.

An alcoholic grocer out to avenge his son.

A Muslim linked to Al Qaeda and stalked by Serious Crime.

A love struck shopkeeper, retired.

Not your typical Glasgow crew.

"How much you put in, Eileen?"

With no obvious money bags leaping out, Aulay had made an assumption. Eileen owned property. Lots of it. He'd no idea how much she was worth. Pub speculation put a lot of zeros in the total. Not a flaunter, Eileen dressed well, even at the Jessie Street car boot sale where, most Saturday mornings, she can be found rifling through the piles of crap for a bargain.

"About fifty grand, so far," she said.

"Much left?"

"Thirty five odd."

"Is there more, if needed?"

"For you, Aulay? Of course."

"What's in it for you, Eileen?"

"I owed Eddie big time." She coughed. "A private matter. When he came to see me...any amount, no questions asked. We started a bottle and he laid out the scheme. In hospital, when he knew the worst, he said you'd take over. Said your army training would come in handy."

"Eddie's gone, Eileen. What you got going here now?"

"Truthfully? It's thrilling. The most exciting thing I've been involved in since, well, you don't need to know when."

"You telling me you're in this for the malarkey?"

"Aye... and the possibility of getting into your pants."

Add to the list...

Eileen McCloy; thrill seeker and sexual predator.

It was time for a bout of devil's advocate.

"How long since the Cellists formed?"

"Four months, give or take," said Eileen.

"Rehearsals?"

"Eh?"

"How many times you ran the plan?"

"Three. Would have been four but it was raining."

"Not expecting rain on the big night then?"

Silence.

"Many changes?"

"The odd tweak. I'm sure Eddie updated the script."

He had but the black hole in the Fifth Testament was there for all to see.

Aulay ran the crew through the routine from start to finish, twice. Each band member did well. No virtuoso performances but impressive. When he threw in a couple of realistic hiccups, no-one hit a bum note.

"C'mon, Aulay, try another," purred Meow who was kneeling on the bar pretending it was a roof.

Aulay paced the floor enjoying his first cigarette in a boozer for a while. It was time. Feeling like a team building instructor after the tree hugging and before the abseiling, he pulled the first rug.

"Who's got the IP cameras?"

Puzzled expressions.

"The log-in?"

From puzzled, the looks changed to puzzled with a bit of worry.

"Are the passwords changed every day? Every hour?"

He had them now. It was a technique from his Special Ops training. Get them high then blow the plan away.

"To access beyond the hatch is it swipe card, number code, fingerprint or retina recognition?"

The cellists needed time to retune.

"I need a pish," said Aulay. "Do the bogs still work?"

He stubbed his cigarette out on the floor and headed for the gents. The lights didn't work, so God knows what state he left the place in.

Back in the dim lounge, Osama was first. "Tell us. Are we screwed?"

Osama should have been more up to speed but then, bank jobs are in-out, bells ringing. Who gives a shite, if you're quick. The Fifth Testament was a six-hour armed kidnapping.

"No' yet," said Aulay.

In the dark toilet, his reasoning had been... 'The Polmadie will be up your arse in five minutes. Thanks for a fun evening, and goodnight.'

Where did, 'Not yet' come from?

Two days before, Aulay had paid a visit to The Polmadie Consigliore's flat. The Consigliore wasn't there at the time. He and his lady were having the buffet at the New Anand curry house.

***

Taking along Bandit, a pal of Aulay's since school and a wiz in the world of I.T., they'd slipped into the Consigliore's flat where Bandit hid his gizmos. Later, in Bandit's spare bedroom, the extent of The Polmadie's IT revolution was revealed.

"Forget PC1." Bandit pointed at one of the screens on his desk. "It's linked to the internet and used for the usual bollocks, surfing, music and film downloads etcetera."

He pointed to another screen. "PC's 2 & 3 are bouncers and mirror a server."

I.T. Multiple Choice Test.

Q1:

What is a server?

A tennis player.   [ ]

A big computer.   [ ]

Someone behind a counter.   [X]

Server? Bouncer? Mirror? Aulay had no idea.

"There's one server in The Bull's office and the other... not a clue."

"Why not?"

"PC 1 accesses eight IP cameras. One of them looks onto a big fuckin' sign which reads, 'The Bulls Security Ltd'. No' a bad clue, eh?"

Aulay nodded.

"And, although I'm a genius, I've still to master the art of seeing down cables and following digital data. This is not Hollywood. On the other hand..." Bandit glanced to where his left hand would have been, if he'd had one, "...we have the IP address of server two and we could get lucky."

"I know where it is," said Aulay. "The Depot. It's on West Street. Sandwiched between a wholesale outlet and a Scot Rail works."

Bandit's next sentence had fourteen words in it. Aulay recognised three.

"Give me what you have in English, Bandit. Preferably words of one syllable."

"The Depot server logs all the ins and outs. It controls access to three separate areas and monitors its own bank cameras. The cam-signals are encrypted, so we can't see them. There's random password generation every hour, received via text message, to four mobile phones, on two different networks."

"What are the three areas in the Depot?"

70

"Goods-in, collation and goods-out. Goods-in has a weighbridge, number plate recognition and identification software running on two cameras."

"Fuck me."

"No' tonight," said Bandit. "It took me a while to latch on. Every driver is 'recognised' and the weight is checked before the up and over door kicks-in."

"A van full of bodies is going to set off the fireworks?"

"Aye, and the gates behind you will already be closed. You'd be stuck."

"Jesus H Christ. This is some setup and we're no' even in the place yet."

"If you get through goods-in, the next up-and-over gate lowers before the hatch to collation is activated."

"Only from the inside?"

"Think so. There will be a master entry-code for the hatch. I'm calling it a hatch. Similar to the in-out hatches on a security van. Too small for a man."

"Goods-out follows the same script?"

"Aye."

Aulay stayed quiet. Repeating 'fuck me' all the time would get annoying.

"This is a serious operation, Aulay. I've set up a few systems but this is run by one geezer sitting in collation, monitored by a mirror PC in the Consigliore's flat and one other location. Yer man has mobile text warning activated. Wherever he is, the Consigliore can shut the whole thing down. Every driver, in or out, will be warned off."

"Any good news?"

"Maybe. The geezer in collation has a get-out clause. At the evacuate signal he legs it. I'm making an assumption here but, I don't think the bloke calmly exits the premises,

71

climbs into his Mondeo and drives home. Oh, and when the polis get in they'll find lots of ash."

"Ash?"

"Aye, the heating, lighting and ancillary equipment are controlled via the server. Deposited cash runs on a conveyor into an incinerator where the drugs are stored. The cash stays there until goods-in is empty and goods-out is secure."

"The collation geezer, how does he get out?"

"The sewer, the roof, no idea, but he does and not through a door."

"How's that?"

"The evacuation signal shuts everything down, lock, stock and all the doors. If there's a body with a pulse, infra-red sensors will stop the bonfire. Otherwise, the drugs and the cash go up in smoke."

Destroying the evidence is always a good plan.

"What happens after goods-out?"

"Same script. Text message acknowledgement of receipt. Same when the cash reaches its destination. I've counted 63 money laundering sites on the monitoring system. A slip-up, time delay, whatever and The Polmadie will shut down, crawl into their burrow and wait it out... or Skulk, as they call it."

"Skulk?"

"Aye, a recipient misses a drop off, a laundry doesn't text receipt of the cash, anything dodgy and they fire up Skulk. Everyone goes home after dropping their load in a safe place... just think... sometimes there's a good many geezers skulking about stashing serious amounts of cash and drugs in graveyards or behind hoardings all over Glasgow."

Eddie's Fifth Testament only had one flaw. This wasn't 1978.

***

Aulay left the cellists in the fusty lounge of the Fotheringay with an agreement to meet again.

Splitting up the band wasn't in his best interest, yet. He could let the cellists get to the gig then, before the fat lady sang, reveal the scheme to The Polmadie. It could be his way into the gang.

Chapter 10   pub quiz

Pub quizzes weren't Aulay's thing. Too many people get overly serious about whether the Isle of Man is part of the British Isles. Who gives a shite?

But, Shaz promised to fill a spot in her pal's team.

"It's an emergency. Someone's called off."

"You'll owe me."

Their date got hijacked.

Aulay nursed a pint, with irritation chaser, in Sammy Dows' back-bar. It was a place he knew. Every Thursday night the venue hosted a jam session where ageing rockers climbed onto the small stage to plink and pluck their stuff. Uncle Eddie was a big fan and used to drag Aulay along. He'd begin the evening bored beyond tears. By shutting time, he'd be screaming along with everyone else for one more rendition of a bygone melody.

Tuesday night was quiz night and the place looked different. The lights were on.

"Those four auld blokes call themselves, The Brat Pack," said Shaz. "They're the favourites."

The Brat Pack showed their superiority by ignoring everyone else. The No Hopers, four women more interested in a blether and a few Bacardi Breezers, were giggling already. A pair of husbands and wives made up the Odd Couples, the second favourites. Behind the mask of... it's just for a laugh, both husbands kept glancing at the Brat Pack, hoping for a heart attack maybe?

Aulay asked Shaz's team, "What are you guys called?"

"Last Week's Winners."

Aulay's aloof detachment cracked.

Sally was the head of trivia with Posh Spice and Cheryl Cole her specialist subjects. Nan was the acknowledged science expert and not too shoddy at geography either. Natalie worked in the Daily Snot canteen so held the current affairs brief. Shaz was stepping into Greg's shoes, the only bloke in the team, in charge of sport. This was a shame.

"What do you know about sport?"

"Nadal's got a nice bum and that Ronaldo too."

After the first general knowledge round, Aulay slipped down to the main bar to watch Montrose play Elgin City. Anything with a ball was better than the riveting spectacle upstairs. They also had Stella Artois on draught.

Before half-time, Shaz appeared.

"Well, hello Aulay...*what river goes through Baghdad?*... how are you?"

"Shaz, you *Tigris*, how you doin'?"

A little later...

"Aulay, you still here...*who wrote Brazzaville Beach?*...on your own?"

"Aye, Shaz. My night out with the *Boyd*s fell through and *William* couldn't make it."

Montrose won two nil, Aulay felt the pleasant glow of a few Stella and his earlier irritation had been replaced by a cockiness sponsored by two sharp answers. He made his way upstairs for the finale. He felt the tension. Crossing the lounge, he spotted one of the Odd Couples speed texting under the table. Was phone-a-friend allowed?

Last Week's Winners were neck and neck with the Brat Pack and the Odd Couples. It was the last round with two questions left.

"What band does Gwyneth Paltrow's husband play in?"

The Brat Pack's huddle tightened as the quizmaster played back the scores to crank it up.

Should he, thought Aulay. What the hell. He wandered over to the Odd Couples.

"Excuse me?"

Husbands one and two looked up.

"You will get the last question wrong."

"What the-"

"Do you want me to expose your mobile phone scam."

Both husbands looked, em ...Aulay racked his brain. Aghast is a good word. Both husbands looked aghast. Wives one and two curled up with the humiliation of it all. Caught cheating, here, in Sammy's.

Shaz popping down to the bar wasn't the same thing and anyway, Stella had said it was alright.

Aulay returned to his seat as the quizmaster held up a blank A4 sheet.

"I will turn this photograph round for five seconds. The question is; who is it?"

With a dramatic flourish he revealed... Aulay's brain scrambled, he'd never seen one without the other. Was it Ant or Dec?

Aulay nodded to acknowledge a couple of daggers thrown by husband number two, but hey, the man got caught.

Letting everyone stew as he slowly counted up the totals, the quizmaster milked his moment in the spotlight. Even Aulay's bum squeaked.

Last Week's Winners became this week's winners and they jumped about like Olympic gold medallists. The Odd Couples upped and left. One of the Brat Pack got sent to Coventry for insisting it was The Arctic Monkeys when it should have been Coldplay.

And it was Dec, or...

Husband number two loitered outside the pub. "Think you're a smart bastard then?"

"No' really," said Aulay, "just playing by the rules."

Husband number two moved close, too close. Aulay finished rolling his cigarette and fired up his lighter. "You know what rules are?"

His intimidation technique not working, husband number two turned away. "Watch yourself, son. I'll be keeping an eye on you."

Last Week's Winners emerged still charged with the glory of it all.

"You upset the DI then, Aulay?" said Shaz.

"The who?"

"Detective Inspector McCaw." Shaz looked at the retreating husband number two.

"You know him?" asked Aulay.

"Aye, hard as nails. I've defended more than one of McCaw's arrests. One or two came to court straight from hospital."

"They deserve it?"

"No doubt, but I think DI McCaw enjoys it a little too much. There's a lot of 'resisting arrest' or 'the accused fell down stairs'. My favourite was a couple of months ago, 'the accused self harmed'." Shaz snorted. "The guy had a broken nose."

Shite, thought Aulay. A wee bit of gamesmanship and he'd ended up with a detective inspector monkey on his back. Things looked up when This Week's Winners turned into Shaheds on Pollokshaws Road. Nothing like a proper kebab to cheer you up.

It was after midnight when they got back to the cupboard. Belly full, good full, Aulay anticipated two spoons with Shaz before sleeping the sleep. **It was not to be**. The pink panther melody drifted up from his phone.

"Aulay, you better get over here." It was Bandit.

"See you in ten," said Aulay. "Sorry Shaz-babe, got to go."

"What you up to, Aulay?"

"I've got something going with Bandit, and you know him, no clocks. I'll tell you later, promise."

Explaining his predicament to Shaz was getting closer. He was editing the 2nd draft. Aulay reached his car without his car keys. He re-entered the cupboard to find Shaz bending over to re-arrange the bed covers.

"I thought you said ten minutes?" said an irate Bandit.

"Sorry," said Aulay, "something came up."

Bandit sat at his control-centre underneath the poster of his hero, Spencer Tracy in the filum, 'Bad Day at Black Rock'. Electronic equipment thrummed and buzzed. Little blue, red and green led's flashed intermittently, as black boxes did what black boxes do.

The one-armed Bandit looked at life through a different lens. That part of the brain that most people reserve for putting up shelves, Bandit honed from an early age.

In primary school, Aulay remembered when Bandit asked Julie McCorkie to hold his pencil sharpener. For the next six months, Julie followed Bandit about in social-carer mode. Following that episode, Bandit put one of his vices on permanent pencil-sharpener gripping duty.

Of all the Bandit's vices, Aulay's favourite was the shoe lace adding machine. Football boots don't come in a slip-on variant and when it rains, trainers are as useful as ice skates on a beach. Bandit needed something, not someone, to tie his laces. The Mk I SLAM was enormous, all springs and angles. The Mk IV, with its pad and a single hook-clamp meant Bandit's other foot could tension the spring, and one lace. Genius.

Bandit sailed through school and tech with ease. A freelance consultant, he took on the funnies, the technical problems conventional engineers looked at and scratched their heads.

He pointed at one of his screens. "See this?"

"What am I looking at?"

"We've been traced. The Polmadie's system has a tracker loop, a really small one. I didn't spot it."

Aulay gave Bandit the evil-eye.

"It means they know we're in. They're watching us watching them."

"Do they know who we are?"

"They'll have our IP address and the level of our penetration."

Aulay's thoughts drifted to Shaz... stop it.

"Are we in danger?" Upsetting The Polmadie was way down Aulay's list.

"An IP address search will lead them to Budapest then up a blind alley. My current blind alley has a locked gate and should hold... for twenty-four hours."

Jeez, the techno lingo. "Should?"

"I've pulled the plug. Any intrusion after the locked gate will be drained off."

Aulay'd had enough. "Bandit, let me spell this out. This is The Polmadie we're fooling about with, no' Mothercare. If they find us, we're well and truly fucked. Tell me if we need to catch a plane to Rio in the morning."

The Bandit got it.

He'd been playing cyber tech wars, pitting his wits against the brains on the other side of digital-land, and loving it. Turning to one of his weird keyboards, Bandit started typing. The keys, arranged in a sort of semi-circle around a roller ball mouse, clicked gently as Bandit's only hand flitted over them.

"Hungarian keyboard, great design," he'd told Aulay. "There must be lots of one-armed people in Hungary. They even have one for lefties."

The Bandit woke Aulay as he lay in the middle of a debauched congregation of nubile surf babes. Dawn had switched on

"How we doing, Bandit?"

"We're safe. I instigated a reverse thrust and..."

The geek-speak continued until Aulay made coffee. Sitting at Bandit's kitchen table, they talked football.

Forty minutes late for his date with Shaz, Aulay met two frosty stares as he slid into his seat at Zorba's, on the High Street. Gregorio, the grumpiest waiter in Glasgow stood behind Shaz. He got away with outlandish treatment of his diners by maintaining a consistent level of abuse. The punters loved it. Leaving someone like Shaz waiting put Aulay at the bottom of Gregorio's food chain.

Aulay's tepid lamb finally arrived with a crash, and a look of contempt. One of Gregorio's finest.

"You've no' been arrested yet." said Shaz.

"No' yet."

"You're on thin ice."

"Why?"

"You know and I know."

"What do you know?"

"I'm no' an idiot. You're running here and there. Your mobile's stuck to your ear and you've got a tremor on the go."

Bandit almost stepping into The Polmadie's digital snare had ramped things up. Only Shaz could spot the tremor, now Uncle Eddie was gone.

Aulay sat back. What did he want? He wanted Sharon Curren. They walked the walk. Losing her, again... eek. She needed to know enough to trust him, to stop asking questions. Not easy. His knight in shining armour and secret agent testimonies would be inadmissible, even though one of them was true.

"I've got a few things on, but if I tell you, you'd be put in a position."

Shaz's fork froze. "Me...? I'd be put in a position?"

Aulay watched as Shaz trawled through her filing system. It didn't take long. Her fork hadn't moved.

"My firm's clients are the fuckin' meanest, nastiest bastards on the planet and you're dickin' about with them?"

"It's something I need to do." Aulay sounded like Gary Cooper before he stepped onto the street, alone, to face the gun slinging baddies.

"How deep is the shite?"

Aulay shrugged.

Shaz's fork moved to an inch from his chest. "You get caught and receive a custodial; I don't do the hanging around, waiting thing. We tried that once before..."

Aulay met her gaze.

"...remember?"

"Shaz-babe..." He knew before it left his lips.

"Fuck the Shaz-babe shite, Aulay."

Gregorio was all ears and smiling.

"I will not let you fuck me about. Before it starts, I'll be off."

Aulay bit the bullet. Shaz needed to know. He took a deep breath and... The pink panther theme played. It was Bandit.

"Sorry," he said, "I need to take this."

If they'd been having a lovey-dovey giggly evening would he have been caught out? Who knows? As soon as Aulay arrived on the pavement, the dark cloud appeared. He woke up in the boot of a small German car.

***

Aulay sussed out the rear wheel drive, a sporty model from the throaty rumble and snappy acceleration. The boot was cramped. He had it down as a small Audi or a 3 Series BMW. A two door after the front seat shifted to let the third guy out. During his time in the dark, Aulay flicked through the interrogation manuals. Abduction = assume a level of abuse.

A boot up his arse followed by, "Move, fucker!" proved the point. Aulay shuffled forward with the wary gait of the blind. Another kick. Another instruction.

"Stop."

Aulay took in his surroundings. The hood over his head flapped in the breeze and the cable ties round his wrists were tight. The air tasted salty. Gravel or pebbles ground under his Doc Martins. There was a hum from a generator or a big freezer. He was at some remote seaside cottage or round the back of a fishmonger's.

A key went into a lock, no, a padlock. A door opened with a metallic screech Aulay recognised. A container. Shite, this wasn't good. A quick flash of a coolie discovering his remains in distant China flitted through his mind. Another push and Aulay tripped over the container's lip. Falling blindfolded, with your hands behind your back, is a bit scary.

Dragged up onto a chair by two of the three blokes, Aulay made sure his breathing remained steady. Why would there be a chair? His vision of a slow trip to the Far East faded. The chair was good. The hood stayed on. Another positive. If he was going to suffer life ending grief, his abductors wouldn't worry about being seen. It was a tip the British army passed on to every westerner in the Middle East. Hoods are good. They mean you're worth something. Some western hostages knew this by instinct, protecting their hoods more than their crotch. Others made the mistake of removing the hood, to put their captors in a position. The new position? Kill the fucker and kidnap someone else.

"Well, Mr Mackay, you've been busy."

Aulay recognised the voice, a vague thing. He couldn't put a face, good education, north side of the city. He'd not been asked a question so kept quiet.

"Do you miss your Uncle Eddie then, Mr Mackay?"

"Aye, you?"

"Yes, I do. We had an arrangement."

"So, you're the fucker. I've been waiting to hear from you."

Aulay braced without moving. The blow was not as bad as it might have been but he made sure he toppled to the floor. The way they hoisted him back onto the chair was a relief, these guys were pro's. Aulay's first thought, that he'd been picked up by The Polmadie, a bunch of amateurs. Amateurs have a poor hostage/kidnap survival ratio.

These guys must be the police, who kick the shite out of people all the time, yet few die. Aulay now recognised his questioner as DI McCaw, husband number two of the Odd Couples.

"I'm here to tell you one thing, Mackay."

"Keep it short. I'm on a date."

He braced. There was movement but Aulay sensed the one about to strike stopped. Amazing what you can pick up with a hood on. With the eyes out of action, the ears and the hairs on the back of the hand do what they normally do but the brain pays more attention.

"We know you've taken over Eddie's crew."

"The Cellists?" said Aulay. "String quartets are not my scene. Opera though, that Bocelli geezer. He's got the voice of God."

If DI McCaw knew of the blind Italian tenor, he'd get it. Inside the hood, Aulay would sing.

"Cut the crap, Mackay."

The backhand slap was severe, not vicious. They wanted him unmarked.

"We have it all. You will carry out the raid on The Polmadie's Depot and we'll take 50%. How you split with the rest of the crew is up to you. Anything happens to upset this and you'll be fucked. Do you understand me, Mackay?"

Another slap. Aulay tasted blood. Poor technique. The back of the hand is more likely to mark someone. He stayed quiet, waiting for the next slap.

The low sound of cotton on cotton as an arm swung out. Tut tut, the backhand again. Opening his mouth Aulay caught a finger, a good grip on a knuckle. As his head swept to the side with the force of the blow, he felt a delightful 'snap' followed by a howl. Backhand man would need a splint.

On the floor, Aulay curled into a ball. He took a few in the ribs.

"Shite, Graeme, leave it!" barked McCaw. "Fuckin' hell, stop, both of you. Now! Get him back on the chair. Christ almighty."

Aulay smiled, ignoring his aching jaw. He had two names.

DI McCaw, Graeme and the third policeman left for a confab. They had two options. Leave it where it was or get rid of him. Murder is a different sport with another set of consequences. Corrupt police want money, easy money. If Aulay didn't play along they could pick him up again.

After Shaz's assessment of DI McCaw: a no nonsense operator, bit of a thug but no mug, Aulay suspected the DI was looking for his retirement score. Muscling in when two criminal organisations clash makes for a sound plan.

Footsteps approached.

"We'll be watching you, Mackay. The next time we meet things may not be as, em, comfortable."

"You mean I'll have to sit on the floor?"

"You're good, Mackay. Keep it up."

A heel came in. Aulay bent double and toppled to the floor once more. The DI cut the cable ties on his wrists.

The scrotum defence paragraphs, Aulay knew by heart. What to do? His upper thighs took the kicking and hurt like hell but he wasn't disabled. With his hands free, should he tackle the McCaw?

An Uncle Eddie lesson flashed through his mind.

***

"Bent polis are powerful, Aulay. They can make life difficult."

They were in the Curren's sitting room. Mrs Eddie and Shaz sang along with Elvis somewhere else in the tenement flat. Aulay put away the cards after a game of bridge. Mrs Eddie and Shaz had won, again.

"How so?"

"Och, they can stop your car every day, check the tyres, breathalyse you. All legal and a right pain in the tits."

"Doesn't sound too life threatening though."

"Aye, but they can up the ante by sticking their noses in elsewhere. Drop a hint to the vat man or the revenue people. You end up paying accountants to keep your paperwork sorted. An expensive nightmare."

"You havin' trouble, Eddie? I thought you'd retired."

"It's no' me I'm talking about. Someone came to me for help."

Past tense meant a lesson. Aulay stayed quiet.

"This polis man screwed whatever he could get from... we'll call him, Mr Blue. Any idea how to stop a guy like that?"

At fifteen, Aulay's Machiavellian strategies were limited to beating up the guy. He didn't think Eddie needed a playground answer. He shrugged.

"Ok," said Eddie. "What's the polis guy's big problem?"

"He needs cash."

"Good ...what's he need it for?"

"Is his Mrs a gimme gimme gimme?"

"No' bad."

Aulay whispered. "Is he a greedy bastard?" Mrs Eddie didn't stand for any swearing in the house.

Rolling a slim one, Eddie smiled. "Its no' that simple."

"Drugs?

"Good... or?"

"He a gambler?"

"On the nose, Aulay."

Shaz and Mrs Eddie appeared with tea and biscuits. It was a Sunday afternoon.

"You giving Aulay your pearls of wisdom," said Mrs Eddie as she poured.

"Just going through the recent polis bung script," said Eddie reaching for an Abernethy.

"Well, I'm sure Shaz'd like to have a go too," said Mrs Eddie sitting down with a Penquin biscuit.

Uncle Eddie started again. Shaz got to the nub before Aulay by missing out the 'gimme gimme gimme' and the 'greedy bastard' options.

"So," Eddie continued, "how do you deal with a Bent polis with the law on his side?"

Shaz piped in. "You stop him being a polis."

Mrs Eddie smiled. Eddie said, "Gimme more, Sharon."

"Catch him doing something illegal. End of problem polis."

"Aye," Aulay chimed in, "but not with Mr Blue, something else."

"Yea," said Shaz, "'cos he could trade what he knows about Mr Blue to get a lighter sentence."

Mrs Eddie said, "He could trade Mr Blue anyway, dear."

Shaz and Aulay looked at each other for inspiration. Shaz got there first.

"You need a double whammy. Get the goods on bent polis for two offences and let him know, the minute he starts blabbing about Mr Blue, you'll offload the evidence of the second crime."

Shaz's future profession was already poking through.

"Aye," said Aulay, "and the second offence needs to be bigger, more serious."

"You think that would work?" Eddie looked at Mrs Eddie.

"Depends, it comes down to scale," she said. "When a corrupt polis goes to court there's all the press and TV. Too much drama."

Eddie and Mrs Eddie waited.

"Ok," said Aulay, "... force him off the force. Get bent polis sacked for... something not too dramatic."

"Aye," said Shaz. "Get him on something where he'd need to resign. Keep the serious offence as backup. No hassle from the media."

"Right, time for the filum." Eddie reached for the remote.

For the next two hours they watched John Wayne don his eye patch and play the grizzled Rooster Cogburn dragging Katharine Hepburn across the West. Shaz and Aulay were out in the open by then. They held hands on the couch.

Another Sunday afternoon at the Curren's.

Two days after True Grit, Aulay asked Eddie for the details.

"Bent polis stashed the bung money in three accounts in three different banks. All his betting was on line using credit cards tied to each account."

An unsigned letter, with a copy of a bank statement from the smallest account, arrived on the desk of an honest Detective Inspector.

Aulay raised an eyebrow at this but Eddie insisted. "There is the odd honest polis-man."

On the same day the letter arrived on the honest policeman's desk, bent polis received a letter outlining the contents of the honest DI's mail and the prospect of the details from his two other accounts being forwarded to the same DI. As a freebie, copies of all three statements would also be sent to the Daily Snot.

Bent polis was asked to resign for, 'income anomalies'. He did, quietly.

"How'd you get the bank account info?" asked Aulay.

"Och, banks are like wet paper bags, son. From a distance they look solid but, close up..." Eddie shrugged, "... and yer bent polis was a wanker without a shredder."

"You rummaged through his bins-"

"No' me, Aulay," Eddie laughed. "I've got other people for that."

***

Lying on the floor of the container, Aulay didn't have a double whammy. He let DI McCaw go on his way.

It wasn't a fishmonger's or a remote cottage. Aulay emerged into a yard in Ibrox. It was dark. The sea smell and the generator hum came from a refrigerated lorry carrying shellfish from the far northwest to Spain. A light flickered in the driver's cab. Some late night viewing before going down

89

for the night. Aulay called a taxi. On his way to the cupboard he wondered what he would tell Shaz. Abandoning your girlfriend in a city centre restaurant would take some explaining. Getting kidnapped wasn't a viable excuse. The taxi ride to the cupboard wasn't long enough for him to come up with an answer.

"What the hell happened to you?"

Shaz sat on Aulay's fold down bed reading case notes. She looked fabulous in a big jumper and jammy bottoms.

"I bumped into someone."

"Who?"

"No one you know."

"Try me."

"Not now."

Aulay left a furious Shaz and went off to the communal bathroom. In the shower he worked out a plan. He'd tell Shaz everything.

Dreaming it would all come right during a post coital cigarette, Aulay dried off and inspected the damage. His bruised thighs looked worse than they felt, good. He'd play these up during the TLC thing. The cut to his lower lip was minor.

Aulay re-entered the cupboard, scrubbed and ready for action. He slipped into bed where the silk sheets did a career best to envelop him in their erotic envelope.

"Turn the light off."

An ardour killing phrase. A pissed off Shaz is not to be tampered with. Any two-spoons manoeuvre, especially with an advance guard, would not be tolerated. Aulay reviewed his plan. He'd launch a dawn attack.

He woke in an empty bed. There was a note.

'Aulay - you're a wanker. See you in court.'

There were no kisses, fuck, fuck, and fuck. DI McCaw's timing had been perfect.

Chapter 12   costly swim

Aulay moped about all day before searching for the answers in a glass. Towards shutting time he decided to skip getting rat arsed and said cheerio to his new best pal.

"See you later then..."

He'd forgotten the guy's name. The guy didn't care, he'd passed out. The barmaid encouraged Aulay's courageous decision to stop drinking.

"It's well after time, Aulay. Come on, I've got to lock up now."

A kebab on a well-done naan bread would cure him. By the time he'd finished the Yadgar's finest, along with two cans of Irn Bru, things were looking up. On his way home along Calder Street, Aulay walked in a reasonably straight line.

He'd tried to drink his way out of trouble before. It never worked but felt good, for a while. During his time in the army, especially in-theatre, they'd go at the booze like blunt razor blades, raucous and loud, daring each other to be alive after the next patrol. Thinking about 'patrol' triggered it.

Suspicious people tend to cover themselves in a cloak of the stuff. The geezer slinking up to the door of the Govanhill Baths would be less noticeable if he wore a mask, stripy jumper and carried a bag marked 'swag'. The guy did a full 360 before giving the secret knock. Aulay watched Mr Incredible slip a poly-bag through the open door, say a quick 'bye bye', turn and saunter casually up the road, whistling. Honestly, the bloke whistled.

If Mr Incredible hadn't been mid-forties, Aulay would have moved on. Mid-forties meant something more than childish pranks or mindless vandalism, and the shape of the poly-bag suggested fish-suppers. What would three or four grown men be doing in an abandoned swimming pool? And be there long enough to need fed at midnight?

Aulay walked round the block. The arse of the boarded up swimming pool was just that, a solid Victorian bum with no access. Didn't go in for fire-escapes, the Victorians. It meant the roof and getting there was a joy. He made it in under two minutes. Still in no man's land between drunk and a false sobriety, Aulay felt better than fine. Sober, he'd have taken ten minutes. Tonight, he was Spiderman.

A dim glow shone from one of the many skylights. In stealth mode, Aulay made his way across the roof. Reaching the glow, he put his ear to the glass, nothing. He waited.

He woke up convinced he was in Basra. He grabbed for his guns. The night's escapade returned and the now sober Aulay felt like a tosser. He was ready for the off when he heard the sound of men in a heated debate. Inching forward, no longer the rampaging superhero of the night before, Aulay looked through a broken skylight.

"I say we go for it. What do we have to lose? We're dead anyway."

"Listen, the posh geezer isn't a killer, believe me."

"It's not him I'm worried about. It's their Top Banana, this Chancer MacKinnon. He's the killer and when he gets back..."

Aulay looked up at the night sky, shook his head and contemplated the laws of coincidence. How the fuck did Charlie Weathers get to be a prisoner of The Polmadie? Shite. Why hadn't he ignored the dodgy fish-supper man, gone home and curled up in bed.

All of Aulay's blinkers were intact when Charlie Weathers introduced himself...

***

"Hi, I'm Charlie."

A large negro held out a hand. Charlie Weather's parents escaped from the Congo when times there were bad. Times there are always bad. Born in Hackney, Charlie grew up in the ghetto among the knife wielding gangs. When he was eighteen, a judge gave him two options. Charlie joined the army. Charlie is very black. Like the inside of a bin-bag stuffed into a velvet sack hidden in a cave at the bottom of the ocean.

With his hand out to be shook, Charlie clocked Aulay's millisecond of reticence and ignored him for months.

The whole blinker thing gave Aulay no end of trouble. Convinced he could spot a catholic at a hundred paces, he fell in with two lads who dragged him through the worst of commando training. Without them, he'd never have made it. He was nonplussed when they told him they'd done their schooling at St Catherine's Church of the Rosary... something or other.

Aulay's black blinkers fell off during a brawl outside a pub. The pub's plasma screens showed England against Sweden. Convincing the English trainees of his inability to support England at anything, took a while, but they got it. That night it was a Special Ops co-ordinator he struggled with. The guy was German.

"I don't understand, Aulay. You are British," said Otto. "You should be on the side of England."

Christ, thought Aulay, this could take a while.

"Aye, that's true, but there's a difference. Especially when it comes to football."

Aulay launched into a long harangue about the history. "You seen Braveheart?"

Twenty minutes later, Otto still wasn't getting it. Fed up, Aulay played his trump card.

"Listen, Otto. We fought the English more often than you have... and we won a couple."

At the full time whistle, Aulay celebrated Sweden's victory a tad on the strong side. When he left the pub for a smoke, two English Neds pounced. With the head of one Ned in an arm lock, Aulay wasn't letting go 'cos he'd join his mate who was trying to lever Aulay's eyeballs out. Things got desperate... then... someone dropped the gouger with a beautiful one in the crotch; a true moment. The crippled Ned put two hands to the affected area and sank to the ground, with a look beyond pain on his ugly face. Aulay released his Ned from the head lock. He did the smart thing. He ran away.

Aulay understood the irony. He was getting the shite kicked out of him because he was Scottish and Charlie Weathers, a black Englishman, came to his rescue.

His subsequent attempts to gain Charlie Weather's respect fell on the sword of once bitten, twice shy. Aulay felt shame for the first time.

After the night of the Neds, whenever Aulay met someone new, he worked to ditch the stereotyping bollocks. Ingrained racism and bigotry is a heavy load. It wasn't easy and took time.

Everyone's at it though. On a bus in London, Aulay sat in front of two old Chinese women who prattled away in dialect. When he got up to leave, the bloke in front of him did too. The man rounded on the sweet old ladies with an outburst in their lingo. Horrified, the women covered their faces and burst into tears. The bloke jumped off the bus. Aulay wasn't having any of this and caught up with the guy.

"What the hell do you think-"

"Ah," the man said, "you are the second ugliest man on the bus. Nice to meet you, I'm the ugliest."

"Eh?"

"Sorry, old chap. My name is Connor, Connor O'Connor. Spent twenty years in Hong Kong and speak the lingo." He pointed at the retreating bus. "I'm afraid those two old hags were dissecting everyone on the bus, with brutal frankness. They compared the coloured gentleman on my left to a... well, you don't need to know."

Aulay spent a pleasant hour in the pub with Conner O'Conner. He received an education on the Chinese view. Very enlightening.

As they parted, Aulay asked, "What did you say to the crones on the bus?"

Conner smiled. "Two old witches, with cunts drier than the Gobi desert, should mind their manners."

Aulay lost it.

"Remember," said Connor. "By tomorrow, those two old buzzards will be using that one on each other."

Aulay liked Connor O'Connor.

For the rest of commando training, and for a couple of tours, Aulay battered away at Charlie Weathers' filters without success. Charlie clocked him on day one as that class A1 wanker, a racist.

Thinking back, easy thing hindsight, Aulay was a racist with a small 'r'. Ignorance is the defence of a... Aulay couldn't remember the expression but he was guilty through ignorance, not experience.

***

Back on the Govanhill Bath's roof, he looked through the cracked skylight at a patch of tiled wall. A white captive with a designer beard surrounded by days of stubble walked across his line of sight.

His way in? The stubble meant a few days in-stir, which should breed complacency in the guard. One guard? With three prisoners and four fish suppers, it was a reasonable assumption. Aulay's watch said 4am. The guard should have read the Daily Snot three times and fallen asleep with a full belly.

After his earlier Spiderman moment, Aulay checked his sobriety level before making his way down and round to the front of the building. When Mr Incredible delivered the fish suppers, the door opened and no light appeared, none. Aulay decided on a subtle approach. He battered the front door with his fist.

The door opened a crack. "What-"

Aulay pulled the heavy oak with both hands. It moved enough for him to squeeze through, shouting... "Geez a fuckin' break fer Christ's sake, I've been oot there fer..."

Pushing the door closed, Aulay ranted in the dark, in drunken arsehole mode, in case there were two or more. There wasn't. He turned the guard to the wall and rammed a cigarette lighter into his back.

"Keep fuckin' quiet or your dead, ok...OK!"

"Yea, no problem."

"You alone?"

"Aye, pal. I'm on my own."

"What do they call you?"

Talk to your captive. It stops them freaking out.

"They call me, Paddles."

"Why?"

Aulay pulled the back of Paddles' jumper up and over his head.

"'cos I run like a bird with a tight skirt on."

That was good. Aulay disguised his chortle with a heave to remove Paddles' belt before using it to secure the man's hands. Sitting Paddles on the floor, Aulay cracked the big doors open to let a little street light in. On a table was a well read Daily Snot, a few sad chips, a mobile phone, a big torch and keys.

"Can you see anything, Paddles?"

"No, mate. No' a thing, honest."

Aulay swung a Doc Martin in his direction. The man didn't flinch.

"Paddles, don't move a fuckin' muscle."

Lifting the torch, Aulay pocketed the mobile phone and locked the front door.

He had a bit to go. Wandering along the wide corridors reminded him of times as a kid, when a torch was an instrument of adventure. Across the prisoner's door lay a big steel bar nestling in heavy 'L' brackets. They'd need to ram-raid the door from the inside to break out. No need for a proper guard either. Paddles, probably one of The Bulls Security people, would be more used to snoring the night away in some portakabin on a half-finished building site.

Aulay put his ear to the door, silence. As he wondered how Paddles got the fish suppers through, he kicked it. The crude cat flap returned home with a light screech. Careless; most booby-traps are at floor level.

"Hey, Paddles," said a bored sounding Charlie Weathers, "why are you wandering about at this time of night?" A shadow moved under the door. "You going to remember to get my smokes in the morning?"

Charlie's voice was at the door now. Aulay lay on the floor next to the cat flap.

"Rainman," he whispered, "this is a public building. You can't smoke in here."

He could almost feel Charlie's brain scrabbling, at 'Rainman' in particular. Charlie Weather's was an excellent card player.

***

Most of his fellow army recruits could play pontoon and poker. Charlie couldn't hold a hand or shuffle a deck.

"What did you do on a long train journey?" someone asked.

"Never been on one," said Charlie. "Furthest I ever travelled was to here."

After a month, Rainman ruled the roost. He mastered cribbage and bloody canasta in about five minutes. Aulay never got him onto bridge. Finding two others to make up a rubber proved beyond him. Fast, an adult version of snap, remained Aulay's sole success. Fast came down to hand-eye speed, nothing to do with mind games or number crunching skill.

***

"Who are you?" whispered Rainman.

Aulay switched mode to 'talking to foreigners'. He pronounced his T's and left out the vernacular.

"Aulay MacKay"

"Red Five. Is that you?"

Aulay smiled. He hadn't heard Luke Skywalker's call-sign for a couple of years. "Aye, Rainman. You free to talk?"

"There are three of us. They're asleep. You with this Polmadie crew now?"

"Not exactly. What are you doing here?"

"Freelance muscle for a London crew. We fucked up big style."

"Tell me."

"Now?"

Aulay wanted to hedge his bets. "We've got time."

"It was a take over operation for the DSH. Same as ones they've carried out in Derby and Rotherham."

"Christ, Rainman, Derby and Rotherham?" said Aulay. "This is Glasgow for fuck's sake."

"Tell me about it."

"Who's the DSH?"

"The big boys. The Drug Super Highway. They control the crack and heroin routes from Afghanistan and South America, worth billions."

"They based in London?"

"Partly. The main man and the finance runs out of southern Spain."

"What are they doing getting involved in Glasgow? Did The Polmadie screw them over?"

"I don't know. I'm a low-life heavy here."

"What went wrong?"

"Our Glorious Leader thought it would be a walk in the park. He went straight for The Polmadie's Consigliore before we were set up."

"Set up?"

"We were supposed to kidnap the Consigliore's lady first and..." Rainman stalled.

"And what?"

"...kill the Top Banana."

"Wooa there." Aulay took a step back. Hard to do when you're lying down.

"Jesus, Rainman what the fu-."

"This was my first gig, Aulay. I was muscle for leaning on people. I knew naff all about any killing."

Aulay let the silence stretch. Rainman needed to suffer.

"Aulay, you still there?"

"Aye. What happened in Derby and... wherever?"

"The Derby Banana retired. The Rotherham bloke had a heart attack. He dropped dead during the... em, negotiations."

"Why'd The Polmadie's Banana make the hit list?"

"A change of plan. Orders came from Spain. Take out the boss. Something about speeding up the process."

"How'd you end up here?"

"The Consigliore, a geezer called Freak Johnston, you know him, Aulay?"

"Never met the guy."

"My job was to keep pace with him. I followed him for a day. When he walked into his local pub, I called it in. Glorious Leader decided to make his move. It was a disaster. When we breezed into the pub, Freak Johnston invited us to join him for a drink."

"You didn't think to recce the place first?"

"I wanted to but Glorious Leader marched us in without a recon. Three shotguns pointed our way."

"Do the Polmadie know about your em... takeover plan?"

"Fuck, yea, Aulay. They kept us strung up overnight before I caved in. I gave them everything."

"Strung up?"

"You know, wrists tied above your head, feet off the floor. After three or four hours your shoulders, wrists, every fucking thing is screaming. A dentist with a blunt drill would be great, and the woman they used, she's the best."

"Woman, what woman?"

Aulay knew what women. There was only one.

***

Jocelyn Brodie, Lady Barb to her regulars, ran a lucrative S&M operation out of her large sandstone detached in Pollokshields. The basement resembled your worst nightmare, or the peak of eroticism, sometimes both.

101

The sixteen year old Aulay joined the team Uncle Eddie had put together to carry out the basement conversion. He did wonder why every team member was a True One. He soon realised, it wasn't the sort of work that went out to tender.

***

"Know what goes on here?" asked Eddie.

Aulay took a breather from lugging timber down the basement stairs.

"Geez a minute," wheezed Aulay. "Yon things are steep."

Eddie laughed "This'll help, breathe deep." He held out a lit roll-up.

Aulay leaned against the wall and took a long draw.

"Jocelyn, the lady upstairs, is a... a specialist in...," Eddie hesitated, it wasn't like him, "...c'mon, I'll show you."

Stubbing out the cigarette, Aulay followed Eddie up to the ground floor.

"Go soft, Aulay. Joss is off to the shops but Deirdre's about."

"Who's Deirdre?"

"Joss's... em, partner."

"What? They're a couple of old lezzies?"

"Weesht, Aulay, keep it down. Takes all sorts."

Eddie opened a grandfather clock and fished about. "Got it." It was a key. He slouched at a door in the main hall. It swung open and there it was; the apparatus.

"Fuck me, Eddie, it's... it's a dungeon."

The instruments and chains shone. There were straps, buckles and objects Aulay couldn't place. A full size crucifix dominated, with shackles.

Along with Shaz, he'd dabbled with the leather and ropes thing, on the Internet, as you do. On his own, Aulay would resurface on web sites with fit birds having a good time.

"What's this do?" Aulay held up a shiny chrome thing. He recognised the shape, it was the straps attached to it he couldn't..."

Eddie didn't have to answer; Aulay got it.

The crunch of rubber on gravel. They scurried out. Eddie managed to re-stash the key before the front door swung open.

"Ah, Eddie," said Miss Jocelyn Brodie as she removed thin leather gloves, "...and who is this, another of your clan?"

"Aye, Joss, this is Aulay,"

A touch of sweat appeared on Eddie's top lip. "Aulay, meet Jocelyn."

"How do you do?"

Aulay took the proffered hand. Smooth delicate fingers like the piano playing Miss McLafferty from school. Their eyes met. All sorts of images danced through Aulay's head.

"Aulay's a good name."

Joss held onto his hand.

"From Macaulay. My mum's maiden name."

Miss Brodie wasn't a stunner although she did look more than all her bits put together. She had presence. Over the next few days, Aulay bumped into her in the hall, the kitchen, out for a smoke.

"You should give that up," she said.

"We all have our crosses to bear."

She looked at him, not in passing, an inquisitive look, with an edge to it. With a hand reaching for the door of her old Nissan, there was a Mercedes in the garage for 'formal wear' as Eddie put it, Joss stopped, turned and walked back.

"You have a girlfriend." It wasn't a question. "You are besotted. She's the big light in your life."

She stared at him, or was it through him. Without a question to answer, Aulay stayed silent, returning her gaze.

"Resolute too."

The hint of a smile?

"So," she said, putting fresh leather gloves on, she had lots of pairs. "Eddie's told you... no," her eyes narrowed. "The auld bastard's let you look."

Not many could see through Aulay's straight face, not even Uncle Eddie. Dad could, but on a different level.

"You're not my type," said Joss. "You know it and I know it, so... there's a thing."

With both gloves secure, she strolled back to her car. Aulay knew 'My type' had nothing to do with Deirdre.

Approaching fifty, or it could be sixty, with black hair kept short, long nails and the figure of a fit thirty year old, Jocelyn looked every bit the cool well-off professional, which she was. Always leather with a discrete stud or two, a skirt with the gleam that screamed expensive or knee length boots, the heel a tad short of outrageous. Aulay's favourite? The tattoo. A cat's paw design hidden in the palm of her left hand. Lightly drawn, the feline claw expanded and contracted as Joss opened and closed her hand.

"You know the trouble with your uncle?" Joss asked one day. She was dressed to kill.

"What?" said Aulay.

"He's a blusterer."

An odd word but he knew what she meant.

"It's just for show," said Aulay. "Uncle Eddie hits the target when he needs to."

"I know, I know." Joss buttoned her leather coat, "but all men are see-through. You only have to look."

"Look for what?"

"Patience, Aulay. You're a natural see-er. A little insight and you'll get it."

He'd half an inkling of what she meant. He'd stumbled over his 'see-er' thing a few times.

"I'm doing some marketing today," she said, "fancy it?"

"You're doing what?"

"The amount your Uncle is charging necessitates additional clients, Aulay. You want to get paid, don't you?"

"Aye, but Uncle Eddie-."

"I've spoken to Eddie, it's alright."

Aulay asked Eddie about it later.

"Joss'll teach you stuff I can't, son. She's taken a shine to you, says you have potential. I'd grab it while you can."

Jocelyn took Aulay, 'sight-seeing'.

"Where we goin'," he asked on their first trip.

"The sad-bastard aisle in M & S is always good."

Her first target was an ordinary looking bloke with a shopping basket. Most sad-bastards don't use a trolley, they buy one-offs. Men advertised their thirst for her services. Joss could spot a potential client in a bus queue. She taught Aulay how to read the signs.

With unwavering eye contact, Jocelyn approached sad-bastard. If he didn't flinch, Jocelyn would back off. Backing off was rare and never happened while Aulay was there. Sad-bastard flinched. Jocelyn moved closer, invading his space. If eye contact faltered, this was a naughty boy, someone who needed disciplining, a little spanking at £100 for fifteen minutes. Jocelyn had dozens of regulars. Aulay watched another join the list.

Snaring a devotee didn't happen often. Aulay only saw it once, in the third week of his apprentiship. A fat bloke in expensive, mismatching golf gear grabbed the odd tin here and there.

"Him," said Aulay indicating stout golfer.

"What do you see, Aulay?"

"I don't know... but inside he's frantic."

Stout golfer looked anything but frantic as he sauntered down the beer and wine aisle. Was he right?

"Let's see," said Jocelyn. She marched straight at the man.

Stout golfer spotted her. He flinched when the adrenaline kicked in, a cheek muscle twitched... Jocelyn moved in, face to face now... eye contact never wavered... at last... a devotee.

Joss bought Aulay Italian leather shoes as a graduation present. He's still got them. They've walked no more than three hundred metres.

A devotee became compliant only after the negotiations were complete and the session under way. Their requirements would shake the foundations of anyone who knew them. For £900 an hour, devotees demanded exquisite levels of service. There were eighteen on Jocelyn's books, nineteen now, a who's who of Glasgow. Two regulars came up from London and another flew in from New York.

Stout golfer's requirements were... no, the man's on TV.

Jocelyn's clients varied. Married men whose wives' bedroom enthusiasm had waned, when more important things took precedence, like status or the committee. A few led conventional sex lives, too embarrassed to mention their secret desires for fear of... lots of reasons. The odd naughty boy didn't ask for anything. Fifteen minutes in a room with another woman was enough.

Was Aulay abused? He'd argue for the defence. He didn't get to watch, or meet a client and Joss never laid a finger on him. He was a pupil. As to the running of her enterprise, Eddie filled in the details.

Jocelyn ran an exclusive guest house. You could never get a room and no one ever stayed, but the taxman didn't know that. All the legitimate deliveries of food and alcohol were carefully logged, and paid for, before slipping out to several of The Polmadie's pubs. Jocelyn mixed in the same circles as many of her clients, with Brian on her arm. For performing this service, Brian got a 'freebie'. He was a naughty boy who squealed with fright and delight when Jocelyn shaved his nether regions with an open razor. Joss never slept with her clients, ever. It added to the mystique. Not even the American, who offered an obscene amount of money for the privilege.

Deirdre, Joss's long time partner, kept house and quiet, rarely venturing out.

When work in the basement dungeon finished, Joss gave Aulay another present.

"For your lady." A tear trickled. "They're not for wearing out."

A pair of the softest leather gloves. Shaz loved them. So did parts of Aulay.

"You know where I am, if you ever need anything."

Aulay, a bit choked himself, said goodbye. His see-er sense worked as before, but now he understood what it was telling him.

Mrs Eddie tried to explain the origins of his see-er sense. Sitting in a cafe one day, they watched a young drunk bounce up to the news stand opposite, grab a newspaper then drop it. The drunk slapped the blameless Daily Snot seller. The girl fell to the ground.

"That's an evil one," said Mrs Eddie.

The drunk screamed at the cowering girl. Mrs Eddie started to get up.

"Hold on, I'll go," said Aulay.

"Be careful..."

He was outside before she could finish.

"Excuse me."

The drunk put on his best stare but giving Aulay the evil eye lost out in the battle to stay upright. His balance mechanism needed constant recalibration.

Swaying, he managed. "Go an' take a flyin' fuck to yoursel', pal,"

A good line. Aulay always remembered it.

The drunk's fist missed and kept going. Aulay forced the youth's face against the tenement wall. He already knew whispering worked better than shouting.

"Was it your Da' or an Uncle?" he asked. "Did he come in the night?"

"What the fu-"

"Remember the smell of sweat, of fear, the pain? Is he still alive? You still remember, still wake up at night? You still wonder... don't you?"

The drunk got a wee bit distraught. "Ge' aff me, you..."

He staggered when Aulay released him. The stumble was more than a balance mechanism glitch.

"How in the name of Christ did..." Tears hung from the young man's eyes as he tottered up the road.

Aulay helped the Daily Snot seller to her feet.

"Cheers mister. Here's a paper, take it, it's free. I'm Bunty."

"Thanks, Bunty. I'm Aulay."

He took the red top, smiled and returned to the café.

"What did you see?" asked Mrs Eddie.

Aulay gave her the diluted version.

"While he was screaming at the girl, his right arm flinched to a rhythm. He's too young to have kids of a beatable age, so I figured he was a victim once."

He sipped his Irn Bru. "Oh, there's something else."

"What?"

"His team lost the Old Firm game today, four nil. He was really pissed off."

Mrs Eddie frowned. "How'd you know which team he-"

"Tattoo, right forearm."

Mrs Eddie took the afternoon to tell what she knew about Dad.

Aulay is half Gypsy.

***

The tiles on the floor of the Govanhill Baths' were hard. Aulay shifted to ease the cramp in his shoulder.

"...and when she..." Rainman was on the home stretch. Aulay could hear him shiver.

Joss had said, "Find the right button, and push it. Men are easy. They have a penis."

Rainman ended his painful reminiscing with, "...suffer permanent damage for my Glorious Leader? Fuck that. I told her everything I knew."

Rainman's shivers slowed down. When they stopped, he asked, "How deep is the shit, Aulay?"

"You're fucked, Rainman."

Aulay coughed. "Who else did you speak to apart from the woman?"

"Freak Johnston, the Consigliore. He's ok. A smart bastard, but no thug. He's treated us well since I spilled."

One thing bothered Aulay. "How did he know you guys were coming?"

"The dossier."

"What dossier?"

"The DSH have some clout, Aulay. A full Intelligence Ops Manual, recent photographs, addresses, known movements, the full bollocks. We had Freak Johnston's eBay account details for Christ sake."

"Any clues to the source?"

"Not military like the ones we had in Iraq."

"Could it be polis... sorry, police, Special Crime stuff?"

"Could be, I've never seen one but..."

"But what?"

"The terminology fits, you know, police language."

Someone in Serious Crime was leaking stuff to the DSH?

"I'm still missing the link, Rainman. How'd The Polmadie know you guys were..."

"Freak had a copy of the same dossier, with attachments, our photographs and our flight arrival time. We were tapped from the moment we got off the London plane."

Obtaining Special Crime dossiers, then following three individuals in a big city is a major logistical undertaking. Uncle Eddie would be impressed with the new Polmadie. Aulay was.

"Can you get me out, Aulay?"

Aulay mulled things over. He could walk away by returning the night watchman to normality. Paddles would keep quiet as long as his three charges were intact. If he took Rainman with him, what then? A big black man in Glasgow sticks out like blood on snow. There were Negroes about, but not enough to be normal, Glasgow is not London. To get Rainman safely away would involve holing him up at his place then driving him out in the black of night. Dodgy.

"Can you leave on your own?" asked Aulay, already regretting it.

110

"The only thing I owe my Glorious Leader is a bullet in the head."

Handy. Leaving Glorious Leader behind might rub salve into The Polmadie wound.

"And Number Three?"

"He's an innocent, Aulay, like me. I'd take him, if you can."

"Fuck me, Rainman. You passing the buck?"

"You were always in charge, Aulay, remember?"

Aulay made Sergeant in record time. He stopped there despite overtures from above. These were his guys and he wouldn't leave them. Special Ops by then, with two dead and three wounded. It creates a bond.

Aulay wondered how to make the bond go and take a flying fuck to itself.

After Rainman woke Number Three, Aulay slipped the iron bar off the L brackets and let them out. The bar slipped back on with a piercing screech. Glorious Leader woke up and panicked. They retreated down the corridor to the sound of banging and obscenities.

Paddles hadn't moved.

"You're two prisoners short, Paddles. Might be better for you to remain tied up."

Paddles grunted from inside his jumper.

Rainman hadn't mentioned the day-glo overalls. He now had to get two bright-green blokes to his place without being noticed. No chance. Dawn was breaking. They needed a hiding place.

Down a bit and across the road was an alley. The sign above the entrance demanded 24 hour access and invited all comers to Tracy Nolan's Irish clog dancing lessons. Like a lot of tenement quadrants, the alley led to a series of old

111

workshops and lock ups. Aulay found a derelict and shoved his two charges in.

"Keep low and quiet. I'll be back with a van and some gear."

"How long, Red Five?" asked Rainman.

Number Three didn't need to know Aulay's name.

"Car hire place opens at nine. I'll be back before ten."

"You want a recon signal?"

"Aye."

Rainman took a loose brick and placed it on a broken window sill. Aulay checked the line of sight.

"Ok, see you."

Three hours later, someone let Aulay in at 68 Calder Street.

"Sorry, pal, rang the wrong bell."

Aulay climbed past the disgruntled first floor tenant. On the third landing, he checked the brick, it was still there. He reversed a van loaded with blue overalls, boots, jackets and baseball caps into the alley. They took the day-glo overalls with them.

It was an ideal van, a Peugeot Partner with windowless rear doors and a bulkhead behind the front seats. Both passengers remained out of sight. Aulay drove south to Hamilton Services on the M74. They dumped the day-glo gear and ate the all-day breakfast. It was crap and bloody expensive. They chewed manfully in silence before locking an acquiescent Number Three back in the van.

Over weak coffee, Rainman asked, "Where are we?"

"Deepest darkest Lanarkshire. The London train stops at Motherwell, just up the road.

"Options?"

"It comes down to how desperately The Polmadie want you back. There's a motorway hotel a mile away. You could hole up there for a couple of days then jump a taxi to the Motherwell station."

Without identification, Rainman hiring a car was out of the question.

"Do you know people here, Aulay?"

"This is Lanarkshire. Jesus doesn't have any friends here."

Rainman looked worried. Aulay tried to hold the words back but his one millisecond of reticence at their first meeting still rankled.

"I'll drive you to London."

As they shook hands, Aulay felt himself drift through Charlie Weathers' last wanker filter.

From the frying pan...

Aulay's cat nap on the roof of the Govanhill baths cost him. Watching the London train gaining on them was the last straw. He pulled the van into a motorway services.

"You drive for a bit, Rainman, I'm knackered."

"Is it safe?"

"Who's going to spot you here, a runaway couple?"

They were in Gretna Green, a mile from the English border.

Aulay woke up south of Birmingham where they did another stop. Again, Number Three quietly did what he was told. Aulay took the wheel.

"What's the plan when you get home?"

"Get into bed with Darina. You can sleep on the couch."

They discussed old army pals, dead pals, for a while. A conversation only those who'd been there would understand.

"Remember the crossroads in Sector Eight? We got lucky there."

"Aye..."

That was it. No more needed saying. The horror, the fear, and the elation remained.

During his time in Special Ops, Aulay's squad did a few crazy things, leaving a trail of dead people. Mostly insurgents.

After the London sign drifted by, Rainman directed Aulay on a tortuous route from the end of the M1 to Brixton. It took an hour.

London. The big smoke. To Aulay's mind, the place was too big and too small. On his first visit, he walked the city for days before he realised what was wrong. There was no horizon, ever.

On the small side was the space allocated to diners in restaurants. He could listen to four conversations while he rubbed elbows with strangers. A trip to the loo involved descending three levels below ground. Nice place to visit though.

Nearing Rainman's place, Aulay felt uneasy. His 'inside enemy territory' instinct reared up, and not because he hadn't seen a white face for a mile. He pulled the van over. It was approaching midnight.

"It's just along here..."

"There's no one about, Rainman. The street's empty."

Aulay took out his phone. "Ring home."

"But Darina's expecting us."

The lovers had spoken earlier during a stop.

"Just do it, Rainman, for Red Five, ok?"

Charlie Weathers grabbed the phone.

"Hi, honey, it's me."

"Hi, Charles... you ok?"

Aulay watched the blood drain from Rainman's face. A remarkable sight in the poor street light.

"Yea, babe, problem with the car, getting it fixed right now, AA man's here. I'll call you when I'm an hour away, ok?"

"Sure, Charles, see you soon."

Rainman hung up. "They've got Darina. She'd never call me Charles. Knows I hate it."

"Who's 'They'?"

"Turn this thing round, Aulay. I need to get to Theo's."

Theo turned out to be Rainman's uncle. Within an hour, Aulay had stun grenades strapped to his belt and was checking the action of an AK47.

"You'll need this."

115

Rainman handed him blackener. Aulay smeared it over his face. Most people think shoe polish is the stuff. It's bloody POLISH. Be better off with a lighthouse on your head.

"Right, all ready?"

Aulay, Rainman, Number Three and another two heavily armed blokes, climbed into the back of a transit van. Uncle Theo started the engine. They headed for Rainman's place.

Aulay couldn't believe it. One minute he's playing Spiderman, the next, he's about to raid a flat in south London with bullets and explosives alongside tooled up black guys. There were times when Aulay wished the odd blinker had stayed put.

Rainman dialled. "Hi babe, we're at the end of the M1, see you in an hour."

"Ok, Charles, take care."

"Now," said Rainman, "there's Darina and Louis-"

"Who the fuck is Louis?" Aulay didn't need complications.

"Our son. He's three months old."

"Where does he live?"

"He sleeps here."

Rainman spread out a floor plan sketch. He indicated a box room at the end of the hall.

"Darina will have him though, with strangers in the place."

The layout of the flat was simple. A hall with four doors. Living room, bedroom, kitchen and box room.

"Where's the bog?" asked Aulay.

"En suite, in the bedroom."

Aulay couldn't resist it. "Cushty," he said, in as close to a Trotter accent as he could manage. It lightened the mood.

"It got a window?"

116

"Nope, it's vented."

They were parked some fifty yards away now. With an hour's leeway, whoever was inside Rainman's flat would be a few levels below hypertension.

After breaking into a blacked out flat behind Rainman's place, Aulay went to the kitchen window and raised his binoculars. Through Rainman's kitchen window, past the well armed bloke surveying the back gardens, he could see into the living room where another armed bloke remonstrated with a naked woman trussed up like someone on a dodgy web site. The ropes securing her breasts looped round her back to secure both arms. A broom handle tethered to each ankle kept her legs splayed. Darina had nowhere to hide. Still, she looked to be fighting her corner, giving Armed Bloke Two a good mouthful. A small bundle writhed about next to her. That would be Louis.

How to get heavily armed men into a first-floor flat when the enemy has someone looking out the front and the back?

[Two armed so far] Aulay whispered into the two-way radio. [One at the kitchen window; One in the living room; Big Parcel and Small Parcel unharmed]

Aulay didn't know why he whispered, he was alone in an empty flat. He didn't mention Darina's predicament. He needed Rainman to remain calm.

Opening the window a crack, Aulay heard the subject of Darina and Armed Bloke Two's remonstrations. Baby Louis had a fine pair of lungs on him. Armed Bloke Two lost the battle. He untied Darina, slowly, ankles first. He looked to be enjoying himself. When her breasts finally rippled free, Darina stood for a moment to let the blood flow. She picked up Louis and marched into the kitchen.

Aulay barked into the two-way. [Go Transit]

With Louis in one arm, Darina opened a kitchen cupboard and took down a wee brown bottle. That'll be the Calpol. Aulay recognised the baby-soother from many nights babysitting with Shaz. She earned some money and they got to canoodle in central heating.

Aulay ran down the stairs to Homer, one of Rainman's mates. In the back garden they listened to the squeal of rubber on tarmac followed by an almighty thud. In Rainman's kitchen, Armed Bloke One tore his eyes from the voluptuous Darina's fine arse and left to see what the commotion was out front.

Uncle Theo's job had been to smash the Transit into a Vauxhall Cavalier parked outside Rainman's living room window.

[Rainman; You in position]

[That's affirmative]

What's wrong with [Yes] Aulay wondered. Strange the way the mind works when it's wired to the moon. Immediately following the crash, Rainman and Number Three had successfully slipped inside the block of flats.

Standing below Rainman's kitchen window, Aulay could see Darina and Louis. The infant was trying his best to interfere with the neighbour's TV signals.

[Rainman; Hold back; Wait at the front door]

[What the fu-]

No time to explain. [Rainman; This is Red Five; Hold back]

Jumping up and down, Homer and Aulay waved their arms. Darina spotted them. Great tits, thought Aulay. She recognised Homer and opened the window.

"Throw the baby," Aulay hissed up at her. "Drop Louis then yourself."

Modern flats are tiny. In Shaz's place, Aulay could change a light bulb without going on his tiptoes. The drop from Rainman's kitchen to the garden was minimal. Still, asking a mum to throw her baby out of a window stretched things a bit.

"Homer," hissed Darina, "you drop Louis and I'll slice your black balls off."

Darina leaned out, lowered the wee man to arms length, took a deep breath, shut her eyes and let go. Considering the pressure he was under, Homer carried out his task with aplomb. Aulay almost missed it though. What a sight, those outstanding orbs, dangling and swaying.

"Homer," said Aulay. "Take Louis to Recovery."

Aulay didn't think Homer, as a pal of Rainman, should be around for the next bit. Darina was already half-way out the window. Aulay's mouth gaped. A part of him wanted everything to slow down.

In a disappointing flash, the nubile Darina crashed into his arms. They hit the ground. Catching Darina was out of the question. A dropping human body weighs a ton. It was a pleasant, cushioning manoeuvre, Aulay was after.

Darina leaned over him. "You ok?"

"Och aye." Aulay kept his eyes firmly on her face. "Let's go."

Shouting from above. Aulay looked up. The barrel of something moved their way. Pushing Darina, he swung his AK round and blew the back door of the flats away. Inside, he grabbed the two-way.

[Rainman; I've got Big Target; We are inside the rear entrance; Small Target is at Recovery. Status?]

[At station, Red Five; Ready to go in]

[No Rainman. We're getting out of here]

[But, Aul-]

[Fuck me, Rainman; We've won]

We've won? It was poor, but the best Aulay could come up with. In Special Ops, everyone did exactly what they were told. The merest hint went unquestioned. If the chief died, the next in line became chief. For all Rainman's gigs, Aulay had been the chief.

He understood Rainman's anger but, revenge and retribution make for a poor hand in this game. Cool, precise achievement of the objective is the thing when you're up against big boys with big guns. Anyway, the sirens were getting louder.

Darina grabbed the two-way. [Charlie, get your fat nigger arse down here. Now!]

A pause.

[Descending now]

Aulay just had time to scramble out of his combat jacket and pass it to Darina. When Rainman reached them, his eyes asked questions. No one spoke.

Rainman's other pal covered the front of the flat from a roof on the other side of the road. At Aulay's signal, he put a quick burst through Rainman's living room window. The occupants were reluctant to show themselves after that.

Another uncle had been roped in. He waited in another van at Recovery, an alley behind a late night chip shop. Aulay was starving.

"Anyone fancy a supper?"

He stuffed a fairly decent haddock down his throat on the way back to Theo's. In the back of the Transit, sitting opposite, Darina filled Aulay's jacket. On the pot holed roads, it was like watching two Labrador puppies fighting in a pillow case. Ah, the smell of fish.

Back at Uncle Theo's double garage, they had a pow-wow. Kitted out like a saloon, with a pool table and a corner bar, the large space had three couches round a big coffee table.

From Darina's description of her captors, Rainman worked out the play.

"The Polmadie let Glorious Leader go."

"In Glasgow, were you blindfolded the whole time?" asked Aulay

He watched a switch go on inside Rainman's head.

"Yea."

"What are you two talking about?" asked Darina.

Aulay explained about hoods and hostages.

"The Polmadie were going to let all three go. They got everything they needed."

Not taking Glorious Leader along had been a mistake. Ah, hindsight again.

"Quick flight and Glorious Leader's in London hours before we are." Rainman looked at Number Three. "He's put the blame for the Glasgow fuck-up onto you and me."

"The DSH," asked Aulay, "do they know about your Uncle Theo, and this place?"

Homer butted in. "Sure, but no white boy's goin' to get within a mile of here."

"Homer," cackled Darina, "you got three lily-livered white trash here right now."

Number Three and Aulay were still blacked up but Darina's whiteness glowed. Homer stomped over to the fridge where he plucked out a bottle of Carling. Aulay suspected the guy was a trifle put out. For an hour, he'd had to take orders from a white bloke. Rainman laid out the ground rules before they left in the Transit.

"Red Five's the man. What he says, you do, no shit, ok?"

Everyone nodded, even Uncle Theo.

"Why Homer?" Aulay whispered to Rainman, "he a Simpsons fan?"

"No, his name's Izzie, and he's odd."

Stress does funny things to different people. In the heat of it, some go mad. Others crawl into their shell. Post stress is the same. Aulay? He found little things hilarious. It took him ten minutes to get the Homer definition out of his system. Even then, whenever he caught a glimpse of the ancient story teller, he struggled to keep it going.

Uncle Theo returned. The police had accepted his broken brake hose story.

"I sent some of the boys to your place, Charlie. It was trashed. I've organised replacement windows and for the locks to get done."

"You can't go back there," said Aulay, "you need to lie low."

"You think?" The sarcasm dripped.

Aulay commiserated with Rainman's suffering. Their swift exit, with a naked Darina, would grind away for a time. But hey, no one died.

The other van driving uncle walked in. He took Uncle Theo aside, whispered in his ear, then left. Uncle Theo wandered over.

"The word's out. The DSH want you two dead." He indicated Charlie and Number Three. "Everyone with a gun is aiming at you."

Right, thought Aulay. Time to go.

"Well, Rainman," he said, "I've stuff to do."

Homer put a hand on Aulay's chest. "You leavin' now the fun's about to start?"

Aulay had to look up. Homer was six five, all muscle. Aulay leaned in and whispered, "Where's your stash of gay porn?"

Homer blinked. It was enough. Spread-eagled on the floor, Homer lacked oxygen. Rainman moved. Aulay stopped him with a bark. The tension rose.

"Red Five," said Rainman. "Homer's an idiot, let him go."

"Fuck me, Rainman." Aulay rose from the choking Homer. "You need to control your people."

He checked his pocket for the van keys. "Right, I'm for the offski."

"Before you go," said Uncle Theo. "There's something you can do for us."

A mix of sucking and groaning came from the floor. A wide-eyed Homer stared. Aulay knew what he was thinking. How did the white bastard know he was gay?

At Aulay's school, people sensed he knew stuff, and left him alone. Jocelyn Brodie shaved the rough edges off.

Aulay looked at Uncle Theo, "What can I do for you?"

"The DSH are fighting on two fronts..."

Military terminology. Aulay loved it.

"...Glasgow and London. Down here, they'll splash a lot of cash about to get rid of you two." A nod to Charlie and Number Three. "And after tonight's escapade, the DSH will know they're up against us."

"Who are you?" asked Aulay.

"We're not to be tampered with," said a shrugging Uncle Theo.

Aulay believed him. Any group who could kit an assault team and launch an operation five minutes after a prodigal son appeared at the back door were title challengers.

"Do you know The Polmadie?" asked Theo.

"Let's say I know the older generation. None of this new crowd, why?"

"I want to talk to whoever's in charge."

Aulay was planning to rob The Polmadie one minute, and now? Shite. That was it, he needed a shite. "Excuse me," he said. "I need to use your facilities."

Neck muscles in knots, Homer had to turn his shoulders to keep an eye on him. A gay man in a Caribbean gang? That must present a few challenges. Aulay kept his eyes front.

The last time he was in a toilet making up his mind, in the Fotheringay with the Cellists, Aulay returned to the fray and nearly blew it. What to do now? Introducing The Polmadie to this Caribbean crew could be another way into the gang.

Back on the couch, he scanned their faces. "What's in it for me?"

Uncle Theo smiled. Not in a cruel or smart way, more a benevolent thing.

"We won't mention to The Polmadie it was you who got Charlie and Number Three out."

They had him there.

"Ok," said Aulay. "Give me your contact details. I'll pass them along."

On the long-haul back to Glasgow, Aulay sent Shaz a few texts. No replies. Déjà vu.

Chapter 14   Aulay passes

Aulay watched Jemima MacAskill bend over to load stock into low cupboards. He was in the Greasy Spoon where Jemima worked the weekends. Standing up, Jemima tugged at some unseen structure to bring her formidable brace of breasts under control.

"Hi."

She turned sharply. Aulay watched two thoughts flash across her face. 'Does my bum look big in this?' and 'Did he catch the breast rig manoeuvre?'

He almost said 'no' and 'yes'.

Keeping the leer level below perceptible, he stared at Jemima's chest.

"Hi, Jem." He raised his eyes from the plastic name tag.

"Good morning, sir. What would you like?"

Her accent was a couple of notches above Polmadie, but short of Newton Mearns. Maybe Shawlands, or Cardonald.

"Crispy roll and square, soft roll and egg with a white coffee, please." Aulay used his middle Rutherglen. Good choice. Rutherglen had posh and scummie bits. "Some hot sauce, if you have it."

Watching Jemima bustle about, Aulay focussed on the contents of the leopard print skirt as her fine arse filled and emptied the material. Like watching a magician repeat an illusion again, and again, he worked it out but remained mesmerised.

A Ned crashed into the Greasy Spoon wearing the uniform, white tracksuit with sparkly white trainers.

"Oi," he said, "geez a pie an' blanket lifters."

The slur was there. Bit early, thought Aulay, but druggies live by a different clock.

"A drink with that?" a dead tone from Jemima, with no 'sir'.

"A can o' Bru."

The Ned slumped in a corner booth where he kept glancing at his reflection to check the angle of his baseball cap. From the look of him, pale and wide-eyed, heroin was his morning caffeine substitute.

Aulay tackled his breakfast. It was hot, spicy hot. Jemima's bottle of peri-peri sauce would take paint off a skirting board.

"Pie and beans." Jemima put the plate down in front of the Ned.

"Hey, doll," he said. "You got some pair o' jugs on you. Fancy gettin' them out for the boyz?"

"I only get them out for wankers," Jemima snapped. "On my web cam."

She turned and slipped behind the counter.

The Ned stood. "Hey, ya bitch, who you think you iz-"

Aulay caught the Ned's foot, the one he'd raised to leap over the counter. Twisting his grip, Aulay checked on Jemima. She held a foot long carving knife in one hand. Good girl, he thought. The Ned landed on the floor. Still holding one sparkly trainer, Aulay stood on the Ned's throat. The youth produced a knife from somewhere. Aulay stepped away. The Ned got to his feet with renewed confidence. His knife was king. Leaning over the counter, Aulay grabbed two implements of the kebab trade. With a foot long fork in one hand, a breast of chicken and green pepper laden skewer in the other, he faced the Ned.

"Come on, come on then," said Aulay. "I'll slice you to fuckin' pieces." He spoke louder. "Fancy a Glasgow smile? COME ON THEN."

The Ned dropped his knife and ran. He squealed when the door of the Greasy Spoon stuck for half a second.

Aulay's Errol Flynn antenna, the dashing knight to the rescue of the distressed damsel, and his Gary Cooper antenna, the nonchalant, shy hero not seeking reward or recognition, fought each other for prominence.

Jemima held up the Ned's plate. "You goin' to pay for the pie and blanket lifters then, or what?"

"Ok, doll."

Jemima dropped her accent a couple of notches. "My names no' Mary an' I'm no' yer doll."

Aulay put his hand in his pocket. "How much you owed?"

"Look, don't worry and... thanks."

She had a great smile.

"That's ok." Aulay headed for the door.

"What's your name, by the way?" asked Jemima.

"Name's Aulay, Aulay Mackay."

She came up and gave him a peck on the cheek. "Thanks again, Aulay."

Now, if anything happened to Shaz? Not many made Aulay's reserve list. The odd one shoved Shaz into the shadows, for a bit. This time, Aulay pressed the delete button, then the erase button, just to be sure. Dickin' about with a Top Banana's bird was mad crazy.

Aulay stepped out of the Greasy Spoon and into the Barras Market, a square half mile of covered and uncovered stalls, selling everything. The Barras is what you want it to be, full of junk or antiques, rough as hell or a jolly jape. In the tourist info, it's 'quaint'. To insiders, it's where serious business gets done. For Joe Public, it's the place to search and find that thing to make the thingy work, from washing machine bits, to windup record players.

127

All of society came to the Barras. Well-off types from the burbs try and convince themselves they're part of this Glasgow. One hand stays on their wallet, the other remains poised to fend off a slashing sword. Smoking policemen send their brother, father, sister, anyone to the Barras to buy their illicit tobacco. Tracksuit wearing waifs with a wean, weighing only slightly more than the child in the pram, draw on their cigarettes as they survey the world from wizened faces. The waifs are the lookouts. They can stash a cargo of illicit cigarettes, DVDs or computer games into the bottom of a pram, and disappear into the melee, before a uniform can get within fifty yards.

The Barras hierarchy has four levels; A-Lists, Minor Celebs, Worker Bees and Waifs.

Worker Bees deliver the goods and pass information along, they are the gofers. Few Worker Bees make it to Minor Celeb. They usually fail on - thick, stupid, drugs, alcohol, dishonesty and the greatest of these is, any one, or either, or, or.

Minor Celebs keep an official stall in the market, to launder cash. A-Lists stay in the background, appearing in various pubs to make the wholesale deals. It was an A-List who cornered Aulay as he bartered over a 1958 Oor Wullie annual. It was a bit tatty, but readable. The stall holder wanted a tenner for it. Aulay offered a fiver...

"You Aulay Mackay?"

"Who's askin'?"

Aulay turned to face an enormous bald bloke wearing blue jeans and a leather bomber.

"Come wi' me," said the Hulk.

It wasn't a request. The man mountain waddled off. He had a quick waddle. Aulay reluctantly handed over a tenner, took the Oor Wullie annual and made after him.

"Where we goin'," he asked Gigantor.

"Blue Parrot."

"What for?"

Silence.

The two blokes sitting in the Blue Parrot's dim snug looked ordinary, late twenties, well turned out without being flash. They both stood when Aulay emerged from behind Behemoth's shadow.

Goliath introduced him. "Aulay Mackay."

"Man of few words," said Aulay indicating the retreating Tsunami.

"Who, Fat Bastard?" said the taller man. "FB's no' paid to talk."

Aulay shook the offered hand. The man was five ten, slim with an ordinary face. Shaz had been spot on; The Polmadie's Top Banana would disappear in a crowd.

"I'm Chancer, and this is Sim."

The muscle on his right nodded. Short, about five foot five, Sim had bulk. His neck reminded Aulay of an oak banister.

"Take a seat, Aulay. Drink?"

"A Stella, cheers."

There was an Irn Bru and a Coke already on the table, but Aulay wasn't in the gang.

"Ferrari," called Chancer, looking over Aulay's shoulder. "A Stella."

The hovering bartender responded. "Sure, Chancer, back in a sec'."

This was a first for Aulay, waiter service in a Glasgow pub.

"So, you know us?" asked Chancer.

"Aye."

"You a collector?"

An Oor Wullie annual is hard to conceal.

"No' really, I like a giggle though."

Chancer's mobile buzzed. "Me too," he said checking the screen. He rose and made his way to the bar. Aulay didn't see the signal, but four men picked up their pints and left Chancer space to take his call. Sim kept silent. Aulay knew he'd been with Chancer since school. The rumour was, The Sim had taken a hand in the killing of the old Banana.

In the wait Aulay got it. Blue Parrot + Ferrari = Casablanca.

Chancer returned. "You're one of Eddie Curren's lot."

It wasn't a question.

"You knew Eddie?"

"Only to see, one of the old crew. Sorry about the news."

"Aye."

A second or two passed to let the deceased float back into the ether.

"You did a proper job in the Greasy Spoon," said Chancer.

"Och, the Ned was an arsehole... and drugged up."

Word of the stramash in the Greasy Spoon had spread faster than Old Firm football results. To track him down in under half-an-hour was good too and, they knew who he was. There was more.

"You between contracts the-now?"

"Aye."

The Polmadie knew what he did for a living = a gold star.

"When you goin' back?"

"Don't know, maybe never, I've no' decided."

Aulay couldn't go back. Did Chancer MacKinnon know that too?

A bloke hovered. Chancer ushered him in and introduced him as Belgy. Aulay later discovered that when Belgy was twelve, his mum and dad took him on holiday to Brussels.

"Yer Ned at the Greasy Spoon was one, Paul 'Tosser' Macalpine," Belgy began, reading from notes.

"Lives at the Bridgeton Cross with his ma' and da'. Da' works at the airport and ma's a cleaner in the toon. Tosser's a druggie who thinks he's a hard man. He's out of it most of the time, a proper Gasgcoine. His Da's been in touch a'ready. Says he'll get the boy to his uncle's in Kilmarnock. For as long as you say, Chancer."

"Why's he called Tosser?" asked the Banana.

Belgy hit his Blackberry and went to another page. "Tosser's ma' was on a night out with pals and some went back to the Macalpine gaff for a wee voddy. Ma' Macalpine shooed her mates into the living room where they found our Paul sitting with headphones on watching a porn film. He was starkers with the TV remote in his left hand."

"Jeez" said Aulay.

"Fuck me," said Chancer. They all lost it.

At the tail end of his last guffaw, Chancer said, "Tell Tosser's da' to get the boy sorted before he comes back, however long it takes. And, the Da's to go to the Greasy Spoon every Saturday. He's to say fuck all and leave a good tip."

"Righty-o." Belgy upped and left.

Letting Tosser off lightly put another brick in the wall of the new regime at The Polmadie. The old Banana would have castrated Paul Macalpine.

"How come you know about me?" asked Aulay.

"I don't, still scrapin' the surface."

Chancer and The Sim stood.

"Come with us."

At the door, The Sim put a hand on Aulay's shoulder.

"You wait here. There's plain-clothes outside."

Chancer crossed the street to two men.

"Hi, Colin, Jimmy."

Both policemen nodded. "Hi, Chancer."

"I'm goin' home. Get your car. I'll wait for you."

"Cheers," said the taller of the two. They made off in the direction of London Road.

Chancer walked back. "No need to get you onto Special Crime's radar, eh, Aulay?"

The Banana walked on. Worker Bees raised an eyebrow as they scurried past. Waifs flicked their cigarette ash in a familiar manner and snarled nicely. Minor Celebs pointed to the sky; the equivalent of the tugged forelock? A-Lists hovered in case there was something they could do for their Top Banana. Chancer acknowledged people here and there. A calmness Aulay hadn't noticed pervaded the place.

A man with one arm shorter than the other walked towards them.

"Hi, Clockface," said Chancer, "what's the score theday?"

Clockface looked at Aulay. Chancer said, "He's ok."

"Fair, fair is all I'll say. New stuffs good but havin' a few probs on the D side with three R's on the sick. I'll huckle a few guys to double up, should be fine."

"A'right," said Chancer, "any hassle, geez a buzz. All set for the do on Saturday?"

"Dead right. The misses is buzzin', cheers."

Clockface waved his shorter arm and left.

"What you doin' Saturday, Aulay?"

"Nothin' can't keep."

"Come round the Pennant, know it?"

"Aye."

132

"Come about two. Bring Shaz."

The Banana knew that Aulay was shagging his lawyer.

Chancer stopped next to a shiny red Alpha Romeo.

"Jemima MacAskill, the girl in the Greasy Spoon, she's important to me."

Shaz had been right again, the guy was bilingual.

"Don't blame you, she's game," said Aulay. "If Tosser'd made it over the counter, he'd have had something sharp stuck up his arse."

The Banana held out a card. "I owe you one, here."

Aulay took the card, no name, just a mobile number.

"Leave a message. I'll get back to you."

"Cheers."

"You never know, Aulay. I might need someone with your skill set one day."

With that, Chancer and The Sim climbed into the Italian thoroughbred and roared off.

The Polmadie had Aulay tied down in under an hour. Tooled up with more than muscle and cocaine, the gang would give the spooks a run for their money in the technology stakes. Despite Bandit's demonstration of their capabilities, Aulay still lived with Uncle Eddie's Polmadie, where sending a message involved a pencil.

He flicked through the results of his see-er scan of Chancer MacKinnon. Stress = nil, concern = nil, worry = nil, assured, confident and calm – all 10.

"I don't need you to take me to the Pennant," said Shaz. "Half my firm's clients are going. You think I'm no' invited?"

"I know, but it'll help with what I'm workin' on."

Pleading over the phone is never easy.

"Fuck you, Aulay. That stunt you pulled with Jemima MacAskill. Christ."

Shaz was convinced he'd set up the episode in the Greasy Spoon.

"Don't screw around with The Polmadie," she said. "They don't take fuckin' prisoners."

Aulay could have pointed out the opposite.

"What if we turn up at the same time. You do your thing and I do mine?"

The silence dragged on. Shaz played the game well.

"Listen," said Aulay. "I'll tell you everything... after the bash, ok?"

A hundred questions hung in the air.

"I'll hold you to that."

The line went dead.

They arrived at the Pennant without a ticket. The only bouncer, the formidable FB, looked inside, got a nod from The Sim and lowered his arm to let them pass. Shaz headed straight for the ladies.

"Yer man, Tosser Macalpine. He's done a runner," said The Sim.

"Oh, where too?"

"Magaluf."

"He's got a few brain cells left then."

"How so?"

134

"I'd put a few more miles than Kilmarnock between me and an angry Banana. Wouldn't you?"

"Aye, maybe. You're in the clear anyhow."

Aulay gave The Sim a mild questioning look but didn't chase it. The Polmadie had someone in Magaluf, or flew someone out there, to question Tosser Macalpine. Very thorough.

Shaz returned. "Hi, Sim," she said, "how you doin'?"

"No' too bad. Now, youz enjoy yourselz. The bar's free, though we'd appreciate a wee donation for the weans, at Yorkhill."

The Polmadie were having a charity bash. The Sim returned to his post. There were people waiting and FB needed more nods.

Aulay whispered in Shaz's ear. "They tracked Tosser Macalpine down and persuaded him to tell all. I passed muster."

"You are one jammy bastard." Shaz grabbed his balls and squeezed.

Keeping Shaz happy had benefits. They looked around.

"This is where me and the girls took tango lessons. Changed days. The place was a dump."

The Pennant is a big boozer with a bar, lounge and a basement function suite. A down and out's hovel until Chancer Mackinnon spent a serious amount of money to bring the place out of the dark ages. The bar, black and chrome glossy, had big screens showing any sport you fancied. One had cricket on, a first. A ponytailed pensioner plinked away on a guitar doing a mix of Dylan and Scottish folk. He was good. A four piece jazz combo played in the lounge where the older generation mixed drinking and a finger buffet with a burl round a small dance floor. A mix of pop and hip hop splayed from the function suite where the younger generation revelled beside tables of pakora and pizza.

After a quick recce, Shaz decided on the bar. Aulay ordered a Stella and a Gin 'n' slim. He slipped five twenties into a bucket labelled, Yorkhill Children's Hospital.

Shaz knew more people than he did.

"There's a bunch of Banana's here," she said. "That's Paisley Bob of The Buddies."

Aulay looked over at a tall man sipping blue liquid from a glass with an umbrella.

"And there's Bubbles Souter, The Drum Banana." Shaz pointed to a short bloke dressed to the nines in a pin stripe suit and cravat. "He took over The Drum when his dad, Soapy, retired."

The Drum Banana walked their way. A big geezer brought up the rear.

"Shaz doll, you're lookin' the business."

"Hi, Bubbles," smiled Shaz, "this is Aulay."

"Ah, the white knight." They shook hands.

A tight knit community; Glasgow hoodlums. The Greasy Spoon incident had done the rounds.

"Shaz," said Bubbles, "can I steal you for a wee minute, a bit of business."

Bubbles took Shaz by the elbow and led her off to a quiet corner.

"What do you go by?" Aulay asked Bubbles' minder.

"They call me Squeak."

Squeak's face didn't move. Must be one of the attributes required of a Top Banana's minder. The Sim was made of granite too. Squeak kept one eye on the door, the other on Bubbles. He was working.

The Polmadie, Drum and Buddies' Bananas were all in the same room, and no bloodletting. Changed days. In Uncle

Eddie's time, the gangs carved up the city, and each other. Under Mad Rab Smillie's tenure, The Polmadie held its ground, brutally stamping on any encroachment into their territory. The turf wars stopped after Chancer MacKinnon took the helm. Aulay didn't know why.

The very man appeared from a door to the right of the bar. Their eyes connected. On his way over, Chancer did the host thing, shaking hands and slapping backs.

"Where's yer man?" he asked Squeak.

Squeak indicated the corner where Shaz and Bubbles were deep in conversation.

Chancer looked at Aulay. "Much in demand, your Shaz. You got a sec?"

"Sure."

Chancer led Aulay out of Squeak's earshot.

"Can you come round to The Bulls Security yard, in the morning. Know it?"

"Aye."

"Ask for Freak Johnston."

With a nod to Squeak, Chancer threaded his way back through the throng.

Aulay went outside for a smoke. It was difficult to tell with Chancer Mackinnon. Did The Banana know he'd set Tosser Macalpine up? Tosser didn't. He was at the Greasy Spoon to meet a new heroin dealer. Returning to the fray, Aulay found Shaz discussing the issues of the day with Jemima MacAskill.

"No," said Shaz, "Freak's much better looking than Brad."

Jemima spotted Aulay. "Ah, my guardian." He got a hug.

"Hi Jem. Have you two sorted out who you're goin' home with?"

"There's the dish over there," said Shaz. "I've no' decided between him, and a few others."

Aulay followed her gaze to his Sunday morning appointment. Freak Johnston was tall, blond with a face chiselled to an almost feminine beauty. He'd heard the rumour. Women melted when Freak Johnston entered the arena. Aulay didn't believe it.

Jemima, Shaz and Aulay spent three hours discussing the pros and cons of the blokes crossing their path. They downed large amounts of the 'free' booze while Aulay kept one eye on the comings and goings at the door next to the bar. Paisley Bob and Bubbles Souter went in together, and stayed for an hour... mm.

Aulay poured Shaz into the taxi just in time, she was squiffed. During the ten minute journey back to her place, she gave him garbled messages in-between bouts of tears.

In her flat, Shaz put a finger to her lips, "Shush now."

She put the gas fire on, dimmed the lights and tottered over to the hi-fi. The powerful opening bars of 'Always on my Mind' brought them together and they clung on, swaying back and fore, tinkering with buttons and clasps, not saying a word.

An hour later, Elvis was into his eighteenth ballad and they were still moving slowly round the living room. They'd inherited Elvis from Mrs Eddie. A lifelong disciple of the King, she booked her pilgrimage to Graceland on the day she was diagnosed.

Aulay would have carried on, but nature's calling broke the spell. Shaz's bathroom was a mystery, or a temple, with oils and bottles, jars and potions. Strange things hung in the shower, and a fluffy pillow waited at one end of the bath.

When he emerged, a solemn Shaz pulled him to the carpet. She put her arms round his neck.

"So, how deep is the shite, Aulay."

She'd sobered up.

"It's pretty deep."

"Tell me."

He told her the whole story. The murder charge, the detention, the threat hanging over him, and the deal he'd made with the spooks. It took a while.

"Can I help?"

No why's or queries. She believed him.

"In the taxi, you said something, 'Chancer's a goodie', what did you mean?"

"Chancer's caught between the polis and the bad guys."

"The Polmadie going legit, it's real then?"

"Och aye, listen, I've been working on it for months, we're nearly there. Chancer's ended the war with The Buddies and The Drum. The final switch-over is in the diary."

"What switch-over?"

"The Polmadie are pulling out of the hard drug business. A lot of people's futures are riding on it."

"Jesus."

Shaz wasn't finished. "... and Chancer needs to be lucky. I need you to be lucky too, Aulay. Promise me you'll be lucky."

"I promise."

Another long silence as each contemplated their situation in the gas fire's dancing flames. Shaz perked up when Elvis began, 'Always on my Mind', for the fifth time.

"This song reminds me of Da'."

"How so?"

"In the back of his car, I was about fourteen. Da' stopped when he saw Gerry Struthers. Remember him?"

"Aye."

"Well, Gerry came up to the driver's door and leaned in, 'Always on my Mind' was playing on the radio. Gerry didn't see me."

"Know where I was when The King died, Eddie?"

"No, Gerry," says Da'."

"In my Cortina getting a blowjob from a bird from Castlemilk. The geezer on the radio interrupted the broadcast to announce the awful news. I was devastated, Eddie."

"Didn't know you were a big Elvis fan, Gerry?" says Da'.

"I'm no', but the bird from Castlemilk was. The bitch was too upset to carry on."

Aulay didn't believe a word of Shaz's little anecdote, but she had the knack of bringing him out of himself. Slipping Uncle Eddie into the gag, worked too.

Aulay ran his fingers through her hair, along her shoulder, thigh, breast, ankle, toe, shin, neck, cheek...

The sky was no longer black when Shaz took her head off his shoulder.

"It's always been you, Aulay."

For days he'd been slogging along the hope and longing road, fearing the post Kenny Finlayson shag fest was only a band aid... but now, he started shaking. The cold selfish bastard part of him whispered, 'Thanks, Eddie.'

Shaz drifted off. Aulay carried her through to the bedroom. She still sucked her thumb and he took her picture with his phone. Back in the living room, he tried Bandit's number. No reply, again. Shite, something was very wrong. He grabbed a bottle of red wine and listened to Bruce Springsteen's Nebraska. He skipped every second track. A trick he'd picked up from a depressed Corporal MacKechnie.

"Mr Johnston."

From Aulay's research, the man he faced owned an I.T. company, with accounts registered at Company House. The firm had one employee, and one customer.

"Mr Mackay, good to meet you."

Freak Johnston spoke with an English accent. Not London but close. After the hand shaking and coffee refusal, he opened with a bazooka.

"Mr Mackay." He paused to check something on one of the many screens filling the portakabin. "Can you tell me how you came to know three members of the DSH were being held in Govanhill Baths?"

Freak's gaze remained steady, his tone conversational. Out of several options, from denial to complete confusion, Aulay picked honesty.

"Your man delivering the fish suppers needs a few lessons."

"Lessons?"

"Och aye, he had *Amateur* and *Secret Mission* tattooed on his forehead."

That brought a smile. "Please continue."

Aulay told the whole story. Rainman was an ex-army buddy. Aulay owed him. The trip to London and the fracas with the DSH, he left out the bit about falling asleep on the roof.

Freak Johnston's attention, even with the odd glance at a PC screen, never wavered. He took notes. Aulay's story finished when he entered this portakabin.

"Quite a tale, Mr Mackay. Taking such a risk for a friend is commendable and... you passed on Uncle Theo's contact details?"

141

"Uncle Theo had me by the short-hairs. Said he'd blow the whistle if I didn't. It seems the old bastard dropped me in it anyway."

"Not quite right. I have not yet spoken to Uncle Theo."

"Then how did you know-"

Freak indicated a screen on another desk.

Aulay watched himself lying on familiar white tiles talking to a cat flap. The infra red camera was top drawer. A pop up window had the flickering audio as he and Rainman discussed their options.

Another Uncle Eddie-ism on his part. Of course The Polmadie would have the place bugged. Listening in on hostile prisoners is standard bloody practise. Aulay couldn't put it down to being Spiderman that night because he hadn't thought about it since. He needed some time off.

"Fortunately for you," continued Freak, "your actions fitted with our intention, improved it somewhat. Instead of releasing three men who could disappear, we released one who, we suggested, might want to blame the other two for his situation."

"Now," He leaned back, "about the Strathbungo Cellists and your intrusion into our security system."

Another bazooka. Aulay hadn't seen him reload. Playing with the Cellists was foolhardy at best, and crazy stupid the rest of the time. How did this guy know so much...? Shite. The Polmadie had Bandit. The one-armed wanker played too many computer games. In real life there is only one level.

"Listen, Mr Johnston. Bandit did it 'cos I asked him. He didn't know who he was dealing with... my fault. I should have stopped him. He's an innocent. I'm the one you should... em..."

Freak lifted a phone. "FB, come in here, please."

The cabin buckled when Colossus entered.

That's it then, thought Aulay. Taking on Fat Bastard would be easy. Getting out into the yard? Dodgy. He'd counted six Bulls Security guys in the cabin joined to this one. From the yard to the street? Winning the lottery, i.e. no chance.

"FB, could you-"

Aulay interrupted. "Mr Johnston, can I say someth-"

Freak interrupted his interruption. "Please." He raised a hand. "FB, would you mind asking Bandit to come in here, please."

Ask? Was this some over polite bollocks?

"Sure, Freak." The cabin righted itself.

Freak flitted across a keyboard as Aulay worked the odds of charging the window. The metal bars would impede his progress but it was looking like the favourite.

"Hi Aulay. Howz it goin'?"

Aulay looked round at a healthy and unmarked Bandit.

"Bandit, howz you, you ok?"

"Aye, no' bad. You should see the system these guys have. No wonder we couldn't get the complete script from the Depot scan. They've fire-walled their inner sanctum with beetle juice."

"Where you been the last few days? Your mobile fall off the pier?"

"Ah, em... sorry, Aulay. Freak suggested he keep hold of it, for a bit."

"Bandit," said Freak, "would you mind letting myself and Mr Mackay have a little word. You two can catch up shortly."

"Nae bother, Freak," said the infuriatingly still smiling Bandit. "See youz later."

Freak leaned back in his chair. The guy never seemed rushed. Aulay? He couldn't figure out what was going on. Was Bandit an unknowing hostage?

"You seem somewhat disconcerted, Mr Mackay."

Aulay shrugged. "Aye, an inner sanctum lined with beetle juice. I've no' a scooby, you?"

Freak's light smile reappeared. "Your friend Bandit is very good. Indeed, if he had two hands, I never would have tracked him down."

"How so?"

"Your friend leans more to the right side of his ingenious keyboard. A subtle thing but enough for me to pre-empt him... eh, pulling the plug."

Aulay considered his options. Could he take his host hostage?

"Now, Mr Mackay, may I call you Aulay?"

"Sure... Freak." Where was this going, the pals act?

"The Polmadie's Depot is as secure as I can make it? What were you and the Cellists planning? I'm curious about your proposed methodology."

The guy spoke a select brand of English.

"The Cellists came to me with a half baked idea about raiding the place. It was a load of cack."

"Cack?"

Must be a new word on him, thought Aulay. Hard to pick up all the vernacular. A good word, cack, an old word. Uncle Eddie used it all the time.

"Two meanings," said Aulay. "If you cack it, you're dead. If it's cack, it's shite."

"Thank you." Freak repeated the word a few times. "I know Eddie Curren's plan was, as you say, cack, but the Cellists have not disbanded."

144

The guy knew it all. Aulay made a mental note to search up his arse for the hidden microphone.

"If it wasn't for the current situation," said Freak, "we would have rounded up the players."

Aulay wondered what 'rounded up' meant. "What does 'rounded up' mean?"

"My leader suggested making an example of their leader."

If it wasn't for the DSH barging into Glasgow, Aulay would be missing body parts.

"Listen, Freak, the Cellists believe the script will follow Eddie's original plan. I was going to come good on the entry / exit stuff...em, the bits that me and Bandit worked out. I didn't get the chance 'cos I was day tripping down south."

The timetable fitted but would he go for it?

"Let me put something to you..." Here it comes, thought Aulay, the price. "... I believe you have an alternative to Eddie Curren's scheme. However. No matter. Please disband the Cellists, for now. When the small matter of the DSH is out of the way, I'd like the Cellists to reform and implement your plan."

"You want me to rob you?"

"Attempt, Aulay, attempt. No live bullets, no guns at all, preferably. You are a resourceful individual and I would like to pit my security regime against you. As an academic exercise. So, let us say you are successful. Whatever you and the Cellists blag, you can keep."

Aulay wondered what planet the guy came from. His Top Banana is in deep shite with Serious Crime, the biggest drug running organisation in Europe were banging at the door, with guns, and he wanted to play games. Blag? No one said 'blag' anymore, surely?

"I'd need Bandit," said Aulay.

"Of course," said the lunatic. "Lunch?"

Bandit didn't know anything about Uncle Eddie's plan. There must be a band member playing solo.

Lunch was a burger van on Scotland Street. The girls working the van waved.

"Hiya, Freak."

No one in a burger van ever waved at Aulay. He watched the girls check aprons, straighten skirts. Both wore makeup. In a greasy van?

As Freak made his final approach one girl squealed. The other jumped into the air.

"A very good afternoon to you, Chantelle," said Freak, "and to you, Marbella. It's a beautiful day."

Both girls preened with the thrill of it all.

"You havin' the usual the-day, Freak?" asked Chantelle with cooking implements poised.

"Please and for my friend here..."

"A roll and black pudding," said Aulay, "with coffee, white, no sugar."

Chantelle scooped a dried out black lump off the hot plate, slapped it onto a roll and handed it over. A polystyrene cup of weak brown stuff followed.

"Thanks," said Aulay, to no one.

Freak's usual was a roll and square sausage with a can of Irn Bru. The three or four limp sausages lurking on the grill were ignored. Chantelle retrieved a sample from the fridge, placed it in fresh, sizzling oil surrounded by Marbella's newly diced onion. The can of Irn Bru got a wipe to clear any condensation.

Aulay was no Brad Pitt, darker, nearer the George Clooney end of the scale. He received his fair share of looks and shy smiles. Today, he felt like an old slipper on Christmas morning.

"Like my new hair-do, Freak?"

"Fabulous." Freak said it like he meant it. Chantelle glowed.

Aulay'd had enough. He walked to a low wall and sat alongside his jealousy. They both chewed.

Freak walked over to join him. During the next while they were interrupted twice. Once by Chantelle who walked over with a Tunnock's Tea Cake for Freak. Nothing for Aulay. And once by Marbella who was all aquiver.

"Freak, you no' finished with that bird o' yours yet?"

Aulay couldn't believe it.

"Sorry, Marby... but, as I promised, you will be the first to know."

A distraught 'Marby' made her way back to the van.

Freak turned to Aulay. "It is an almighty curse, my friend."

Aulay believed him.

They finished lunch in a silence without any awkwardness. Neither attempted discussing the weather. When the last of Freak's Irn Bru slipped down, Marby appeared to take away his empty can.

'Thank you, Marby. That was delightful."

"You be back the 'morra then, Freak?" It was almost a plead.

"My undying wish," said Freak who got up and headed for the Bulls yard.

Aulay followed, still holding his empty poke and limp Styrofoam cup. A curse indeed.

In the portakabin, Freak checked his various screens.

"Why did the DSH launch a takeover?" asked Aulay. "The Polmadie upset somebody?"

"The DSH want to take over the street distribution of their commodities in various cities. They've had some success to date and, I assume, they felt our recent change in leadership gave them an edge."

It made sense but Aulay wasn't much on global strategy.

"Who's your favourite Cellist then?" he asked.

Aulay needed to know who was hitting the bum notes if the game of 'rob you charades' was ever to take place.

"Would you answer that question, in my position?"

It was worth a try... hold that thought. Freak was on his feet, a cold look on his angelic face. His fingers flitted across a keyboard.

"Excuse me. I'll be a few moments." Freak glided round the desk and out, closing the door behind him.

Aulay dondered round the desk to see if any of the LCD screens would give him a clue. The largest one had an ongoing game of chess. It was Freak's move. Maybe he was a lunatic. The other screens had a variety of screen savers running, red motorbikes mostly. He returned to his seat.

After a few minutes, he heard a commotion. People shouted. Not in anger, more of a hurry up thing. The door opened and FB filled the frame. "Go wander in the yard."

"Can I see Bandit?"

"Naw."

Uncomplicated answer, and final.

Two guys came in and hit the keyboards. Crossing the yard, Aulay spotted Freak patrolling the western fringes with a mobile stuck to his ear. He pointed at the phone then at Aulay and mouthed, 'won't be long'. Aulay waved back. He sat on the bonnet of his Daewoo Leganza.

The car wasn't much of a limo. Drab silver, the four door saloon oozed family car. Cars bored Aulay to death. He bought the Daewoo at auction, one of the big outfits in the east end. He'd enjoyed the day. The rattle of sabres as dealers competed for bargains. When the lazy Daewoo burbled onto the stage there was a shift, boredom from the throng as they checked to see if the next car on the list would be worthy of their attention. Aulay placed the only bid.

The previous owner was a mum with young children, or one child who grew up in the car. Among ancient spillages, an atrophied lolly lay marooned down the back seat. A Tele-Tubby filled the rear ashtray.

"Aulay Mackay, what you doin' here?"

Aulay rose from the Daewoo's bonnet. "Hi, Tadger, you with these scumbags now?"

"Aye, I work security on the nightshift. I'm no' involved wi' anythin' dodgy."

He offered Aulay his tobacco tin.

"Anythin' in this, Tadger?"

"Naw, yer fine. If yea fancy a blaw, I've got some in the motor."

"No, ta, this'll do."

Aulay and wacky baccy only met in Amsterdam coffee shops. He liked to sample the local colour wherever he went.

They filled the gaps in their lives. When Tadger started laughing, Aulay knew the story before he started... The pair were having a smoke outside Sammy Dows...

***

When Sledge MacQuarrie turned the corner at the bottom of Nithsdale Road, Tadger squeaked, threw his cigarette away and dodged back into Sammy's where he slid into the gents.

Sledge entered the pub. "Where is the wee shite?"

A hush floated through the place. A punter froze with his pound coin halfway to the puggy machine. The barman let the pint he was pouring overflow. The four auld geezers in Bullshit Corner looked up from their routine silence. Everyone watched the furious man at the door. Sledge MacQuarrie was not a man to cross.

"Who's you lookin' for, Sledge?" asked Aulay.

"Tadger Pirrie. I heard he was here."

"Tadger's been gone a wee while."

Aulay watched the man's disappointment.

"Shite."

"Fancy a drink, Sledge?"

"A wee rum."

Lowering his massive shoulders, Sledge lumbered over. He put his nail-gun on the bar. Technically, Sledge was banned from Sammy Dow's, and all the other pubs in the area. Barmaids got away with not serving him but it was a brave, or foolish, barman who refused the big man a drink.

"So, howz you?" asked Aulay as a tot of dark rum and a glass of water arrived.

"No' bad. Been working regular. You?"

"Go back in a few days, then Iraq. What's with you and Tadger?"

Aulay noticed the barman sneak into the snook. The police would be here soon.

"Och, I got three up at Doncaster an' was just at the bookies. Tadger, the wee bastard, never put my bet on."

"How much you down?"

"About three hunner." Sledge gripped the nail-gun. "I'm goin' to nail the wee shite's balls to the floor."

"Doesn't sound like something Tadger would do."

"Here."

Aulay scanned the bookmaker's slip. Sure enough, an accumulator. A crazy bet at those odds. All three needed to win for a payout, they did.

"How much you put down?"

"A tenner."

Sledge thrust the tot of rum down his throat then took a delicate sip of water. Throwing back rum like the ex-navy man he was, Sledge took his water gently, one pinkie in the air.

Sledge waved his forefinger. More drinks arrived.

Aulay got up. "Goin' for a pish."

In the toilet, he gave a trembling Tadger, two hundred and ninety seven pounds.

"Now, you little wanker. Stay here until I come back, right?"

"Sure, Aulay, sure," squeaked Tadger. "Thanks, I owe you one."

Aulay returned to the bar as the police car pulled up outside. He put one hand on Sledge's shoulder and the other on the nail-gun.

"Let's put this away before the polis come in. I'll hang on to it for now, eh?"

Sledge looked at him then glanced outside. Two young policemen climbed out of the car.

"I could snap them like twigs... but..."

Sledge swallowed his rum. Aulay slipped the nail-gun under his jacket.

"Ok, officers?" Sledge smiled at the approaching PCs.

"Mr MacQuarrie," said the taller one, "you know fine you can't drink in here?"

"Sorry lads, blame him." Sledge pointed at Aulay. "He insisted I stay for one."

He faced the policemen. "Any chance youz could drop me off at the Black Prince, on the north side?"

The PCs looked relieved.

"Aye, Sledge, sure," said the smaller one, "c'mon."

Sledge winked at Aulay.

Later, Sledge fell for Tadger's 'placing Sledge's bet with a different bookies' script. Aulay kept the nail gun.

***

In the Bulls Security yard, Tadger smiled. "That was the closest, eh?"

"Aye," said Aulay. "What's with Sledge these days, you see him much?"

"Och aye, he works here too. Nearly blew it with the new Banana though, didn't rate the no drink policy. It was back at the start, about six months ago. If it wasn't for his Mrs..."

Tadger launched into the story.

***

Sledge and Tadger approached the Star Bar at Eglington Toll. They were looking for some light refreshment before starting the night shift.

"If the new Banana expects me to spend all night in a Baltic portakabin without my regular supply," Sledge patted the bottle of Asti Spumanti poking out of his jacket pocket, "he's aff his head."

"The Banana's no' all bad," said Tadger. "The new shift rota's fair an' what about this holiday pay malarkey, eh?"

"Aye, suppose so, but," grumbled Sledge, "no' allowing an honest drink through the night, is a step too far."

"The wage rise is handy."

"What's the chances of Mrs Sledge no' hearing about it though, eh? Fat chance and fuck all."

Both men knew that 'more dosh' would permeate the marrow of the district in minutes.

As they entered the Star Bar, the barman waved them over.

"Now you boys are gettin' more dosh, I want a twenty off each of youz, against yer tab."

"Fuck me, TB. We're just in the door. Can we no' take our coats off first?"

Sitting with their pints, Sledge shrugged. "If Tight-Bastard already knows the script, I'm screwed. Mrs Sledge'll have my wages spent before the 'morra."

Around 2am, the sleeping Sledge turned round to try and blot out a consistent knocking. The regular beat transformed his dream from a pleasant sequence of sexual debauchery to one of galley slaves rowing to the rhythm of a big lug beating the shite out of a drum. Fear gripped Sledge as the galley tipped over. Sledge couldn't swim. He was going to drown.

He landed on the portakabin floor. "What the fuck."

Sledge looked up into a face he recognised. His drowning panic submerged beneath a worse fear. Sledge was no shrinking violet but The Sim's reputation quelled any thoughts of hitting out.

The Sim forced something into Sledge's mouth.

"Eh, wa…" garbled Sledge.

"Blow, fucker," growled The Sim.

Sledge blew.

A minute later, The Sim told Sledge to get his stuff and go. He was sacked.

Sledge didn't get fired for sleeping. With Tadger out on patrol, Sledge snoozed until it was time to swap. Accepted practise on the nightshift. Sledge was over the drink driving limit. Tadger escaped, he was just below the limit.

Next morning, Mrs Sledge barged into a meeting at the Bulls yard.

"Listen, Chancer," she said, "my Sledge is an arsehole. He thought you was jokin' about the booze thing."

A powerful woman, with bingo wings made of muscle, Mrs Sledge filled the doorway.

"I'll keep him on the straight and narrow, honest. If he fucks up again, it'll be me who does the damage, ok?"

A younger Sledge got the nickname because he kept getting pulled by dogs. The current Mrs Sledge filled the bull mastiff slot down to the thick neck and slobbering.

Sledge got his second chance.

***

Aulay laughed. It was a good tale.

"Changed days from Mad Rab's time then, Tadger?" he said.

"No' half. The Bulls men used to spend most of their time stealin' stuff off the sites an' selling it back to the builders."

"You miss it?"

"It was exciting, don't get me wrong, but... we worked the edge all the time."

"The polis?"

Tadger laughed. "The polis took their cut. Naw, it was Mad Rab. Towards the end he would prowl the sites looking for trouble. Two blokes working a site in the Gorbals got caught with a hooker. It's been a year now an' they're still no' back at work. As for the hooker..."

"What about her?"

"She'll never work again, if you know what I mean."

Aulay made a show of stubbing his cigarette out. Tadger took the hint. No more details were required.

"So, changed days," Aulay said again.

154

"Aye, this is regular work. Full PAYE. Keep your nose clean here and there's bonuses, sick pay. Jeez, Aulay, I'm a proper member o' society now."

Like a lot of people Aulay grew up with, Tadger flitted in and out of juvenile detention and seemed destined to travel the road to nowhere but prison.

"What's this guy like?" Aulay asked, nodding his head in Freak's direction.

"Get past the plums in his mouth an' he's alright, for an English bastard. Doesn't look up or down at nobody. He's the Banana's main man and Cosi rates him on the board."

Cosi Fan Tutte, a chess playing fanatic from school, went to opera lessons, his mum insisted.

"Cosi still singing?"

"Och, aye," said Tadger, "most Tuesday nights at the Opry."

Aulay remembered the sign outside the venue at Paisley Road Toll.

Karaoke with a difference – First Prize – A Tenor.

"This guy Freak, can I trust him?"

"Aye."

Aulay searched Tadger's face for signs. Nothing. An honest answer to an awkward question.

Freak arrived.

"Sorry, Tadger, got to go, business," said Aulay.

"Nae bother. Aulay, you go easy." Tadger nodded at Freak. "See youz around."

"You know our Mr Pirrie?" asked Freak as they crossed the yard.

"Aye, known Tadger for yonks."

"His nickname intrigues me."

155

"It's enormous. Like a baby's arm holdin' an apple," said Aulay. "At school we called him horse 'cos he kept taking it out in public, like the real ones do."

With Freak on a wide grin, Aulay threw another onto the fire.

"All Tadger's girlfriends are called Filly."

Freak roared. Aulay felt good without knowing why.

Back in his office, a serious Freak asked, "Can you do something for me?"

"Shoot."

"Is gunfire on the streets of south London something you could throw some light upon?"

"When'd it happen?"

Freak looked at his watch.

"Sometime within the last hour."

Aulay called Rainman.

"They got Number Three and Homer. Rammed their motor and started blasting, with shotguns. They didn't stand a chance."

"Anyone else hurt? Darina and Louis OK?"

"Yea, yea, we're holed up in a pokey place in Brighton. Aulay..." A chill came down the line. "...we should have gone into the flat."

"Rainman, we don't do regret, remember?"

It was weak, but true. "What's the plan?"

"Uncle Theo's tooling up. It's war against the DSH."

"You joining up?"

"Dam right, I owe it to Number Three."

Aulay ended the call and gave Freak the facts.

Freak thought for moment. "Can you reach em... Uncle Theo? I would appreciate an introduction."

Aulay looked up Uncle Theo on his phone.

"Hi, Uncle Theo, it's Aulay Mackay. Just heard the news and spoke to Charlie. Sorry to hear about Homer."

"Homer was an idiot who wouldn't listen," said Uncle Theo. "Him and Number Three decided to go out on a jolly."

"I've got The Polmadie's Consigliore with me. Ok if he wants a word?"

"Put him on."

Aulay handed his phone over and made to leave. Freak ushered him back to his seat.

"Uncle Theo, Freak Johnston here. My condolences, sir."

The tone was solemn and sincere. There followed a series of "uh huh, yes, mm."

"Uncle Theo, I understand your reasoning. Can I however, ask you to delay any action for seventy two hours?"

Freak paced the floor with the same beat he maintained out in the yard.

"Our situation is delicate and the timing is important. It could help both our causes, without putting your people in jeopardy."

Good word, jeopardy, thought Aulay. Not used much these days.

A couple more "uh huh."

"If you don't hear from Aulay before then... well, our plan will not have achieved its objective."

Aulay was in the loop?

More "uh huh."

"Thank you, Uncle Theo. Can I pass you back to Aulay now? Uh huh, uh huh...I look forward to meeting you too. Thank you."

Aulay took the phone. "Hi."

"This Freak geezer," said Uncle Theo, "do you trust him?"

157

With 'This Freak geezer' looking straight at him, there was only one thing Aulay could say.

"I don't know the guy, Uncle Theo. We just met. If you want a first impression then... I'd say yes."

"My boys are itching, Aulay. I need more than that."

"Ask Rainma... Ask Charlie. He was Freak Johnston's guest for a few days."

"Ok. I'll do that and call you back."

As they waited, Freak turned his attention to one of the LCD screens.

"Rook to queen four," said Aulay.

Freak didn't blink. "It is the obvious move, nevertheless... I feel he wants me to make it."

"Who's he?"

"Don't know, could be a she. It's a blind online game. You obviously play?"

"I've handled a few chessmen. My dad taught me."

He didn't mention that Dad was twelve and could still run rings round him.

"We must have a game when..."

The pink panther theme sounded. "Hi, Uncle Theo."

Freak got his seventy two hours.

"What you need three days for?" asked Aulay.

"Peace and quiet." Freak sat forward. "Up until now, we... The Polmadie, have scraped through this episode more by luck than design."

His fingers tickled the keyboard. "Aulay, would you consider working for us?"

"Doin' what?"

"A trip abroad."

"Where abroad?"

"Spain. The Costa del Sol."

"To do what?"

"Provide backup. Chancer needs to get out of Glasgow for a while."

Aulay suspected the 'while' was seventy two hours.

"Because of Serious Crime?"

"That... and the DSH."

"Why me? You've an army out there." Aulay indicated the door.

"We need someone with air miles."

Aulay's look said he didn't get it.

"Our troops are not em... well travelled. Two weeks drinking lager in the Lion Rampant Bar in Torremolinos doesn't qualify."

So, the Polmadie were homely types. Take them out of Glasgow and they'd be as much use as a get well card in a funeral parlour.

"You are well travelled," said Freak. "Five years in the army, then two years babysitting wealthy American businessmen."

"Businessman," said Aulay. "My first and only boss died from a bullet through the head."

"Not your fault, I believe."

Freak didn't know everything. Anyway, where was this guy getting his information?

"I don't kill people," said Aulay. This left a myriad of other things.

"Agreed."

Freak handed over a thick envelope. Aulay peaked in at airline tickets and a healthy wad of Euros among other bits and bobs.

"When do we leave?"

"You're flying solo, to stay in the background. You're booked on the same flight and into the same hotel as Chancer and The Sim. I want you to watch their backs"

He wanted Aulay to play Harry Lime, and The Sim could take care of anything outside Aulay's 'myriad of other things'.

"How do you wish to be paid?" asked Freak. "I believe a thousand pounds a day is the going rate."

Aulay took a business card from his wallet. "Payable here."

"Your accountant?"

"Aye."

"Ask him to bill my company, for consultancy work, keeps everything legal. I'll transfer the money today. A month in advance?"

Aulay nodded. Freak knew his 'terms & conditions'. Another thing; The Polmadie had this trip tied up before Aulay woke up this morning. Did he have a choice? Not really. With the Govanhill Baths and the Cellists hanging round his neck, he'd work for free. Paying him was a good will gesture and they both knew it.

They discussed a few minor details... communications / chat room addresses / mobile numbers – it was all in the envelope.

It was time for Aulay to leave. He wanted to check something. "You know a DI McCaw?"

"In what regard?"

"He fancies muscling in on the Cellists."

"Mm." Was all Freak Johnston said as he shook Aulay's hand.

Aulay now worked for The Polmadie. Shaz would be pleased. The pink panther sounded as he drove out of the Bulls yard.

"Hi, Eileen Doll, howz you?"

"No' bad, Aulay. Where you been hidin'? Was expecting you at rehearsals."

"Been busy, Eileen. Should've called, sorry." He checked his watch. "Where you at in an hour, Sammy Dows?"

"Ok, and Aulay, fuckin' turn up."

Aulay's phone went dead. He smiled. An angry Eileen McCloy is worth seeing.

Aulay walked into Sammy's. The rain pelted down but he wasn't too wet, he'd found a parking spot right outside.

"The wanderer has returned," said Eileen. "What'll you have?"

"Coffee."

She raised an eyebrow but made no comment. Aulay sat in the window seat next to Eileen's whisky and ginger ale. He watched the kafuffle behind the bar as they struggled to get the coffee machine working. Gone were the days when Sammy's had a cook and did pub lunches.

The barman walked over. "Instant awright, Aulay? The machine's fucked."

"Aye, Gob, instant's fine."

"Why do you call him Gob?" asked Eileen when she sat back down.

"It's quicker than saying grumpy old bastard."

Eileen laughed.

Aulay looked around the half busy bar. Through a collection of six or so student types, he spotted them.

"Back in a mo'."

He wandered over to his mum and dad. "Hi, guys, anyone want a drink?"

"I'm fine, Aulay."

"Beer please, son," said Dad.

Aulay returned with a ginger beer and a straw. "So, what you guys up to?"

"We're meeting Stan the Man then goin' to the pictures," said Dad removing the straw.

Dad liked straws. He had a drawer full of them, well, nearly. Mum sneaked a few out every now and again, to

162

make room. Mum looked good. She'd had her hair done, a younger cut.

"Hair looks good, Mum."

She smiled and did the hair patting thing that woman do after a coiffure complement. There was something else but Aulay struggled to pinpoint it. His mum wasn't a female in the general sense, the gender repartee didn't apply, and what remained was elusive.

Earrings. His mum's ears were pierced. Jesus, how to handle it? Another woman and Aulay would launch into it no problem. This was sticky. He was saved when Dad headed for the gents. Mum leaned over.

"I'm worried about Stan, Aulay. He's not himself."

Before he could ask for details, the pub door opened and a scraggy wet dog dragged in a drenched bloke. Both Stan's looked done in. Why Stan called his dog, Stan was a mystery. After a quick hello, four legged Stan went on patrol, lots of things to sniff at today.

After a quick 'Hi' to Eileen McCloy, two legged Stan walked over. Under his raincoat, he wore a blue blazer and grey slacks. Stan was a bowler and wore the uniform.

"Bloody weather, one minute fine, the next, cascades of the wet stuff."

He still hadn't caught Aulay's eye.

Mum smiled.

"Hi, Stan," said Dad returning from the loo.

"Hi, Dad."

Aulay didn't get a mention.

"You got time for one, Stan," Aulay asked, standing up.

"No." Stan looked at Mum then his watch. "We need to move. Got to drop Stan off home first."

Aulay remained on his feet. He watched two legged Stan marshal his defences before turning to face him.

163

"What's new with you then, young Mackay?"

"You don't know, Stan? I'm surprised. A lot of interesting people know exactly what I've been up to."

Mum gathered her stuff. Dad finished his beer, pocketing the straws. At the pub door, Aulay whispered in Stan's ear. "I'll see you after the matinee. Be available."

"Love the earrings, Mum," he said.

He got the big smile then.

"Aye," said Dad, "they're cool."

Aulay sat down heavily.

"What's up?" asked Eileen.

"One of the Cellists is breaking strings all over town. DI McCaw has our complete repertoire."

Stan the Man was the obvious choice. Bag and Stash is a passive roll. Not a street guy, Stan would squawk at the first hint of a threat. Aulay nipped to the bar and returned with a house whisky. He poured into his crap coffee. He needed a hit.

"You think its Stan the Man?" asked Eileen.

"I know it's him."

It was Aulay's own fault for not disbanding the Cellists on day one. Now his mum's fiancé was in deep doodie, right up to his neck.

"What do we do, Aulay?"

"Fuck knows. I'm seeing Stan later so not a peep about anything. I'll let you know. No more band practise, ok?"

"Aye," said Eileen. "Fancy another?"

"It's my shout. You want a whisky and ginger?"

"No, a brandy, large." Eileen wore a weak smile. "Should I be scared, Aulay?"

"No, Eileen. You should be very scared."

Aulay returned with her drink and another crap coffee.

"You on the wagon?" said Eileen.

"No, I'm working."

"At what?"

"Security Consultant, for The Polmadie."

Eileen's nervous tension exploded in a big guffaw. Rolls of fat rippled as her chins did the cha cha. Aulay joined in. A stressful day and it was only lunchtime.

***

Stan the Man led Aulay into his kitchen. He offered whisky. Aulay took a can of coke. Stan has a proper kitchen with two armchairs on either side of a working coal fire. The always spick and span had slipped. Aulay noticed the full sink. Grime coated the worktops underneath a few empty tins. A pile of newspapers climbed up the wall. He caught the whiff of rotting waste as he past the bin.

Four legged Stan finished his welcoming manoeuvres and curled up on the hearth carpet, a millimetre from scalding.

"I was going to tell you," said Stan. He looked tired.

"Tell me now."

"Me and your Uncle Eddie go back to Gory McGlorry's time. The family shop was on Polmadie Road then. My father let out one of the storerooms. Eddie paid the rent every week. I started running little errands for him. I was only twelve."

Aulay looked at his watch. He didn't have time. "Skip the history lesson."

Stan took a deep breath and burst into tears. Aulay waited, embarrassed.

"That fucker, DI McCaw. You know him, Aulay?"

"We've met."

"He did this..."

Stan lifted his shirt to reveal the livid remnants of a good pummelling. Aulay's Stan rating rose. He'd held out for some time.

"McCaw's been dripping information to The Polmadie since Eddie's time," said Stan. "He's on a bloody retainer, for Christ's sake."

"How'd he find you?"

Stan shrugged. "He rang the bell. I opened the door. There were three of them. I was wanted at the police station. Some bollocks about identifying stolen goods. In the car they put something over my head and forced me down."

Aulay knew the next bit. Sitting on a chair in a container behind Ibrox Park.

Stan started to cry again. "I tried Aulay, I did... it... it was too much. I told them everything."

"What's the threat, Stan? If you talk to me or anyone else."

"Your mum..." he sobbed now, "please Aulay, if anything happened to..."

DI McCaw was playing a different game. Family were non-combatants, and sacrosanct, or used to be.

"Anyone else been to see you?"

"Who?"

"From The Polmadie?"

"No, Aulay, I swear..."

There was another Cellist playing bum notes or McCaw's team leaked, which would fit with Rainman's DSH dossier story.

"Ok, Stan." Aulay stood up. "Give me your cheque book."

Worry caressed Stan's face as he fumbled in a drawer. "Here."

Aulay noted the account number and sort code.

"Here's the plan, Stan. By the 'morra you'll be a few grand richer. Take Mum and Dad to the airport and fuck off for a couple of weeks. Don't go to Spain. Ok?"

It took a couple of seconds before Stan grasped it. He was out. The big hole he was in was going away.

"Jesus, Aulay, I..."

Aulay headed for the door. "Tell Mum you need a break and nothing else."

"Ok."

"Leave your mobile phone here. Do the same with Mum's. Buy a couple of pay-as-you-go mobiles at the other end."

"Will do, Aulay, thanks."

***

£682,756.12 appeared on the computer screen. It looked good. Personal Security for American millionaires paid well, and he'd spent nothing during his time with the Waincross family. He transferred £5000 to Stan the Man's account, paid the extra to make it instant, and logged off.

The downside of all that money? The bank's pestering by phone, email and letter to make him do something responsible with it.

***

Aulay couldn't remember the last time he'd been in a phone box. It took him a minute or two to work out how the contraption worked. He remembered the smell.

"I'm in, Hector," he said into the huge handset. "I'm playing the 'third man' to the Top Banana and The Sim. We're taking a trip to the Costa."

"A quick summary, please," said Hector

Aulay ran through the events of the past week. "You mentioned bigger fish. Would they be the DSH?"

Hector ignored the question. "Do you know Chancer MacKinnon's plans? His objective?"

"Nobody here's spelt it out but I can make a guess. The Banana doesn't want the DSH to try another takeover. He's going to make a deal."

"Aulay, the DSH don't deal, ever and..."

"The Banana doesn't strike me as an idiot, he'll have a plan."

"It'll need to be a good one."

"Any advice then, Hector?"

"Keep your head down. Be alive to testify."

"Testify to what?"

"That Ricky Temple, the head of the DSH, ordered the hit on Chancer MacKinnon."

Hector told Aulay that his passport would be removed from the blacklist, and hung up.

Aulay called LJ. They were at school together. He joined up too. LJ lost a foot in a fire fight with the Taliban during their first tour. He retired to the Costa.

"Hi, Long John, its Aulay, howz you?"

"Red Five, shit man, long time, what's happenin'?"

"I'm heading your way, LJ, need a favour."

"No sweat, anythin' at all, man."

LJ always did have the hippy thing going.

A relieved Aulay finished the call. There would be guns in Left Luggage at Malaga airport.

Happy days.

Feeling the comfortable weight of his new holdall, Aulay followed the throng through Malaga airport to where Chancer MacKinnon and The Sim stood getting their bearings. They had too many clothes on. Outside, the heat hit them properly.

Aulay overheard The Sim complain, "Now I know how a kebab feels."

The Galoots got into a taxi. Aulay climbed into the next one. The Galoots? The tag Chancer and The Sim picked up during their school days when they rarely strayed from each other's side.

Aulay had travelled the road from Malaga airport many times. Building sites off to the right, as the sprawl of development crept further inland to scar the orange soil with ugly outcrops of white concrete. Other memories of this part of the world were vague. Alcoholic binges, the consistent dum dum dum beat of late nights spent in grotty nightclubs chasing birds from Sheffield who wore nothing much and were as drunk as he was. Ever the optimist, Aulay would begin the week looking for a Shaz, only to crash and burn on the poor fare of a Claire from Livingston, or a Michelle from Doncaster. The two years he'd spent chasing Shaz's shadow equalled the average term of bereavement. He'd read that somewhere.

Arriving at the Hotel Sol in Puerto Banus, a platoon descended on Aulay's Taxi. Two guys with umbrellas made his three steps to the shade bearable. Others removed his two small bags from the boot. Yet more hung around waiting for something to do.

Opulence, decadence, filthy rich, call it what you like, the Hotel Sol catered to those with obscene amounts of money.

The foyer's marble and steel drew the eye to a thirty metre waterfall. Immaculately turned out waiters, porters and reception staff glided along anxious to cater to every need. A little ahead of Aulay, the Galoots mastered the checking-in palaver before walking to the lifts with a posse of porters. The foreign tipping trauma went away when Aulay read the sign at Reception.

The tipping of staff is <u>Discouraged</u>. Please feel free to make a donation to our Staff Fund at the end of your stay.

Aulay shooed the gaggle of porters from his room where they'd been checking the shower, the toilet et al. Alone, he removed both of LJ's guns and checked them over before getting the lift to the top floor. He knocked on the door of the Banana's penthouse suite.

"No' bad digs eh?" said Chancer.

Looking round the enormous space, Aulay spotted The Sim on the balcony with a bottle of coke in his hand. Aulay's room, opulent but pokey in comparison, faced the orange hills.

"Great," said Aulay keeping the adolescent envy from his voice.

The Sim came in from admiring the vista. "Beer, Aulay?"

"Aye, cheers."

Sim walked over to a big American style fridge. He pulled out a bottle of San Miguel.

"You got a plunge pool on yer veranda?" The Sim asked as he held out the beer, "'cos I've got one on mine."

As Aulay reached for the San Miguel, The Sim dropped it. Aulay made a grab with both hands. In a blink, he was face down on the floor with his left arm desperately trying to get out of its shoulder socket. One of LJ's guns poked the dodgy bit behind his left ear.

"Tooled up, Aulay?" The Sims mouth was a few millimetres away. "Where'd you get this?"

The Sim was good, fast. Aulay had a decision to make. It was taken out of his hands.

"Let him up, Sim," said Chancer.

Sitting up, Aulay took a pull from the bottle of cold beer. He smiled. "Look. Didn't spill a drop."

Taking up one trouser leg, Aulay unclipped the ankle holster and removed LJ's other gun. The Sim had the good grace to look embarrassed. Aulay could have blown his head off.

"What's with the artillery?" asked Chancer. "You planning on shooting someone?"

"Aye, anyone who's shooting at me."

"How'd you get it through the flight?"

"I didn't. I know people here. I arranged for a drop at left luggage."

The Sim put both weapons down on the coffee table. "They're neutral. No markings."

"Very enterprising," said Chancer. "What makes you think this trip might involve em... trouble?"

"Nobody pays me a grand a day to watch their back for the fun of it."

Chancer did a half shrug half nod. "Let's check the comms."

They sat round the suite's dining table confirming the pay-as-you-go mobile phones did their thing. Laptops were hooked into the hotel's wireless network. They ran through the communication channels with Freak Johnston via a series of internet chat rooms. Everything worked.

"Now," said Chancer, "the DSH know we're here. They'll be in touch."

171

This was news to Aulay. "What's to stop them blowing you away?"

"This is business, Aulay. Their takeover failed. Why waste resources? They'll want to hear what I've got to say."

Aulay kept quiet.

"Sim," said Chancer, "I'm going to talk best-telephone while we're here. Easier on the locals, OK?"

"Nae bother, chief. I'm goin' tae dae it an' all, cheers."

The Sim took a swallow then sprayed it all back out. Everyone laughed.

Aulay was curious. "How'd you manage to pick up best-telephone?"

"My mum overdosed when I was six. I moved in with my grandparents. I'd get a clip round the ear if I brought street talk into the house."

Made sense.

With nothing due to happen until the DSH made contact, The Sim decided on the gym. Chancer settled into a seat at one of the pool bars and world watched. Aulay stuck with Chancer. Taking a seat within hearing distance, he read a Washington Post.

It wasn't difficult to work out the hotel hierarchy. Porters and cleaners were Arab or African. Barmen and waiters were Spanish. Reception staff and above were Brits with the odd Aussie. Aulay hadn't heard a word of Spanish since the 'buenos dias' from his departing taxi driver.

"Excuse me, Senor MacKinnon?"

A porter offered a silver tray. Chancer read the card.

"Two gentlemen would like to meet with you, Senor MacKinnon. I can ask them to leave, wait in reception, bring them here or show them to your suite."

"Ask them to join me here, please."

The two gentlemen approached. Big guys in light weight suits, garish shirts and sandals. Ex soldiers who carried adrenaline residue from, 'the time of their lives'. How did Aulay know? An ex-squaddie can spot another ex across a football stadium.

Well groomed with slicked back hair on one, shaven on the other. The nails, their nails were manicured. A quick peek confirmed the toe nails too. Aulay picked up the faint scent of boredom. Messenger boys sent out by the gaffer to make sure The Polmadie's Top Banana was comfortable.

"Mr MacKinnon, howza," said Slicked Back, "welcome to the Sol." He introduced Shaven.

Chancer shook hands with both and a false bonhomie overflowed. Backs were slapped. Purple and yellow drinks, with sparklers, appeared.

"Mr Temple sent us down to see you alright and with an invitation for dinner at the Copacabana. Say, 9 o'clock?"

"Thank Mr Temple. We'll be there."

The Sim arrived.

"Guys, this is Sim."

"Howza," Slicked Back shook Sim's hand.

Hand out, Sim turned to Shaven. Aulay sensed a girding of loins. Shaven was going to show the pip squeak who was boss. Their hands met. When the onslaught arrived, The Sim responded.

Patting Slicked Back and Shaven on the back, The Sim ushered both heavies out to the hotel reception area with, "Nice tae meet youz guyz, see yeez later."

Shaven did well to keep the pain from his face.

Aulay joined the Galoots in the lift.

"Much damage?" he asked The Sim as they hurtled skywards.

"Naw. Broke his trapezoid. He'll be fine in four to six weeks. Great gym here, by the way."

Aulay smiled.

In their suite, the Galoots found an invitation to The Sol's Albertino Lounge, 7pm, smart casual.

"What's a cocktail party?" asked The Sim.

"No' too sure," said Chancer, "Aulay?"

Cocktail party was a foreign phrase in Glasgow. Aulay sensed a reticence in the air. The Galoots would have been to the odd swanky place. Their table manners a few rungs above pigs at the trough but... a cocktail party at the Sol would mean mixing with high flyers, international high flyers.

"It'll be a posh do at a place like this," said Aulay. "It's where a load of strangers meet and introduce themselves."

"To who?"

"Each other."

"I'll give it a miss," said The Sim. He picked up the Sol's TV & Movie guide.

"You up for it?" asked Chancer.

"Sure." Aulay resigned himself. He'd attended dozens of these tedious events with Coulfield Waincross III. He preferred listening to air-conditioning.

"What do they mean by smart casual?"

"No shorts or T-shirts," said Aulay. "You got a suit, wear that. Take a tie, just in case."

Just before seven, an Armani'd Chancer bumped into Aulay in the poolside bar.

"The Sim's worried about falling into the mire," said Chancer after they'd introduced themselves to each other.

"The cocktail party thing? How so?"

Chancer explained.
***

For a recent first date, The Sim booked the Wok Way, a posh Chinese restaurant in Giffnock where getting a table involved waiting for weeks, or lots of cash. Everything went smoothly until the pudding arrived, the house speciality, elaborate sculptures arranged around a dollop of ice cream.

"Whit dae ye think it is?" Sim pointed at what looked like a bird about to take off.

"Looks like it's made of turnip tae me," replied his victim, Babs.

"Och well, I've never had turnip an' ice cream afore."

The Sim started hacking the wing off a swan.

A scream went up followed by Mr Chow careering through the tables. All eyes followed.

"No no no," screamed Mr Chow, "only for decolation. For decolation only."

When Aulay stopped laughing, Chancer looked around. "In a place like this, The Sim would stand out like a first day apprentice among the time served." He smiled. "Want to hear my apprentice story?"

"Sure."

"I was eighteen..."
***

Lydia, almost thirty, was determined to have her evil way with the young Chancer. The seduction arena had candelabra, chandeliers and a menu with no prices. Their waiter wore a tux.

"I felt like David Attenborough on his first day with the gorillas."

Lydia ordered mussels to start. An extensive perusal of the wine menu ensued with Guy, the wine waiter, who dismissed Chancer, with his cheap haircut and denims, as a philistine.

"Madam is a connoisseur," said Guy. "The Batard Montrachet. An exquisite choice." With a withering glance at Chancer, Guy asked Lydia, "Shall I bring two glasses?"

"Aulay, I swear. It was three hundred quid a bottle."

Guy presented the label, de-corked with a flourish then poured a dribble into Chancer's glass. He stood back with an eyebrow raised. Lydia came to Chancer's rescue.

"Pour please, Guy. I'm sure it will be excellent."

With an exaggerated, "Oui Madam", Guy filled both glasses before slipping the bottle of Batard Montrachet into a floor standing ice bucket.

The mussels arrived. Chancer followed Lydia's cutlery choices and her shell fish technique. He felt he did OK. Guy returned, launching into a brouhaha about red wine regions, year, constant temperature of 19 degrees blah blah - to complement the filet mignon main course.

Most of the Batard Montrachet was inside Chancer by this time. He wasn't used to wine of any region, or vintage. He felt good though. He'd negotiated the mussels with aplomb and was on the verge of getting into the knickers of 'gorgeous with the tits'.

When the filet steak arrived, Chancer was the cock o' the north, only dimly aware of Guy's performance with a bottle of deep red Claret, the filling of lower, fuller glasses.

As Guy turned to go, Chancer paused in his delivery of a riveting anecdote.

"That wine waiter hasn't got as clue," he said in a loud whisper.

176

People at surrounding tables turned to watch as Chancer grabbed the nurtured bottle of red and plunge it into the ice bucket.

***

Another bout of honest laughter. Aulay warmed to the Banana and felt obliged to recount his 'blowjob in public' debacle. Chancer paid attention, wincing as the climax approached.

"Fuck me, Aulay. That blows me and The Sim's gaffs into the weeds."

The sign to the Albertino lounge led down a corridor to a sinister purple curtain. A tall blonde stood at a lectern. Aulay and Chancer checked their flies before sauntering down. The blonde beamed the big smile.

"Good evening, gentlemen. Are you here for the Albertino cocktails?"

"Aye, eh, sorry, yes," said Chancer.

"May I have your room keys, please?"

They handed over the wafer thin devices. The blonde whisked them thru a machine. Photographs appeared on her screen. She did a cursory glance at each, beamed the big smile again, returned the pass keys and drew the curtain back.

"Thank you, gentlemen. Have a very good evening."

A waiter offered flutes of champagne. Another, slimy grey lumps on shells. Aulay and Chancer took a flute, body-swerving the grey lumps. People stood around talking. The men wore light suits, open neck shirts. The woman wore dresses, short, flouncy numbers, bling jewellery matched tiny handbags. Everyone seemed to know someone.

Chancer nodded at the waiters. "Those slimy grey things, oysters?"

"Aye," said Aulay, "and they taste like puke coming back up."

Chancer swallowed a snort. A couple approached.

"Good evening. My name is Clarence De Bencheur and I'm a stockbroker. This is my wife, Edith. We're from London, well, Surrey actually."

Clarence held out his hand. Edith smiled.

"Good evening, Edith, Clarence. My name is Alec MacKinnon. I'm in the ice cream business. This is..." Chancer paused, "... I'm sorry, we've only this minute met in the bar..."

Aulay reached out a hand. "I'm Aulay Mackay, good to meet you."

Chancer continued, "...and we're from Glasgow."

Edith joined the party. "Lovely, we were up in Glasgow last new year, hogmanay, had a lovely time. Do you get down to London at all?"

"Sorry, no, not too often," said Chancer.

"What sector of the Ice Cream business are you in, Alec?" asked Clarence.

Edith and Clarence were an experienced cocktail party tag team.

"Manufacture and retail distribution," said Chancer.

Aulay put his nurse maid cap away. The Banana could take care of himself.

"Seasonal workload I would imagine?" This from Edith.

"Och, children don't care what the weather's like when the ice cream van plays the tune."

"And Aulay. What do you do?" it was Clarence's turn.

"I fix tanks."

"Water tanks, oil storage tanks?"

"Chieftains and Challengers mostly."

Aulay's stand-by occupation, an artificer in the Royal Electrical & Mechanical Engineers.

"Must be varied and interesting work?" From Edith.

There was no phasing this couple, they were pro's. The chit chat continued until an unseen bell tolled. The De Bencheurs turned smartly and walked towards another couple.

There was no time to reflect before the house building Smethicks, from Yorkshire, faced them. Then it was the turn of George and Sybil Tomlinson, from Brighton, who were chemists with a string of outlets along the south coast. On and on it went. Chancer expanded his list of questions and responses. Somewhere along the line, he won a coveted UK award for his vanilla.

A potential blip, when Rupert and Jeremy, the only other all male couple at the bash, made their way over.

"Ah, you must be the Glasgow boys. Action man and Ice Cream man. We've heard about you. Received a few warnings even."

"Warnings?" asked Chancer.

"Some reckon you must be criminals who've hit the big time and came to see how the other half live."

"Is it that obvious?"

"... or, one of you is a Lottery winner and brought along a pal for back up."

"Why here and not Thailand, or Jamaica," said Chancer, "where a young man with cash has a myriad of more eh..., adventurous options?

"See, told you," this from Jeremy. "I was right. They've bumped off the original guests, took over their identities and are staying one step ahead of DI Taggart."

Everyone laughed and Chancer's voice returned to its higher, normal pitch.

Some unspoken rule indicated the event was over. Chancer and Aulay did the 'nice to have met you' dance and went their separate ways. Aulay would make his own way to the Copacabana.

The Sol had a fleet of BMWs available for guests. Aulay climbed into a 7 Series. Following the sat nav along the coast road, he perused the last few days. The Top Banana had depth, and not just the kind needed for killing. Chancer MacKinnon was likeable and smart but, what the hell was he doing walking into the DSH's lions den?

Aulay parked in a spot where he could monitor all the comings and goings at the Copacabana,. Opposite the club was the beach, still busy with the full spectrum of British holiday maker, from pale blue first day-ers, to scarlet masochists. A steady stream, carrying limp children and the remains of a hot day, passed Aulay's beemer on their way to the high rise hotels and apartment blocks.

A low but consistent dum dum dum announced the beginning of nightclub mayhem. A few dolled up girls appeared. In their bright eyes, Aulay saw two or three vodkas, the bedrock for an evening's debauchery. He pined for his lost weeks here, or here abouts. It wasn't all atrocious. Take Mandy from 'uddersfield for instance... another time.

The Galoots climbed out of a chauffeur driven Mercedes limousine and climbed the steps to the Copacabana. Aulay followed. The Galoots were met by two girls, who slipped on like limpets.

The Sim's bimbo was small with dark eyes and legs that went all the way up to her arse. Aulay could tell, her thong didn't hide anything. An oriental stunner, with a gold tooth, slipped and slid round Chancer.

A man appeared with a camera. He took half a dozen snaps before staring at the remnants of his digital pride and joy splattered about the marble floor.

"Get a new one." The Sim slipped a wad of Euros into the stunned photographer's open mouth.

Both limpets scurried off when a fifty something bloke appeared. Dressed a tad young, his hair receding and ponytailed, he laughed off the situation. He looked at the still speechless photographer.

"Hernando, how many times do I have to tell you, ask permission first, Christ... Mr MacKinnon, it's a pleasure to meet you, I'm Ricky Temple. I'm so sorry abo..."

They shook hands.

"Mr Temple, don't worry, no harm done," said a smiling Chancer.

The Top Banana of The Polmadie and the CEO of the DSH entered the Copacabana Nite Club & Casino.

The camera above the door was discreet but not invisible. Aulay pulled his sun hat low, kept his shades on, and followed them in. The Copacabana was laid out like the spokes on a wheel. Aulay sat on a stool in the Hub Bar.

Ricky Temple took the Galoots on the executive tour. The bars, two night clubs, four restaurants, both bistros and the Casino. The Casino ran to three levels. One arm bandits led to the gaming tables before the 'Members Only', where a dress code of 'must wear socks' was strictly enforced. The tour ended in the Beluga Restaurant.

Aulay ordered chicken in a basket from one of the Bistros. It wasn't bad.

The Galoots left the restaurant after an hour. They looked tense. A waiter ran ahead to organise their limo. Wandering across the lobby, Aulay looked into the Beluga. He watched Ricky Temple bark out orders to Slicked Back and Shaven.

181

Something was in the offing. Both Slicked Back and Shaven left the restaurant with a sense of purpose that Aulay recognised.

Before the Banana's limo appeared from the Copacabana's underground car park, Slicked Back and Shaven appeared in a silver Audi. Aulay followed. At the coast road, he pulled over to wait for the Banana.

The stretched Mercedes manoeuvred round a mini roundabout. Aulay pulled out, forcing the limo driver to screech to a halt. Aulay had his .45 pointing at the chauffeur's face before the car stopped bouncing. The Sim and Chancer got out.

"Get in my car," said Aulay.

The Sim made to do... something. Chancer raised a hand. They climbed into the back of the BMW.

Before the coast road climbed the cliff, Aulay pulled into a side street.

"I take it we're not going back to the Sol?"

Aulay looked at the Banana in the mirror. "Not right now."

"Why use the gun?"

"The limo driver might have been in on it."

"Was he?"

"No."

The Galoots' limousine glided by on its way back to the Sol. Aulay pulled out and followed, keeping his distance. Near the cliff top sparks flew as lead pierced the shell of the two ton Mercedes. Shoot the driver first, Aulay remembered. The chauffeur, no doubt still shaken at being relieved of his passengers at gunpoint, had been going along at a fair old lick. The Mercedes sliced through the crash barrier and disappeared.

"Well, Aulay, you seem to have a nose for this stuff."

Aulay slipped into reverse and slid down the hill. He backed into a break in the rock face, took out the makings and rolled up. His passengers didn't smoke so he dropped the driver's window. It killed the air conditioning.

All three sweated in the humid air as they listened to the cicadas' regular chirping. Post-stress cigarettes are great, thought Aulay. Up there with post-shag ones.

Slicked Back and Shaven's Audi cruised by.

"Back to the Copacabana," said Chancer, "we're going to pay Mr Ricky Temple a visit."

"How we going to get into the place?" asked The Sim.

"We're not. Mr Temple is coming out."

This should be good, thought Aulay. He dropped what remained of his third cigarette out the window. The BMW's straight six burbled into life.

Parking several streets away from the Copacabana, they made their way to the beach where people milled about admiring the glorious red sky. It didn't take Chancer long to find what he was looking for. A dozen youths lounged, smoking and drinking in a small depression in the sand. A stag party from the north east of England. The night was young.

Chancer despatched The Sim on an errand. "Go to a quiet place, no rush."

"So, what's the plan?" asked Aulay.

Chancer explained the outline. It was cheeky enough to work.

The Sim returned with two dozen bottles of beer. The Galoots strolled over to the stags. Aulay sat in the sand a short distance away.

"Any of you English bastards mind if we join you?"

The stags looked up. They saw a couple of pale blue Scotsmen loaded with beer.

"As long as you Scottish wankers concede you will be in the presence of superior beings," said the group leader.

This brought a laugh from all concerned.

"Listen pal, youz are a race of Danes, French and Romans," said Chancer. "We was never conquered, remember?"

Aulay later discovered that the only thing Chancer enjoyed at school was history, and not because Miss Connaught was a stunner, well, maybe at the start.

The banter continued. Soon Chancer and The Sim were part of the crowd. All they needed now was a Likely-lad who wasn't too drunk.

Sat in the Copacabana's Hub Bar when the fire alarm went off, Aulay waited for the mayhem to start. The only bedlam came from the screaming klaxons as the croupiers and other staff calmly escorted the gamblers and diners to the exits.

"A ten euro voucher to every guest when you return," Ricky Temple shouted through his smile as he heralded people out the front door. The smile disappeared when the sprinklers came on.

The local fire station wasn't far away. Fire fighters ran up the steps, clearing people away from the front of the building. They set up a cordon.

Arguing with a gas mask wearing Spanish fireman, in cockney, was ambitious. Ricky was forcibly removed to the chaos of the street where he felt a slim blunt object thrust into his back.

"Don't say anything, don't look round. I want you to cross the road and stroll down to the beach..."

It took Ricky a second to decipher the accent. He shivered, then scanned the crowd.

Aulay poked his ribs. "I can kill you now or later. It's up to you, Mr Temple."

Slicked Back was thirty metres away, eyeing up a pretty little thing wearing little more than a hanky. He sidled up to the girl. It kept him upright. The Sim, in hoody and shades, stood a couple of metres away holding a wine bottle in a polly-bag. Good weapons, wine bottles.

"That the guy who took your money?" Likely-lad pointed at Ricky.

"Aye," said Chancer, "and here's the other half, as agreed. There's a wee bonus for the sprinklers."

"Cheers, mate. Next time you want a fire alarm to go off, you let me know"

Not as well dressed as the rest of the stag party, who wore designer gear, labels to the fore, bling watches, Likely-lad sauntered along the beach to find his mates. 500 Euros for setting off a fire alarm was not to be sniffed at.

"Right, Mr Temple. Let's go," said Chancer.

"How much do you want?"

"We don't need your money, Mr Temple. Now move."

Slicked Back and Shaven arrived as the BMW left the kerbside. The first bullet came in through the rear window and left through the windscreen. Aulay floored the pedal and the big motor died. Fuck. Where's a Daewoo Leganza when you need one. A second bullet grazed Chancer's cheek as the restarted engine picked up speed. A third bullet exited via the front passenger window and into the large posterior of Mrs Arabella Ramos, who was doing a little late night shopping. The shopkeeper serving Mrs Ramos died instantly, a ricochet entered his mouth, leaving through the back of his head.

More bullets thudded into the car. The BMW limped along billowing blue smoke. Something was wrong with the steering.

"There, over there." Chancer pointed to a narrow opening between two tall apartment blocks. Aulay swung the stricken car into the alley.

The Galoots got a shaking Ricky Temple out of the boot. Ricky wasn't looking good. His eyes stared off into the distance.

"He's lost the plot," said The Sim who struggled to keep the shaking Ricky upright.

Chancer gripped Ricky's wrist, placing it against the open door frame. Ricky returned from wherever he was. "No, please no..."

The Sim slammed the car door shut. Ricky shrieked the place down. He stopped when Chancer gripped his throat. Ricky opened his eyes. His hand was fine, no pain, he moved his fingers. The pain did come, from his face, after a vicious slap.

"You with us, Mr Temple?" asked Chancer.

Ye...yes. Please... please don't hurt..."

"Mr Temple, I'm only going to say this once, do you understand?"

"Yes... I..."

Chancer leaned in.

"Anything happens to me, or mine, Mr Temple, and you will die fuckin' slowly."

Ricky dipped his toe back into the water of losing it. The glint from a blade forced him to resurface.

"I... I understand. Please..."

They left him there and made their way into a rabbit's warren of lanes behind the high rise holiday apartments.

The Sim asked, "Why'd you pull the wanker's hand away?"

"If he's any sense he'll understand the gesture, and back off," said Chancer. "If he doesn't, well..."

The Sim nodded, but Aulay wasn't so sure. Letting the head of the DSH away with attempted murder didn't smell right. Neither did Ricky Temple when they left him.

"Let's get as far away..." Aulay stopped. "Sim, you ok?"

The Sim's face was set and covered in sweat. Aulay was sweating too but not dripping from nose and chin.

"Took one in the leg," The Sim muttered.

"Let me see," said Aulay.

In the dim light of a street lamp, The Sim dropped his jeans.

"I don't do this for everyone," he said.

Aulay prodded and probed. "The bullet went clean through."

Removing his only Paul Smart shirt, Aulay ripped it into strips. There wasn't enough blood to justify a tourniquet so he bandaged the wound as best he could. His field dressing badges were still up to date.

"That'll do 'till we find somewhere to hole up."

The sirens were getting louder. The three moved through the quiet streets. It was the slow time. The old and young would be asleep. The inbetweeners would be getting drunk. A squeal of tyres made Aulay haul The Galoots into a shop doorway. From the shadows, they watched Slicked Back slowly drive by weaving his head from side to side.

"Reminds me of Cruella de Ville searching for the Dalmations."

The Sim didn't say much, but when he did, it was worth it.

They turned to face a Spanish shopkeeper.

"What can I get you, Senor?"

The guy seemed unfazed. He must be used to British tourists arriving late at night in various states. They were in a Tabac. One of the many slotted into small gaps between regular shops.

Aulay surveyed the shelves. "Lucky Strikes, please."

Decent rolling tobacco can be hard to get in the US. During his time there, Aulay found Lucky Strikes to be the best of a bad bunch. A carton of two hundred, a box of matches and a bottle of vodka appeared on the counter. Aulay looked up.

"For your friend's leg, senor. Vodka is a good, how you say..."

"Disinfectant?"

"Si."

"Why?"

"The man in the car, he searching for you?"

Aulay nodded.

"He an animal."

Aulay decided not to push it. After a little song and dance, he remembered the Spanish for thank you and good night. The shopkeeper refused the money offered. Aulay threw a few notes onto the counter.

They made slow progress. Sirens milled about as the melee created by the shoot-out was attended to. Where to go? Where to hide? Three blokes, one unable to walk, wouldn't stand out at 3am, but now? Aulay was on the point of suggesting a break in when...

"Hey you, stop!"

"Chancer," whispered The Sim, "Leave me; I'm nae use, holdin' yea back."

Aulay gripped his .45 and made ready. Leaning The Sim against a wall, Chancer turned, fists clenched.

Likely-lad ran across the road. He wore a wide grin.

An hour later, The Sim's wound was clean, wrapped in vodka soaked bandages. He was unconscious, the vodka helped here too. Chancer leaned back in a big chair sharing the night's exploits, and the last of the vodka, with a thrilled Likely-lad. It was Aulay's first time seeing the Banana take alcohol. The champagne flute in the Albertino remained full.

Aulay spent twenty minutes in Likely-lad's small kitchenette on his pay-as-you-go.

When the vodka kicked in, Chancer took a Lucky Strike, lit up, drew in more smoke than a seasoned pro, and coughed for ten minutes. It sobered him up.

The parents of one of the Likely-lad's party owned the holiday apartment. Their son was out on the razz with the rest of the stags. He returned in the early hours, took no notice of the bodies in the lounge, staggered into the toilet, puked up a fair percentage of the night's booze, and some kebab. He retired, fully designer clothed, onto his bed. It was a one bedroom apartment.

"What's the plan?" asked a pale Chancer after Likely-lad drifted off to sleep on the fold down couch next to The Sim.

"A mate of mine, he of the guns in left luggage, is coming in the morning to pick us up. LJ's got a place in the hills, about an hour away, safer than here."

"Right, good. We'll figure out what to do tomorrow. I'll fill Freak in." Chancer turned then stopped. "They'll trace you to the BMW."

"I reported it stolen."

Chancer raised an eyebrow.

"I arranged the car through the Sol. I called them and told them I'd been out on the town. When I got back to the car, it was gone."

The look remained.

"Nobody's seen my face," said Aulay, "I made sure of it."

"The Spanish polis will latch on."

"Aye, I know, but not right away."

Chancer borrowed Likely-lad's laptop, plugged in a memory stick and spent some time in chat rooms with Freak Johnston. Aulay fell asleep to the sound of a clicking keyboard.

Next morning, Likely-lad returned from breakfast shopping.

"You guys are screwed," he said and threw a copy of the local paper onto the coffee table.

Chancer and The Sim stared out of the front page. Likely-lad switched the TV to Sky News. Chancer and The Sim were everywhere, the prime suspects in the murder of a local grocer and the attempted murder of one Mrs Arabella Ramos, currently in a stable condition in hospital. A pretty news anchor filled in the details.

"In an interview with our reporter, the Copacabana's owner, Mr Ricky Temple, outlined the details of the attempted robbery which he and several of his security guards foiled. As the robbers made their escape, they kidnapped Mr Temple and shot their way out before Copacabana security staff caught up with them in Murcia Street."

"These thugs are bringing the name of the British down and must be caught," said a solemn Ricky. "Thankfully, I managed to outsmart them and, badly injured, escape with my life."

Ricky waved a bandaged hand to confirm his bravery, winced and took a long breath before manfully carrying on.

"I'm offering a reward of 100,000 Euros for information leading to the capture of these villains."

A dark faced Chancer didn't take his eyes off the screen. "Likely-lad. Did you know about the reward?"

"I... em, aye."

"Why are the police not barging through the door?"

Likely-lad pointed at the bedroom door where last night's refugee still hadn't surfaced.

"Crashed out in there," he said. "He's my best mate. I couldn't risk it"

"Risk what?"

"You know. You guys have guns and... It could get hairy if the police turned up."

Chancer stood. "You got a good memory?"

"Aye, 'spose."

Chancer read out an eleven digit number and made Likely-lad repeat it, twice.

"When this is over and we're all back home, text me a Sort Code and Account Number. You'll get the reward. Now, I need access to your laptop again."

"Sure, Mr MacKinnon," said Likely-lad, whose casual banter with the Chancer of the previous evening was forgotten.

The TV reporter continued..."It is believed one of the gang brutally ejected a local resident from her car to make his getaway..."

Cut to an interview with a distraught Spanish girl.

"Slicked Back must have hijacked her car to search for us," said Aulay.

191

"Police have located the other getaway vehicle. There is blood on the passenger seat and in the foot-well." Cut to dilapidated BMW with both doors and the boot open. "One of the fugitives is assumed to be injured. All hospitals have been notified. Security at the ports and airports has been stepped up."

Cut to film of machinegun carrying police on patrol.

"Police in the UK have identified both men in the photographs taken by the Copacabana CCTV cameras as, Alec 'Chancer' MacKinnon and his bodyguard, 'The Sim' Simpson.

Cut to photographs of the grim looking killers, this time clinging to scantily clad young ladies outside the Copacabana.

"Both are notorious criminals from the city of Glasgow where they head The Polmadie criminal gang..." Cut to ancient footage of Glasgow's industrial past. "... believed to be responsible for 70% of the drugs in the city amongst a host of other unlawful activity. Both fugitives are thought to have fled the UK after the mutilated body of a local business man, a Mr Robert Smillie, was dredged from the River Clyde. Scottish Police are promising full cooperation with the Spanish authorities."

"It's no' that bad, Chancer," said The Sim, "They haven't mentioned you've no' paid yer TV licence yet."

A loud pop echoed through the flat. Aulay was at the door before the stun grenade's first echo. Silence from the stairwell. A few more pops.

"Aulay..." Chancer was at the window.

Men in black pointed a range of weapons at the apartment block opposite. Smoke poured from two windows on the second floor.

"What's over there?" Aulay asked Likely-lad.

"A few retired English people as far as I know."

"You connected to any of them?"

The word 'connected' seemed to inspire Likely-lad.

"Aye, man. We use one of their wireless routers for our internet connection. There's no password."

"Shite."

The authorities had traced Chancer's chat room link with Freak and raided the apartment associated with the IP address. The Spanish police would guess the situation soon enough then troll through the apartments within wireless range.

"We need to move, now."

Chancer turned to Likely-lad.

"When they find you, say we broke in, ok?"

Chancer ripped the cord from the curtains. He tied Likely-lad's hands behind his back. Likely-lad's pal snored in the bedroom.

"Hit me, it'll look more realistic."

Chancer smashed a fist into Likely-lad's face. One eye started to swell.

"Again."

Chancer smashed a right into his nose. The blood pored. Likely-lad slumped to the floor. Chancer's murmured 'thanks' fell on deaf ears.

Leaving the block via the rear door, all was quiet. The Sim wilted from the exertion of the stairs, his borrowed trousers already stained with leaking blood. Aulay looked over a low wall. They were in a quadrant of clothes lines and bins. He checked the windows. Nothing. The residents would be watching the commotion out front.

"You see that Temple geezer with his bandaged hand?" said the Sim, "Fucker plays the media game well, eh?"

"Aye," said Chancer, "The man's confident."

A car turned into the quadrant and flashed its headlights twice. It was LJ. Thank fuck.

"Sorry, didn't catch that," said Shaz into her mobile phone.

"Miss Curren, you've seen the picture?"

"Yes."

"Recognise the man?"

"No."

"Come now, Miss Curren, take a closer look."

"Why don't you tell me?"

"I'm sending the next one, enjoy." The caller hung up.

Shaz grimaced when the next photograph appeared on her screen.

She answered the next call. "You guys are good at doctoring photographs,"

"I can send you the video, Miss Curren."

"What to do you want, Mr...eh?"

"Let's say I'm looking for you to provide me with a little information," said the voice. "I'll be in touch."

The line went dead. A drip of perspiration left Shaz's hairline on its way down her neck. The photographs weren't in high definition but... Shaz was on her knees giving head to a black man. The second shot, a close up, focussed on Kenny Finlayson from the waist down with Shaz in the foreground doing what lovers do.

She recognised the location. The Hilton Hotel in Paris during her firm's annual weekend bash. She'd taken Kenny along, why? To show how far she'd come from her lowly beginnings, to bask in the light of her liberal, born again beliefs? Shaz dismissed Kenny. Would it be any better if she'd been caught on film blowing Angus Semple from accounts?

They'd got tipsy, Kenny downing the free wine like it was... well, free. Shaz'd slipped into good time girl mode, flirting outrageously with her senior partners and a judge or two. A great weekend.

Her eleven o'clock appointment waited. Shaz shook herself and hurried along. Her private dilemma would have to wait.

Looking round the posh coffee shop, Shaz spotted Freak Johnston at a corner table.

"Tea?" asked Freak.

A hovering waitress almost pounced in her eagerness to serve. Shaz understood the woman's enthusiasm. It wasn't every day you served a god. With tea ordered, Shaz coughed to shake a recent image from the front of her mind.

"You look serious, Freak?"

"We've run into a few problems in Spain," he said. "I take it you haven't seen the news?"

"No."

The tea arriving gave Shaz a few unwanted moments to run down a list of possible, 'few problems'. The waitress poured and preened. A patient Freak refused biscuits, scones, pancakes, tarts, cupcakes and a slice of chocolate sponge. As a last resort, he accepted a piece of shortbread.

"I made this myself," the waitress squeaked before launching into a soliloquy on her prowess in all matters female.

"Excuse me," interrupted Shaz. "My husband and I need to discuss my chemotherapy regime, so, if you don't mind."

The waitress's smile split in two. Concern for Shaz and a glimmer of hope. She turned away.

"Shaz, you are the mistress of the double edged sword."

"What about Spain?"

Freak leaned forward and told Shaz what he knew.

"Where are they now?"

"They were picked up by a friend of Aulay's," Freak looked at his watch, "a couple of hours ago. They're safe."

"Who's the friend?"

"Old army pal called LJ."

"Is The Sim the only one injured?"

"Yes."

"Has there been any connection between Aulay and The Banana?"

"None that I can see from the media coverage, but it's only a matter of time."

"How did they trace them to Likely-lad's apartment?"

"Serious Crime are all over us. They must have sent Chancer's IP address to the Spanish. We were in various on line chat rooms into the early hours."

"Do they know what you were saying to each other?"

"No, everything's encrypted."

The full force of the situation hit Shaz then. Aulay facing a long prison term in Spain put her Paris Hilton moment in perspective.

"How the fuck did the IP address..." Shaz stopped. Now was not the time for recriminations.

Freak's face remained passive. "I thought we had everything covered. Someone is spending lots of manpower, energy and money to keep tabs on us."

"How so?"

"To follow seemingly random chat room access involves extensive monitoring, or amazing good luck."

"Have Serious Crime got the capability?"

"No."

"Who else..." Shaz stopped to follow Freak's gaze.

A TV hung from a bracket in the corner. The sound was off. They watched in silence until the news bulletin changed to some scandal about a Tory MP accused of having sex with a dog. The Kennel Club were up in arms. Shaz stayed quiet. The news item contained video footage of Chancer and The Sim covered in two almost naked females. Aulay strolled in the background wearing a sunhat and shades.

"What do you want me to do?" she asked.

"You're Chancer's lawyer, and he's wanted for murder and kidnapping."

Having Freak point out the bleeding obvious, in his fucking placid tones, brought Shaz back from where she'd been since Aulay made his debut on Sky News.

"I'll fly over and engage the best lawyer they have."

"There's a Prestwick flight leaving at two, you're booked on it," said Freak. "It'll be full of sun seekers, so ditch the gloves."

She glanced down at the patent leather, a present from a long ago Aulay. Shaz ignored the twang at her heart strings and grabbed the rising Freak's arm.

"Who has the necessary... to carry out that level of surveillance?"

"Have you seen Hector lately?"

"He's abroad... Jesus."

Shaz's brain went into overdrive. Headline grabbing international crime brings resources to bear. Known associates of associates of the chief suspect's second cousins would be found and investigated.

"There's a connection," said Shaz. "LJ is Dougie MacAllister. Dougie and Aulay joined up together. If the powers that be find out..."

"I know," said Freak, "but The Sim's condition is the limiting factor at the moment."

198

Freak took something from his pocket.

"My pay-as-you-go number." He handed Shaz a small card. "Get one when you arrive in Malaga and text me, ok?"

"Sure. What's the plan? Can you tell me?"

Freak looked round the small cafe.

"I have to disappear. Set up somewhere remote with virgin communications. Keep in touch."

Freak's lack of eye contact told her everything. She watched The Polmadie's Consigliore leave with a gracious smile to the hovering waitress.

Shaz cobbled together a timetable. Taxi to the flat, keep it waiting, then the airport, shite, what to pack? Nothing was the answer. The Polmadie could well afford a bout of retail therapy when she arrived on the Costa.

During the hour long taxi ride to the misnomer, Glasgow Prestwick Airport, Shaz cleared everything at BD&P. The Polmadie paid a healthy retainer so no problem there. Mr Birltoni himself would take charge of her current caseload. He asked Shaz to pass on his regards to Mr MacKinnon. Shaz could feel him smile through her phone. High profile shenanigans provided untold publicity.

"Make us look good, Sharon," he said before hanging up.

Crossing the border into Ayrshire, Shaz stared out of the window at the passing traffic and remembered her last meeting with the tall man with the stick.

***

"Hector."

"Sharon, delighted, as ever."

Their get-togethers were public, pubs and restaurants, never the same place twice, in the evenings, with no paperwork. Shaz looked forward to them like a schoolgirl anticipating the weekly tutorial with the cool Geography teacher. For months they'd delved into the machinations of

The Polmadie's hectic structure picking at the bones of what was legal, on the edge of legality, and downright impossible to drag out of the range of HMRC's blood hounds. They worked well together.

**

Shaz rang Hector's number, straight to voice mail. She left a message. As the black hack approached the airport's terminal building, Shaz moved Hector from the 'goodie' pile to the 'maybe's aye, maybe's no' pile. She would need a wee bit more than Freak's speculation to place Hector with the 'baddies'.

On the plane, it didn't take Shaz long to change her seat. A scruffy teenager in dilapidated trainers accepted the offered £50 and made his way to 32b. During the short negotiation, Shaz caught the eye of the sweaty man sitting in 32a. John Maclean could go fuck himself.

Chapter 20   a pirate to the rescue

After the Galoots and Aulay slid under the security cover in the rear of the mother's favourite, Long John cruised past the police cordons outside Likely-lad's apartment and pointed the Volvo estate west. He put an Elvis CD on.

The King launched into 'It's Now or Never',

Aulay asked, "What happened in the Beluga restaurant?"

Chancer told him...

***

"The Copacabana is some setup and... that was excellent."

Chancer put down his fork after a delicious seafood paella.

The fourth man at the table had been introduced as, 'arvey Lemoy. Ricky Temple didn't have a problem with his H's, Harvey did. The DSH's Consigliore kept quiet throughout the meal.

"Nothing like shellfish from your neck of the woods," said Ricky who went on to describe the tortuous route the prawns served up in Spain took from Scotland.

The polite chit chat continued until coffee. A waiter regularly topped up Ricky's brandy glass.

"Now, Chancer," said Ricky, sitting forward, "'arvey tells me you detained our Glasgow delegation before they could begin negotiations."

In the Volvo, Elvis joined in with 'Suspicious Minds'

"Your delegation were amateurs," said Chancer.

Ricky smiled. "You know how hard it is to get good people."

"Why us, anyway. Why The Polmadie? We're small potatoes?"

201

"Are you familiar with franchising?" Ricky didn't wait for an answer.

When the Copacabana Complex hosted the European Franchising Association's annual bash, Ricky saw the light. The DSH were stagnant and in the ever increasing demand for growth, he decided to follow in the footsteps of Starbucks and McDonalds.

"We already supply and control most of the south east so it seemed the way to go. We have several successful UK franchisees up and running."

To prospective franchisees, Ricky's sales pitch was persuasive, backed up by a lot of guns. Some Top Banana's resisted, at first, one died. The survivors ceded overall control to keep their position at the top, with a significant drop in earnings.

"The DSH control everything from supply to the street price. It's the future."

Ricky expanded further. His impressive setup at the Copacabana fronted a floor in London's docklands where analysts, accountants and lawyers do what these people do for big organisations. Laundering huge amounts of cash involved complex deals with rogue investments in nonexistent mines in the Congo and petro-chemical plants in Nigeria. The DSH made some dodgy government officials very wealthy.

"It's not The Polmadie who are small, Chancer. The DSH are too big."

Ricky sat back resting his hands on his middle age spread. He was enjoying himself, as successful business people do when they get the opportunity to wax lyrical about their achievements.

Mr Presley reached the chorus, 'I'm Caught in a Trap'

"Your plan included taking me out, Mr Temple?"

Sensing a change of pace, Ricky sat forward.

"All you Bananas resist and that costs me time and money. I changed the plan. Cut the Top Banana out before the negotiations. Mr MacKinnon, you need to understand who you're dealing with. I'm giving you my time tonight because you had the balls to come to the Costa." Ricky paused for another hit of brandy. "You return to Glasgow working for me, or in a fucking box."

"I've put together a business plan of my own, Mr Temple."

Ricky shrugged.

"The Polmadie, The Buddies and The Drum have formed an alliance. You move against one, you move against all. My Consigliore is currently talking to Lanarkshire, Edinburgh and Aberdeen. We've received enquiries from Dundee, Leeds, Manchester, Birmingham and a few others."

Ricky regrouped. "I'll turn your tap off."

"That's not good business, Mr Temple. Anyway, the Jamaicans are itching to expand and they have the capacity."

Chancer stood. He placed two hands on the table.

'Treat Me Nice' warbled from the Volvo's speakers.

"Mr Temple, The Polmadie is not Rotherham or Derby. You send another takeover team to Glasgow and they will disappear."

"Who the fuck do you-"

"When was the last time you were on the street, Mr Temple? Twenty, thirty years ago? The word is, you can't get out of bed without chemical help"

Ricky stood up, face flushed. "Listen, cunt, I've-"

Chancer and The Sim left Ricky talking to the room.

***

The Volvo swung off the tarmac onto a dirt road. The big Swede didn't have the suspension for off-road work and bounced along.

Elvis sang 'I'm All Shook Up'.

"I now see why you went into the lion's den," said Aulay. "I thought you were off your head. You should have told me you had ammunition. Something to negotiate with."

Aulay didn't make a habit of criticising an employer but hey, once in a while kept them on their toes.

"Aulay, I needed you on your toes. You thinking I was an idiot was a good thing."

Aulay mulled that one over. The bastard was right. "Still," he said, "it was some risk."

"The script needed a face to face," said Chancer. "Ricky's ego guaranteed a meeting. I expected him angry but not drunk enough to send the dogs out right away."

"Now you know who you're dealing with, what's the plan?"

"Three things. Get off the front pages, get off the Spanish most wanted list, and stop the DSH invading my city."

The Volvo pulled in and stopped.

Aulay asked, "The business plan you put to Ricky, how much is true?"

"Some."

The tailgate rose and they were blinded by the Mediterranean sun.

All in all, both Galoots handled themselves pretty well, thought Aulay. They'd been shot at and hit. Watched what should have been their coffin fly off a cliff in a hail of automatic fire. Remained calm when the fluke of wireless technology bit them in the bum.

LJ's villa lay off a dirt road which carried on up into the mountains. The place exuded peace and quiet. Long John did the introductions.

"Brokeback, this is Aulay, Chancer and The Sim."

Brokeback lifted the unconscious Sim from the car, moved him to a shoulder and strolled to the villa. The Sim didn't give Brokeback any problems, the man was enormous.

Mrs Brokeback dispelled any connection to gay cowboys. She ministered to The Sim's leg. An ex-army nurse, she met her future husband in a field hospital in Afghanistan. With The Sim getting seen to, Long John produced a decent plate of cheese, cold meat and bread before expanding on a few details for Chancer's benefit. Aulay knew the story well.

Brokeback and LJ shared long dreary months in hospital. Brokeback did indeed break his back and both men climbed the steep hill of recovery together. From wheelchair to re-learning how to walk.

"When Aulay phoned last night," said LJ, "I figured we could use a little help. A-"

Nurse Brokeback interrupted. "Your man won't be on his feet for a while, but no permanent damage."

"So what kind of trouble you in?" asked Brokeback.

There was no TV.

"Well-"

There was a knock at the door. Chancer jumped. Aulay did too but only on the inside. LJ let in a couple of lean types, one limped. Another two ex-wounded ex-marines, from the same military hospital, had received word from Long John and made their way over.

Both men stared at Chancer. They had TV's.

"Fuck me," one said, "do you know who you are?"

Chancer told his story.

"So," said Brokeback. "All we have to do is get this Ricky Temple to confess to the police that it was his men who carried out the shootings?"

"Aye, that's about it," said Chancer.

They battered various ideas and scenarios about for the next few hours. Nothing jumped out.

Aulay approached Chancer. "I'm going back to the Sol, to check out. It would be better if I stay legal."

Aulay parked LJ's Volvo in Fuengirola and jumped a taxi to the Sol. Passing through the foyer, he spotted Hector sitting behind a Financial Times. Hector waggled a finger. Aulay turned. An angry Shaven walked his way. Anger, thought Aulay, a debilitating emotion to carry around during an operation.

"You," barked Shaven. People turned.

Aulay put some fear into his eyes. He backed into the reception desk.

"Eh... can I help you?"

"Were you with Chancer Mackinnon last night?"

"Eh... I..."

"In the Albertino Lounge."

"Yes... yes..." He put a tremor in his voice. "I met Mr MacKinnon in the bar and..."

Shaven backed off. Aulay looked too shit scared to be connected with anything. Shaven turned and stomped out of the hotel's entrance where a young couple had to be quick to move out of his way.

The little spat with Shaven gave Aulay an idea.

"Busy night then," said Hector. They were in Aulay's hotel room. "Don't suppose you have any malt?"

Hector's Dapper Dan look shone. Chino's and sandals topped off with a pale blue blazer. Hector looked every bit the... the what?

Aulay hadn't opened the fridge, or made an inventory. It wasn't like him. He found a Glen Livet miniature and a crystal tumbler. "Ice? Water?" Both met with a shake of the head. Aulay took a can of lemon ice tea, it was good.

They ran through the events of the last twenty four hours.

Hector did a quick, "Excuse me," and pulled his vibrating mobile phone.

"Hello... yes... Hotel Sol, Puerto Banus... OK... see you then, bye."

"We getting a visitor?"

Hector ignored the query. "Has Chancer got a plan?"

"Tell me something first."

Hector raised an eyebrow.

"Is it Ricky Temple you want, or the DSH, or both?"

"Both."

"And what about Chancer Mackinnon?"

"Are you getting too close to the Banana?"

"Well, he's not what I expected."

"What do you mean?"

Shaz set the ball rolling with her – 'he's a goodie' remark and Aulay was coming round to agreeing with her.

"He's got a way about him. He's no thug and ... smart, you know? You need to meet him."

"I've already met Mr Mackinnon." Hector looked at his watch. "How much time do we have?"

Aulay shrugged. He settled into a chair.

"I was in Glasgow before the previous Banana, Mad Rab Smillie, departed this life," Hector began. "Late one evening, I was accosted outside a corner shop by three of his minions."

***

"Listen, Gimp. Yer wallet or you'll need a white stick by the 'morra." Ugly Grant held out a serrated gutting knife.

Hector surveyed the three young men. Two hung back, the watchers. All six eyes blazed with alcohol. On centre stage, Ugly Grant wanted to add another notch to his reputation.

Hector remained calm and quiet.

Ugly stepped forward, knife low. "Listen, ya auld fucker, times wastin'. I'm goin' to gut you."

Two seconds later, Ugly still held his knife but it looked different, there was an eyeball on the end of it. As he tottered to the pavement, Ugly tried to put his eye back into the empty socket. He woke up in hospital.

Runner 1's instinct let him down. Charging in screaming, he met the elbow that smashed his jaw. He woke up next to Ugly.

Runner 2s' instinct was to get the fuck out of there. He took one step before Hector's cane intervened, snapping a kneecap. Runner 2 didn't have any luck. He remained conscious, and suffered until a paramedic put the needle in.

***

Aulay grinned.

"You put Ugly and his two runners in hospital. I'm impressed."

"I was going to leave it there until Bunty revealed all," said Hector. "I met Bunty in the Lochan. Know it?"

"Aye."

The Lochan Hotel. The only licensed premises in Pollokshields. Blue tartan carpet crashed into green tartan wallpaper. Guests lounged on red tartan upholstery. A Monarch of the Glen print hung above the B&Q fireplace and the barman, wee Harry, wore a kilt. The Lochan catered for wealthy tourists. Americans mostly.

***

The cream of Pittsburgh society sat up, raised an eyebrow and whispered loud enough for Hector to hear. The

209

whisperer had been trying to entice Hector to join her little coterie of eyelash fluttering spinsters for an hour.

"Jeez Louise, what have we here?" she said.

A small, wide woman in a white track suit stood at the bar. A heavy satchel made her lean to one side

Bunty announced her presence. "Anyone wan' a paper?"

Hector ignored the sniggering and raised his arm. Bunty shuffled over lifting a copy of the celebrated rag from her satchel.

"Fifty Pee." Bunty ignored the American sniggers.

"Are you the regular girl?" asked Hector.

"Aye, every night but Saturday."

"What's your name?"

"Bunty."

"Right, Bunty, let's make a deal. I'll arrange with Harry..." Hector nodded towards the barman, "to pay you on a Sunday night. Ten pounds cover it?"

Hector slipped a tenner onto the bar.

"I'd like a newspaper every night. If I'm not in the bar you can leave it with Harry, OK?"

"Cheers, mister," said Bunty, "you got a deal."

She put out her hand and they shook on it.

"What's that yer on?" she asked.

"Malt. Fancy one?"

"Naw, I'll have a cooking whisky though, a wee one."

Harry produced a glass of blended. Hoisting her satchel onto the stool next to Hector, Bunty pulled another stool along and climbed on. She was taller sitting than standing.

"Are you just starting out?" asked Hector.

"Aye, this is the first stop from the Ibrox depot. I cover Pollokshaws Road, Victoria Road an' The Battlefield, about sixty pubs all told."

"That'll keep you fit."

"Och, it's more the bloody rain that gets you, you know?"

A car tooted and Bunty frowned. "Need to get a shift on, that's my gaffer."

She downed the last of the whisky and left with a, "cheers," and a wave. She kept her special smile for conceited from Pittsburgh and her menagerie.

In the mirror behind the bar, Hector followed Bunty's progress. At the reception desk, she stopped to ask Greta a question. Greta looked in Hector's direction before both girls giggled the way girls do.

Hector rose from his seat, there was a shuffling and a straightening of the spine, an emphasizing of breasts along with more eyelash fluttering from the Pittsburgh flock. Placing his folded newspaper neatly under his arm, Hector winked at wee Harry and left the hotel bar.

***

A vague memory tickled. "I think I've met your newspaper girl," said Aulay.

"Bunty is the star of this show," said Hector. "There's a journalist too, John Maclean, he has a supporting role, along with Ugly Grant."

Aulay sat back nursing his ice tea. Hector was proving to be a decent raconteur.

***

"Three get Hospitalised – Police chasing shadows," ran the Daily Snot headline – by Crime Reporter, John Maclean.

Mad Rab Smillie growled down the phone. "This is embarrassing, Maclean."

"You got anything for me to go on, Mr Smillie?"

"Bugger all. Nobody saw a thing, even when my boys asked nicely. Whatever team smashed up Ugly and his runners, they were good and quick."

"Ugly piss anyone off? The Drum maybe?"

"You think the fucking Drum would come into my backyard and put three of my boys in A&E?"

"No, Mr Smillie."

"How much you into me for, Maclean?"

"About fourteen grand."

"You find me the fuckers who did this to ma boyz and we'll work a deal."

Mad Rab's next statement burled around Maclean's head for days.

"You talk to anyone but me, Maclean, an' your balls will be rammed so far up your arse, I'll have a job setting them on fire."

After a day trawling through his usual suspects, Maclean had nothing. Three members of The Polmadie don't get beaten up and no one knows anything. This is Glasgow. He finally got the wire in the Pandora.

"Some auld geezer called Hector," said Snitch the barman, "just left the corner shop. This Hector geezer must have seen it all."

Mad Rab was informed.

When Bunty walked into the Pandora, Maclean nursed a half pint.

"Any one wan' a paper?"

With the latest football scandal plastered all over the front, and back pages, business was good. Juicy and salacious stories sold newspapers. Juicy and salacious footballer stories sold lots of newspapers. Gordon 'Deano' Dean went to his manager's house to complain about being dropped. Before he knew it, Deano was rolling about with the daughter. Then the mum came home, and joined in.

"What could I do?" Deano was quoted as saying, indeed, wonderful stuff.

Bunty was a good place to start if you were looking for someone on the south side. Maclean would normally cross the road to avoid Bunty, and her ilk, but Mad Rab Smillie called the shots here.

"Bunty, how's it going, hen?"

Bunty stood her ground. Nobody got anything without a business transaction.

"Ok, geez one then." Maclean handed over a pound.

Bunty retrieved a copy of the Daily Snot. Maclean threw it onto the bar. She didn't offer any change.

"I'm looking for an older bloke," said Maclean, "well dressed about sixty odds, might be new in town, name of Hector, anything come to mind? Oh, and he's got a stick, thin with a wee silver tip."

"Don't ring any bells," said Bunty. "Sorry, I'll keep my eyes out and let you know."

"It's important," said Maclean, "good bung in it for you."

"I'll remember."

Bunty started round the bar.

After the Pandora, Bunty made her way to the Staffs where the buzz was Deano's shagging exploits and The Polmadie crew getting a good kicking.

"That wee bastard Ugly Grant's in some state, by the way," commented a smiling Statler.

"His two runners an' all," echoed Waldorf.

Bunty sold Statler and Waldorf a Daily Snot each.

"Anyone hear anything about how Ugly got done?" she asked.

"I heard some auld geezer wi' a stick left the shop just as it happened," said Waldorf.

Bunty looked at the pub door in an effort to stop the snort. Some auld geezer? Statler and Waldorf, permanent fixtures in the Staffs, were Methuselah's older brothers.

"Anyone know who this auld guy is?" Bunty asked.

"Nup."

In the New Anand, Bunty tied it up. The restaurant's owner bought a Daily Snot every night. He scanned the problem page before leaving the paper out for customers to look through as they waited for their take away.

"Hi Bunty, how are you?"

"Hi, Deepa, no bad, quiet the night?"

Deepa checked his watch. The last rush of the day wouldn't start until throwing out time, when the Glaswegian curry obsession kicked in.

"Och, another fifteen minutes and all hell will break loose. So, what's new, Bunty?"

Bunty retold the events at the corner shop, and the damage inflicted on The Polmadie crew.

"The word is some auld guy must have seen it."

"What time you say this happen?" asked Deepa.

Bunty told him.

"We have new regular customer, lamb bhoona with extra chilli, special salad, side order saag aloo and well done naan bread, no rice. Charming fellow, been to my country, speaks the lingo, enough to discuss finer points with Girda, the chef."

"He use a stick?" asked Bunty.

"Och aye," said Deepa, "mm, and the gentleman left here similar time, walked in right direction."

"Know anything about him?" asked Bunty.

"Lives in the Pollokshields. Postman Ronnie, chicken chat, vindaloo sauce, side salad an' two chapatti, spoke with

214

him. They recognised each other. I remember now, customer is called Mr Chalmers."

Bunty had Hector nailed.

In the Lochan, Hector followed the story in the paper. The Daily Snot demanded action in the search for the vicious thugs who carried out the horrific assault on three innocent young lads whose only crime was to be out for a stroll of an evening.

Sipping a decent Islay, Hector glanced up. Bunty approached.

"Hi, Bunty, how are you?"

"Fab, Hector. You battered any more Neds lately?"

Hector stopped. "I'm sorry?"

"Oh, so you're no' the geezer with a stick everyone's looking for. Och well, catch you the 'morra night then."

"Hold on, Bunty. Time for a quickie?"

Hector glanced at Harry who nodded and reached for a blended.

"What's all this about then, Bunty, I'm curious?"

Bunty relayed the events of the past twenty four hours. Hector sat with teeth together but slack jawed. The girl was good. She asked the right questions in the right places. Having to be there made Bunty invisible, yet all seeing and all hearing. Hector lifted a tenner from his wallet. He handed it to Bunty under the bar.

"Don't want yer money," she said. "Just wanted to let you know."

Bunty explained who Ugly Grant was, and his connection to The Polmadie. She dismissed Hector's assurance that he was unconnected with the affair.

"If I can find you, so can Mad Rab. He's The Polmadie's Top Banana. His minions will come after you, and there's a journo called John Maclean..."

Bunty pointed to the crime reporter's name on the front page of The Daily Snot.

"... he's a fanny but, he'll no' be far behind me."

"Bunty, this is fascinating-"

"Listen, Hector. You're no' invisible... what I'm sayin' is, even the polis might get on to you."

Bunty gave Hector a wink then swallowed her whisky.

A nonplussed Hector put on his biggest smile. It wasn't difficult. "I em... would be delighted if you could keep me up to date with any developments."

"Watch how you go."

Bunty hadn't noticed Hector slip five twenties into her jacket pocket.

***

Back in the Sol, Aulay laughed out loud. This was great.

"So, Hector, you were working in Glasgow with Serious Crime. Against The Polmadie?"

"Amongst other things."

"Undercover?"

"More... incognito than undercover."

"Not only do you hospitalize three Neds from the gang you're investigating, you're exposed by a Daily Snot seller. How the mighty fall."

"Wait, Aulay. There's more..."

***

Ugly Grant pleaded. "But Rab, this Hector witness geezer, I can deal with him. It was me and my crew got stood on. It should be us deals with it."

"Cool your jets, Ugly. We'll find him. We'll get the info on the crew that did you and yer runners"

216

"Jeez, Rab, can I no' just..."

"Shut it, Ugly. Here's a few quid. Get you and yer boyz a few bevies, we'll sort it. Now, fuck off."

Ugly and his crippled runners left the Bulls Yard. Ugly Grant was worried, very worried. Did Mad Rab Smillie doubt his story of an outside team ambushing him and his crew? Ugly's whole life had been one long struggle to be seen to be hard. To be accepted by The Polmadie. If word got out that he and his crew were taken apart by one auld bloke with a walking stick – shite. And would you fuckin' believe it. With the press involved, everyone and their granny was looking for the same auld bastard.

Ugly's crew had seen better days. Scaffold held Runner1's fixed grin together. Runner 2 sported shiny new crutches and cried like a baby when a fly landed on his knee.

Ugly looked for luck in a glass. It's never there, ever. Next morning, lady luck arrived in the shape of six year old Britney. Ugly was in the Stew Pot having a hangover curing full Scottish breakfast. Full Scottish differs from a full English breakfast by virtue of the square sausage. The Stew Pot was busy. Sharing Ugly's table was Britney and her dad's only option. The weather bollocks was followed by the football bollocks. Ugly was in no mood for any of this but Britney was the one firing the questions.

"What's with the patch then?" she asked.

"Snooker cue," said Ugly. He checked the eye patch was sitting square.

Britney turned to her dad. "Your pal Hector's got a snooker table, aint he?"

Ugly's ears burst into flames.

"He's no' a pal, Britney, he's on my rounds."

217

Postman Ronnie turned to Ugly. "Sorry about this. I'm a postie and do the Shields. Britney's always askin' about the big houses and the people in them."

"The Shields, eh," said Ugly, "you might know a customer o' mine, older bloke, he goes by Hector, don't know his second name, uses a stick. I owe him money."

As an employee of Her Maj's Postal Service, Ronnie was under no obligation to reveal information about the members of the public on his rounds. He was only persuaded when the pressure on his scrotum went beyond endurable.

With number 9 Shields Gate imprinted on his mind, Ugly left the table.

A curious Britney asked, "Dad, why are you crying?"

At the counter, Ugly threw a few extra quid down to cover Ronnie's roll 'n' egg and Britney's burger. How good could it get? He went through his options. Round up his crew? No. Runner's 1 & 2 were not the backup team of yore. A solo mission. His crew would be his alibi. He knew where the gun was, easy. What about the getaway? Steal a car? Ugly couldn't drive and Runner 2 was the motor man so that was out. Bus? No, too public and unreliable. Bike? Aye, he'd borrow his wee brother's mountain bike.

Ugly caught his reflection in a shop window. The eye patch stood out like a dwarf in the long jump. What to do? Wait 'till dark? That was it. Arrive late, ring the bell. When the door opened, he'd start blasting, doddle.

Waiting for the sun to go down had one fatal flaw. It gave Ugly most of the day to ponder the 'what ifs'. Getting the gun from its hiding place should have eased his fears, it didn't. Ugly took a little white powder to settle his nerves, a little more to bolster his resolve, then another hit because he was starting to feel brilliant.

218

Hoody up and high as a kite on the mix of pain killers and cocaine, Ugly wheeled the bike behind a hedge at 9 Shields Gate. The bike was expensive. Ugly had to hand over the username and password for www.harlotsville.com before his wee brother would unlock the chain. The wee shite would be screwed when Ugly got home. Changing the password would take seconds.

Hitching his jeans, Ugly patted the gun. A .45 something or other. He couldn't remember. Other things were going a little awry too. What was his name? Ugly's brain curdled as he approached the front door. A shrill squawking pierced his ears and the sweat poured down his face. Out-with Ugly's addled sphere of influence, all his preservation alarms were going off. A snort of coke would fix everything. Sitting on Hector's front step, Ugly opened his bag of Delight.

Once more 'delighted', Ugly stood with gun up, potato ready. The potato he'd gleaned from an episode of C.S.I. Potatoes made good silencers.

He forgot a crucial bit of the plan, to ring the door bell. After a time, the big .45 started waving about. This gun's fuckin' heavy, thought Ugly. He considered returning with a lighter weapon. Who's got a wee gun? Wasn't Clockface always mouthin' off about a stash of weapons? Ugly didn't trust Clockface. You can't trust a guy with one arm shorter than the other.

After twenty minutes, Ugly's right arm ached. Before his arm gave up the ghost, he moved the .45 to his left hand. A tricky manoeuvre with a potato going the other way. Maybe Clockface was the thing. Was it worth a go? Aye, definitely. He'd waltz off and get something smaller than this howitzer, and a cabbage maybe. After snorting another line or two, he'd come back. Plan B. A relief.

When the door opened, Ugly raised the potato and fired. He looked at Hector, then at the potato, trying to figure out why it hadn't gone off.

Hector leaned forward and slipped the .45 from Ugly's other hand.

"Fuckin' heavy fucker aint it?" said Ugly.

Hector nodded.

"I'm offski, by the way," said Ugly. "Going to come back wi' a smaller one, OK?"

Hector led him inside. Ugly spotted a computer screen through an open doorway.

"Can I borrow your PC, just for a wee minute, I need to change a password. Is that OK?"

"In a while," said Hector.

He led Ugly down to the basement.

The following day, the police were called to a disturbance at the Aldi supermarket in Govanhill. A dishevelled Ugly Grant was remonstrating with a security guard when the police car swung in.

"Listen, that wanker's no letting me in." Ugly told the constable.

The PC looked over at the shrugging security guard.

"Look." Ugly held up a banana skin. "All I want is a refill, and these buggers insist I have to buy a new one. It's no' fair."

The concoction Hector injected, mixed with the cocaine already swimming around Ugly's system, severed a few connections in his frontal lobe. Ugly would live out the rest of his life in another world, and be no threat to anyone. He'd never quite get the banana thing.

***

Aulay looked puzzled. "How'd you know Ugly Grant was coming to your door?"

"Ah, this is where Chancer MacKinnon comes in," said Hector. "He paid me a visit earlier that day."

***

When the door bell rang, Hector opened the CCTV channel on his PC. A young man loitered with a baseball cap pulled low. He seemed innocent enough. Camera 2 pointed at a shiny red Alfa Romeo.

Pressing 44 on the keyboard put Hector through to the door entry intercom. "Can I help you?"

"I'm looking for Mr Hector Chalmers."

"In what regard?"

"Saving his life."

Hector recognised the figure. It was Alec 'Chancer' MacKinnon, a Polmadie Capo.

"Please, come in."

Selecting his small Beretta, Hector tucked it between his belt and spine and left his study.

"You Hector Chalmers then?" asked Chancer.

"Indeed, and who might you be?"

"I think you know who I am, Mr Chalmers."

That got Hector wondering. "What makes you say that?"

"I've a copy of the file you guys have been putting together."

Hector's wondering increased. "What file?"

Chancer reached for the bag he was carrying.

"Be careful..." said an unmoving Hector.

"Here, you take it." Chancer held out a Thomas the Tank rucksack.

Hector peaked in. The official letterhead, the off-white paper with the Serious Crime logo. He felt some relief. It wasn't something his people could have leaked. Still, how on earth did this guy get his hands on it?

"Do you drink, Mr MacKinnon?"

"Aye."

"Fancy a malt? I've a varied selection." Hector turned and entered the large sitting room. "Know your malts, do you? I'm an Islay man, myself."

"I'll have an Irn Bru, or something... please," said the following Chancer.

From the file, Hector remembered, Chancer MacKinnon didn't drink on the job. "Let me see now." He opened a small fridge behind a well stocked bar. "Diet?"

"Full fat, please. If you have it."

Another fact confirmed. Chancer spoke best-telephone. Hector's in-head data processing searched for the why.

"You are in luck, Mr MacKinnon. Here we are. Ice?"

"No, thank you."

Got it. Grandparents from the Western Isles...em, Isle of Lewis. Common name on the island, MacKinnon, no no, MacKinnon was the father's name and he originated from, from... Garscadden. After pouring a good measure of Scotland's other national drink into a whisky tumbler, Hector handed it to his guest.

"Sit, please." Hector indicated a leather couch.

Chancer had joined The Polmadie ten, no, twelve years ago. He'd overhauled their drug distribution network by using the Fat Controller Ice Cream vans. It took Serious Crime eleven months of intensive surveillance to crack it.

"Don't suppose you can tell me how you got your hands on this?" Hector glanced at the rucksack.

"Sorry, Mr Chalmers, that's a tin of pigeon."

Hector nearly lost it. He'd not heard that line for years. The old Chic Murray gag. A bloke asks a Chinese shopkeeper for a tin of pigeon. The shopkeeper gives the regretful reply, "Velly solly, no can do." Great stuff.

Hector's analysis of what the young man was doing here ground to a halt.

"So, Mr MacKinnon, what can I do for you?"

When Hector lowered himself into his favourite chair, the barrel of the Barretta pierced the skin in that sensitive bit at the bottom of his spine. Bloody hell, it was sore. Calmly putting his right leg over his left, shifted the pain from excruciating to acceptable.

Chancer sat up straight, cradling the glass of orange liquid in both hands.

"It's a comprehensive file, Mr Chalmers," he began. "Serious Crime have enough there to make a lot of arrests, today. I'm wondering why they've not started locking people up?"

With Serious Crime's latest progress report in a bag next to him, Hector didn't waffle.

"It's called the Al Capone quandary, Mr MacKinnon. Yes, we could arrest Mr Smillie and a good many others but, the charges against those at the top would be minor. Fraud, tax evasion and money laundering."

"Those at the bottom?"

"Ah, the hierarchy," said Hector. "Long sentences for possession and distribution of hard drugs. It's always the way of it."

"You telling me you're waiting around for a smoking gun?"

"As a matter of fact, yes, we are."

"What if the situation changes and there is no smoke, Mr Chalmers."

Hector's curious needle flicked to interested.

223

"You will know, from the file, Mr MacKinnon, that we have very little on you personally. A few uncorroborated rumours. We might have enough to charge you with something, but you have no criminal record. You'd walk away."

"I'm not thinking about me."

A piercing lunge from the Berretta made Hector sit forward. He watched Chancer assume the new posture meant avid interest. Hector was avidly interested but would rather have kept the fact quiet.

"You pull the plug and The Polmadie crash and burn, true?" asked Chancer.

"Yes."

"Take another look in the bag. Open the zip."

In the internal compartment, Hector found sheets of paper stapled together, about a hundred of them. "What is this?"

"Look through it."

Hector did, it took half an hour.

Chancer spent the time scanning the room. Hector's house was one of several hundred sandstone mansions in Pollokshields. Monuments to Glasgow's lucrative slave trade with the Americas. The Glasgow tobacco barons never sent an empty ship to collect the Virginia crop. A stopover in West Africa made good business sense.

The original interior had been retained, tall sash windows, ornate plaster ceiling. Hector's style was minimal, no bric a brac, no family photographs, no photographs at all, except one of a dog, a black collie with a white flash down his face. It was a loner's house or temporary accommodation.

Hector put the sheets down, stretched and rubbed a truly aching back. He moved the Berretta an inch or so, relief.

***

In the Hotel Sol, Aulay asked, "What was it then, in the rucksack?"

"The outline of Chancer's plan to turn The Polmadie round. The Polmadie own twenty-three businesses from pubs, bookies, ice cream vans, tanning shops and security companies. They all launder drug money but, essentially, they are going concerns. The plan was good."

Was Hector's use of the past tense significant, 'the plan was good'?

"Ok," said Aulay, "tell me more."

***

"Why bring this to me, Mr MacKinnon?"

Hector's assessment of the young man had risen but the immovable object, Mad Rab Smillie, still stood in the way.

"You're not polis, Mr Chalmers. You're a spook."

"The difference being?"

"When the polis find Mad Rab's body, they'll need to act."

Mad Rab Smillie was dead! The revelation sparked. Hector almost showed a smidgen of surprise.

"Can you reveal the details of Mr Smillie's em... demise?"

"You recording anything, Mr Chalmers?"

"No, I'm not."

"Let's go out to the garden anyway."

Hector led the way out to a decked area. They made themselves comfortable in oak garden furniture.

"You don't shop at B&Q then?" commented Chancer as he sat down.

"So, Mr MacKinnon, tell me about Mr Smillie?"

So Chancer did...

Despite the broken and bloody bodies of Runner's 1 and 2 lying in a heap at his feet, Mad Rab Smillie's fury level remained high. Ugly Grant and his crew had lied to him. They weren't beaten up by an outside crew but some auld geezer with a fuckin' walking stick. If this got out, The Polmadie would be a joke. Mad Rab would be a joke. With no Ugly Grant to rip apart, Ugly was nowhere to be found, Mad Rab made a move on Freak Johnston, ostensibly for letting Ugly get his hands on the gun.

Chancer stepped in. "Everyone knew where the gun was, Rab."

Mad Rab glared. "Listen, you get out ma way or I'll send you to the butcher's."

The butcher's? A reference to the old days. During a bitter turf battle, Mad Rab knifed Jack Hainey Jnr then had his body put through a mincer. The Scotch pies containing their son's remains were delivered to the Hainey Haulage yard. Mad Rab phoned and got Ma Hainey. He told her the news. Ma and Pa Hainey puked up all over their office and retired to a little cottage in Ullapool. They never ate meat again.

Chancer tried again. "Rab, listen, we all knew where the gun was."

There were six Polmadie Capos in the room, nobody moved.

"Son, you've crossed a fuckin' line."

The Sim stepped forward and caught Mad Rab's fist before it reached halfway to Chancer's face.

Something flashed. Chancer shouted. "He's got a blade."

Mad Rab slashed and kicked, he didn't make any connections. The Sim gripped the back of Rab's neck with one hand. He held on to the knife wielding wrist in the other.

A Capo stood up. Freak Johnston stepped forward. "Dourface, I'd really rather you didn't." Dourface Smillie sat down.

Bellowing like a bull in the wrong field, Mad Rab went mental. The Sim held on, letting Mad Rab go was not in his best interest.

Chancer's mind worked full tilt. Soon he, The Sim and possibly Freak, would be dead. There was no way Mad Rab would let them walk away after this. He made his decision, and struck.

Mad Rab stared at Chancer in incomprehension, then understanding. He looked at the handle sticking out of his chest, smiled and died.

No one said anything. The only sound, the ringing in their ears and The Sim's panting. Chancer approached Dourface.

"Am I goin' to have a problem with you?"

"No' me, Chancer," said Dourface, "never liked the fucker. Been tormentin' me since I was wee."

"Any other body got a problem?" Chancer searched the faces.

Belgy shook his head. Each Capo in turn did likewise.

"Fat Bastard, you got yer limo?"

"Aye," said FB.

"Right, Clockface and Belgy; get Ugly's two runners into FB's limo. Drop them at A& E. Don't let any bugger see you. When you're done, nick a wheelie bin and bring it back here. Sim, you get some bin bags and stuff to clean this up."

Mad Rab died quickly, most of the blood belonged to Runners 1 & 2.

Everyone took to the new regime with a collective sigh. Mad Rab had been getting madder.

The Nissan estate reversed up. FB, Chancer and Dourface slid the wheelie bin out and dragged it to the riverbank. They watched it drop the thirty feet to the cold dark water. For a nerve jangling few seconds the bin floated jauntily in the lapping waves before the weight took over and, expelling air in a profusion of bubbles, Mad Rab Smillie sank to his penultimate resting place.

"Good fuckin' riddance," murmured Dourface.

It was a well organised dump, it needed to be: it was still daylight. The route and place had been reconnoitred first, two cars made the trip. The first, to check the area was still clear before the Nissan turned in. Headlamp flashing signals were rehearsed beforehand. It was the Capo's introduction to the new Polmadie.

Mad Rab wasn't simply turfed into the wheelie bin. His teeth were removed with pliers. A blowtorch scorched the fingerprints before removing his face.

"Chancer," said Dourface during the blowtorch faze. "Better check his arse."

"What for?"

"Well...em, Rab's got a birthmark, a real corker."

The purple star like thing was removed. What was left would never be identified as Mad Rab Smillie, well, not easily. Chancer needed all the time he could get.

Back in the Nissan, Dourface said, "Green wheelie bins are for organic stuff, aint they?"

Everyone laughed the laugh of men with PTRS. Prolonged Tension Removed Syndrome.

Runner 1's face, already broken, recovered. He never heard anything in his left ear again and the teeth he used for opening annoying plastic bags, no longer met. He reluctantly took to using scissors.

Runner 2 was the lucky one. He had three broken ribs, a cracked skull, lost four teeth, cracked three more and fell for Moira, the plump and happy hygienist working for the dentist putting his mouth back together. Runner 2 thanked Mad Rab. He never came back.

***

When Chancer finished the story of Mad Rab's demise, Hector sat back a little star struck. Chancer MacKinnon was on the periphery of Serious Crime's radar, allocated somewhere in the thinker category. A strategist, not a soldier. Killing is not easy, Hector knew. OK, there were mitigating circumstances but, to slide a blade into a man's chest is, well... cold blooded.

And this happened when, a few hours ago. The young man opposite showed no outward sign of arguing with a traffic warden, never mind using a knife on a Banana.

Next came Ugly Grant having a gun.

"I assume, Mr MacKinnon, that you feel I'm under threat from Mr Grant."

"Aye, word is he's on the prowl. No one's seen him since the gun went missing. Unusual name you have. Not too many Hector's about."

"How did you find me?"

"Ugly was seen threatening a bloke in a cafe this morning. We traced the guy. He's your postman, Ronnie something. I spoke to him in A&E. His encounter with Ugly didn't go well. He gave you up."

"Where is Ugly now?"

"Don't know. Last we heard he'd scored some Delight."

A tooled and coked up Ugly would be working himself up to it.

"You didn't know Ugly and his runners were Polmadie?" asked Chancer.

"My mistake, I'm afraid. Members of the lower order."

Hector retreated to the house and returned with refills. Sitting down, he asked, "What do you want from me, Mr MacKinnon?"

"Time. There are too many good people involved. People who've done... whatever, to protect their families, and themselves. Mad Rab was the terror. When he suggested you do something, it got done. The consequences of not doing it... well."

"What makes you think I have that much influence?"

"The polis are polis. They investigate crime. You guys, the spooks, you sift and search. You're the boss. You can sift and search a wee bit slower."

"And why should I do this for you?" asked Hector. "I mean, I'm grateful for the heads up re Mr Grant, but..."

"You get awful tired walking down the street with one eye behind you."

A good threat, thought Hector. "Are you threatening me?"

"Aye."

"Has anyone ever given you good advice, son?"

"My Grandda' did," said Chancer, "he told me to always buy black socks."

"Why?"

"No need to pair them off after the washing."

Hector struggled to maintain his air of calm indifference.

"Mr Chalmers." Chancer leaned forward. "When you go through my proposal, you'll know it's the right thing for The Polmadie."

"How do you propose to...em, report progress on The Polmadie's transition from the dark side?"

"Through this lady." Chancer reached over with a card. Miss Sharon Curren of BD&P.

Hector led Chancer through the house. At the front door, Chancer turned.

"By the way, we no longer use The Fat Controller ice cream vans for distribution."

"I know," smiled Hector, who didn't. He made a mental note to kick someone's arse. "I'm curious about one thing, though, why use a Thomas the Tank rucksack?"

"Last thing a burglar's going to bother with."

Chancer walked to the waiting Alfa.

***

Aulay's hotel fridge was down another couple of malts by this time.

"When was all this?"

"Six months ago," said Hector. "I stalled things at my end but when Mad Rab's body turned up, Serious Crime threw everything they had at The Polmadie. Chancer in particular."

"Why?"

"There's a new guy heading up Serious Crime. Ambitious chap. He wants to make his mark and there's none bigger than the Top Banana of The Polmadie."

Aulay still wasn't clear in his own mind where the boundaries were. A serious spook teams up with a Glasgow hoodlum, for why? OK, warning Hector about Ugly Grant being on the rampage sounded plausible but, to hinder a Serious Crime investigation on the back of it? That didn't wash... and Chancer threatening Hector also had the ring of bollocks about it. Then there was the news that Shaz and Hector were connected. Interesting or dangerous?

Something else niggled.

"Chancer got his hands on Serious Crime's Polmadie file before Mad Rab was killed."

Taking a good swallow from his glass Hector wiped something invisible from his knee.

231

"...and you still haven't plugged the leak in Serious Crime. It's been more than six months..."

Aulay stopped. Hector had made a mistake. The knee wiping manoeuvre. He'd never hesitated to corral his thoughts before.

"...you're the fuckin' leak."

Hector sat back. "Not in the beginning. I took over when circumstances gave us a chance of getting at the DSH."

Hold on a minute. "Chancer's plan to go legit gave you an idea?"

Hector nodded.

"... and you kick-started the DSH takeover of The Polmadie by sending a copy of the Special Crime dossier to Spain?"

"A doctored version," said Hector, "amplifying The Polmadie's weaknesses."

"...and then passed details of the DSH's takeover team to The Polmadie? To make it fail?"

Hector nodded.

This was mind boggling stuff. See spooks? Never trust one.

"...all this to get Chancer MacKinnon into the DSH's face. To force a confrontation?"

Hector nodded again.

"That still doesn't explain this morning, when the Spanish polis lobbed a few stun grenades into an apartment across the road."

Hector looked contrite. "When Chancer's picture appeared on the news, Special Crime released everything they had to the Spanish. Including my organisation's monitoring of Freak's traffic which... was unfortunate."

"Unfortunate? That's fuckin' dandy. I could be getting unwanted attention from depraved Spanish inmates 'cos your stuff is available on Google?"

Aulay stopped for a breather. Hector stayed quiet. To let him calm down?

"Where am I in this fuck up? Do Special Crime or the Spanish know about me?"

"No, Aulay, nobody knows about you. You're mine alone."

"How did Freak Johnston know my employment history? Is your original leak still up and running?"

"What do you mean?"

"Freak knew my previous employer took a bullet in the head, and my day rate."

Hector went all business like.

"You being charged with murder, and your time in prison, is blanked out. The Americans agreed. Your Anfursati suicide bomber escapade bought your anonymity. I've checked and rechecked, but..." Hector shrugged. "Aulay, you're a part of recent history. Anyone with internet access could find out a lot about you, right up to Mr Waincross's death."

Hector was right. Before, on Ops, Aulay didn't give a shite. If he died because some intelligence bod made a mistake, hey ho. Now was different. A Miss Shaz Curren populated his diary.

"Does Chancer know he's a decoy, to flush out the DSH?"

"No."

Other details would have to wait. "I'm going to have a shower and head back to LJ's."

Hector stood up. "What's your assessment of the DSH so far?"

"They're fat, lazy, arrogant and think they're untouchable."

"Use it against them."

Hector closed the door behind him.

Under the scalding water, Aulay turned pink thinking about the scheming minds of spooks. A chauffeur and a grocer were dead. Mrs Ramos and The Sim each took a bullet while Hector Chalmers drank malt fuckin' whisky and schemed some more. There were holes all over Hector's story.

A knock on his hotel door. A mumbling as someone came in. Aulay levelled his .45 as the en suite door swung open.

"Hi, Aulay. I'm bursting." Shaz pushed past him dragging her skirt up.

Finished, she pecked him on the cheek and whispered, "Turn the water temperature up, it'll help."

In a luxurious Sol bathrobe, Aulay went to his suitcase, it was empty. In the wardrobe he found recently pressed jeans, shirts hanging in poly bags, even his y-fronts and socks had been ironed. Shaz cradled a gin 'n' slim.

"Well?" he said.

She'd checked in, a room on the eighth floor. She told him about her morning meeting with Freak Johnston.

"I've an appointment with Senor Sebastian Gallardo tomorrow morning, at seven."

"He any good?"

"Aye, according to my office he's the best. You should have heard him when I told him I was Chancer MacKinnon's lawyer. Yes, Miss Curren. No, Miss Curren."

She told him about the intricacies of the Spanish legal system. She'd read up on the plane.

"Did Freak say anything about how his communications with Chancer got into the hands of the Spanish."

"He suspects The Polmadie's friendly spook."

"Hector?" said Aulay. "You just missed him."

"I met him in the lobby. He gave me your room number."

"You've never mentioned Hector's name before."

"Neither have you."

"Touché."

"Hector claims the IP address leak to the Spanish was a fuck up."

"Do you believe him?"

"Aye. Hector wants the DSH. Chancer getting arrested wouldn't help his cause."

"What would help?"

"A dead Chancer, with me as a witness."

Shaz stared at him, cogs turning. "This whole thing is a set up?"

Aulay's time in the shower hadn't been wasted. About now, Chancer and The Sim should be getting dragged from a limousine at the bottom of the Med. Aulay would be earmarking Slicked Back and Shaven as the shooters. They'd give up their boss, Ricky Temple.

Aulay's guess? Ricky would squeal if he faced thirty years in Spanish stir. Result, end of Ricky Temple and life threatening dents in the DSH. Explaining all this to Shaz didn't take long.

"How much does Hector know about The Polmadie's plans to go straight?" asked Aulay.

"General progress," she said. "What are you thinking?"

"I think Hector's been planning this DSH gig for a long time." He left it there.

Shaz stood and walked to the window. The stark red hills loomed up to the sky. After a minute, she turned, forehead creased.

"The old bastard's been stringing me... everyone... along for months. If this Costa thing goes tits up, The Polmadie will collapse."

"Regardless of what happens here, The Polmadie are screwed. What about you, Shaz. You in the clear?"

"With Hector? There was no paperwork, ever... and anyway, I'm Chancer's lawyer and client confidentiality blah blah."

"Did he record anything? You've been caught out before."

"We met in public places, I chose them."

Her mobile beeped. After reading the text she closed the flip phone.

"That was Freak. Chancer needs to get away from LJ's place."

Aulay raised an eyebrow. "No one's going to connect Long John to this; I'm invisible."

"No, you're not. You're up for best supporting actor on Sky News."

Christ.

"Where'd you get the phone?" he asked.

"At the airport, pay-as-you-go."

"Credit card?"

"Shite. I'll dump it and buy another."

Aulay explained about the amount of shite they were in. The British, Spanish and Americans would be all over this 'international incident'.

"Why the Americans?"

"The DSH buy 80% of the Afghan crop."

He gripped Shaz's shoulders.

"You need to stay above everything. No more contact with me or Chancer. Everything needs to go through Freak. If Freak gets rumbled, you need to break all links with him too."

A look crossed her face. Did she get it?

"Shaz, they know who you are, that you're here in this hotel. If they don't, they soon will."

"Who's 'they'."

"The goodies and the baddies and... you and me, we're dispensable."

"But..."

"Fuck me, Shaz. There are two dead bodies already and the DSH have more money than God. They'll have people in the Spanish polis. What they know, the DSH will not be long in finding out. If they get an inkling that you're in touch with Chancer..."

"I can't hang about doing nothing."

"You got any connection with the media here?"

"The journo Maclean was on the flight."

"The Daily Snot guy?"

"Aye."

"Fuck him. Go to Sky News, or the BBC. Issue a statement. Hold a press conference. Make yourself public."

Aulay pulled her to him and grabbed her delicious arse.

"Get this Senor Gallardo to investigate the Murcia Street shooting, it's full of holes, and... Shaz babe, keep yourself safe."

Her eyes looked straight at him.

"Where do your loyalties lie, Aulay?"

He didn't blink. "With you."

He'd never said a truer word, or words.

The taxi dropped Aulay off a street away from LJ's Volvo. Paying the driver, he noticed a Seat hatchback pull in up the street. Two men got out. One walked off, the other loitered. It only took a minute for Aulay to know his followers were good, they split up, hung back, swapped places. He needed a diversion and found one in Raul Mendez. The street entertainer juggled four knives as he scooted about on a unicycle. His name was on a bucket half-full of coins.

Raul was good. The large crowd shrieked when he lost control, and careened towards them, blades twirling. He'd recover at the last second, straighten up, smile, bow, lean into the middle of the circle, before charging towards squealing kids on the far side.

Aulay stayed on the periphery, moving anticlockwise. With his back to an alleyway, he waited until Raul scared the bee-gee-bees out of the people in front him. Ducking low, he scurried into the alley and ran, weaving round bins and piles of black bin bags.

Aulay hated running, a boring occupation, unless there was a ball involved. He hit the smell of burgers and stopped. Slipping into the rear of the burger bar, Aulay waved at three sweating teenagers in McDonald's uniforms. At the street entrance, he checked up and down before making for a beach-wear shop across the road. He needed to blend in.

At LJ's, Aulay climbed out of the Volvo with a baseball cap on backwards. His blue shorts were wide enough for two. The sleeveless pink t-shirt clashed with his purple plastic sandals but matched the John Lennon shades.

Aulay told Chancer about his day. Soon, he was once again three spooned between the Galoots in the back of the

Volvo. The Sim climbed in unaided, sweating like a badly injured man clambering into the back of a car.

"The guys that followed you, DSH?" asked Chancer.

"They were professionals. Maybe Spanish spooks on the DSH's payroll."

"How'd they find you?"

"Could be my walk on part on Sky News, or you and me teaming up at the Albertino Lounge..." He mentioned his run in with Slicked Back in the Sol's foyer. "... or they followed Shaz from the airport. Whoever they were, it means I'm on the wanted list now too."

The Volvo drove to an English couple's isolated villa. The couple only visited over Xmas. They left keys with LJ, in case of an emergency. This was an emergency.

In the dark rear of the Volvo, Aulay remembered Hector saying, 'Use it against them'. He put his half baked plan to the Banana.

Chancer's cheek looked sore from the bullet that grazed along on its way into Mrs Ramos's bum. Covered in oilskins, baking in the late Spanish sun, the Banana suffered from more than a sore cheek.

The small boat inched closer to the cliff. The swell increased as the waves rebounded from the rock. Chancer turned green. He'd been purple up until then.

"No' much of a sailor then?" asked Aulay.

"Naw," said Chancer, "been round Rouken Glen pond in a pedalo once or twice."

Chancer leaned over the side.

"Not long now," yelled Brokeback as he hauled on a length of rope, connected via a myriad of metal things, to somewhere beyond Aulay's knowledge. Aulay's time on the water had been spent in metal boats with engines, not this sailing malarkey.

Brokeback shouted commands to the other ex-marines who carried out mystical manoeuvres with a range of props, and their own ropes. Before stepping aboard, the three began speaking in tongues. The words were familiar, but the sentences pointed nowhere Aulay knew.

The noise from the crashing waves increased. To give the queasy Chancer something to focus on, Aulay gave him a rope.

"Grip this and don't let go," he ordered. "It's important."

Chancer clung on with both hands.

The sharp end of the boat pointed skywards before plummeting into a white cauldron of foam. The noise of the boat's agonised shrieking drowned out everything else. Aulay too began to suffer. With his insides about to let go, it all changed. Calm, the water an undisturbed pool.

"We're in the lagoon," said Brokeback as he lowered the sail.

Before long, the pointy end hit bottom. Aulay took the rope from Chancer's white knuckles and cast it aside. Cast it aside, a good nautical term, he thought. After leaping onto the narrow pebble strip, Aulay watched Chancer trace the other end of his life saving length of rope. It was tied to his comfort blanket, a metal ring bolted to the deck. Chancer looked at Aulay, got it and laughed out loud.

The boat was dragged up onto the pebbles.

"When the tide comes in," said Brokeback, "she'll be smashed to pieces."

The plan didn't include a return voyage. Brokeback's crew removed weapons, and a stack of other equipment, from four holdalls.

"Where's the path?" asked Chancer.

The narrow inlet was just that, a thin strip hunkered down beneath a sheer face. Both ends looked like dead ends.

"No path," said Brokeback, "we climb."

Chancer looked at Aulay. "I can't go upstairs on a bus."

Aulay helped Chancer into a rock climbing harness. The rig secure, he edged him to the base. Brokeback and the others had already begun their accent.

The graze along Chancer's cheek was white. He was shaking.

"You're connected to me," said Aulay. "Tell me the story as we climb."

If his sea legs were day trippers, the Banana's head for heights imploded many moons ago.

***

A man dangled a four year old boy from a third floor tenement window. Chancer's stepdad wanted his wife's meagre earnings from her council cleaning job.

"Geez it, or I'll drop the wee shite onto the fuckin' railings, woman," screamed Crazy-out-of-it.

"You'll get it if you bring him back in the window."

Chancer's mum approached Crazy-out-of-it with hand outstretched.

"Geez it, here!"

"No' until he's inside the window."

Getting his hands on the money for his next fix could make Crazy-out-of-it forget what he was holding onto. He dropped Chancer on the floor. Cash in hand, Crazy-out-of-it left with a spring in his step.

Chancer's mum reached for her shopping bag and pulled out a bottle of vodka. She bought the essentials before returning home on payday. A good swig would calm her down, followed by another, then another... The abandoned Chancer cried under his bed. The safest non-high place he knew.

The dangling thing happened three times before Crazy-out-of-it left for pastures new. The adolescent Chancer researched his fear of heights, something a-phobia, to get a handle on it. He couldn't go up a ladder, but understood why not. He called it P.D.S.D. Post Dangling Stress Disorder.

Chancer saw Crazy-out-of-it again. Taking a shortcut across the railway track, he spotted the winos under a bridge. The Salvation Army uniform distracted him, at first. Crazy-out-of-it served up hot soup as well as the righteous path.

During his first meeting with Mad Rab Smillie, Chancer faced the dreaded height thing again. He was still at school. At Polmadie Comprehensive you went through the Galoots for drugs, cigarettes, rolling tobacco, alcohol, condoms, porn on DVD or memory stick. The Galoots stayed off the hard stuff. A wee drink or a toke was ok. Sim's porn rating became a standard. Hiring a Sim-9 wouldn't disappoint.

Don't be surprised they stayed on at school. It was too profitable, and there was nothing else to do.

When the Galoot's success came to the attention of The Polmadie, Mad Rab scheduled a meeting, for the roof of a high rise in Tory Glen.

"It'll be dark," said The Sim. "You won't be able to see fuck all. That should help."

On the night, The Sim got Chancer onto the roof early. It was overcast. Low clouds blocked out most of the city. The Sim positioned Chancer with his back to the night sky.

"It's goin' to be ok, honest," said The Sim.

"If it gets too much, I'll collapse and pretend something, ok?"

"What? Feeling dodgy after a Ruby, like?"

"Aye, that'll do."

The Smillie brothers arrived.

"Youz boyz got a good deal going through the school, but next year, you're out on your ear," said Mad Rab. "Any plans?"

Concentrating on the solid concrete behind Mad Rab's head, Chancer orchestrated a detailed response.

"No."

"Youz fancy coming to work for me?"

Again, Chancer skipped any unnecessary waffle. "Aye."

"There someone at the school who can take over from youz?"

The need to come up with more than a one word answer overloaded the circuits Chancer needed to stay upright.

"We thought of Ronaldo," said The Sim.

Mad Rab looked at his brother.

"Tam Wilson," said Dourface, "he's solid, Rab, I'd go with him."

Mad Rab asked, "Why's he called Ronaldo?"

The Sim stepped in again.

"School dance lessons. He tripped and pulled down Cassie Broxburn's skirt. One step-over too many."

Mad Rab roared. He was still laughing when they moved inside, to get out of the rain.

"You look more relaxed, son," he said to Chancer. "Were youz nervous about meetin' up?"

Chancer's equilibrium had returned.

"Aye, Mr Smillie but... you seem ok. We heard rumours."

"Listen, Chancer. You stick to my rules and everythin'll work out fine. Cross me, and you'll wish you'd fallen off the fuckin' roof. An' call me Rab."

"Right... Rab," said Chancer, "...why meet on the roof... just curious?"

In the lift, Mad Rab hit number 9.

"Got a date with a supplier. He's been a little short. Youz fancy comin' along?"

Chancer looked at The Sim, who nodded. "Aye."

On the 9th landing, Mad Rab hung back. Dourface rang the bell.

There was a mumble from inside. "Johnjo, it's me, Dourface."

More mumbling. "Naw, Mad Rab's no' here, come on, open up."

The door moved. Dourface put his shoulder to it. He barged in with Mad Rab and the Galoots close behind. Johnjo was a little man. Mad Rab simply lifted him off his feet and threw him against the wall. A framed family portrait crashed to the floor. Johnjo landed on it, smashing the glass. Mrs Johnjo came into the hall, screamed, ran into another room where two or three children started howling in tune with their mum.

"Rab..." said Johnjo. He stopped speaking when a steel toe-cap rammed into his rib cage... followed by another... and another... and another...

***

Back on the cliff, Aulay waited. They'd made it halfway up the face.

Chancer froze. "I'm scared shitless."

'Don't look down' is the old adage. Aulay hadn't said it often enough. Below them, the dying sun splayed patterns on the sea. It looked like the door to hell. Aulay retraced a few steps.

"Look at me," he whispered. It's best not to bark orders at a scared shitless.

Chancer didn't move. Aulay put his hand between the Banana's shoulder blades and gently pushed him into the cliff face.

"Look at me."

Chancer turned his head.

"What else you scared of Chancer? The dark, spiders, what?"

"Nothing like this. I mean... when Brokeback explained the route, it sounded good. Simple even. Sally forth, stroll up a hill, and hey ho. If he'd said 'scale a cliff' I'd have raised my hand and suggested I go with LJ."

LJ was in an unmarked van running the jammers. Without taking the pressure off the Banana's spine, Aulay turned and leaned with his back to the cliff. It really was a cracking view.

"You ok for a bit?" he said. "I fancy a smoke."

Chancer nodded.

"Close your eyes. Think about Jemima."

Aulay pulled his tobacco tin, rolled up, lit up and took a deep draw. For the benefit of the terrified, make it look like a

245

stroll in the park. After a couple of draws, Aulay reapplied the pressure to Chancer's spine.

"So, without looking down, tell me, how'd you and The Sim team up?"

Aulay'd been with seized-up recruits many times. He'd been one himself. Best to keep them talking.

Opening his eyes for the first time in a while, Chancer spoke.

***

The Sim's mum moved to Glasgow from Fife, after her husband skipped off leaving them in a pile of debt. The unmarried mother of three accepted the Council's first offer, a one room tenement flat in Polmadie's Wine Alley. The Sim's first day at his new school remained uneventful until ten past nine when thirteen year old Andrew MacKinnon was rushed into the medical room. He had a broken cheekbone, two squinty teeth and would never slag off a Fife accent again.

The lad explained to the teacher. "I tripped over a hole that was sticking up."

At morning break, another Fife accent teaser, with bruised genitals, was discovered lying in the toilets.

"...I was pulling up my kegs when someone kicked the cubicle door."

The Sim's preferred method? Grab his tormentor's hair, force the head down to kicking height, and stick the boot in. When he felt their resistance weaken, he'd raise the head until the genital area became a reachable target. Not too many came back from that.

Later that day, at High Noon, Sim sealed his reputation by kicking the shite out of the older brother of his first victim. In a Glasgow school, High Noon is both a time and a place. At Polmadie Comprehensive it was the west gate, at four o'clock.

Come the time, the entire school looked forward to the wee runt from Fife getting a proper kicking. The rumour mill ran red hot throughout the day with odds presented and bets taken. There is a formal air to these proceedings. After the initial surge to the west gate, the silent herd form a circle round both combatants. A shout goes up...   "Fight!" "Fight!" "Fight!" The shouting grows to a cacophony and the human circle contracts.

The Sim stood and waited. Chancer, two years older than The Sim, and several kilos heavier, dangled a three foot bicycle chain from his right hand.

"You put my wee brother in the hospital?"

"Aye, the wanker tried it on."

"Tried what on, your dress?"

In stressful situations, crap patter can work well. The surrounding herd laughed like that was the funniest thing they'd ever heard. In the midst of the guffawing, Chancer swung his chain in a high arc. Before it reached vertical, The Sim's forehead broke its second MacKinnon bone of the day, a nose this time. Chancer staggered, howled then brought the chain into play once more. Again, The Sim was too quick. He landed a boot to the groin, which sucked out every breath Chancer had drawn into his lungs since a week past Tuesday. Chancer crumpled, and stayed crumpled.

It was all over. The gathered throng wanted action, not a four second knockout, and blood, where was the blood? There was plenty of blood. Chancer had to swallow copious amounts of the stuff to keep his airways clear.

The aficionados knew they'd witnessed something exceptional. Street fighting made simple, in, out, bim, bam.

247

Cool as fuck. It was The Sim's last fight at Polmadie Comprehensive.

***

On the cliff top, the ex-marines waited.

"Two days later," said Chancer, I went back for another go at the wee shite. With my bust nose, and all the bruising, I looked like Zorro."

As the Banana giggled at the memory, his knuckles lost some of their whiteness.

"When I called him out the second time, the wee shite said, 'You're a right chancer. I can break somethin' else, if you like'."

More giggling. "I've been called Chancer ever since and... I still haven't managed to shake off the wee shite."

The younger Sim moved into Chancer's classes. Nobody said a word. It was that kind of school, a shelter from the rain, and boredom. A meeting place before deciding what to do that day.

***

They reached the cliff top.

"Thank fuck for that." Chancer hugged the ground.

Leaving him to his prayers, Aulay stripped off his climbing gear, checked the weapons and nodded at Brokeback.

[Seadog at Summit] Brokeback whispered into the two-way radio.

Why the whispering, thought Aulay, there was no one about.

Ricky Temple's pad followed the same principle as Tantallon Castle, in East Lothian. That old fortress is three sides of a square. The fourth? A sheer drop to the sea.

The house loomed over the swimming pool, tennis courts and other rich man's paraphernalia. The official way in, from the landward side, Aulay was getting into this nautical patter, meant negotiating armed security at two sets of gates, electric fences, and the rumoured dogs.

Brokeback mumbled some more gobbledegook into the two-way before secreting it somewhere. "Right, Long John's in position and the jammers will be ready in two."

Three dark figures slipped away in the direction of the garage complex. Chancer and Aulay made for the only ground floor window with a light on.

Raiding is what commandos are good at. This raid came about after one night's bar chat. Aulay and the Banana were in the Thistle Bar in Benalmedena. The pokey place catered for sunburnt Scots looking for a bit of home. 'An Audience with Billy Connolly' played on one of the screens, on repeat.

"Where you fae?" Aulay asked a swarthy guy nursing a beer at the bar.

"Drumchapel, you?"

"Govanhill."

With all the media attention, referring to Polmadie could trigger the wrong reaction.

"You on holiday?"

"Naw, I work here," said Swarthy, "you?"

"Been here a week. Go back the-morra."

Aulay caught Chancer looking at himself in the mirror behind the bar. Blond wasn't his colour, but Mrs Brokeback insisted. The big earring did its job too.

"People can't help it," she'd said as her hammer forced the needle through Chancer's ear lobe. She ignored the Banana's screech. "An earring draws their eye, especially on a bloke. As good as a mask."

Swarthy pointed at the plasma screen hanging in one corner. "I'd shag that one."

Sky News had the latest on the Murcia Street shooting. Walking down the steps of a grand looking office building, Shaz looked the business in a light gray suit, hair lightly muddled, reporters all around.

"Miss Curren, you'll be aware that your client is also wanted in the UK in connection with the death of a Glasgow business man, Mr Robert Smillie?"

"Yes," said Shaz.

"Are you in contact with Mr MacKinnon?"

"No."

"What are you doing in Spain?"

"I'm here to help my client."

"If he's innocent, why does he not give himself up?"

"He will, when he's ready."

Shaz climbed into a waiting car which sped off.

The reporter turned to the camera...

"That was Sharon Curren, Alec 'Chancer' MacKinnon's lawyer, leaving the offices of Sebastian Gallardo, chief public investigator in the Murcia Street shootings. Back to you in the studio."

"Aye, yon's a babe," said Aulay, "and that Temple geezer got off light, eh?"

"No' half. He dicks about wi' a Glasgow Banana and walks away, fuck me."

"This Temple bloke, he a big noise round here?" Aulay took the stool next to Swarthy.

"Ricky Temple's a tight fisted fuck." Swarthy warmed to it. "He lives off a big reputation built on a shooting twenty odd years ago. He's well connected though, know what I mean?"

Swarthy finished his beer.

"What's that yer on?" asked Aulay.

"San Miguel, cheers."

Aulay was in.

Earlier that day, Brokeback followed the first likely vehicle to leave Ricky Temple's estate. Swarthy's Fiat van was it.

"You know this geezer Temple?" asked Aulay as Swarthy's San Miguel arrived.

"No' really, done some work at his place, and seen him about. He's got people to deal with the likes of me."

"People?"

"Aye, yon's a rich bastard. Two security gates before you get near the place, guards are armed too. I go through 'arvey. He buffers Ricky from all the day to day shite, know what I mean?"

"What do you work as?"

"Satellite TV. The Brits here can't last two minutes without Eastenders. I was up there today."

Swarthy took a swig. Aulay stayed silent. Blokes didn't need prompting to talk about themselves.

"Mr Temple's out to impress some bim-bette tonight, he wants to look his best?"

"How'd you manage that?"

"New Hi-Def camera and a fuck-off 60 inch LCD mounted over the bed. Now when he's on screen, you can see the plooks on his arse from the other side of the room."

Over the next half hour, Aulay gleaned a fair amount from the talkative Sky-man, enough to get the gist of the house layout, and the numbers present.

Titbit from Sky-man 1, "...there's 8 staff, all Spanish, cooks, gardeners and what not. They live in-between gate 1 and 2.

'arvey's the bloke I deal with. He lives in an add-on to the big house. A couple of hard types live above the garage."

251

"Hard types?"

"Aye, big guys, English, ex army if you ask me, mean fuckers."

Slicked Back and Shaven stayed close to Ricky Temple.

***

Looking in the lit window of the add-on to the big house, Aulay recognised the bloke from the Beluga restaurant. Ricky's Consigliore worked his laptop.

Aulay opened the door. Harvey leapt from his chair.

"'ow the fuck-"

Harvey stopped when Aulay raised a finger to his lips. The AK47 helped too.

"Don't move, 'arvey. It is 'arvey, aint it?"

Harvey nodded, then swallowed when he recognised Chancer.

"Sit down and stay quiet, 'arvey. We don't want any fuss."

"Do you know-"

Aulay moved to an inch from Harvey's nose. "I said sit down."

He sat.

Aulay slid Harvey's lap top away, did a cursory body search, pulled a roll of gaffer tape from his combat trousers and strapped Harvey to his chair.

"You alone 'arvey?" asked Chancer.

Harvey didn't respond.

Chancer smashed the butt of his AK47 into Harvey's left foot. Harvey only had slippers on so the odd bone broke. He screamed into the t-towel stuffed in his mouth.

The mood had changed since Chancer's terror on the cliff face. The Banana was back in charge.

"You goin' to answer now?"

Harvey nodded. Tears ran down his red face.

"Ok. 'arvey." Chancer pulled the gag out. He let the whimpers die down.

"Ricky's girlfriend still here?"

"Yes."

"You expecting anyone else?"

"No... 'onest."

"Can you turn off the alarm to the big house?"

Titbit from Sky-man 2, "...there's 14 TV's in the place. You need three separate security codes for Christ sake, main house, staff quarters and external. It's a major pain in the tits because they keep changing the codes."

Harvey hesitated until the AK twitched.

"... no, only from the inside."

"Where's the telephone exchange?"

Titbit from Sky-man 3, "...you need to dial '9' to get a fuckin' outside line. The exchange is in a room beside my aerial amps and other electronic shite like fire and smoke alarm gear. There's a serious security system with CCTV and all sorts."

"Down the 'all. The exchange is in the Plant room. Second door on your left."

"And your walkie-talkie?"

Titbit from Sky-man 4. "When I go to leave, they call Gates 1 & 2 on the phone, or by walkie-talkie."

"In my jacket pocket," said Harvey, "it's 'anging over there."

Aulay retrieved it.

"When do you need to check in?"

Titbit from Sky-man 5, "...one time, 'arvey left his walkie talkie behind and before I knew it, two bulls came charging in with shooters. 'arvey needs to check in or the shite hits the fan."

"...about 'alf an hour," said Harvey.

"Don't fuck..."

"Ok, ok... em...," Harvey glanced at a clock on the wall, "...when I go to bed."

"What happens then, 'arvey?"

Titbit from Sky-man 6, "...there's four or five of them, vicious lookin' fuckers, Dobermans."

"I 'ave to let the dogs out," said Harvey.

"How?"

"From the computer. The kennels have automatic gates."

Chancer tapped a few keys on Harvey's laptop.

"That the only way?" asked Chancer after the interminable wait for Windows to shut down.

"If you 'ave no will to live," said Harvey, "you can let the dogs out yourself."

Aulay went to find the telephone exchange.

"Boss, it's me," said Harvey into the phone.

"What the fuck is it, 'arvey," grumbled Ricky.

"We 'ave... em... a situation, boss."

"It better be fuckin' good."

A click. The door opened. Chancer and Aulay followed the hobbling Harvey down a corridor and into the big house. At the master bedroom, Harvey knocked and went in.

"Cut to the quick, 'arvey," said Ricky who wore a rather fetching silk dressing gown.

Harvey stepped aside.

"Mr Temple, remember me?"

Ricky looked on the verge of heart failure. Chancer lifted his AK47. Ricky looked down the barrel, and passed out.

The enormous dimly lit room had different shades of suede covering the walls. Off-white deep pile carpet, deep enough to trip over, encircled an oval waterbed which was big enough for a family picnic. A blank plasma screen angled down from the ceiling. Half a dozen mirrors pointed at the bed. Ricky liked to view his sexual exploits from all angles.

Aulay moved to the three doors on the other side of the room. The first opened into a kitted out gym with expensive looking equipment still covered in cellophane. Behind the next door, a dressing area with row upon row of suits, shirts and shoes. The third door fed Aulay into one of his favourite fantasies. The gold toothed oriental stunner, who'd slipped and slid round Chancer in the entrance to the Copacabana, stood in the shower. She looked his way and squinted. Oriental-stunner was short sighted.

Aulay said nothing.

Naked, apart from patent leather stilettos, Oriental-stunner selected a shiny object from a selection to her right. She switched it on.

If someone had suggested installing up-lighters in the floor of a shower, Aulay would have dismissed the idea as bonkers. Now, they were on his shopping list. They'd make a mess of Shaz's tiled bathroom floor, but fuck it.

The gentle beat from the hidden speakers changed to a hip hop frenzy. Oriental-stunner moved her lithe body into a myriad of positions, all-out to galvanise Ricky's libido. Slipping one hand into a leather loop fixed to the top of a polished, floor to ceiling pole, she hoisted herself up and began making good use of the now buzzing 'item'.

Aulay might get away with installing up lighters, but a lap dancing pole? No chance.

Pole dancing and related studies are part of the military lifestyle. Aulay considered himself a good judge. He gave oriental stunner a 9.9. The missing 0.1? Shaz had a delicious dimple on her bum.

Aulay retreated, pulling the bathroom door closed behind him. He was in time to see Chancer pour a bottle of Courvoisier over the spread-eagled Ricky's face. The now naked Ricky spluttered and coughed himself conscious. Stripping your captive is good technique, makes them more vulnerable. Other tips Aulay had passed on, work the guy quickly, and make it painful.

"Light," said Chancer.

Aulay threw his lighter over the bed.

"You with us, Mr Temple?" Chancer poured the last of the brandy over Ricky's left foot.

"Mr MacKinnon, you need to listen... nooo."

Ricky's outburst ended in a grunt as the stockl of the AK47 crashed into his mouth. Bits of teeth and blood dripped onto the silk sheets. Chancer flicked the lighter and dropped it. Ricky's left foot burst into flames. He made a terrible noise but the AK rammed down his throat kept the volume down.

Aulay was aware that some amateur torturers get carried away, destroying the victim before anything useful comes out. Chancer looked in control.

The smoke detector started blinking. Harvey looked at Aulay, then cottoned on. He'd tampered with more than the telephone exchange during his time in the plant room.

Plant room? In a house? The mega rich spend lots of money on security, CCTV and other 'toys'. Ricky's plant room had lighting and heating control panels, Swarthy's Satellite distribution kit, audio and video servers, 64 way telephone exchange, main PC network hub, routers, patch panels, fire and sprinkler controllers. Control boxes connecting everything to everything else.

Coulfield Waincross III introduced Aulay to 'Home Automation'. Touch screens in every room controlled anything and everything. The rich don't have six remote controls on the coffee table. Coulfield installed the same automation system all his houses. Wherever he was in the world, everything worked the same. On boring days, Aulay would spend hours trying to get the automation systems to crash. He's hit the virtual buttons in random sequences, looking for a bug in the software. His favourite was the mansion in Charleston, Virginia. If he switched from lighting scene 3 to lighting scene 6, then satellite channel 47 to channel 8, the garden sprinklers came on.

In Ricky's plant room the patch panel ran to three, two metre high, 19 inch racks, well labelled, in English. After disconnecting the master bedroom, he'd pulled the telephone exchange link to each security gate, the garage living area and the staff quarters. They could talk to each other, but couldn't dial out. The zoned fire and sprinkler panel was a doddle. Aulay switched off the button marked master bedroom.

Using his other foot, Ricky managed to manoeuvre the available sheets to put out the fire. His relief was short lived. Removing the AK from his host's smashed mouth, Chancer selected another bottle from the bedside cabinet, a Hennessy XO; Ricky enjoyed only the best, and liberally splashed some over the poor bastard's crotch.

Problem. Aulay's only lighter was a charred plastic ruin. Ricky didn't know this. He crumpled, wailing like a new born, begging and pleading as best he could with a swollen tongue and wrecked toothless gums. Ricky curled into a ball.

Repelling the urge for another peek at oriental stunner, Aulay whispered into his two-way.

[Red Five to all; Status]

[Pink Cowboy; they're watching TV; we're in position]

Brokeback was monitoring Slicked Back and Shaven's digs.

[Silver; all quiet]

LJ was in a lay-by outside gate 1.

Chancer pointed to the en suite. "Is someone in there?"

"Your gold toothed oriental from the other night is em... cleaning up," said Aulay.

With Chancer playing Mr Ruthless pretty well, Aulay hadn't wanted to distract him.

"Is there another way out?"

Extreme exotic dancing hadn't prevented Aulay checking the en suite. A walk in shower, a sunken bath with space for six, two sinks, each with an LCD screen, one on BBC News24, the other on a porn channel, both screens had a cracking picture; Swarthy was good at his job. The toilet pan and bidet sat behind an opaque glass modesty screen.

"One door in and out. No windows," said Aulay. "I'll lock her in for the night."

The en suite door opened into the bedroom. Aulay dragged one of the lounge chairs from the palatial seating area and wedged it under the door handle.

"Right 'arvey," said Chancer, "lets fire up your computer."

Chancer led the hobbling Harvey from the master bedroom. Aulay followed pulling a meek Ricky along by the belt of his Armani dressing gown.

"Nice," said Aulay.

Ricky didn't reply.

With Harvey limping, and Ricky's left peg looking like a well done pork chop, Aulay wondered if the Banana had a foot fetish.

Back in the add-on, they gaffer taped Ricky and Harvey to two chairs. To stop the incessant moaning, Aulay filled a basin with tap water for Ricky's roasted foot.

Harvey's laptop started up pretty quickly.

"Right 'arvey, you're off to bed, what now?" said Chancer, "and be careful, no fuck ups, and no dogs tonight."

Holding the phone to Harvey's ear, Chancer flipped the button.

"Jonesy, I'm calling it a night. Anything 'appening?"

"Nope, quieter than a nun's dream. Is the boss up?"

"Miss Japan's trying her best," said Harvey. "I'm leaving the dogs in tonight, Jonesy, she's a swimmer, remember?"

"It'll take more than a swimming pool to wash the old fart's sweat off," said a chuckling Jonesy. "Night 'arvey."

Aulay and Chancer grinned. Ricky didn't.

"You're good 'arvey," said Chancer, "now, let's look at what we have here."

Chancer plugged a memory stick into the laptop and fiddled about. Fifteen minutes later, Freak Johnston had remote access to the Harvey's computer and, via the house's wireless network, to the server in the plant room. Before Freak could gain the roaming rights to the entire DSH in Spain, London and Lagos, they had to go through the password rigmarole. There were three levels. Both 'arvey and Ricky gave up their secrets without any trouble.

Harvey's three passwords were revealing, Godfather; Godfather2; Godfather3.

Ricky's more so, Debbie; Does; Dallas.

After the IP address stun-grenade incident, Freak had disappeared. He re-emerged with a PC World bought computer, an external terabyte hard drive, in a hotel room in Edinburgh. If the DSH did have remote monitoring of Ricky's home system, they could trace Freak's link, and turn up his IP in a 320 room hotel. This was the dodgy part. If all went to plan, Freak would download enough to screw the DSH.

Chancer looked tired. Aulay suspected bloody violence didn't come naturally to the Banana. As good as he was, Chancer suffered along with his victim.

Most men fell into two types. Normal, everyday blokes suffer after the violence. Some have sleepless nights and fret for ages. Others drain mentally, as well as physically, but recover quickly. Aulay put Chancer in the latter group.

Aulay could take it or leave it. Unnecessary violence left him cold. Necessary violence? If it needed doing he could do it. Had done it.

The phone rang. To disguise his jump at the noise, Aulay walked over to the clanging demon. [Ex 24] flashed in blue.

"What's extension 24, 'arvey?"

"En suite in the master bedroom."

"Shite."

Aulay ran to the plant room. Of course there would be a phone in Ricky's bog, behind the modesty screen? What if he was in the bath and ran out of coke or brandy. Aulay hadn't noticed the en suite extension plug on the patch panel in the Plant Room. He hadn't looked.

The odds of Miss Japan calling security first were low. Aulay pulled his two-way out.

[Red Five; Status]

[Pink Cowboy; All quiet]

[Silver; All quiet]

Aulay felt bad. When you fuck up, it crawls into your head and burns. He remembered people dying because someone didn't check a wardrobe. The suicide bomber waited until the house was full.

In the en suite, he walked into the range of Miss Japan's vision. She put hands on hips, thrust out her surgically enhanced breasts and glared at him. "Who the fuck are you?

"I'm the burglar."

"Where's Mr Temple?"

She ignored Aulay's .45 automatic. AK47's are good, for killing fourteen people in three seconds. Too bulky for a wrestling match with a naked oriental.

"Ricky's a bit tied up."

Aulay smiled. His stress management kicked in. He laughed out loud. Miss Japan didn't smile. Aulay spotted handcuffs amongst the chains and brackets on a shelf in the shower. Still giggling, he wandered over to examine them. They were real.

Something made him duck. A sound? A feeling?

Miss Japan's stiletto'd heel whizzed past his ear. Her jab to his throat, he caught in his left hand. She was quick. Twisting her hand, Aulay spun her round. To stop her wrist from snapping, she had to go down. On the floor, Aulay put one knee on her spine then clicked the handcuffs on. She didn't make a sound.

"What was that all about?"

No reply. He lifted her up. Her skin was smooth, oily. Keeping behind her, a knee in the balls is worth preventing; Aulay held her elbows in. They shuffled over to the shower. Reaching the pole, he forced his body up against hers, undid

261

the cuffs, snuck both her hands round the pole, and clicked the cuffs back on. Stepping back was a struggle.

She shivered. It wasn't cold. There was genuine fear in her eyes. He understood. Miss Japan's boss was nowhere to be seen. The pervading smell was of recently burnt human flesh. A demented armed man had appeared, laughing hysterically at nothing. No wonder she lashed out.

"I'm not going to harm you," said Aulay. "In fact, that's all the bodily contact finished, honest. Was that Jujitsu? You're very good."

Another tremor. Aulay took out a packet of Lucky Strikes. He'd nicked Harvey's lighter.

"You smoke, Miss Japan?"

"I gave up three months ago, and I'm half Chinese, half American."

"Want one?"

"Yes."

"Tipped or plain?"

"Plain."

He snapped off the filter and put the lit Lucky to her lips. She thanked him with her eyes. Aulay lit another.

"Do you stay all night?"

"No," she said after a deep draw.

"When do you normally leave?"

"Straight after."

"What time?"

"Depends, Mr Temple can be em... difficult. He drinks."

"What's your name?"

"They call me Suzie Wong."

An alarm went off in Aulay's head.

"You swim in the pool... after?"

"No."

Aulay was out the bathroom door before he had time to say 'Shite'. Harvey had told security it was Miss Japan. Was it code for 'attack attack attack'? Charging down the corridor, Aulay ripped out the two-way. Worst case scenario? Everyone was dead, but him... not again.

***

It was a cold night somewhere near the Pakistan border. A forward sighting group were out to pinpoint Taliban positions for US airstrikes. For three days they'd watched the village. Nothing moved, ever. Most of the hamlet's roofs were caved in from earlier conflicts with rubble and debris strewn everywhere, the residents long gone. The cold nights bit into the marrow making the retreat for morning ablutions excruciating.

On the fourth morning, Captain Hardy ordered them in. As the best marksman in the squad, Aulay stayed with the radio. When all five reached the killing ground, the Taliban opened up with rockets and mortars. IED's blew the ruins further apart. It was a massacre.

It was the day the Allies learned; Taliban fighters don't retreat for morning ablutions. They pissed and crapped where they lay, for days, surviving on nothing.

On a freezing mountainside, with a dozen Taliban ex-statues homing their fire power onto his position, Aulay radioed in his own coordinates and waited for the cavalry.

Inside an airstrike is surreal. The once solid ground rises and falls, buckling into huge waves and the noise, Jesus. Aulay got lucky. The first rocket buried him alive, sheltering him from the storm. The noise level remained below bleeding. Not long after the last explosion, the scraping of boots broke the silence as the Taliban searched for his remains.

With enough room to move his chest, Aulay adopted the Taliban regime and stayed underground for the next four days. Body heat kept his tomb from freezing. On the fifth night, he dug himself out. The radio lay in tatters. He crawled back to Recovery. There was no one there.

It took another five nights, he holed up in the daytime, to make it back to base. He'd lost a few pounds and looked like Robinson Crusoe on a bad hair day. He should have died.

***

If Harvey's Miss Japan line to security had brought in the silent ninja killers, Aulay planned to take a few with him.

[Red Five; Status]

[Pink Cowboy; All quiet]

[Silver; All quiet]

Nothing from Big Yellow. Was the Banana dead? Captured?

Aulay slowed down. No point charging into Harvey's kitchen. If they had Chancer, they'd have his two-way, and know he was coming.

[Zero – one – niner] Aulay ordered.

'Niner' was the signal to change channel, to the reverse of the first two numbers.

Aulay waited on Channel 10.

[Pink Cowboy; Check]

[Silver; Check]

No Big Yellow.

They had contingencies. LJ would drive up to gate 1 and start blasting, hoping to draw security from gate 2. Brokeback would lob a few grenades into Shaven and Slicked Back's digs above the garage, again, drawing security from gate 2.

[Hold; Expect Trouble; Going to silent]

He switched off the corridor lights and crawled to Harvey's kitchen door. Silence, well, not quite. With all the gismos and electronics, rich people's houses hum. Lighting control systems are never off, even when the lights are. Another thing, all internal doors are heavy. No hardboard panelled crap here. Harvey could be holding a rave and Aulay would be none the wiser.

Aulay turned the handle and pushed. A still trussed up Ricky and Harvey turned their heads, searching behind their blindfolds. All was quiet except for the drone of light snoring. Aulay stood up, dimmed the lights and closed the blinds on all the windows. Big Yellow was sleeping on the floor. OK, thought Aulay, the man had recently been shot at, sailed across rough seas, climbed a terrifying cliff and tortured another individual, but still... Aulay kicked the Banana.

Chancer tried to scream. He couldn't, Aulay had his hand over his mouth.

"Where the fuck is your two-way?" Aulay's heart beat like a train but it was coming into the station.

Chancer pulled his radio from a pocket. The fucker was switched off. Commando training takes months. Chancer had an hour. His AK47 didn't have any bullets; he'd never fired a handgun, never mind a rapid fire killing machine. He understood that, on operational matters, Aulay was the chief. If he couldn't hear instructions via the radio, he was a liability to himself, and to the rest of them.

Aulay asked for an update. [Red Five; Status]

[Pink Cowboy; All quiet]

Chancer fiddled with his two-way.

[Silver; All quiet; Big Yellow's status?]

[Red Five; All ok]

"We're on channel 10."

The Banana had the good grace to acknowledge his lapse with a cough.

Aulay ripped the gaffer tape from Harvey's mouth.

"What's the 'swimming pool' script, 'arvey?"

"What?"

"Suzie Wong's not a swimmer." Aulay raised his AK.

Harvey flinched. "... 'onest, I thought Miss Japan was 'ere."

The man trembled. Could it be a simple mistake? It happened during operations. The smallest things can cause mayhem.

"Jonesy at gate 1. Was he on duty when Suzie Wong arrived?"

Harvey looked at the clock.

"No, 'e came on at eleven, she arrived at ten. I never saw 'er. She went straight to the front door, Ricky let 'er in."

After re-wrapping Harvey, Aulay explained the situation to Chancer.

"If the 'swimming pool' line was a signal to Jonesy at gate 1, we'd be in a fire fight by now. There's another thing, Suzie Wong leaves em... after she's all done."

"Do they have a sign in / sign out log?" asked Chancer. "What if Jonesy looks it up?

The phone rang. The receiver was next to Harvey's ear in seconds.

"Jonesy?" said Harvey in a reasonably cheery tone considering it was the third time gaffer tape had been ripped from his face..

"Sorry to disturb you 'arvey. I've got Suzie Wong signed in, not Miss Japan."

"Ricky must 'ave felt the need for a little punishment tonight," said Harvey.

"That little bitch can punish me anytime," said Jonesy. "Any idea when she'll be signing out?"

"No, but there's enough lube in the master bedroom to get a torpedo up Ricky's arse, if that's what it takes."

Jonesy snorted. Aulay pictured the array of objects next to the shower, painful.

"'arvey," said Jonesy, "how much does Suzie Wong charge?"

"Depends. A grand for some light tinkering. Two if you want a full re-bore."

Jonesy whistled. "It'd be worth it. Night 'arvey."

Aulay's paranoia meter worked overtime. Harvey and Jonesy's conversation could be a dissertation on the current situation.

Felt the need + a little punishment = The threat is real

Enough lube + torpedo up his arse = Ricky was in deep shite

Light tinkering + full re-bore = Bring reinforcements

Aulay re-wrapped the now red red raw Harvey in more gaffer tape. He'd look barbequed in the morning. Aulay lit a Lucky. Chancer having his two-way switched off was a minor misdemeanour compared to his howler, leaving Suzie Wong capable of communicating with the outside world. Another thing, kicking a Glasgow Banana awake, with attitude, wasn't in any survival guide Aulay had read. There would be consequences.

The flat above Ricky's garage lay in darkness.

"Any joy?" Aulay asked Brokeback.

"You were on the button. There's an L7 machinegun hidden in the boot of the Audi. The magazine's empty."

After blasting the Sol's Mercedes off the road, Aulay suspected Slicked Back and Shaven wouldn't ditch their British army L7. With any luck, the guns that killed the grocer, and inconvenienced Mrs Ramos, wouldn't be far away.

Extending across the twelve car garage, Slicked Back and Shaven's palatial digs had bay windows overlooking the sea. Getting in was a doddle. Aulay turned the handle and opened the front door. He walked into the smell of pizza, beer and stale cigarette smoke.

Some squaddies leave the army and go to seed. Not physically, but in their heads. As reliable in a scrap as a pit bull terrier, they leave the service, step off the pavement and get hit by a bus. Slicked Back and Shaven were supposed to be on an operational footing. Their boss had recently been kidnapped, they'd shot up the streets, killed a chauffeur, one civilian, punctured another and their adversaries, meaning The Galoots, were on the loose.

Empty beer bottles covered the living room coffee table. Pizza boxes and their remnants littered the carpet. Two overflowing ashtrays lingered by reclining chairs. Porn DVD's lay scattered. Aulay was embarrassed.

Five minutes later, they had Slicked Back and Shaven handcuffed to the Audi. Four handguns joined the L7 machinegun in the boot.

Back in Harvey's kitchen, Chancer was at the PC.

"How's it look?" said Aulay.

"Finishing up. Freak's got everything he needs."

Chancer spent the next hour going through the script with Ricky Temple. Ricky quibbled at first. His Consigliore persuaded him. Harvey understood the scale, and consequences, of the data now resident with Freak Johnston back in Scotland. The DSH were stuck between a rock and a stack of diverted funds.

All were ready when the phone rang. It was mid-morning.

"'arvey, there's a convoy of vans here. Sky News and some local TV people."

It was Jonesy at gate 1.

"Let them in, Jonesy. Ricky's going to make a statement. Let gate 2 know."

"Fuck me, 'arvey, nothing like this..."

"I'll get Mr Temple, 'old on."

A now silk-suited Ricky took the receiver. "Shonesy, open the fuffing fate."

The rearranged architecture in Ricky's mouth made hard consonants difficult.

"... and feep it open."

"Sure, boss."

The Armani'd Top Banana looked ready for the cameras.

"Ok, I'm offski," said Aulay.

They shook hands.

"It's Hector Chalmers next."

Aulay nodded.

Suzie Wong sat on Ricky's waterbed wearing a simple t-shirt and cut off jeans. Aulay returned her mobile, along with 20,000 Euros silence money. She slipped the envelope into her shoulder bag without comment. They made their way out to her waiting MX5. Suzie put the roof down after slipping into the driver's seat. Before the key entered the ignition, the media convoy swung into the courtyard. A smartly turned-out Shaz jumped from the first vehicle. Two beefy types handcuffed to a silver Audi took her attention, she didn't notice the wee Mazda.

Suzie slipped on a pair of designer shades from the glove box. Aulay hoped they were prescription. In among the cameramen, technicians, about three miles of cable, Shaz looked cool. She ushered the waiting reporters to her.

"No camera is to filum anything until I say so. Nothing. Not even to check the light."

All three reporters nodded.

"I will be meeting with my client first. Then, and only then, will you be allowed into Mr Temple's villa."

More nods before the trio of reporters went back to checking their hair and makeup.

Shaz looked round the courtyard. She saw through Aulay's disguise. They shared a long look as she walked over. Aulay removed his John Lennon shades. Shaz eyed Suzie Wong, from the painted tip of her toes, to the sheen of her jet black hair.

"If you're in charge," said Aulay, "would you mind asking someone to clear the entrance. We have an appointment."

"Of course."

Shaz signalled to some gofer who rushed over. He took his instructions and raced to the media van blocking the courtyard exit.

Under the noise of the Mazda's engine starting Aulay said, "This is Suzie Wong, she's my alibi."

Shaz hid her one fingered reply inside her suit jacket.

Suzie Wong could handle a car. They screeched through the gate, tail sliding, tyres spinning. Brokeback and his two mates didn't stand a chance. Their Land Cruiser, kindly offered up by Mr Temple, loped along in the distance.

Chancer MacKinnon was on his own, with Shaz and the world's media.

Aulay pointed to the lay-by. Suzie executed a lovely 180 degree handbrake turn, thrashed the throttle to continue the spin and slid the wee car in behind LJ's VW Camper.

"Rear wheel drive," she said.

"I bet there's a lot you're good at."

Suzie Wong wore a smile. Reaching over, Aulay took off her shades to see if it was genuine. It was.

"The bitch in charge back there, is she yours?"

"Aye."

"Lucky girl, now, Red Five, get out."

Waving at the tail sliding MX5, Aulay felt a whiff of what it must be like to be Freak Johnston. He just managed to get his big head in beside LJ in the camper. They waited for the Toyota Land Cruiser to show up before heading for the hills. Their borrowed English couple's villa had Sky.

A sober Ricky was a smooth operator. His bruised and bloody face kept still yet portrayed an undercurrent of humility. He began by indicating the handcuffed Slicked Back and Shaven before pointing to Harvey. "My F.A. 'arvey Lefoy will fead a frefared sfafemen'."

Harvey shuffled the papers. "I'm speaking on be 'alf of Mr Temple." He coughed...

"I received my facial injuries during the capture of these two gentlemen, my employees. They planned and carried out the robbery at the Copacabana. They kidnapped me and dumped me in the boot of Mr MacKinnon's car."

Aulay had taken Ricky on a tour of Slicked Back and Shaven's gaff above the garage. Sacrificing his employees didn't give Ricky Temple any trouble. His highly paid personal security had been boozed up, watching porn, while Ricky's crotch lay soaked in brandy. Passing the handcuffed duo he let fly. Aulay waited until Ricky got several good

271

kicks in before dragging him off. Having the sacrificial duo bruised up, fitted Shaz's script.

"During my kidnapping I 'ave to admit to not seeing my assailants. A 'ood was placed over my 'ead. After my escape I took my people's word that Mr Mackinnon was the mastermind behind the plan. Mr MacKinnon has graciously accepted my sincerest apologies."

A nodding Banana appeared on camera.

"The shooting on Murcia Street was their..." Harvey pointed to Slicked Back and Shaven. "... attempt to kill myself, Mr MacKinnon and 'is associates, who were innocent decoys."

"I also understand that a second attempt was made on Mr MacKinnon's life. The car he was supposed to 'ave been travelling in, was blown off the coast road by 'eavy machinegun fire."

The time line for this was all wrong, but who'd know?

"Luckily for Mr MacKinnon, 'e'd told his limousine driver to take the night off."

Harvey indicated the weaponry lying beside the silver Audi.

"These are the guns used in the Murcia Street, and the coast road shootings. The Spanish authorities have been notified and are on their way. That is the end of my statement. Thank you."

Behind the clamour of questioning reporters, Chancer, Ricky and Harvey re-entered the villa. Shaz remained to pacify the rabble, giving yes and no answers until she too turned for the villa. Aulay smiled. Shaz was a natural.

Ricky's statement, written by Shaz, was ambiguous and teasing. The media went nuts. Over the next 24 hours, Sky interviewed anyone and everyone who could speak English.

They followed the Spanish news teams, translating their interviews with the locals. The media built the case to match the statement. The woman dragged from her car on Murcia Street identified Slicked Back as the culprit. A nice old couple from Renfrew, out for a stroll, put both Slicked Back and Shaven on Murcia Street with guns blazing. Two cycling students came forward. They were setting up their tent when a silver Audi parked up. Two men got out. They set up something on a tripod. They watched the shooters blast a big black car off the road, and over the cliff. They couldn't give an exact time. Both students spoke with Scottish accents.

When Aulay got off the Spanish plane, a text message asked him to go straight to The Bulls Security.

"Aulay Mackay, I bow to your superior knowledge in all things military," said Freak Johnston.

After the mutual back slapping, Freak sat down heavily. "There's a problem. The Russian wants his money back."

"Eh?"

"It seems the DSH is 70% owned by gangsters from the old east. Like all international conglomerates, there have been buy outs, amalgamations, takeovers."

"How much money we talking?"

"One hundred million."

Aulay whistled. As The Polmadie's insurance policy, against future attempts by the DSH to 'interfere' in Glasgow, Freak had lifted that amount from various DSH accounts.

"What's the script?" asked Aulay.

"A delegation will arrive to discuss the situation."

Freak glanced at a screen and flicked his mouse.

"You got a chess game going?"

"With quite a smart chap, want a look?"

Freak twirled the LCD round. He was in trouble. Both rooks were hemmed in.

"Take his queen," said Aulay.

"But that would..." Freak stopped and stayed quiet for a bit. "You are quite correct." He flicked the mouse. "We really must have a game sometime."

"So, this delegation..."

"Yes, a Mr Chevnenko is flying in."

"Alone?"

"I doubt it."

Swapping queens was the only way to play for a draw. Freak not seeing it gave Aulay a whiff of how deep the doodie was.

"When?"

"As soon as Chancer is released from Spanish custody."

Chancer was still helping the Spanish police with their enquiries.

"What's the plan?"

"The Polmadie will be going to the li-los."

"The what?"

Freak put his lazy smile on.

"You remember The Godfather. When the Five Families went to war? Well, times change, we don't go to the mattresses anymore."

Aulay would have laughed if he hadn't understood the strategy. Russian gangsters are notorious for shooting first and thinking later. The Polmadie were going into hiding. Deep deep doodie right enough.

"Can't you just give them their money back?"

"We offered, less commission and expenses, but it seems we have dishonoured this Mr Chevnenko. We've made him look a fool in the eyes of many."

The cult of 'face' in Russia is keen. You embarrass a Boris you need to be ready. Ask an Afghan.

"What bargaining chips do you have?"

"The DSH download. Their money trail from Afghanistan to West Africa and back to Europe. We have all of it."

"Why are you telling me this?"

Aulay helped on the Costa, job done. He was now a free agent.

"We need help."

"Explain."

"I want you to go to Mr Hector Chalmers. We need to negotiate."

Freak knew about him and Hector?

"When did you find out?" Aulay shifted in his seat.

"We always knew. Hector recommended you before you pulled that stunt with Jemima MacAskill."

"Christ." Aulay remembered the Banana's, 'The girl in the Greasy Spoon, she's important to me.' Aulay's temperature dropped.

Freak appeared relaxed as he flitted about on one of his keyboards. He looked up.

"It appears Ricky Temple was the DSH's front man. Apparently he's been going downhill for years. The Russian kept him in place to give the authorities someone to aim at."

Aulay stood up and paced the portakabin. Ricky Temple never did strike him as the dynamic chief gangster type and Slicked Back and Shaven were rank lazy bullies.

"The Costa show was a scam to flush out the real boss, this Chevnenko?"

"Seems so," said Freak. "We only understood the plan when the Russian made contact with us directly. I don't think Hector quite expected The Polmadie to be holding the DSH's purse strings."

Aulay kept pacing. "What does Hector want, the DSH download?"

"Yes. If we don't deliver he's promised to pull the pin."

Pin, not plug... explosive.

"What pin?"

Freak sat back, flicked the mouse and tapped a few keys.

"My opponent accepted the draw. Lunch?"

Chantelle and Marbella missed out. Aulay insisted on the Yadgar. Spanish fare is fine but the Scottish curry fire

276

burned. Over chicken chat with vindaloo sauce, Freak explained 'the pin'.

Hector had someone inside The Polmadie, a Capo, a witness to Mad Rab Smillie's death throes. If Freak didn't hand over the DSH download, Chancer and The Sim would go down for a very long time. Freak for a good amount of time, and the other silent witnesses, for a time. With everything else that Serious Crime had, The Polmadie would disintegrate and more people would go to jail.

Freak continued. "Hector offered us a deal. He'd bury the eye witness account and go along with Chancer's intention to de-criminalise The Polmadie, if we helped him snare the DSH."

Blackmail forced the Banana into Ricky Temple's lion's den, and Freak was at it again, de-criminalise and snare? Was he a budding writer of crime fiction, circa 1954?

Holding a bright red chicken wing, Freak said, "This tastes exceptional and... if the Russian learns that we gifted the DSH download to the authorities, everyone in the DSH's dossier, and their families, will be killed."

"The Russian said that?"

"Yes."

"Can he do it?"

"Not if you stop him."

Aulay wasn't getting it, and it showed.

"Hector's holding out. He won't pass on any information on this Chevnenko. What he looks like, how he travels and..." He looked at his watch. It gave away his stress level. "...time is of the essence."

Freak leaned forward. "Aulay... whatever Hector has on you, The Polmadie can do much better."

Sipping his sour lasse, Freak gave off the impression he threatened people all the time, twice before breakfast.

Aulay sank a chicken wing into the vindaloo sauce, up to his fingertips. It burned.

Back in the portakabin, Freak threw across a folder of photographs and newspaper cuttings. The pictures were of dead people, men, women, children, all shot and mutilated.

"From the Russian?"

Freak shook his head. "From Hector."

"To prove what? Mr Chevnenko doesn't negotiate, or take prisoners?"

Freak shrugged.

"I've researched the newspaper articles. Each one relates to either a flawed narcotic deal, bad debt or someone not too keen on outsiders muscling in."

So, Ricky Temple's 'franchise revolution' was the Russian's modus operandi. Shite, Aulay was delving into dodgy patter now.

"Time scale?"

"All in the last fifteen years. All mainland Europe."

The photographs were not pleasant. A family of nine had been eating outside, on what looked like a big veranda, with a beautiful view of some mountains. They died where they sat, from the matriarch to the toddler in a high chair. A couple were caught in-flagrante in the back seat of a Mercedes. He was still in position with her legs wrapped round his arse. A father and son, both wearing Barcelona football tops, lay beside a toppled over scooter, the boy looked about eight. There were lots more pictures. Aulay skimmed through the newspaper cuttings.

Aulay pulled his phone. He looked at Freak. "Where's your girlfriend?"

Freak hesitated.

"And Jemima MacAskill. She around?"

One of Freak's spark plugs must have broken.

"...and Shaz is on the Costa. It's the Russian's fuckin' back yard."

Freak lifted his phone. All eight cylinders running again.

In the newspaper articles, before the Russian orchestrated the main event, someone on the periphery died. Not as a threat, more a precursor. Good tactic. Makes everyone jumpy. Cool heads go out the window. Those closest to the Top Banana were most at risk.

Shaz answered after seven rings.

"Aulay, hold on a mo'... Gracias Senor... Sorry, Aulay, our drinks have just arrived. Howz you?"

Shaz stayed in Spain to 'facilitate' Chancer's 'helping the Spanish police with their enquiries'.

"Have you heard about the Russian?"

"What Russian?"

"Who's with you?"

"The Sim."

Wounded or not, The Sim was good. "Ask him."

Freak shook his head so Aulay already knew the answer. Shaz came back on the line.

"Sim doesn't know what you're talking about."

"There's a serious operator out to..." Aulay was on his regular phone, calling Shaz's regular phone... "Shaz, put The Sim on."

"Hi," said Sim, "there a problem?"

"Don't go back to your hotel. Can you get on line with Freak?"

"Tell Sim to go to chat room four," said Freak.

Aulay passed the message on.

"Ok, twenty minutes."

"Put Shaz back on."

"Shaz, do what The Sim tells you, no arguing, ok?"

279

A direct order? Shaz's weak point. "Why?"

"Remember Clatty Pat's?"

Shaz killed the call.

***

The old story went; in Cleopatra's night club, if you arrived without a weapon, the bouncers gave you one. Aulay, Shaz and their crowd loved it. At sixteen, they could act grown up and pretend to be whoever they wanted to be. In those days, Aulay and Shaz were known as The Couple.

"Who's goin' tonight?"

Tam the Bam, Fiona Two Fannies, Kenny Short Arse, the Smirnoff sisters and The Couple.

Thursday night was their night. Without the underage drinkers, the vast cavern of a night-club would only have a few sad souls scattered about, the insomniacs and those who crave more alcohol after pub shutting time. In Clatty Pat's, the last Thursday in the month was special. Nurses from the nearby training hospital got paid and vodka guzzling flocks would descend on the place between eleven and midnight. By sheer coincidence, the last Thursday in the month also happened to be 'Ugly Bastard' night. Lonely single blokes manned the nooks and crannies, ogling the gyrating students. Lone females walked safely through the city's parks on Ugly Bastard night. Even the flashers had to leave their raincoats in the cloakroom.

The only menace came from out of town all male groups. Salesmen in Glasgow for a conference or a trade show. On the lookout for a little action on an otherwise quiet Thursday. Tanked up on bonhomie, away from suburbia, the missus, the kids, they could step over the line. Too full of back slapping tequila shots to understand the consequences.

Shaz and Two Fannies moved together on the still threadbare dance floor. Darren from Shrewsbury approached

280

the girls, who dutifully turned and gyrated in his direction. All through Yazoo's 'Only You', a Shaz favourite, Darren from Shrewsbury tried his best, leaning in to chat. He ignored Two Fannies. Keeping her distance, Shaz gave noncommittal responses. Alison Moyet sang the last haunting line. Darren kept at it. He took Shaz's arm and led her over to his applauding pals. He placed a tall glass in her hand.

Something bothered Aulay. It wasn't jealousy. It was Darren. He looked wired, and not with the glory of getting the blonde bomb back to mix it with his mates. It was something more and, at sixteen, Aulay couldn't place it. Darren looked quite old, mid twenties. Tall, slim with the look of a runner or gymnast. He carried himself well, with confidence. How much was natural and how much down to alcohol, or other substances, Aulay couldn't be sure.

He watched Shaz take the drunken compliments from all and sundry. She'd had a few drinks and was in the zone, a place she was still exploring. A rave hit started up and talking became impossible. Shaz made her excuses. Darren kissed the back of her hand. She left her gaggle of admirers.

Sitting down, with glazed eyes and flushed cheeks, Shaz scooped up her drink. She gave Aulay the big smile. At sixteen, Shaz was all woman, think Britney Spears in her schoolgirl outfit.

Shaz often attracted adolescent males struggling with hormones, and life in general. When the odd one didn't take 'no' for an answer, Aulay would intervene. Darren was a man, and therefore... what?

"I've got a feeling about that guy."

"He's Darren," said Shaz, "from Shrewsbury. He's doing some show at the SECC. Said he'd put a bet on with his mates that he could get me back for a drink, pleaded with me. So I did, what's the harm?"

Brandy and ginger ale flooded Shaz's preening receptors. How could Aulay explain without sounding like a jealous wanker?

"He looks... wired..."

"Aulay, we're here for a good time, come on..." Shaz stood and led him to the dance floor.

Later, on the way to the gents, Aulay spotted Darren's crowd downing little glasses on fire. Sambucas?

The big venue filled up. Nurses in all shapes and sizes began doing what they do, flirting, dancing, shouting above the loud music. The temperature rose. Ugly Bastards crept from their lairs for a closer look.

Aulay had all but forgotten Darren from Shrewsbury until the guy approached their table. He tapped Shaz on the shoulder.

"Your Royal Highness, may I have this dance?"

"Why, certainly," said Shaz who quickly downed the last of her drink.

Shaz took Darren's hand and sashayed to the dance floor. A Gangsta Rapper track began... 'Fuck them bitches' blared from the PA system.

Aulay looked at Darren from Shrewsbury's group. They were expectant. Aulay started for the dance floor signalling everyone at his table to follow. He was too late. Darren had one arm round Shaz, gripping her left arm at the elbow, pinning her right arm to her side. His other hand was fumbling about under her short skirt. Shaz's screams went unheard in the mayhem.

Darren had his back to Aulay, so dropping him was a doddle. His right boot crashed into Darren's scrotum. The man collapsed.

"Two Fannies," shouted Aulay, "you and the Smirnoff Sisters get Shaz out of here."

Tam the Bam, Short Arse and Aulay turned to face Darren from Shrewsbury's crowd as they surged forward. They didn't have any knives, so they stopped. Aulay's crew had one each, long slim and shiny. Aulay had never used a knife in anger, but, it was part of the uniform back then.

Glasgow bouncers are good. They can smell a stramash through a concrete wall and came charging into the space, barrelling revellers out of the way. They concentrated on the writhing Darren and his phalanx of angry suits. Aulay and his crew slipped through the peering crowd.

Aulay met Darren from Shrewsbury at the SECC the next morning.

"So," Aulay said, "give me the pitch then."

Darren worked the Grangemount stand in Hall 2 of the Scottish Caravan and Camping Show. Grangemount manufacture the high end of the mobile home market. Their entry level camper comes in at £90,000.

"Are your parents with you, Sir?" Darren asked Aulay through late night redeye.

"No, they're dead, left me a bundle. I really fancy one of these." Aulay pointed at a six berth Horizon Seeker.

Darren wasn't moving as smoothly as the night before. He looked Aulay over and his salesman's sense kicked in. Aulay wore a Nike beanie hat, Joss's Italian sleeks, a ridiculously expensive shirt, designer jeans and the Rolex.

Aulay had phoned Uncle Eddie that morning.

"You want to hook a salesman, mention your loaded first. Back it up with expensive clobber and he'll bite your hand off."

The Horizon Seeker wasn't a camper, it was a Winnebago. During the tour, they got chatting. Darren played squash at county level, had two kids and supported Arsenal. After half an hour, Darren invited him into the Grangemount's V.I.P. room. "To discuss the details."

The V.I.P. room had glass fronted fridges stacked with an array of German lagers and white wine. Two leather sofas opposed each other across a marble coffee table. Aulay noticed the heavy looking cut-glass ashtray. An espresso machine gurgled.

Aulay declined coffee, beer and wine. "I'll have an Irn Bru, please."

The Grangemount hostess frowned. "I'm sorry, sir. We have Coke, Fanta and Seven-Up."

Aulay frowned in turn.

"If you don't mind waiting, Mr Muir. I'm sure Linda can get you some... eh, Irn Bru."

Linda got the message. She left with a weary smile.

Darren produced the paperwork. Aulay took out a packet of Dunhill's.

Aulay bumped into Linda on his way out of the VIP booth, she looked surprised.

"Darren's nipped off to the toilet. When he gets back, tell him I'll meet him here at two."

"Do you want this?"

She held out a tin of the hangover cure.

"Thanks, Linda."

Short Arse waited in the Gents with Aulay's 'day' clothes. Back in denim jacket, jeans and trainers, Aulay carefully wrapped Joss's sleeks in their protective sheepskin. He finished the Irn Bru then dumped it, and the Dunhills, in a bin. They got the bus home. He'd spent every penny he had on his 'disguise'. The fake Rolex alone cost him £26.

Heavy glass ashtrays make good weapons. Darren from Shrewsbury took one to the base of the skull. Next, his right hand, the one he'd put up Shaz's skirt, would never hold a squash racket again. Even a fork would be a struggle. After squeezing Darren's limp body into the cupboard under the bar, Aulay slipped a CD of assorted gangsta rapper female abuse tracks, he'd spent most of the night on his PC putting the collection together, into the salesman's suit pocket.

***

During the time it took The Sim to get to an internet cafe on the Costa, Freak started another chess game. As Aulay paced the portakabin he pondered, 'whatever Hector has on you, The Polmadie can do much better.'

In the army, he'd been a pawn at the whim and favour of people he didn't know. Everyone joked about it. Back then, he had nothing to look forward to.

Something pinged, one of Freak's PCs. The Sim had logged in. Freak typed Aulay's instructions.

"Hire a car with cash. Drive to the channel using A roads. If they need to, stay in cash only B&Bs, and do it now."

Freak looked up from his screen. "Shaz only has a bikini and a towel."

"Tough shite."

"... and what about Chancer, the Sim's asking?"

"Get Shaz onto Senor Gallardo. When the Banana's released from custody, he'll need protection until he gets on the plane."

Aulay paced the floor. Was he over reacting? It was 24 hours since the media scrum at Ricky Temple's. Too soon for the DSH to tool up a team and hit Glasgow... but Spain?

With Shaz organised, Aulay stayed in operational mode. "Explain the li-los."

"I stay here and keep communications open."

The Bulls Security Yard had four metre high walls topped with razor wire. Ramming the wrought iron gate with a tank might work.

"Each li-lo has a Capo with up to four men." continued Freak. "They stay in select accommodation and wait for instructions."

"Select?"

"Furnished flats rented from various letting agents."

"Armed?"

"Not particularly. A few shotguns and small calibre hand guns mostly."

"Can you get more?"

Freak shook his head. Aulay stabbed his phone.

"Rainman, its Red Five. I need lollipops and a dozen bean tins in Glasgow."

Rainman agreed to drive a load of weaponry up from London, along with twelve two-way radios.

Aulay dialled another number. "LJ," he said, "the forecast isn't good."

LJ would be on the next plane. Aulay paced some more.

"Go to the li-los now," he told Freak. "All Capos, and anyone else mentioned in the DSH dossier, need to get their families out of the city. The Polmadie's closed."

Freak nodded and walked through to the next portakabin.

How did this happen? Aulay was now in charge of Glasgow's biggest drug gang. Under duress, he reminded himself. He brooded. The Russian had names, addresses, all kinds of shite, and Hector was keeping quiet, why?

Freak reappeared. "What now?"

"I need to talk to the Drum and Buddies Bananas. Now would be good."

Freak reached for his phone.

Aulay's mobile rang. He struggled. It wasn't a good time.

Earlier, he'd been stir frying a tinned Thai concoction for Shaz. The Sim and Shaz hadn't stopped. Sharing the driving, they'd made it back to Glasgow in less than a day.

During the gastronomic finale, Aulay managed to pour boiling fat into the sensitive crevice between his pinkie and ring finger. The pain was excruciating. No amount of leaping about did any good. His ardent libido, usurped by his inability to wield a wok, petered out. Debauchery cancelled, and polite chit chat a no no, the evening collapsed. Shaz understood her flat was out of bounds. She went to a hotel.

After finishing the celebratory bottle of Moet, Aulay attempted sleep by keeping his throbbing hand submersed in a jug of water. An endeavour fraught with trial, error and damp sheets. After three jugs and four large whiskies, to dull the pain, he lay insecurely in the land of nod when the pink panther sounded.

Aulay reached for the bedside lamp. The cold damp patch spread and his scalded hand returned to centre stage. His stomach tilted. The evening's mix of champagne and whisky found no scaffold to cling to. He choked, then gagged as the rancid blend of alcohol breached his throat's defences. The first blast filled the tiny sink. Thrusting two fingers down through the carrot filled shambles, Aulay forced the crud down the plug-hole before his guts reloaded. He just made it.

It was then he decided he needed a bigger place. Somewhere without a shared toilet.

Head pounding to the mixed beat of burnt flesh and vomit, he was reminded why he was awake, his mobile trilled to the sound of a received text.

'Call me.' It was Shaz. It was 6.30am. He called back.

"Hi, Shaz."

"Ricky Temple's dead. Shot in his car outside the Copacabana,"

Aulay's various ailments withdrew behind the balm of the Russian's precursor.

"Where's the Banana?"

"In the air. Chancer and Ricky were released at the same time... and Aulay?"

"Aye,"

"Best of luck with Hector."

"Thanks... and Shaz?"

"What?"

"You keep out of sight... and another thing. They're still full."

"I'll ease your suffering when you stop crying like a baby."

He found Freak in chat room 7. Three Polmadie Capos were already at Glasgow airport to meet the Banana. Aulay went back to bed and tried to sleep. He failed.

On his way to Hector's house, the pink panther sounded.

"They arrested Chancer at the airport," said Freak.

"Christ. For what?"

"Mad Rab's murder and... Dourface has disappeared."

Hector's pin.

"Where are they holding the Banana?"

"Cardonald."

"Does Shaz know?"

"Yes. She's heading there now."

Shaz would be safe. Cardonald police station on Paisley Road West looked like the Alamo. It would hold out longer than Davy Crocket.

Aulay parked the Daewoo in Hector's driveway.

"Aulay, please, come in." Hector smiled. "Drink?"

It was 9am.

"Stella, if you have some." A hair of the dog might work. Aulay sat in a big leather couch.

"I have Grolsch. Will that do?"

"Aye, fine." Needs must.

After passing over a cold bottle, Hector splashed a smattering of malt into a tumbler and sat. Aulay had a strategy for this meeting. Ask questions until he ran out. He thought he knew the answer to question one, but...

"The Polmadie knew I was on your payroll?"

"Both parties needed to assess your capabilities."

"I thought I'd passed muster with your people?"

"Indeed, in a war zone. This is civilian territory, in the UK. I wanted to see how you operated. Your methods proved to be unorthodox. The hostage situation in London, for instance, very well executed. The Polmadie were particularly impressed with your penetration of their Depot systems through, what was it, The Strathbungo Cellists?"

It took Hector twenty minutes to lay out the drift of his overall plan. Yes, Ricky Temple was only the front man. Yes, luring Chevnenko out of his lair was the main objective. Yes, The Polmadie had been too smart on the Costa. Yes, he believed Chevnenko was now on his way to Glasgow.

"You know, Aulay. I had three teams in Spain waiting for Chevnenko to peek over the parapet. Cost a bloody fortune."

"Teams?"

"We want Chevnenko pretty badly."

"At any price?"

Hector had the good grace to cough.

"Who is this Russian anyway?"

290

"Yuri Chevnenko, old Russian mafia. After the demise of the USSR, he expanded."

Hector rubbed his gammy leg. Aulay sensed a chink. "You got a personal beef with him?"

"Chevnenko killed my wife and daughter."

"How?"

"Car bomb. My wife decided to drive. She turned the ignition before I got in."

That explained the limp.

"When was this?"

"In '98."

"Why won't you give The Polmadie what you have on Chevnenko?"

There should have been a little respite, to remember the dead, but Aulay wasn't in the mood, and the Grolsch wasn't too bad.

"I've given them all they need to know."

"How so?"

"The photographs and newspaper articles."

That information was enough to make The Polmadie go to the li-los, nothing to help counter any moves Chevnenko might make. Aulay put The Polmadie's only bargaining chip on the table.

"The Costa download. How badly do you want it?"

Hector shrugged.

"We'll be able to prosecute a few bankers, and government officials in faraway places, in time. The DSH are already re-organising. Within a day or two, the Costa download will be old facts."

This was about Chevnenko. It was personal. Aulay was running out of questions.

"What do you have on Dourface Smillie?"

"His car meandered all over the road. Traffic did a stop and search. Dourface was high, and they found two kilos of cocaine in the glove box."

"Dourface is a three time loser," Hector continued. "He'd go down for a very long time... he talked."

"Why arrest Chancer now?"

Aulay couldn't figure it. Hector's six month old 'pin' could have been pulled at any time.

"The Banana is a killer."

"So are you."

An eyebrow rose.

"A Spanish grocer, a chauffeur and now Ricky Temple."

The list of the dead didn't produce much of a ripple.

"Yuri Chevnenko doesn't like failures," said Hector. "Ricky was living on borrowed time. His drinking-"

"What's the real reason for Chancer's arrest?"

Hector took a swig of whisky before answering.

"Is Chancer MacKinnon a match for Chevnenko?"

"Aye, in a poker game."

"Up against Russian Mafia wet-teams?"

Aulay kept quiet.

"The Top Banana was smart enough to know he needed you on foreign soil. Here, in Glasgow, he'd think he had the advantage. I couldn't let that happen, not with Chevnenko. I need you to run The Polmadie."

The dice had rolled for Chancer MacKinnon. What about Aulay? Decision time. He could walk away. Where to? Staying in Glasgow wouldn't be an option. Running out on a Top Banana reduces your chances of getting a pension. Getting out of the UK would be a doddle. The UK Border Agency budget is spent stopping people getting in. Would Shaz come with him?

"It's all working out for you, Hector?"

An edge of a smile reached one side of the auld bastard's mouth. Something still niggled. The Russian obsession with 'face' stretched beyond what was on the table.

"Why doesn't the Russian take his money and go home?"

"Chevnenko is coming after me."

Aulay sat forward. This should be good.

"I nearly got him in '2003 and again in 2008."

Hector went to the drinks cabinet. He topped up his tumbler with another splash of malt. As the bottle of Jura returned to the shelf, Aulay couldn't help feeling a pang of guilt. It was The Order of the Blootered Knights of Jura that got him into this bollocks.

Aulay accepted another Grolsch. "How 'nearly' did you get him?"

"He leads a charmed life does Yuri Chevnenko. Unfortunately we blew up his family, all of them."

"Jesus."

Hector leaned forward. "We had a man on the inside, in the Balkans. He made a mistake and the RAF blew up the wrong house, the mansion. Chevnenko lived alone, in the gate house. He liked to present himself as one of the staff, a chauffeur."

An old ploy but a good one.

"It took a year for the dust to settle. The official enquiry concluded; no more wet operations, unless sanctioned by the very top."

"So you decided to use civilians?" Aulay missed out 'expendable'.

Hector shrugged. "The current DSH dossier has me at The Polmadie's top table. Chevnenko knows I'm behind the Costa operation, my regular meetings with The Polmadie's lawyer for instance..."

Aulay had been right; Shaz had been sunbathing in deep shite. His hackles rose.

Hector sensed it. "Sharon was never in danger. I had a team round her the whole time."

Aye, thought Aulay. Watchers, whose objective was to pinpoint Chevnenko, not protect Shaz.

"What about the no wet-ops clause?"

"We had two very competent Spanish wet-teams in the vicinity. They want Chevnenko as badly as we do."

Hector had it all covered. What were a few civilian casualties when the prize was El Bandido Numero Uno. Aulay ran out of questions.

Hector reeled him in. "Ignore Ricky Temple's execution. Chevnenko will select a precursor closer to home, much closer."

"If a hair on Shaz Curren's head is put out of place..." It's the only place she had any hair. Why did sex rear its... "... I'll come for you, Hector."

Hector remained unruffled. Good word, unruffled; a load of ruffles fall from the sky, and miss their target. Aulay threw up another load.

"With Chevnenko, if it gets tight, I'll need you to show yourself."

"Of course."

Again, the ruffles floated harmlessly to the floor.

Aulay stood. At the patio doors he spotted the fancy garden furniture and, sure enough, it wasn't B&Q. It didn't take much working out. Hector wanted Chevnenko dead.

"If I do this for you, get the Russian. Are we clear? No more caveats?"

"Yes," said Hector, "but I can't protect you if it goes badly."

Aulay looked at the scheming auld bastard. The only 'official' action would be the mopping up after two criminal gangs battle it out.

They batted a few other details around. Chevnenko's technique, his weaponry and the precursor.

"Am I in any DSH dossier updates?"

"No."

No hesitation.

"Not even after my walk on part on Sky News?"

"No one spotted it, and anyway, you blew the DSH and Ricky Temple out of the water before the analysts got that far."

Analysts? A quiet reference to the manpower Hector had at his disposal. So, Aulay thought, as well as being 'acting' Top Banana, he was now an 'unofficial' state executioner.

"How long have I got?"

"I'm moving out of here," Hector said looking around the room, "after this meeting."

If a Daily Snot seller, and a spaced out Ugly Grant, could find Hector, Chevnenko wouldn't have much trouble.

"Where will you be?"

"Around."

At the door, Aulay handed him Shaz's mobile number. Hector recognised it but said nothing.

"I need to know who phoned that number last Tuesday. The same person may have sent two pictures to the same phone."

Hector pocketed the card. "Ok."

Another wee black bag that didn't weigh much. Aulay put it on the passenger seat of the Daewoo and made for the Pennant. The big boozer was now Freak's HQ, or was it Aulay's HQ?

Everything Hector had on Chevnenko, everything he thought Aulay needed, was in the wee black bag. Peering out of the twenty year old photograph, Colonel Yuri Chevnenko looked like your typical cold war warrior with big eyebrows and a face flushed with vodka or idealism. If he hadn't expanded into the drug business, the Russian would have made a decent living as a 'heavy' in Hollywood.

According to Hector, there would be two, possibly three Russian wet-teams on their way to Glasgow. Each ran independently under the watchful eye of a 'vista', usually a van, a big one, kitted out with radios and satellite up links among a plethora of other high tech kit. Chevnenko liked to be close to a kill.

Aulay whistled as he drove along, Oh diddle dee dee, a gangster's life for me.

In the Pennant's car park Aulay admired the recently installed, 'Closed for Refurbishment' sign over the street level door.

His pay-as-you-go trilled. It was Hector.

"Two calls from a phone belonging to one, DI McCaw. Miss Curren also received two files from McCaw's IP address."

That was quick.

"Blackmail is illegal, isn't it?" asked Aulay.

"If you have the evidence."

He did. Shaz recorded the second conversation with McCaw. A technical bod, for voice analysis, would be needed to prove the speaker was indeed the good DI. No big deal.

"McCaw's one of your lot."

"Yes," said Hector.

"The DI blackmailing Shaz. It got anything to do with the current situation?"

"No, but if you want me to-"

"Leave McCaw to me."

Aulay hung up and dragged his mind away from what might be in the McCaw pictures. Not something to dwell on, intimate moments between your girlfriend and her ex. A dishevelled Kenny Finlayson still had a walk-on part in Aulay's dreams, a small role. He wanted to keep it that way.

The Polmadie Capos mingled in the Pennant's function suite, all itching and anxious. Their Top Banana was in custody. Their part in Mad Rab's murder would soon be on public record along with whatever else Dourface Smillie could hang them with. The general hubbub died when Aulay walked in.

The Sim limped over, crutch swinging. "Hi, Aulay, howz you?"

"No' bad, Sim, you?"

They shook hands. Freak Johnston joined them. A general backslapping session began. To strengthen Aulay's position with the 'boyz'? It worked. Aulay appreciated the gesture.

"Anyone seen Chancer?" he asked The Sim.

"Naw, they wouldn't let me in. Don't you worry about the Banana."

"What about Dourface?"

The Sim gripped his arm. "Don't you go worrying about Dourface either, OK?"

"You ready?" asked Freak.

"In a minute," said Aulay. "Can you doctor a photo? It's on here."

He gave Freak a memory stick and told him what was needed.

"Sure," said Freak, "I'll work on it as you entertain the troops."

Freak did the introductions.

"Gentlemen," he said. "You know what Aulay achieved during Chancer's recent trip to the Costa. He's here now to organise The Polmadie for what we know is coming. Aulay..." The ever confident sounding Freak left him there.

Aulay needed The Polmadie to man the barricades against Chevnenko's wet-teams, not looking over their shoulders for the long arm of plod. How to gee them up?

Shaz saved him. All eyes followed her entrance. Her bodyguards, Rainman and LJ, remained at the door.

"Hello boyz." She smiled her big hello smile. "FB, any chance of a gin 'n' slim?"

"Sure, Shaz." FB turned sideways to squeeze in behind the bar.

Aulay got a peck on the cheek and a whispered, "Howz your pinkie?"

Shaz removed a laptop, notepad and pen from her shoulder bag, placing them neatly on a table. For someone who'd travelled nearly two thousand miles and slept intermittently during the last forty eight hours, Shaz looked morning fresh. A blue tailored suit, straight from the drycleaner's poly bag, hair an organised shambles, Shaz moved with a hip swaying confidence that kick started the Capo 'gee up' thing Aulay'd been striving for. Her drink arrived. She put her salacious grin on.

"I know you boyz don't drink..." Raising the glass, she downed the gin in one. "...on the job..." The last of the gloom evaporated. "... but, I'm not strictly in the gang."

To roars of approval, Shaz sat down, put her hand to her chin, gazed at Aulay and graciously gave him the floor.

Reaching into the back pocket of his jeans, Aulay pulled out the makings. A whoop went up as the smokers joined him. The Pennant's basement soon stank like a boozer used to.

Aulay introduced Rainman and LJ. A few Capos recognised Rainman from the DSH takeover bid. Aulay explained Rainman's 'innocence' before highlighting his expertise. There were a few appreciative nods and ahs. It's good procedure to begin outlining a mission with positives. LJ and Rainman were his only two. Now. How to explain The Polmadie's predicament?

"Imagine we are the Taliban," he said to a few puzzled looks. "We blend in; we know the terrain, and the locals are friendly."

The Capos started to get it.

"The DSH are the British army. They don't speak the lingo, not in the right accent anyway. They drive on the wrong side of the road and have no idea about local customs. They'll stand out like nuns at the Hajj."

He carried on, going over the logistics, the communications and The Plan.

"We're going to play dead. Everything closes, the boozers, the Fat Controller... everything. The DSH dossier is comprehensive, they can pick us off."

Us? Aulay was getting into this Polmadie thing.

"The DSH want their money back and to make The Polmadie pay for recent events. They also want... a Mr Hector Chalmers."

A few eyebrows rose.

"The money is theirs, they just need to take it. With Mr Chalmers, it's personal. The DSH and Hector go back a long way."

More detail on Hector? No point and no time.

"As for The Polmadie, we're going to disappear into our mountain vastness, on our li-los, and wait it out."

This met with a few grumbles as testosterone bubbled up. Aulay lifted the photographs of the Russian's previous kills and passed them out. He waited a few minutes to let them sink in.

"The DSH kill people for fun."

With no more grumbling, he distributed copies of Chevnenko's picture.

"I want these all over the city, bus stops, the underground, taxi ranks, pub doors. Anywhere people meet or walk by. Freak is getting 50,000 copies made as we speak. This is the guy we want. Get him and this stops."

Cobbling together a wanted poster hadn't taken Freak long. Chevnenko's face now rose above, 'Seen this man? Call free phone 0800400400 - £100,000 reward for a sighting leading to apprehension.'

The 0800 number was The Bulls Security's business enquiry number, now updated to 8 lines. Bulls' staff would be manning the phones on a 24 hour rota.

Aulay kept the best to last. He lifted the lid on the two strong boxes sitting in the middle of the floor. Rainman's weaponry shone. A big cheer went up.

LJ and Rainman took over. The assembly split up into groups for big gun lessons.

Shaz coughed as she made for the corridor leading to the toilets. Gents to the right, Ladies to the left. Shaz wasn't in either. A manicured finger beckoned Aulay from the disabled. He slid the bolt behind him.

"Have you stopped crying like a baby, then?"

Shaz tugged at the zip of her wool skirt to reveal Aulay's favourite. Stockings, suspenders and nothing else. They went at it like hammer drills. Pub toilet floors are best avoided so the handles, levers and other fittings, to help the physically challenged, aided rather than abetted their manic manoeuvres. It didn't take long to exhaust themselves.

A load lighter, and relaxed, the immediate future took a back seat.

"Shaz babe," he said firing up the best post-coital cigarette in an age, "how you doing?"

Shaz checked her flushed cheeks in the mirror. "How soon before they fill up again?"

Aulay'd searched the globe for seven years. There wasn't another Shaz out there. A knock at the door.

"In a minute."

"Aulay, that you?"

It was The Sim.

"Aye."

"The Bulls have been hit."

The Bulls' yard was a shambles with debris scattered over a wide area. Without a gas main, the portakabins and storage hangers were heated by propane gas. The blue propane tank used to be located, as per Health & Safety, in open ground.

The ambulances didn't have any patients. The Bulls' staff had relocated to a tenement flat somewhere in Govan, their phone lines redirected. When Aulay ordered The Polmadie shut down, he meant all of it.

Mingling with the crowd behind the police cordon, Aulay caught a feint whiff of rocket fuel. Modern rocket launchers are light, mobile and laser guided. You don't toss rockets over a four metre high wall. Aulay pointed to the high rise on the Gorbals Road.

"Start on the ninth floor," he told Clockface, "and follow the smell."

Clockface returned with grim news. On the fourteenth floor, a couple in their sixties, a Mr and Mrs Hoy, sat in their armchairs next to tea and scones laid out for visitors. Their throats had been cut.

"Good technique," said Aulay, "quick and quiet."

"No' quite," said Clockface. "There's blood everywhere, splattered up the walls. Mr Hoy's hands are tied to his chair and Mrs Hoy..."

Aulay called Freak. "Is anyone related to a Mr and Mrs Hoy, fourteenth floor Gorbals Road high rise, call me back."

He looked at Clockface. "Show me."

Aulay was no CSI guy but the scenario looked obvious enough. Mr Hoy watched them butcher his wife before they slit his throat. Aulay's phone rang. He was looking at the precursor. Mr and Mrs Hoy were Chancer MacKinnon's grandparents.

Next morning, two things happened. Glaswegians woke to find Yuri Chevnenko's face on every wall, window, railing and Dourface Smillie died on his way to morning ablutions.

Before going down for murder, Steve 'Sweeney Boy' Jackson drove an ancient Ford Granada, owned a copy of every episode of his favourite TV show and forced himself to drink whisky. His wife called him 'Guv'.

The murder weapon, a sharp blade fashioned by tearing a plastic bottle into strips then binding them together, punctured Dourface's heart. The blade stayed where it was as Dourface slumped to the floor. The corridor happened to be the only location in the prison with a broken CCTV camera and, strangely, no prison officer was in attendance.

In Barlinnie Jail, known as the Bar L, most inmates were surprised by the speed of events. Some had drooled over the prospect of a ritual mutilation; Dourface hanging by his thumbs, getting his balls stuffed into his mouth before having his eyes drilled out. Dourface didn't get caught stealing a woman's knickers from a clothes line, he'd squealed on his Top Banana, the deepest doodiest betrayal of all.

Dourface should never have been in the Bar L. His lawyer kicked up a stink until a stranger called his office to let him know that his seven year old daughter looked pretty in her school uniform, in the playground...

A later enquiry discovered a paper trail leading nowhere. The unfortunate incident was put down to one of those things that happen in big organisations. In another odd coincidence, Dourface's lawyer misplaced his notes containing the gist of Dourface's plea bargain.

Sweeney Boy Jackson, in for life, meaning life, got his reward. His wife and two children received a substantial sum and moved to Spain, where Sweeney Boy hoped his two sons would get a better start in life than he did.

On hearing the news of Dourface's demise, Shaz went into overdrive, barging past the head of Serious Crime to the chief Constable. Her client should be released. There are no charges to answer. No witnesses, well, none the police could produce. On her tour of righteous indignation, Aulay drove her about with Rainman or LJ in the back. They kept changing vehicles, arriving in one, leaving in another. By 3 o'clock, they had Chancer MacKinnon, and drove to the Pennant.

The Banana glanced at Aulay as The Sim and Freak brought him up to date. His look gave nothing away, as if Aulay had followed The Polmadie's Deep Shite Manual to the letter. When they got to the explosion at the Bulls, Chancer's face darkened. Even Aulay's robust constitution cooled a couple of degrees. The Banana's head bowed as he took in the circumstances of his grandparent's ugly death.

"Where's Hector?" he said. "I want to see him."

Aulay called Hector's number. No reply. He left a message.

"Get me a drink, Sim," said Chancer. "Freak, use all your channels. Tell everyone I'm out. I want the world to know."

The Sim hobbled off and Freak headed for his computers. Shaz took the hint and made for the Ladies.

Chancer sat up. "You're the expert, Aulay." It was a question.

"We need to get lucky."

"From where I sit, there are two ways out of this," said Chancer. "If we can't get this fucker Chevnenko before he gets us, we give him Hector."

We? Did Chancer assume Aulay was against Hector? The scheming old bastard was the only person between Aulay and years rubbing more than his shoulders with inmates in Jailhouse Rock & Rape, Baghdad.

Aulay stalled.

Chancer's gaze fell on the returning Shaz. He held it for a second too long. Aulay got the message. Shaz was now a pawn in the Banana's game.

Chancer took The Sim's offered can of coke and downed a good half of it.

"Sim," he said, "if this place is closed for refurb, why's the car park full?"

The titular head of Chancer's security, The Sim turned on his heel as best he could. Aulay'd missed it too. Like Suzie Wong's house phone, it's the details. He moved the Daewoo to a side street.

Aulay returned and Chancer ushered him to a seat at the top table. His advice was sought and offered on an equal footing. He accepted an Irn Bru when The Sim offered. There were lager taps on the bar but, hey ho.

The pink panther sounded. It was Hector.

"Chancer would like to meet up."

"Where and when?"

Aulay looked at Chancer. "Where and when?"

"Here and now."

"The Pennant, on Butterbiggins Road. Park somewhere else and arrive on foot."

"Fifteen minutes." Hector hung up.

Aulay wondered why Hector would agree to a meeting. His 'pin' had been blown away.

"How many we got local," Chancer asked The Sim.

"Aulay positioned two li-los across the road and one upstairs. There are four more within half a mile, in cars. There's a fall back, Aulay calls it Recovery, the old Baptist church on Queens Park Drive."

"Ok," said Chancer, "tell the local li-los we're expecting a visitor, single male, anything funny, they scream the place down."

The Sim got up, grabbed his two-way and hobbled off.

Something bothered Aulay. Mr and Mrs Hoy were not in the DSH's dossier and only the Sim had known the couple were Chancer's grandparents. During Aulay's time, if a rocket launch site had occupants, the British army tied them up, honest. To torture, mutilate and murder? It was no fluke. They were missing something.

Aulay quizzed Chancer.

"My Grandda' kicked me out of the house when I joined The Polmadie. I haven't spoken to Grandda' Hoy since I was seventeen."

"What about your granny?"

"Och aye. I'd sneak in to see her when Grandda' was away."

"At Gorbals Road?"

"Aye."

Aulay remembered the cliff face at Ricky Temple's. Chancer acknowledged his raised eyebrow.

"Granny would have all the curtain's shut. When my mum went a needle too far, they lived in a ground floor tenement on Polmadie Road. When it met the bulldozers, they moved to the high rise."

Shaz looked puzzled by, 'have all the curtain's shut' but didn't say anything.

"You visit in the last wee while?"

Chancer caught on. "Since I had the polis up my arse? No."

Aulay went back a bit.

"What did you mean 'when your Grandda' was away?' You mean when he was out?"

"No, Grandda' was in the merchant navy. Retired last year. He wasn't about much."

A dead end.

"You know the funniest thing?" said Chancer. "My Grandda's pals called him 'Landa'."

The Banana burst out laughing, good, therapeutic guffaws. Freak and Shaz joined in and soon, all three were in pain, incapable of explaining the joke. A frustrated Aulay backtracked...

Merchant Navy – Landa – Hoy. The returning Sim found the top echelons of the Polmadie in hysterics.

Hearty laughter pulls different triggers. Chancer stopped.

"Freak, I want the name of everyone who lives at the Gorbals Road high rise. Include the streets around the place."

Freak called Bandit. He was in The Polmadie's Depot, safeguarding the Costa download and bouncing, or was it mirroring, Freak's PC's. Bandit could step in if anything happened to the Consigliore. Freak sent his requirements, told him he needed it yesterday, and hung up.

"What's your thinking?" Aulay asked Chancer.

"In the dim and distant, someone saw me visit my granny."

The Sim showed Chancer a gun, a small automatic. He gave the Banana a quick lesson, how to remove the safety etc. Aulay patted his .45s.

They waited for Hector in silence.

Sporting a tweed sports jacket and pressed grey flannels, Hector twirled his cane as he crossed the Pennant's small dance floor.

"The usual suspects," he said.

Hector sat placing one leg over the other. "That was smooth, Chancer, the move on Dourface. You guys are good."

Chancer shrugged.

"I assume," said Hector, "you want me to offer myself up as bait?" He flicked an invisible piece of fluff from his left knee. "I already have."

Aulay's chair crashed to the floor. Pulling a .45 with one hand, and a two-way with the other, he faced Hector. "Here... at the Pennant?"

Hector nodded.

Aulay barked at the two-way.

[All eyes open; Expect trouble]

He looked at Freak. "Get the li-los on the street, all of them, form the secondary perimeter, now."

After getting the nod from Chancer, Freak hit the keyboard. Aulay sighed. Having his instructions vetted by a third party would be a pain.

"Shaz, you go with-"

"No," said Chancer. "She stays."

The barrel of Aulay's .45 rested between the Banana's eyes.

"Wait." It was The Sim.

Aulay had never given The Sim the smarts he deserved. The Sim's gun wasn't pointing at Aulay. It pointed at Shaz.

Stalemate.

Shaz stood up, "I-"

"Sharon," said Hector, "please sit down."

She looked at Aulay and got nothing. He was busy staring into the black eyes of the Banana. She sat down.

Aulay's two-way squawked. It was Rainman.

[Red Five; Left hand drive Fiat Ducato van; German plates; Parked opposite HQ; One driver; Serious looking]

[Rainman; Assume hostile; Prepare to contain and... Keep me posted]

Rainman and LJ would have cars ready to block the van if it tried to move and, if they remembered their unit's codes, [Keep me posted] told them, 'Their chief was in deep shite'.

The Banana's eyes didn't move. A trickle of seat dripped from an eyebrow.

"Freak," said Aulay, "tell the li-los. If another van approaches the Secondary Perimeter-"

"A Fiat Ducato?"

"For fuck sake, Freak. It's no' a corporate fleet. Any fuckin' van, or a car with four occupants within a mile of here, is to be stopped and searched, OK?"

Freak hit the keyboards. All The Polmadie Capos had smart phones. Instructions whizzed through the ether as SMS. The Rainman supplied two-way radios were in the hands of the li-los round the Pennant.

Time dragged. What did Ugly Grant complain of? A heavy gun? Aulay began to understand his dilemma. "Can we all sit down."

Chancer sat. Aulay's Glock never left his skin. The Sim remained standing, but his arms were like Popeye's.

"Aulay." It was Hector. "A wet-team would try and blend in. Ask about the antennas?"

Shite, he was right. wet-teams were light, mobile and they'd hire something right hand drive, from Hertz. Before Aulay got his two-way up, Rainman came back.

[Red Five; The Fiat van; Domed roof; Aerials]

The Ducato van wasn't a wet-team. It was Chevnenko's vista.

[Rainman; Take out the van; Take out-]

You can hear a Russian made RPG-29 rocket from a long way off. The fuckers go quick though. There's less than a second to get your shite together before it strikes. Aulay multi tasked. He dropped the Glock, screamed, "GET DOWN" and crashed into Shaz.

The Pennant exploded.

The first missile streaked along the Butterbiggins Road and slipped in through the lobby. The two hundred year old Pennant was made of stern stuff. It took another two rockets before the old girl gave up the ghost and imploded.

Location, location, location. It's what saved them. At street level, the two storey structure made a big target. Behind the big boozer, the land fell away. The basement remained upright.

When the mayhem stopped, mayhem started on Aulay's two-way. He switched it off.

Shaz was out cold and struggling, which gave Aulay a few tremors in the immediate aftermath when pitch black and concussed eardrums make it difficult. He checked her body, breathing ok, no blood, nothing broken. As the dust slowly settled, daylight peeked in through the basement's shattered windows.

Impeded by his crutch, The Sim was still standing when the first shock wave hit. He lay still, three metres from his starting point. Freak was unlucky. He'd made it to the floor but falling masonry landed on his computer table. When Aulay reached him, he grunted something.

"Try again, Freak."

"Bandit has the Con."

Con? Was he a Star Trek fan? Freak feinted. Feeling about under the table top, Aulay found two broken legs, there was no blood, clean fractures, good.

Hector moved slowly. Blood leaked from an ear.

"Hector, howz you?"

"I thought we had more time."

Hector stumbled through the back door. Sitting on the tarmac, he tried to wipe the grime from his clothes. He was in shock.

The Banana crawled over to The Sim.

Aulay pulled the two-way.

[This is Red Five; HQ secure; Status]

[Rainman; Vista van occupants held; No Russian; Repeat; No Russian; Status re Posted]

Chevnenko was not in the Ducato van.

[Posted cancelled; Silver; Status]

Long John came back. [Launch site taken; Four neutered]

Ah, some good news. LJ's li-lo had wiped out the wet-team that destroyed the Pennant.

[Titanic; Status]

FB's li-lo manned the ground and first floors of the pub. Aulay waited. Nothing.

[Rainman; Secure all enemy crew minus the top vista; Take him to Recovery; Silver; Bring a car to the car park; Red Five to All; Go to Recovery]

Aulay hit the two-way mute. Shaz moved.

"How you doin'?" he asked helping her up.

"Headache from hell, my ears are on fire and look at my skirt, it's for the bin."

"You need a doc?"

"No, I need my bag."

Aulay heard screaming sirens in the distance. When he got Shaz out, LJ and the car were there. He helped her into the passenger seat. "Drive to somewhere quiet, LJ. I'll be in touch." Shaz blew him a kiss.

The Pennant's car park filled with police, fire fighters, ambulance crews and guys in suits. The suits showed a degree of deference to the dishevelled Hector.

Aulay walked over, relief turning to anger. A big lad wearing a pin-stripe worsted tried to stop him. It would take four ambulance crew to lift pin-stripe's stretcher. Other stalwarts, one in a dark grey wool, the other in a cheap polyester mix, stepped forward. Hector shouted a command. The suits stopped.

Aulay pointed to an Armani wearing dandy. "You. Take notes." He turned to Hector.

"The vista crew are handcuffed and ready for you at 162 Butterbiggins Road. No Chevnenko. One wet-team, all dead, at 202 Butterbiggins Road." He scanned the suits. "Does anyone know the location of the other wet-teams?"

A haggard Hector turned to a minion wearing an awful beige two piece with a loud tartan waistcoat. The man shrugged his shoulders. When Aulay pulled the Glock, even the firemen froze. A couple of suits pulled their weapons. The Glock pointed at Hector.

"Tell me what the fuck just happened?"

Hector walked slowly to the far end of the car park. His cane didn't swing much. Aulay lowered his gun, took out the makings, and followed. They both sat on the tarmac.

Hector took the freshly rolled cigarette from Aulay's lips, sucked in a good draw and held it.

Aulay rolled another cigarette under the distant eye of the suits.

"You had the Pennant sealed tight," said Hector, "with blanket cover of the surrounding area. I couldn't have done it better. I thought we had him." Hector smiled, "What do you call them, your perimeter, the li-los?"

The laugh was genuine. Aulay laughed too. It was the immediate post stress thing again. Hector had the same condition. He finished his cigarette before carrying on.

"I put myself in the spotlight to provoke Chevnenko. I told him where I was going, what time I'd be there. I screwed up, Aulay. Chevnenko had a wet-team already pointing at the Pennant."

"You can talk to Chevnenko?"

"Special Crime's leak to the DSH is still open."

"I don't suppose he'd fall for it twice?"

"With The Polmadie taking out his vista?" Hector shook his head. "Chevnenko is deaf and blind."

"The suits?" Aulay looked at their audience. "They got any idea of Chevnenko's movements?"

"Oh, we'll pick our way through the vista van. If any of his people say a word, their families will be wiped out. I wouldn't hold my breath."

Hector turned to face him. He'd aged. "We've lost him, Aulay. Chevnenko's gone."

"Will he come back?"

"Yes. Not soon, but one day."

Aulay didn't fancy that much. "Chancer was all for tying you to a tree."

"I heard him."

Before being incarcerated in The Polmadie's Depot, Bandit scanned the Pennant for bugs, from top to bottom, twice.

"How?"

"We put a receiver in Sharon's handbag. It was last minute, pretty ropey but I heard what I needed."

Aulay coughed. Shaz had her bag in the disabled toilet.

"Some things were a bit garbled," said Hector. "I deleted a lot of it."

Aulay coughed again. The silence stretched. Hector seemed... his aura had been punctured, he looked deflated.

"I'm finished, Aulay. I'll be put out to grass or into prison after this."

All his scheming to get the Russian within range had went tits up. More civilians dead, screaming rockets fired. The suit gods would want to know why. Hector put his head in his hands. Aulay heard a mumbled groan. A good blub worked. Hector's body shook a little. Aulay stood up to block the suits' view. He rolled another cigarette.

"Fancy a smoke?" He held out a thick one.

"No thanks, I don't."

He'd sucked on the first one like the Marlboro Man. When he got to his feet, something of the old Hector emerged.

"Tell the Banana," he said with a straight back. "If the day ever comes, and he finds a clearing, I'll bring the stake, and the rope."

Hector winked, turned and walked back to the suited fold. On the way, his cane did the two-step.

Chancer walked over. He sat where Hector had been. The Banana's bloodshot eyes stared out of his grime covered face. He'd got The Sim and Freak into an ambulance.

"How are they?"

"Freak'll be fine but The Sim's fucked."

The Banana stared at the bombed out shell of the Pennant. "What about Shaz?"

Aulay had mixed emotions. Chancer putting Shaz on the end of The Sim's gun rankled. The move put half of Aulay's brain somewhere else. It took Hector to point out the vista van antenna thing. Time wasted.

"She's shook up, but ok."

Chancer searched the ruin. Was he hoping to see FB rise from the ashes?

The Banana wiped his face. "In there, you could have shot The Sim... and me."

It wasn't a question. Aulay shrugged.

"Why didn't you?"

"I underestimated the Russian..."

Chancer turned to face him but Aulay looked straight ahead.

"...the Pennant blew up before I made up my mind."

After the deep eye penetration in the 'pre-explosion' basement, Aulay wasn't keen to renew their 'staring' contest. He wasn't sure he'd win. He watched the fire fighters wield their heavy hoses.

Pulling his knees up, Chancer wrapped his arms around them and rested his head. The foetal position? Submission? Aulay felt the tension in the man. It had nothing to do with giving up.

"How'd Chevnenko know about the Pennant?"

"Fuck knows," said Aulay. "He could've put a tracer on Freak's car, or any Capo's car."

It was the most likely explanation. The Consigliore is the hub and the obvious one to keep tabs on.

"Are we fucked?"

Aulay didn't answer right away. There was the question of which 'we' the Banana was talking about.

"Do you mean, you and me 'we' or The Polmadie, 'we'?"

"Both."

"According to Hector, Chevnenko's legged it. He reckons he'll come back, if we don't stop him."

The 'we' in Aulay's statement answered Chancer's first question.

The Banana turned his head. "What's next?"

"Let's get the fuck out of here."

They hauled themselves to their feet.

Despite protests about witness statements, common assault and possession of firearms, Hector cleared their way through the combination of suits and uniforms. On the way to Recovery, Aulay stopped off at the Yadgar. He ordered the entire menu. In the wait, he nipped outside and made two phone calls.

Rainman would 'prime' the captive vista-man, without a hood. When he rang Shaz's number, LJ picked up.

"LJ, don't say a word. In Shaz's handbag there's a listening device. Talk when it's broken."

Aulay waited.

"I'm parked up at the Burrell Collection. Shaz is zonked in the passenger seat. She's OK."

Prime spot the Burrell. In the middle of Pollok Estate; a parkland oasis of several square miles, bang in the middle of the south side. There were some bits where you couldn't hear traffic. Shaz was as safe there as anywhere.

At Recovery, one of the few abandoned churches on the south side not already converted into flats, Aulay wasn't sure what got the biggest welcome, the Banana or Yadgar's finest. After checking the perimeter li-los, Aulay past a sweating Clockface. Most of The Polmadie were sweating. They'd lost four comrades in the Pennant. Others had been involved in a fire fight, wiping out an East European rocket launching crew.

LJ's li-lo, monitoring traffic on the Butterbiggins Road from a ground floor tenement flat, crapped themselves when the first rocket headed for the Pennant. The missile came from two floors above their heads. When the wet-team, three rockets fired and mission accomplished, came clattering down the stairwell, LJ had his li-lo organised. The wet-team met a hail of bullets.

Hail of bullets may sound like a cliché but Aulay had been in a few fire fights, it fitted. Aulay tried to work out the odds of a wet-team and a li-lo taking up residence in the same building. The fortunes of war. The episode proved how good Chevnenko was. His wet-team had been in-situ, pointing at the Pennant, for more than 24 hours.

Chancer linked up with Bandit at the Depot. The latest updates appeared on a big LCD screen. The sightings of Chevnenko from the Polmadie's poster campaign were

317

pinned to an electronic map of the city. There were three clusters. The first over Possil: the second over Sighthill.

Chancer dismissed both. "Possil and Sighthill are full of East European immigrants. Unless Chevnenko's staying in a slum, with relatives..."

The third, and smallest cluster, was in West Pollokshields, the leafy suburb of Victorian monoliths where Hector lived. Belgy came up to the table. He waited for the nod before beginning.

"You remember Tosser Macalpine?"

Aulay swallowed.

"Aye," said Chancer, "what about him?"

"Well," Belgy scanned his Blackberry, "his da' got in touch. He works at the airport. Seems Macalpine Snr reckons our Russian geezer got off a private helicopter. A charter job, up from Newcastle, so no need for immigration or airport security."

Belgy sweated more than the rest of the crew. "I went to the Buddies... for permission, like..."

Glasgow Airport is in Paisley, where The Polmadie need to tread carefully.

"Smart move," said Chancer.

"It was a doddle. Yer man Aulay cleared it with Paisley Bob."

Chancer nodded.

"Well," said a relaxing Belgy, "I went with some of their people. As you know, The Buddies run the airport taxi operation and we went through the whole rota, even woke up the night shift. No joy. I went to see Macalpine Snr and he came good. Seems our Russian had a limo meet him on the tarmac. Macalpine Snr gave us the name... Saltire Prestige Limousines."

"Who are they?"

Belgy flipped a page.

"The SPL are the top division. They do your big politicians and celebs. I went to their office and got the 'client confidentiality' bollocks. I called for handers."

Along with Clockface's li-lo, Belgy returned to the SPL offices and began creating bruises.

"The Russian got delivered to the Central Hotel, but that was a dead end. We're going through all the black hacks that work the Central. Nothin' yet"

"Do the SPL have a return booking?"

"No. But if they get a call, they'll give us a bell. I've left a man there to make sure."

"What about the airport?"

"The Buddies have people checking all the chopper companies. We've got people in Edinburgh and Prestwick checking too, just in case."

"Good work, Belgy. Now, I want two li-los to contact every letting agent on the south side."

Chancer went to the PC. Google Maps appeared on the big LCD screen.

"Anything let in the last week, within this area; I want to know about it. I want every spare man to scour the place, door to door, make up something, canvassing for the Tories, any fuckin' thing. Find me the Russian."

Belgy finished typing and put his Blackberry away. "Sure Chancer."

The Gorbals high rise list of residents pinged into Chancer's in box. He set the printer to work making two dozen copies.

"Is it up to date?" asked Aulay.

"Bandit went through the electoral roll and the poll tax lists. He sent people out to cross off every name by climbing the stairs and knocking on doors. People move, take in lodgers."

He distributed copies. The Polmadie wanted a name, a connection to a name, anything. Chancer spent a long time scanning the list before beginning again.

"The Honeysuckle Guest House."

"Hi, Joss, it's Aulay Mackay."

He held on to the silence as Jocelyn Brodie flicked through her options.

"Do you need my facilities or will I come to you?"

"Can you clear your schedule? I'll be bringing someone with me."

"How soon?"

"Now, and no gloves required."

Recovery wasn't the place for what he wanted Joss to do and the Govanhill Baths had recently been occupied by protestors fighting a campaign to re-open the old swimming pool. Glasgow city council were having none of it.

"Give me an hour and... your guest, I'd rather he couldn't see or hear anything when he arrives... and Aulay... it's good to hear from you."

Aulay backed the Daewoo up to Joss's front door. Clockface helped him lift the bound, gagged, ear plugged and hooded vista-man into the house. The spooks were a vista-van-man short but, fuck it, add kidnapping to the list.

Jocelyn Brodie hadn't changed, straight backed, that aura of control. The aura slipped when Clockface returned to the Daewoo.

"You've grown into a man, Aulay." Joss hugged him.

Why had he not returned, even for a short visit? He'd driven past the Honeysuckle often enough. Was there some remnant of dread... that Joss would 'see' what he'd become?

The vista-man squirmed on the floor as Aulay and Joss did the, 'sorry to hear about Eddie' and 'how's Deirdre'. No weather or football, just personal.

"You're back with Sharon, I hear?"

So, Joss followed his progress.

"Aye, and this one," he indicated the wriggling mass at their feet, "will go a long way to making me and Shaz permanent."

"How is Sharon?"

"Sore head, a bit shaken. She was there when-"

"I'm sure she will be fine. Sharon is made of strong stuff."

"How do you know?"

Joss coughed. "... em, a couple of years ago, I needed discreet legal services. I went to Eddie. He recommended Sharon."

Aulay raised an eyebrow.

"Let's get our visitor down to the basement. I'll tell you the details as we go along."

It wasn't the smoothest descent. At the bottom of the stairs, they dragged vista-man into the basement proper.

"A long time client died on the premises," said Joss. "His heart gave out. He was eighty-three."

Didn't sound like too big a deal. Move the body from the dungeon to one of the 'guest' rooms and bob's your granny. Natural death.

"... there were complications. His daughter sat in the high court, and ..."

Joss removed the standard wrist and ankle straps from the crucifix. Sharp barbs lined the inside of the replacements. If vista-man struggled, he'd tear his wrists and ankles to shreds.

"... the old fool left me a substantial amount in his will... for services rendered."

322

Aulay struggled and failed. The giggles came. They both roared the place down. When Deidre appeared at the top step, Joss recovered enough to signal all was well.

Vista-man fought against them as they raised him to his feet. Joss tightened the first wrist strap. Blood trickled down vista-man's arm. He stopped struggling. Getting the rest of him into position was a doddle.

"Christ, Joss. You had a judge on your tail. How did you get out of that one?"

"Sharon arranged a confidential visit. Lady Murray marched in assuming I was the woman who'd taken her father away from her mother. She'd spent thirty years hating an imaginary 'other woman'."

Joss attached a few other bits and bobs. Vista-man was secure. Any movement, a hiccup and he'd suffer. A moan came from under the hood.

"How did it finish up?" asked Aulay.

"During a tour of the basement, to reassure Lady Murray that my relationship with her father was purely professional, she took a particular interest... in that."

Joss pointed to the medieval stocks.

"What, she..."

"No no, not Lady Murray. A week later her husband called to make an appointment."

Lady Murray's discovery of her late father's needs and desires shone a light on her struggles to keep her own husband tied down. Her feelings of inadequacy, and increasing waistline, had pushed their thirty-year marriage close to the rocks. Long past any interest in the bedroom department, Lady Murray was smart enough to know when the hull was breached. Joss acquired a monthly regular. A naughty boy, Lord Murray needed a little light caning, preferably in the stocks. Another marriage saved.

Returning to the ground floor, Aulay asked Joss another favour. Shaz was in limbo and The Honeysuckle seemed as good a place as any to spend the night.

"We'd be delighted," said Joss. "I'll get Deirdre to spruce up one of the rooms."

Aulay called LJ. He ended the call relieved it wasn't Rainman who was looking after Shaz. He wasn't sure Charlie Weathers could handle meeting Joss again.

Fifteen minutes later, a dizzy Shaz was tucked up in bed. One thing less to worry about. Joss walked him to the door.

"What do you want to know from our guest, and how long do I have?"

He told her, adding, "If the vista-man talks, his family will die." He shrugged. "They're probably dead already."

"That's good to know," said Joss. "I'll be in touch."

Joss and Shaz spending time together was news. Climbing into the Daewoo, Aulay wondered. Shaz had never been a screaming domina, like Isabella from Brechin, who couldn't reach ecstasy without a bruised arse... still, during their manic disabled toilet session, Shaz made demands... which Aulay met... she gave him strict instructions... which he carried out... mmm

The pink panther played.

"Where are you?" It was Bandit.

"Ten minutes from Recovery."

"Can you meet Chancer at the GRH. There's been a development."

"Will do."

The line went dead before Aulay could get any more info, which was a shame. He looked at Clockface.

"Any idea what the 'GRH' is?"

Clockface shrugged. They drove along the road to nowhere. On St Andrews Drive, the tall flats provided inspiration.

"The GRH equals the Gorbals Road high rise."

Aulay swung the Daewoo round. Passing the devastated Bulls Security yard, he spotted a bored PC standing next to miles of gaffer tape. On Comrie Road he pulled up.

[This is Red Five; Two hundred yards from the GRH]

Nothing. They checked their weapons. Clockface didn't need arms the same length. He handled his .32 calibre like a pro.

Aulay asked the obvious question.

"What's the biggest pain in the tits?"

"A one handed wank doesn't do it for me."

It sounded like the stock reply. Aulay let the genuine smile spread.

"No, really, what's the main gripe?"

"When I was younger, I'd have to be on the bird's right, to reach everywhere, know what I mean?"

Aulay nodded.

"The killer was the bra strap. That fucker was always out of reach."

Aulay laughed. "What about now?"

The married Clockface had three kids.

"Och, name your DIY. But, tell you what, yer man Bandit, he's been giving me all sorts of stuff. That fucker's a genius."

A red Alfa pulled in. The driver climbed into the back of the Daewoo.

"The GRH can wait," said Chancer. "Freak's security at the Vicky is two fuckin' traffic polis."

A Polmadie sympathiser who worked in the hospital had sent word.

Chancer gave Clockface the keys to the Alpha. "Tell your li-lo to lie low, then follow us."

Aulay watched Chancer's face in the Daewoo's mirror. The Banana didn't flinch. He stored, 'tell your li-lo to lie low' for another time.

"You got your two-way?" Aulay asked Clockface as he left the Daewoo.

"Aye."

"Get Rainman and LJ to meet us on the Battlefield Road."

On full throttle, the Daewoo lifted her skirts and did a decent impression of a car in a hurry. The roads were quiet.

One name hadn't been mentioned. "Howz The Sim?"

"In the morgue."

Your best friend dying is an expensive business. Aulay mourned for two seconds. "And Freak?"

"Both legs in plaster, but OK."

Chancer held out a photograph. A classic wedding pose with men in kilts, women in their finery, bride and groom all smiles.

"What am I looking at?" Aulay pulled out to pass a bus on Cathcart Road.

"Bloke behind the bride on the right."

DI McCaw, a recent likeness.

"And?"

"One of Belgy's li-lo is a wedding photographer. He recognised a name from the GRH list, MacSporran. Not too many MacSporrans about. He looked through his files. McCaw wanted a deal for his daughter's wedding.

"Have you confirmed this..." Aulay was going to say 'intell' but knew he'd sound like a tosser, "... is the right MacSporran."

326

"Aye, I've just been up there, two floors below my granny. Rang the bell and the bride appeared, eight months pregnant."

Fuck me, thought Aulay. During a visit to his newly married daughter, McCaw spots Chancer on a visit. The Russian needs a precursor so McCaw offers up granny and grandda' Hoy. This was enormous.

"What's the plan?"

"Let's wait 'til we suss out Freak's situation at the Vicky."

Chancer's tone didn't bode well for DI McCaw.

Aulay put everything to one side as he pulled in on the Battlefield Road, two hundred yards from the entrance to the Victoria Infirmary. LJ and Rainman were already there and walked over. Aulay felt a bit better with them in tow. They'd do whatever he said.

After twenty minutes, and three fags, LJ returned. "The security's bollocks. I wouldn't trust those guys to guard a fire."

The suits in Freak's ambulance had been downgraded to two young PCs. One slept in the room next to Freak, the other paced the corridors hunting for nurses. LJ'd breezed past the prowling PC wearing a white coat, stethoscope and clipboard.

"Freak wants out," said LJ, "and from what I've seen, he'd be safer holed up in The Russian's spare bedroom."

"Rainman," said Aulay, "go walk about, check the perimeter. Any funny business, bark on the two-way. LJ, you get back in there, stay with Freak, find a wheelchair, take Clockface."

"You thinking what I'm thinking?" asked Chancer.

"Aye."

Why the change of guard, from armed suited spooks to swimming pool attendants? Did someone gamble on the jungle drums sounding. With the Polmadie at Recovery, or on their li-los, Freak was the only gang member on Special Crime's, and the Russian's radar.

"You want more bodies here?" asked Chancer.

The Polmadie were good, but not at this. This wasn't a squabble over what ice cream van drove down what street.

"No, a big car would help. A Freak in plaster might not be easy to get into the Daewoo."

Chancer pulled his phone. "Belgy's got an estate car."

The two-way vibrated. [Red Five; Transit van; Two occupants; In A&E car park...]

Out of the Daewoo before Rainman finished, Aulay slipped his earpiece-microphone on, it kept his hands free. At A&E, he slowed to a walk. The Banana followed behind. The car park was big and dark.

Rainman appeared. "No change," he said. "They're just sitting there, waiting."

A four man wet-team hit the Pennant.

"Any sign of the other two?"

Rainman shook his head.

Aulay whispered into the two-way. [Silver; Status]

[In situ with Blondie; Both sentinels asleep]

Asleep meant asleep. Glasgow's finest were having a snooze. If LJ'd said 'both sentinels down', he'd be talking interference.

"You got a gun?" Aulay asked the Banana.

"No."

Aulay gave him one of his.

"Don't shoot unless I do, and Chancer..."

"What?"

"For fuck's sake, only shoot what I'm shooting at."

The two-way squawked again. [Blondie mobile; To the Rectum]

LJ had Freak in a wheelchair. They were headed for the hospital's front door.

[Silver; Transport on the way; Wait for my signal before bringing Blondie out]

Aulay turned to Rainman. "Wait here, watch the van. Chancer, tell Belgy I want his tailgate up, back seats down and he's to wait for my signal before pulling into A&E."

Aulay strolled along to the hospital's main entrance, rolled up and discussed the football and the weather with another pariah. They puffed away under a big 'No Smoking' sign.

Through the glass frontage, the hospital foyer was big, bright and quiet.

Belgy cruised past. Aulay signalled and the Citroen C5 swung in.

[Silver; Bring Blondie through the lobby]

Freak looked tired but determined as Long John hovered in front, Clockface pushing from behind. The Consigliore's plastered legs stuck straight out.

Three security cameras whirred into life, rotating towards the approaching threesome. Aulay crapped himself. He now knew where the other half of the wet-team were. Crashing into the hospital lobby Aulay pulled his .45, screamed at LJ to get a fuckin' move on, and waited.

Squawk. [Red Five; Van's on the move]

Christ.

[Rainman; If it heads for The Rectum; Take it out]

Aulay didn't take his eyes off the six doors facing him. Whoever controlled the cameras would have to get past him. The rules of body guarding are simple. Put yourself between the shooters and their target.

Two receptionists and an NHS security guard stared at him. Aulay fired a round into the ceiling. "Get down." Everyone hit the floor.

Door four opened. Aulay nearly shot a nurse. A pretty little thing, she screamed and did the right thing. She stepped back the door. Aulay had a thing for nurses, it was the uniform. Deborah from Luton flashed through his mind. Doors two and six crashed open. Gunfire crackled from outside, some of it automatic, shite. Time slowed.

Wearing the same uniform as the NHS guard hugging the floor, Door two man went down first, a perfect shot to the chest. Door six man got off a few but firing a semi-automatic on the run is difficult. He made a shambles of the hospital's big glass doors though. Aulay's first shot hit the man's shoulder which spun him round. The second took him in the chest and down he went. Aulay didn't check both shooters were dead. He fired a bullet into each of their heads.

Running back through the shattered glass, Aulay caught sight of a Transit van limping along the road with an array of bullet holes along one side, Rainman and Chancer in hot pursuit. He saw a toppled over wheelchair.

Time speeded back up.

In the Citroen, Belgy stared at a small hole in the windscreen. There were bodies under the car. LJ came out first then struggled to drag Freak clear, his foot to thigh plasters made it awkward. A pale Clockface appeared next. He'd been shot through his smaller arm. The pain hadn't hit yet.

"Freak," said Aulay, "you ok?"

"Popped a few painkillers before setting off. I feel pretty dammed good."

Freak was tripping.

"We got the fuckers," said Clockface, his eyes on fire. "You know how, Aulay? Small arms fire." He started giggling. Clockface slipped into shock.

It was an effort but they got Freak into the back of the C5. Shouting at Belgy didn't work. Moving round to the driver's door, Aulay gave the man a good slap. Belgy let go of the steering wheel.

"Move over."

Rainman and Chancer returned from the now idle Transit. Chancer's eyes blazed. The Banana was in euphoria-land, buzzed up with the thrill of combat, the zing of survival and the indomitable truth that he was indestructible. Aulay remembered when he used to feel that way.

A nod from Rainman confirmed the van's occupants wouldn't be giving them any more grief. He handed Aulay a Zrovky two-way but this wasn't the time for a wee chat with Chevnenko.

"LJ, take Freak to a hotel somewhere on the north side. Take Belgy's li-lo along for security. I'll see you back at Recovery."

"Chancer, take Clockface round to A&E. He was a passerby caught in the crossfire."

Chancer accepted Aulay's order without a glimmer and led the still giggling Clockface away. Aulay threw the Daewoo keys to Rainman.

"Wait in the car, I won't be long."

Aulay walked up the hospital steps and into the aftermath where brave medical people were trying to resuscitate two dead Slavs. He approached the NHS security guard. The man recognised him and stumbled backwards.

"You do as I say and everything'll be fine," said Aulay. "Where's the CCTV monitoring suite..." he spotted the name badge. "Harry?"

"Through there." Harry pointed a shaky finger at door number six.

"Take me."

Aulay was on film shooting up an NHS establishment. Ok, two gunmen were trying to shoot him, but Aulay liked his privacy.

The new Victoria Infirmary was in the process of replacing the Victorian sandstone monument on the other side of the road. The CCTV installation wasn't complete. There was no remote on-line storage. Good.

Through tears, a shaking Harry explained it all clearly and simply. The cameras fed a ten terra-byte hard disk storage box. After removing the storage cartridges, only two had any lights flashing, Aulay put an arm round the sobbing Harry.

"It's over, pal," he said, "there's no' going to be any more shooting."

"But... Derek."

Aulay followed Harry's eyes. Blood dripped from a cupboard door. Inside, Derek's eyes stared at the deep cuts in his tied wrists. He'd watched himself die.

"The fuckers said they'd do the same to me if I so much as..." Harry put his head in his hands.

What to do? Aulay didn't have time for this.

"It's over now, Harry."

Harry looked up. "Derek was a dour cunt. I couldn't stand the bastard but, he didn't deserve that."

Harry bucked up. "But you got them good, son. You blew the fuckers away. Cool as fuck. I'm going to be drinking out on this for a bit."

"Harry. I could use a wee favour."

"Sure, son, name it."

Aulay put a little steel in his voice. "I want you to forget me, what I look like, can you do that?"

"Aye, don't you worry. The gunman was blonde, officer, about 5 foot 6, with a limp, and big sideburns."

Harry was his height. Aulay asked another favour. He thanked Harry for letting him borrow his uniform. Harry thanked Aulay for not shooting him.

As he walked back through the scene of battle, a policeman asked Aulay to help set up a perimeter of gaffer tape, to corral the growing number on onlookers. Aulay carried out his civic duty until he spotted the Banana amongst the crowd. He followed Chancer's stare. DI McCaw had arrived. Shite. Making a bee line through the crowd, Aulay grabbed the Banana.

"No' now, its suicide." He huckled the Banana through door four, through A&E and out to the Daewoo.

On the way to Recovery, Aulay counted everything that had went wrong. A royal fuck up. Where else would Chevnenko's wet-team get all points access to the comings and goings of a big hospital?

Chancer remained quiet apart from the sound of grinding teeth. As always happened, the 'indestructible' feeling fades. Combat survivor's can sometimes sink into a deep recess where 'what if's & maybe's' live.

No one spoke until they reached Recovery.

"That could have been worse," said Chancer getting out the car. "Freak was bait and we swallowed it."

The Banana hadn't slipped into post traumatic stress.

"Aye," said Aulay. "The Russian's always one step ahead."

With everyone out looking for Chevnenko, Recovery had a skeleton staff. Chancer sent a runner to get his Alfa.

Caffeine. Aulay made two strong mugs and handed one over. "Any news?"

"We're closing in."

Chancer was logged in checking the latest information from Bandit. Li-los had persuaded the various letting agents to forget the client - letting agent confidentiality bollocks. Of the twelve highlighted properties, ten were innocent enough, a mix of business people and families.

Aulay checked his Blackberry. Three messages waited. The first; someone wanted to upgrade his mobile contract. The second; a shaky photograph of Shaz's bum, very nice. The caption read, 'bruised but intact'. The third; a missed call from Joss. He called her back, picturing the slim chrome handset trilling away in the Honeysuckle's hallway.

There were no preliminaries. "There are three; our guest calls them wet-teams, each with four men. The primary target is a Mr Hector Chalmers. The secondary is Alec MacKinnon, and associates. Our guest does not know Mr Chevnenko's whereabouts but he's local, within a couple of kilometres, something to do with the range of their radios."

"How is our guest?"

"He's em... asleep. There's something he's not telling me... yet. He needs a little time to settle before I can find out what it is."

"Ok, Joss. Let me know when you do."

'Asleep' and 'settle' could mean anything. Aulay hung up with a shiver and relayed Joss's information to Chancer.

"Three options," said Aulay. "We wait it out, we go after DI McCaw, or we can try and get Chevnenko on this."

He held out the Zrovky two-way.

"McCaw's no' going anywhere," said Chancer. "Get Hector."

Chancer's plan was simple. Put Hector in the Honeysuckle, with vista-man and the Zrovky two-way.

Aulay met Hector at The Lochan, three hundred yards from The Honeysuckle Guest House. Hector sipped a malt whisky as he perused a Daily Snot. He looked better than the last time Aulay had seen him. Dapper Dan was back. Aulay had slipped into the cupboard to ditch Harry's uniform. He didn't look too bad himself. There were no suits.

They did the dance around the dead Sim, the safe Shaz and the current state of play. Hector was impressed, especially with Jocelyn Brodie.

"You will have to introduce me."

"Now is a good time."

Hector raised an eyebrow.

"You're going to the dungeon."

Hector ordered another malt, a large one. He insisted Aulay had one too.

Turning the Daewoo into Sherbrooke Avenue, Aulay spotted a parked car near the Honeysuckle. He braked, slipped into reverse and retreated back round the corner.

Hector turned his way. "Anything the matter?"

"This is detached mansion country with tree lined avenues and big driveways. A parked car stands out like a priest at a five year olds birthday party."

The pink panther sounded. It was Joss.

"Aulay, what's a Sputlink?"

"A what?"

"Our guest, he begged me to remove it before he slipped under. I'm not sure I heard him properly. He was a little stressed."

"Joss, I want you, Shaz and Deidre to leave, don't pack. Get in your car and go, now."

"But-."

"Joss. Vista-man has a tracker. His boss knows where he is. Do you understand?"

"My my, Aulay, you can be so masterful." The line went dead.

Commercial satellite trackers are the size of a fag packet. The latest military kit is miniscule. Pop it in a tooth cavity. The vista-man wanted his tracker removed. He didn't fancy a visit from Chevnenko.

Aulay checked his guns as he rolled the Daewoo round the corner and down the hill. The suspect car hadn't moved. Hector pulled a slim Beretta from somewhere. It would be a Beretta, thought Aulay. He pushed the buttons and the front windows slid down. There were three ways to do this. Ram into the arse of the suspect car and start blasting, cruise alongside and start blasting, or cross her bows and start blasting.

"I'm going to cross her bows. You ready?"

"Yes."

They were thirty yards from the small hatchback.

"Aulay."

"I see it, I see it."

The Nissan Micra had 'L' plates. Aulay watched a bloke talk earnestly to someone in the driver's seat. The Daewoo cruised past the irate instructor, the indignant pupil, and The Honeysuckle's driveway.

Aulay pulled in to the kerb. In the mirror he watched Joss swing her Mercedes onto the tarmac before gunning the big German car up the hill.

Aulay turned to Hector. "The latest Sputlink, how good is it?"

"Ten metres; give or take."

Aulay handed over the Zrovky two-way. Hector's face was a question.

"Joss's dungeon," said Aulay, "you wanted a clearing."

Hector nodded. If Hector introduced Chevnenko to his vista-man, on the Zrovky two-way, Chevnenko would know where that was within ten metres.

In the Honeysuckle's basement, Hector admired Jocelyn Brodie's handiwork. There was blood, bits of flesh and the smell of burning. No longer spiked onto the crucifix, the bandaged vista-man lay on a circular water bed. Bound and blindfolded, he slept the sleep of the dead. Aulay didn't blame him. He'd had one hell of a day.

Hector sniffed at the offal lying around.

"Its pork," he said, "your Jocelyn could teach my people a thing or two."

"How so?"

The syringes on one table contained a mix of hallucinogens and anaesthetics. Joss's technique involved a mix of real pain and imagined torment. The real pain came from the wrist and ankle straps, the imaginary pain from inside vista-man's head.

"It's at the extreme end of masochism. Sufferers only achieve satisfaction when they truly believe they are being eaten alive. For every Hannibal Lector there's a willing supplicant."

Christ, thought Aulay. What happened to logging on to www.BigOnes.com and having a wank?

"And the anaesthetic?"

"Before each course, Joss injects a 'local'."

"I'm not with you."

"Let's say, before going under, vista-man knows his manhood is where he left it, after... nothing."

"Why the barbeque."

There was a small butane camping stove set up.

"How do you like your testicles, Aulay, medium... well done?"

Leaving Hector to his admiring, Aulay left the dungeon to call the Banana.

"We've got the Clearing set up."

"I'll be right there."

"No, meet me at The Lochan. Bring LJ and Rainman."

He hung up before there were any questions. This was going down to the wire his way. No more walking into hospital receptions with his trousers down. If the Banana wanted to argue, he was going to have to eat it.

Aulay explained the plan to Hector. For a goat about to be tethered, Hector remained calm.

"Can you bring him round?" Aulay pointed at the prone vista-man.

"I'd need to know what combination of drugs-."

"Here's Joss's number. Ask her yourself."

On his way to The Lochan, Aulay wondered what it would feel like to wake up and find your wedding tackle safe and sound.

Wedding? Where the fuck did that come from? He was getting ahead of himself. More people were going to die before he could think about tomorrow. Maybe a quiet do, Registry Office with one or two... shut up.

In the Lochan car park, Aulay outlined the plan.

"Everyone clear?"

Rainman and LJ nodded, checked their weapons, stuffed them back into holdalls and left the Daewoo.

Of the suspect properties remaining on The Polmadie's 'watch' list, one had been scored off. A Pakistani couple with three kids turned up. The two remaining houses were within half a mile. It was getting dark.

It took half an hour to complete the perimeter, men hid behind hedges or garages, on all approaches to the Honeysuckle. Li-los kept an eye on Property One and Property Two. LJ and Rainman lay buried in the undergrowth somewhere in the Honeysuckle's extensive garden. Chancer took charge of the backup li-lo, positioned mid-way between Property One & Two.

Aulay pressed the 'go' button.

Reports came in. [Vauxhall estate on Nithsdale Road; Turning into...] [Property One; Lights on in downstairs lounge; Curtains closed...] [Toyota van on Dalziel Drive; Moving slowly...]

Too many reports, everyone with a two-way fancied themselves. No one announced who they were, or who they were talking to. [Man walking a dog; A cocker spaniel]. Chaos.

It took an hour to calm everyone down.

Aulay buzzed Hector. [Tethered Goat; Ready when you are].

[[Yuri, this is Hector]]

Hector had the Zrovky two-way on speaker. If Chevnenko replied, Aulay would hear their conversation.

[[Yuri, this is Hector]]

After twenty long minutes, Aulay suspected Chevnenko had legged it. Then... in a clunky accent... [[Good evenink, Hector. What a pleasant surprise]]

Aulay sent the word out. The Russian was within 1-2 kilometres.

[Property One to Red Five; Lights on in the kitchen and dining room; Curtains closed.]

[[Nice to hear your voice, Yuri. Are you well?]]

[[We are getting too old for this work, no? And you, your hip, still givink you pain?]]

The two old warhorses batted pleasantries back and fore.

[[Yuri, say hello to Viktor, your senior vista]]

There followed garbled cursing and sobbing. Silence followed a heavy thunk.

[[Viktor's been helping us. Senor Triatori's murder in May. Mr Mayhew in Zurich last July. Viktor tells me you killed Mayhew personally, with an open razor]]

[[Good, Hector, very good. Now, what do you want?]]

[Property One to Red Five; Lights on all over the house; Curtains closed.]

Aulay decided to move Chancer's backup li-lo.

[Red Five to Big Yellow; Go to Property One; Standby.]

Aulay fired up the Daewoo.

[Red Five to Beehive; Report]

[Silver; No' a sausage] LJ had reverted to his native tongue as soon as he stepped off the plane.

[Rainman; Negative]

[Sutherland Avenue to Red Five; Black Renault Laguna turning into Sherbrooke Avenue]

Aulay watched the French car glide past the Lochan.

[Silver to Red Five; Laguna stopped outside Beehive; Two men approaching on foot]

Chevnenko did want Hector. Why else would he send a scouting party to the vista-man's Sputlink location.

[Nithsdale Road to Red Five; a polis car's pulled up at the junction with Sherbrooke Avenue]

Shite.

[Hamilton Drive to Red Five; the rozzers are here, cruising along at a snail's pace]

[Dalziel Drive to Red Five; there's a fuckin' polis motor stopped outside number 38]

Was Hector playing funny buggers or... was DI McCaw responding to his Russian paymaster's instructions?

[Red Five to Perimeter; Are the polis motors beemers?]

Traffic police drive your average Ford or Vauxhall. Police with guns drive BMWs. They were all BMWs. Aulay called the Banana.

[Red Five to Big Yellow; Two cars to each polis location; Now]

Polmadie vehicles lined the Periphery. The parked car in a wide avenue problem meant the Periphery was half a mile away in the tenement streets of east Pollokshields.

Did they have enough time? Nail biting stuff, the waiting game.

[Big Yellow to Red Five; All in position and ready]

Chancer had done it.

[Silver to Red Five; Two Scouts circled the Beehive; Both Glasgow; Suspect polis; Made no attempt to enter]

The Renault outside the Honeysuckle drove off. This was it. Would Chevnenko go for it?

[Red Five to Big Yellow; No polis BMW to get within half a mile of Property One, Property Two or the Beehive]

Aulay didn't need armed police at his back when he faced a Russian wet-team.

Hector and Yuri continued their duel.

[[You are two wet-teams down, Yuri. I must say, we found it easy. You're slipping]]

[[Casualties in battle become heroes, for the winning side]]

Everything was set. If Property One wasn't the Russian's location, the li-lo on the perimeter would give Aulay some warning. If a wet-team came at the Honeysuckle from somewhere else, LJ and Rainman would hold off any attack until the cavalry arrived.

The wait went on, and on. It was a beautiful still night. Aulay's thoughts drifted. Pulling his Blackberry, he trawled though the received messages until he got to the one of Shaz's bum.

[Property One to Red Five; garage doors opening; Two fuck-off people carriers inside; Men moving about]

Aulay floored the Daewoo.

[Red Five to Big Yellow; If you confirm Boris, take out both vehicles; Repeat; confirm Boris]

This was it. No more learner drivers please. The Daewoo hurtled as best she could. Aulay heard automatic fire. He turned into Milngavie Drive. A shattered people carrier leaned against the kerb. A second people carrier hadn't made it out of the gates.

Aulay's two-way went nuts. Three police BMW's had been involved in simultaneous accidents.

[Red Five to All; Everyone; shut the fuck up; NOW]

[[Tethered Goat to Red Five; Status; I heard gun fire]]

Hector could wait. The ambushing li-los were celebrating, firing their guns into the air. It took Aulay a minute, along with a few slaps, to calm the situation.

Sirens approached. Police responding to their crashed colleagues calls for help?

"Where's Chancer?"

"Over there." Belgy pointed to the people carrier that made it across the road.

"Right, Belgy," said Aulay, "get everyone back to Recovery. Do it now."

Aulay couldn't erase the feeling that they'd wiped out a management team who were heading out on a jolly after a hard day's brainstorming. The array of automatic weaponry littering the VW Sharan dispelled the feeling.

The driver and front passenger wouldn't be making any more trips. Behind them, two more tooled up Slavs stared from dead eyes. Chancer sat in the third row, next to Chevnenko. The Russian had three bullets in his chest and two in his head. The Polmadie hadn't worried about the cost of ammunition.

Aulay lifted the Zrovky two-way sitting in the Russian's lap.

[Red Five to Tethered Goat; Boris has left the building]

Chancer looked pale. "We did it, Aulay," he said. "The fuckin' Polmadie took on the DSH and did the business."

"Aye, but we need to get out of here."

Chancer didn't move. Aulay looked closer, blood seeped from one side of the Banana's mouth.

"I'm fucked, Aulay."

The seep became a cascade. The Banana had taken one in the chest. He was talking dead.

"We did good..."

"Aye, Chancer." Aulay kneeled beside him. "The Polmadie did fuckin' good."

The Banana tried to talk through the flood.

"Get that fucker McCaw. For me."

"Sure, Chancer."

"... and Aulay, tell Jemima I... I spent the penny."

The Banana fizzled out. Fuck fuck fuck.

It took a blood soaked Aulay walking into Recovery to silence the jubilant Polmadie.

Belgy came over. "Where's The Banana?"

343

Aulay sat down at a trestle table, grabbed a glass of something and swallowed. It was dark rum.

"Chancer didn't make it." He raised the glass. "Got any more?"

Someone appeared with a bottle of Trawler, the good stuff, cheap but potent. The li-los closed in, all talking at the same time, asking the same question in ten different ways. The atmosphere heated up. Blame got thrown about. Anger mixed with alcohol makes for dodgy decisions. Aulay's first thought had been to take the bottle of rum and find a hiding place. Decisions. Decisions. 'Get that fucker McCaw' came back to him.

Aulay stood. "All the booze goes back where you got it. We're no' finished yet."

A guy in Belgy's li-lo grumbled. Aulay pulled his .45 and stuck it between the man's eyes.

"You got a fuckin' problem, wee man?"

A couple of metallic clicks followed a whispered, 'Red Five'. LJ and Rainman had his back.

Belgy stepped in. "Right, youz heard the script. The booze goes back in the van. Party's cancelled. Come on."

Belgy took a few empties from a table. He put them in a plastic bag which he handed to the guy on the end of Aulay's gun.

"Here, Shifty, take this to the bins."

A relieved Shifty grabbed his life-jacket and made for the door. With the Polmadie returned to a war footing, Aulay told of Chancer's last moments, The Banana's pride in The Polmadie. There were a few snuffles, the odd 'fuck me'. He didn't mention McCaw.

Belgy described what happened at Property One. Among the men climbing into the people carriers, The Banana eyeballed Chevnenko and gave the order to open fire. He then charged after the first people carrier as it slid to a halt.

It was a common mistake. New recruits are told 'till their brainwashed. It doesn't matter how many bullets you've fired. How destroyed a vehicle, or house, or tank, looks. Not everyone's dead until they're dead. The first dead body you see; shoot it in the head, then the next, and the next.

The Polmadie suffered. After a high, when reality bites you in the bum, the brain can melt. Aulay put everyone to work. All fired weapons needed to be lost, forever, not thrown in the Clyde. Shifty volunteered to take them to Dunure, his cousin ran a small lobster boat. The guns would end up in deep water halfway to the Isle of Arran. Aulay replaced his guns from what was left in Rainman's armoury.

The drivers of the contingency vehicles, arrested after crashing into various armed police response units, would need lawyers, and bail money, by the morning. Belgy took this on. He'd be on the doorstep of BD&P first thing.

Aulay ordered everyone to strip. They took turns scraping every piece of bare skin, in freezing water, before donning new trainers and pristine, scratchy boiler suites.

Returning with the blood stained seat cover from the Daewoo, Aulay overheard someone ask, "Is Aulay the new Banana?"

"Looks like. We could do worse."

It was after 2am when Aulay sent The Polmadie home. The troops trooped from Recovery sad and weary. Rainman left to get his van and start the journey home to the delectable Darina. LJ simply raised a finger, nodded and walked away. After dousing the piles of clothes and shoes in petrol, Aulay set the old church alight. The blaze took a good hold, and the smell? Twenty eight burning li-los gave off some stench. Aulay headed for the cupboard and the sleep of the truly knackered.

Rotten bananas were stalking his dreams when the pink panther sounded.

"Shaz babe, howz you?"

"There's polis here, Aulay."

Ping. Wide awake. "Where are you?"

"Bellahouston Hotel, Room 332. Joss and Deirdre are in room 333. The polis broke in, there's been shouting and screaming."

Shite, 332 meant the third floor, no way out the window.

"Shaz, I'll be there in ten."

He didn't have to get dressed.

"Aulay?"

"What?"

"McCaw's running the show."

Shite. Think.

"You made any other calls since you got to the Bella?"

"No."

"Ok, delete this call from your phone, just this one, do it now."

"Ok." The line went dead.

McCaw would check Shaz's phone. Standard practise.

The Daewoo coughed and spluttered into life. She needed a service. The old girl wasn't designed to go round corners on two wheels, but she managed fine. Aulay stayed off Nithsdale Road for two reasons. It was the obvious route and it would still be crawling with police investigating the stramash on Milngavie Drive. The traffic bumps on Urrdale Drive tore the Daewoo's undercarriage apart. He pulled the wobbling car over next to the pedestrian bridge. He hit the bridge running.

As the eight lanes of the deserted M8 motorway past below, Aulay did some thinking. When Chevnenko traced vista-man's location, he'd have ordered McCaw to trace the Honeysuckle's owner/occupier. When the scouts reported nobody at home, the call would have gone out. An APB on Joss's Mercedes = The Bellahouston Hotel.

His Blackberry vibrated. Shaz. He let it ring three times, to prove his innocence, and to check his breathing.

"Hi, Shaz babe, howz things?"

"Aulay Mackay, good to talk to you again."

"Who's this?"

"McCaw."

"Well, well. How are you?"

"No' bad. Been busy with work, you?"

"Aye, same here. It's never ending."

"Nice job you did tonight, by the way."

"Och, your Russian boss fell into it. It was a doddle."

There was a muffled skirmish in the background before McCaw came back.

"I've been hearing rumours about you, Aulay."

"It's only nine inches. Regardless what Mrs McCaw says."

The DI gave a chuckle. He sounded relaxed. Aulay needed to change that.

"Detective Inspector, what you got planned for your last day?"

"Last day?"

"You going to take a little time to say your goodbyes?"

"Aulay, you're the one looking at the big cheerio."

"Your daughter's a Tania, right?"

Silence.

"Tania McCaw one day then Tania MacSporran the next. Some people have no luck at all. Gorbals Road high rise isn't it?"

Whatever deal the DI was about to broker with Aulay, had been torpedoed. McCaw was dead. The how and when the only remaining details. Aulay closed his phone. McCaw still had the strongest hand, but Aulay hoped he'd put him on the back foot.

Aulay didn't get the 'back foot' expression until his one and only time holding a piece of willow. The NCO's were a man down for the annual NCO v Officers cricket match. Marching out wearing the unwieldy padding, Aulay faced seven balls, was that an over? Captain Smethwick threw the ball so fast Aulay barely had time to get the stick in front of his crotch. The seventh ball, from the slower Lieutenant Chosters, Aulay expected to arrive at the same pace. He swung the club before the ball past the half way line. He was out for a swan. It didn't really matter. He was the last man in and they were miles in front. He spent the second half, bored to tears, near the touchline at... Long Silly Leg rang a bell.

His mobile shook. Shaz. He ignored it.

The north end of the pedestrian bridge landed him in Ibrox. Three hundred yards from the Bellahouston Hotel, Aulay skipped across half a dozen back greens, then sat down to wait.

"Aye," he said into the receiver.

"The Banana's dead. Long live the Banana."

The rumour of Aulay's elevated status had spread.

"You're fucked, McCaw. Every Polmadie gun, knife and spoon is pointing at you."

"I've got Shaz Curren."

"There's more fish in the sea."

"Listen, Mackay, I'm taking Shaz away somewhere safe. You get me a couple of the DSH's millions, and you'll get your girlfriend in one piece. I'll disappear."

Aulay closed the phone to crank it up. Two million was cheap. Aulay called back. McCaw answered in half a ring, which was good.

"You'll get your money."

"Good lad, now-"

Aulay killed the call, put his head in his hands and repeated the Special Ops death mantra.

'Fuck all for one, and one for fuck all.'

Right, brain together, concentrate, put everything away apart from the objective. Move slowly, two, possibly three guns pointed at him. Look over the wall, car park quiet, hotel room windows, most in darkness. Third floor had three lights on, curtains closed. Slip onto the top of the wall, wait, any movement, no, slip to the ground, keep the cars between him and the building, breathe, breathe some more, no lights, no movement, creep forward, they're expecting him, maybe, there's a noise, not far away, something's moving, stay still, wait, wait some more. It's a bloody weasel, or a vole, small and furry, looking to dine out, go easy, no surprises, no more surprises, good, another scan, nothing, hold it, stay still, the smell of tobacco, scan, nothing, scan again, there, by Joss's Mercedes, no, inside the bloody car, front seat, driver's side. The hand holding the cigarette had two fingers strapped together. The back handed slapper from the Ibrox container. What to do?

Crawl, silent, not quite enough, the starched overalls made one hell of a racket as he scraped along the tarmac. Closer, to the passenger side, keep low, a change, freeze, scan, one of the lights on the third floor just went out. Under the Merc now, breathe, wait.

Graeme answered his phone. "Hello, chief. No, it's all quiet here... you need a hand upstairs? Ok, sir. I'll move to the BMW."

Graeme opened the Merc's door. Aulay brushed the nozzle of his Glock along the back of the policeman's neck.

"Hi, Graeme. How's your finger? Healing up? I'll check when you put your hands behind your head."

Aulay had dealt with terrified people many times. This was his first Glasgow policeman.

"To the beemer, Graeme, keep a steady pace. How long 'till McCaw appears?"

"Em...

Aulay slapped the barrel of the Glock against that sensitive bit behind Graeme's right ear.

"Twenty minutes."

He hit him again, in the same place, to set up a pattern. "Convince me."

"He said twenty fuckin' minutes. There's two... em suspects to deal with."

Made sense. Joss and Deirdre wouldn't sit idly by after Shaz left. They would need tying up.

"You married, Graeme?"

"Aye."

"What's her name?"

"Karen."

"Suspect Karen hasn't visited the Bar L much. She's going to be disappointed in you."

A two-door 3 Series BMW sat directly outside the front door of the hotel. Special Crime didn't bother with parking regulations.

"Pass me the keys, one hand only. Any kids?"

"Two. A boy and a girl."

"Clasp hands again. Names and ages, please?"

The car wasn't locked.

"Toby's four and Julie's two and a half."

"That's a lot of birthday parties you're going to miss. The boot or the back seat?"

"Eh?"

The Glock hit the target once more. "Come on Graeme. Is Miss Curren going in the boot or the back seat?"

"The boot."

"Is it to be open."

"Eh?"

Graeme made his move. His right arm came down hoping to jam Aulay's Glock in his armpit. With nothing to stop his downward movement, Graeme folded.

Amateurs wind themselves up, like a golfer taking a backswing. Graeme's 'tell'? A tightening of the shoulders. Aulay wasn't gentle. A sore and bleeding Graeme told him what he needed to know. The BMW lights off, doors and boot open, engine running.

Thirty seconds later, an unconscious Graeme sat in the driver's seat getting his shoelaces removed. After tying a right hand to the steering wheel, Aulay used the second shoelace to fix Graeme's head to the headrest. In the darkness, Graeme looked ready to go.

Graeme's neck wasn't broken. At worst, he'd wear a neck brace throughout the trial and have a few problems looking to his left, until he died. In Barlinnie Jail, as a policeman who'd colluded in the brutal killing of a Top Banana's grandparents, Graeme would be kept alive for a very long time.

Back in silent ninja mode, Aulay slipped up to the hotel entrance and looked in. People milled about. Men in various degrees of sobriety. Women, their finery wilting after a long day. The Bellahouston Hotel had a wedding party staying over and the remnants were refusing to go to bed until they'd squeezed the last vodka out of the night porter, and won the argument over some ancient family grievance. A few slept where they sat. Others nodded in agreement and/or misunderstanding.

Aulay did a quick inventory, guns, tension level, tobacco, lighter, papers, wallet, knife, balls, breathing, Graeme's phone and his police issue Sig 226.

Something behind him. He spun round, almost shooting a wedding guest. That's the thing. You focus on the objective, clear the path in front of any obstructions and forget to scan behind, for fresh, living debris.

"Awrigh' pal, howz it goin'?" The man made a valiant attempt to wipe down his crumpled suit as he got to his feet. The stalk of a flower remained pinned to his lapel.

A wedding reveller who'd decided to sleep it off in the bushes, or maybe it was gravity's decision. Hair on end, shirt hanging loose, shoes scuffed, Aulay could smell the man's booze intake from twenty feet away.

"You got a light?" the man asked after a good rummage came up empty.

Aulay sympathised. A nicotine rush would be a must for a guy in that state.

"Sure." Aulay fished his lighter out. "You got a spare fag?"

Fiddling about with rolling tobacco and cigarette papers wouldn't be good tonight.

"Sure, bud, here." The guy held out a packet of Marlboro Lights. "Have one o' these."

Marlboro Lights only look like cigarettes, but pubic hair rolled in toilet paper would have been fine.

"You the bride or groom?" his new pal asked holding up his lighter.

Aulay followed the swaying flame for a bit, drew in enough to get the gist of a tobacco hit and pointed at the BMW. "Mini-cab."

The guy peered at the car. Looking back, he refocused his eyes. "You got the time, chief?"

Dawn was making its presence felt. "Half five."

Flicking his cigarette away, the bloke hitched his trousers up and wiped his mouth.

"Right, might just have a wee night cap then."

Lurching forward, he crashed into the door jam, rebounded with a quick "oops" before successfully re-entering the fray.

Aulay slipped into his new friend's hiding place. Ideal, pitch black. The bushes allowed a good view of the entrance and the beemer. The only downer? The stench of vomit.

Graeme's phone vibrated, shite. Aulay checked the screen. Karen, Mrs Graeme. Thank fuck for that.

McCaw stepped out, signalling to someone behind him. A handcuffed Shaz appeared, manhandled by a big man. All three headed for the BMW. McCaw and the big man had guns.

Aulay left the bushes with his Glock and Graeme's Sig primed and ready. He'd made up his mind not to kill McCaw. Not an auspicious start to a Top Banana's career, shooting a Detective Inspector. Oh, the people in the know would understand, but the police don't like it when one of their own gets it, however corrupt. The media too, they'd have McCaw on a pedestal before his body was cold.

'D.I. McCaw, a long serving, decorated warrior against Organised Crime, died a hero during the recent war between The Polmadie drug gang and the Russian Mafia, who together brought mayhem to the streets of Glasgow.'

Aulay wanted McCaw to suffer, to join Graeme for years of arse stretching fun in the Bar L.

"McCaw."

McCaw's head exploded. Shaz screamed. Aulay screamed. Time slowed. A bullet removed the right shoulder of the big man holding Shaz. Before the second bullet removed the man's face, Aulay's first ever rugby tackle took Shaz through the middle. They flew across the bonnet of the BMW. More bullets smashed into the car. From the blood splattering, Graeme took a couple.

"Shaz, you ok?"

A few wedding stragglers came out to see who was setting off the fireworks.

Chapter 28   the last chapter

On the Isle of Lewis in the Outer Hebrides, Aulay lived in a bath.

After the shooting at the Bellahouston Hotel the first plane out of Glasgow Airport happened to be for Stornoway. At a letting agent in the town he pre-paid 12 weeks rent on an isolated croft house. A taxi took him to the cottage via an off-sales where he arranged a delivery schedule.

Aulay only left the bath to pay the whisky delivery man. The first dozen bottles lasted six days, the next five and so on. After three weeks, the whisky delivery man didn't get an answer at the door of the croft. He panicked. An ambulance took Aulay to the hospital in Stornoway. It was touch and go.

Even on that alcohol soaked island, Aulay made the local paper. That's when Hector turned up.

The familiar beat of a cane clicked its way along the hospital corridor. Aulay's choice of weapons was limited. The only sharp objects were stuck in his left arm. He pulled one out and waited. With Hector three feet away, Aulay leapt from the bed swinging the needle. He got as far as the floor. He tried to stab Hector's shoes. It took a while, and three male nurses, to get him back into bed.

Seismic alcohol abuse does more than pickle the brain. Biology concentrates on processing the intake as it brawls for survival. Coherence, coordination and bowel movements – hence the bath – are left to their own devices.

Hector came the next day. Aulay was much better, a tad below gibbering wreck with the screaming hee-bee-gee-bees in full flow. The leather straps round his arms and legs limited his options. He ignored the six foot spiders crawling up the walls for long enough to say, "Fuck you."

The day after that Aulay asked Hector a coherent question. He thought he knew the answer but wanted to hear it.

"Why did you take out McCaw?"

"The high ups got involved. It went as far as London."

"What did?"

"A senior detective inspector colluding with the DSH? Imagine the outcry if the public found out. Glasgow Serious Crime working for the Taliban's paymaster, responsible for the deaths of British and American soldiers fighting the war on terror."

"Can't have the Americans thinking the UK is soft, eh?"

"Our intelligence put McCaw at the Bellahouston Hotel. If I'd known Sharon was there too..."

Hector had the good grace to look sad. "And you? We'd no idea you were there. You appeared from nowhere."

The inevitable had happened. McCaw and his crew died heroes, defending a Glasgow lawyer at the top of the Russian Mafia's hit list.

Fewer spiders circled the bed. The ones that remained were bigger. "I warned you, Hector. Remember?"

Hector got up to leave. "I'm truly sorry about Sharon and... I'll be expecting you."

Aulay put his suicide on hold. He couldn't die before Hector.

Day three, withdrawal, day four, withdrawal, day five, withdrawal. Day six was a Sunday where nothing happens on the Isle of Lewis. Something to do with the Presbyterian nature of the place. On day seven he was sober, chemically speaking, the doctor said so.

Aulay had his doubts when an ancillary brought him a slice of toast. The man smelled of his previous night's drinking. Aulay wanted to lick his face. Moving onto toast was a big step. The whisky had hacked through his insides, like paint stripper. He spent another week in a ward with other patients and managed more than toast.

The psychiatrist finished their sessions more confused than Aulay. The doctor nearly got to the nub, once.

"Why not jump off a bridge?"

"Too quick."

"You either lacked resolve or... you felt the need to suffer?"

The doctor was nearly right. The place alcohol abuse took Aulay too had highs and lows. The high of low self esteem is glorious and self pity; a warm gooey liquid.

Lacking resolve? Aulay did jump off a bridge; a high one. The whisky delivery man threw the spanner before he hit the water.

Released from Stornoway Hospital, Aulay caught the ferry to Ullapool, the bus to Inverness then the train to Glasgow.

Directly across from Queen Street station is Dows, an old fashioned boozer. Aulay needed a reference point. Where was he in the alcoholic stakes? He ordered a pint, with a whisky chaser. Sitting in a corner, he worked the odds. Even money he'd leave the pub on a stretcher.

An hour later, he switched his Blackberry on. Ignoring the cascade flooding his month old inboxes, he called The Bulls.

"Is Freak Johnston there?"

"Who wants him?"

"Aulay Mackay."

There was a fumbling. "Freak, it's The Banana."

357

Lightning Source UK Ltd.
Milton Keynes UK
UKOW02f1804300814

237792UK00001B/1/P